W9-CRJ-443

THE
TAVERA LEGACY

Mary Elizabeth Lynn

THE
TAVERA LEGACY

MARY ELIZABETH LYNN

A TOM DOHERTY ASSOCIATES BOOK
NEW YORK

This is a work of fiction. All the characters and events portrayed in this book are fictitious, and any resemblance to real people or events is purely coincidental.

THE TAVERA LEGACY

This book is printed on acid-free paper.

A Forge Book
Published by Tom Doherty Associates, Inc.
175 Fifth Avenue
New York, N.Y. 10010

Library of Congress Cataloging-in-Publication Data

Lynn, Mary Elizabeth.
    The Tavera legacy / Mary Elizabeth Lynn.
        p.   cm.
    "A Tom Doherty Associates Book."
    ISBN 0-312-93136-0 : $24.95
    1. Women physicians—New Mexico—Fiction   I. Title.
PS3562.Y44475T38   1994
813'.54—dc20   93-35851
                                                  CIP

First Forge edition: January 1994

Printed in the United States of America

0 9 8 7 6 5 4 3 2 1

THE
TAVERA LEGACY

One

THE MAN CAST A LONG, NARROW SHADOW IN THE EARLY morning sunlight. His concentration on the notes he was taking kept him perfectly still, even though hundreds of bees swarmed everywhere around him. He knew they wouldn't bother him. They were hungry, not suicidal.

He'd taught them harsh lessons before, at first shooing them, then smashing them, then, most satisfying of all, torturing them. They were like bothersome children. He just couldn't understand Apple Hardy. The reverence the Toya County sheriff felt for *her* honeybees and hives just wasn't natural, at least to a sane person's way of thinking, *his* way of thinking. And he was certainly sane. No one could say he wasn't.

From under the cottonwood branch where he stood near the beehive, he could see what remained of an ancient adobe structure, the melting mud bricks defining nothing more than empty space. Three feet of crumbling dirt was all that was left of what had been the original Tavera family home.

"This is where I want my house to be," he'd once told his father. But his father had discouraged him.

"This is Tavera land, son," he'd said.

That had been his father's final word on the subject. Father had forgotten all about it, he was sure, but that wasn't the end of his own ambitions to live on this beautiful rise overlooking the valley of small, irrigated fields. He'd build his own adobe house, more beautiful than the other many times over.

And he had every right to do so. The Taveras had acquired the land by default, using witchcraft and underhanded methods and dishonest dealings with the crooked and incompetent Santa Fe politicians of pre-1900 New Mexico. For the price of a few dollars owed in back taxes, the Taveras had bought the thousands of acres of the private grant that had been given to *his* family by Governor Gaspar Dominguez de Mendoza in 1739. Lenor Tavera's old book had led him to the truth, and he'd made up his mind. He wasn't going to take the indecency of being swindled lying down, like his ancestors had. His plan to redeem his family's honor was already in motion. Lenor's agony would be much worse than what she was putting him through. He'd succeed. Then, for once in his life, his father would be proud of him.

However, today it was not the plan that interested him, but the verdant hedge that ran straight down the slight incline and seductively waved its luscious pink flowers at his tiny, whirring prisoners. Someone had planted this hedge and tended it through its early stages of growth, probably in much the same way he cared for his own precious plants. These sweet flowers would never have grown wild here, not in this place, not in this arid state of New Mexico. Someone had wanted a break from the wind, had wanted privacy. He looked around. Privacy from what? he wondered. Not another soul or another structure could be seen in any direction.

The clipboard's metal spring creaked in protest as he tried to slip one more piece of lined paper under its sharp edge. Row after row of small, neat, ink-black printing showed through the clean sheet atop the already-thick stack. He was double-checking the

Parkhill work he'd read on honeybee behavior. Did worker bees really tell the others exactly where to find pollen by dancing in a certain pattern? Did a worn-out bee actually leave the hive to die so her remains would not impose extra work on the others? The questions were endless and the answers endlessly fascinating. He permitted himself a smile.

The spring drones had already been born from unfertilized eggs laid by the old queen. Lacking stingers, unable to gather pollen or nectar, their sole purpose was to mate with a new queen. Afterward she could lay fifteen hundred eggs a day during her two-to-three-year life span. Thinking about all that sexual activity excited him so much that he had to stop writing as he impatiently reached under the clipboard to push his hand against the growing bulge beneath his tight jeans. As always, he willed the throbbing to cease, but, as always, it would not. He groaned.

"This is your fault, Lenor," he whispered. "You've got to stop teasing me this way . . . I warn you . . ." His mind played cruel tricks on him. He could see her in the creek where they used to swim when they were kids—but she wasn't a child. His vision was of a full-grown woman emerging from the shining pool, walking casually toward him. She taunted him by slowly removing her scant bikini, teased him by pretending that he wasn't even there as she lay back on a smooth, sun-warmed rock. Her long, dark hair dried to a billowing silken cloud, full breasts glistened with diamond droplets of water, long supple legs relaxed as they warmed. And still she didn't see him standing there, so close he could have reached out and touched her.

The beating of his heart matched the pounding of flesh against thick, restrictive denim. The clipboard dropped from his hand and papers scattered over the ground. "Damn you, Lenor."

Frantically he managed to get the metal studs free from their buttonholes. Just in time. His hand cupped to receive the white fluid that pulsed from the dark red crescent of flesh he'd exposed. The fiery hot skin he touched felt so tender, almost as if the fragile tissues would rip open, shred at the slightest pressure. But the relief made him shiver all over, even in the warmth of the slanting summer sun. And the pleasure made him feel ashamed.

" 'Ah, sinful nation, a people laden with iniquity, a seed of evildoers, children that are corrupters'!" He spoke the words from *Isaiah* in a harsh whisper. *How would he ever be able to explain the enjoyment?*

The pleasure—he was going to have to talk to Lenor about that. Her interference, pleasurable or not, was beginning to interrupt his studies and his work at the most inopportune times. Didn't she realize he had more important things to do than respond to her every whim?

He wiped his hand on his handkerchief, left his jeans unbuttoned—just in case—then squatted down to pick up his papers. Hours of observation were still ahead of him, and he relished the thought of writing down all he would see and learn as he stood perfectly still, while the sun made its daily arc across the perfectly blue New Mexico sky.

Crack . . . crack . . . crack. The CB in the battered 1958 hearse came to life.

"Damn!" He finished scooping the sheets together, jammed them helter-skelter onto the clipboard, then hurried toward the long black vehicle parked at the edge of the dirt road. With one hand he began buttoning his pants. With the other he tossed the clipboard through the open window and onto the passenger seat, then grabbed the microphone. "Emergency One here."

"*Crack* . . . have a pickup . . . Vigil's place . . . *crack* . . . out."

"Vee-hill. Got it," he said, but he knew no one on the other end could hear him. The radio had been on the fritz for a few weeks and was waiting on a mail-order replacement transmitter part. The parts company had probably decided that since New Mexico was a "foreign country," he hadn't sent enough postage. It happened all the time. The *New Mexico* magazine even had an ongoing column about such things, "One of Our Fifty Is Missing." He should probably write the mail-order company a letter.

Sheriff Hardy had said she could fix the radio, make it work again with a little wire and such, but he was having none of her flimsy rigging. Things had to be done right, he thought, as he got in, straightened the stack of papers on the bulging clipboard on the seat next to him, and reached for another clipboard on the dash. He didn't start the engine until he'd noted the current mileage, the date, the time, the weather, his destination into the "next-door" county of Mora, and the particulars of the call. Then he drove west on the almost-nonexistent ruts that used to be a wagon trail.

The Vigil farm was nothing more than a few small fields, fenced off with sagging barbed wire tacked carelessly to piñon poles, and a tin-roofed adobe that zigzagged in a haphazard sprawl of tiny rooms that had been added on as the children came. The living was bare subsistence. Dr. Miller Baldwin's old station wagon sat beside Sheriff Hardy's four-wheel-drive in the dusty driveway, and Mrs. Vigil stood behind the screen door, her youngest daughter clutching at her skirt.

From the way Mrs. Vigil was dabbing at her eyes with her handkerchief, he suspected that Mr. Vigil had finally died. He'd been sick, off and on, for a long time. After making the necessary entries on the clipboard pages, noting that the Mora County sheriff, John Garcia, should have been here instead of Sheriff Hardy, and that the vehicle from the Mora Clinic should have been called instead of him, he got out and walked toward the house. All five of the children working in one of the fields beyond the house waved at him. He waved back.

"Please come in, amigo." Mrs. Vigil pushed open the screen door and pointed to the back of the house. "They're in there."

"Is there anything I can do for you, Mrs. Vigil? I'd be glad to come back and help out any way I can," he said.

"That's very kind of you, son, but we'll be fine."

"You can call me at the store anytime. Remember that," he said.

Dr. Baldwin and Apple Hardy were just coming out of the bedroom. Apple went straight to Mrs. Vigil and put her arm around the woman's shoulder. "I'm sorry, Carmela," she said, then patted the child who still clung to her mother's skirt.

"He's better off now, I know. He was in pain. He's—" Carmela bowed her head and wept silently for a moment, then, "He's better off," she repeated quietly.

In her light tan uniform, pants, shirt, heavy black belt with holster and gun, Sheriff Hardy looked tall and strong beside the tiny farm woman. Yet Apple was as gentle with her as if the sheriff were tending to one of her beloved cats. The woman was a study in contradictions, he thought, strong and gentle, reverent and obscene, tough and tender, beautiful and handsome all at once. Contradictions could mean trouble. His mother, Gloria, had been proof of that. He'd have to observe Sheriff Hardy more closely from now on.

A hand landed on his shoulder. He flinched. It was Dr. Baldwin. He'd have to be more careful about letting his mind wander. "Yes, sir," he said.

"They'll be waiting for Señor Vigil at Taft's," the doctor said softly. "Here's the paperwork to leave at the mortuary."

He looked down. "Cremation?" he asked, as he pulled a small spiral notebook and ballpoint from his shirt pocket and quickly jotted down the time, the place, the date, those who were present, and an aside—eight Vigil children were elsewhere.

"That's what Mr. Vigil wanted, and he has the permission of the diocese," the doctor was saying. "I've called Father Rand, so Daniel's all yours."

"And God's."

Traveling south, the road to Las Vegas didn't have much traffic; a few cars up ahead turned toward Rociada, probably tourists headed for the resort. He took his time and enjoyed the scenery, the Sangre de Cristo Mountains to the west on his right, fertile fields sweeping to the great plain of the Midwest on his left. No hurry. Señor Vigil was a long way past caring, *lucky fellow—all those children* . . .

Children. How could Lenor stand to be around children all

day, maybe even all night? Why would anyone *choose* to be with children? Maybe he'd get a chance to ask her about that when she came home for her grandfather's birthday party. *If she doesn't spend all her time with Apple* . . .

Apple Hardy had been Lenor's best friend since grade school. He'd been part of their circle of friends, but even then he'd recognized his feelings about their friendship as jealousy. He'd kept the feeling well hidden.

Even in high school the two women had practically been inseparable, double dating, spending the night at each other's houses, studying together, competing for the best grades. He had to admit they were both smart, but not nearly as brilliant as he'd been—as he still was. And with all his studies he was getting smarter by the minute. Too bad Mr. Vigil, and all the others who had overpopulated the earth, hadn't been a little smarter.

Daniel Vigil would merit a very long obituary, printed in very tiny type, in the local newspaper. *He is survived by his wife Carmela and their* . . . The list would go on and on and on and on. His mother's obit had been only three lines long. Daniel Vigil was dead at the age of forty-two after fathering nine children, the youngest only two years old. *Maybe all the fathering killed him.*

Fathering—he couldn't help but wonder what Lenor told Apple about the tortures she was putting him through. Just how much did the sheriff know about her best friend's intentions toward him? If she knew anything, Apple would never tell him, of course, even if he had the nerve to ask her. *Fathering . . . all that fathering* . . .

His mind was wandering again, being tugged at, his thoughts becoming disjointed, his body being distorted out of its beautiful slender proportions. "Damn you, Lenor."

He jammed his hand between his legs and pushed with all the force he could muster, while strength seemed to drain from the rest of his body. Why couldn't she communicate through his mind, through his thoughts? Why did she have to attack the one thing he couldn't control? He pulled off on the shoulder of the road, stopped, and undid his buttons.

He usually couldn't bring himself to touch it, but this time he helped it along, first with one hand, then with both hands. Daniel Vigil wouldn't care—or tell. He twisted sideways and glanced back over the seat. "You see, Mr. Vigil? You don't have to make another baby every time." He looked down at himself as he faced forward again. It wasn't a pretty sight, but he'd almost learned to tolerate it. The contrast between the white of his cool slender fingers moving against the blood-engorged flesh disgusted him, but fascinated him so that he almost didn't catch the movement just up the road ahead of him.

He stopped stroking for a moment, just long enough to determine that John Garcia's sixteen-year-old son, Junior, had turned out of the Garcias' long driveway and was walking away from the hearse, along the road. Such a beautiful young man, he thought. So graceful, strong, and tall. He'd be the perfect guinea pig for the test. The stroking began again—slowly—but in seconds the movements were frantic and out of control . . . and painful. "Damn you, Lenor!"

His handkerchief was still sticky from earlier this morning. Better planning was in order. He liked to use a clean one each time, but right now he had no choice and used it anyway, distasteful as it was. This one would end up on the stack with the other soiled handkerchiefs that he threw behind the overstuffed chair in his bedroom. He probably had a full washer load by now. It had been ten days since he'd done the last one.

He buttoned his pants and tucked the handkerchief out of sight. The old engine started on the first try. Junior wasn't too far ahead of him. *Plenty of time.* He rolled forward slowly until he was close enough so that the crunch of tires on gravel made the boy turn around and look back. Junior waved.

"Want a ride?"

Two

"I'M SO GLAD YOU CALLED, HONEY. GIVES ME A chance to slow down for a minute. These women are running me ragged."

"And you're loving every minute of it, aren't you?"

"Lenor! How can you say such things?"

"So how does it feel to be almost eighty-nine, Grandpa?"

"Same way it felt to be almost twenty-nine. Honest to God, Lenor, I don't feel a day over thirty."

Lenor mouthed the words *He's fine,* and gave a thumbs-up sign to the tiny blond nurse standing in the doorway. "That's the best news I've heard today," she said into the receiver.

"In surgery this morning, were you?" Steven asked.

"Emergency room," Lenor said, but didn't miss her grandfather's inference. Surgery was Grandpa's bugaboo. A few years ago, Steven Tavera had been the perfect candidate for a coronary artery bypass operation or sudden death—with the latter far more likely. His paralyzing fear of surgery had sparked his interest in his granddaughter's suggested life-style changes. His wife, Jovita, had demanded he give the changes a try, and set a good example by adopting them herself. "And the party plans?" Lenor asked. "They're going well?"

"Should be my best birthday ever . . . except that Daniel won't be here."

"Why not? Is he feeling sick again?"

"He died, Lenor. I'm working on his coffin now. We'll bury him tomorrow at noon."

"Oh, Grandpa. I'm so sorry. Is Carmela okay?"

"Putting on a good show. But watch out for your mama."

"What do you mean?"

"Magdalena's convinced that if you'd been Daniel's doctor, he'd still be alive." Steven lowered his voice. "She wants you to come home and practice medicine in New Mexico."

"Oh," was all she could manage to say around the instant feeling of suffocation and guilt. Since the day she'd left for the University of New Mexico to become a premed student, Lenor had known it would come to this sooner or later. The debate had been going on in her own head for a long time. Her mother didn't mean to put her on a guilt trip, but she was oh-so-good at it.

Lenor glanced around the doctors' lounge. Much of the furniture was ancient and worn, but, on several tables and desks, computer terminals, monitors, and printers waited to give Foley Hospital's doctors the very latest information on their patients at any time, day or night. High tech, from the latest in bedside computers to hand-held units to the grand mainframe that crunched bits and bytes in the blink of an eye, set Foley apart from every other hospital in the eastern United States, possibly all of the country, coast to coast. *This is where I want to be. This is where I have to be to help the most people.*

"Lenor? Honey, are you still there? I didn't mean to drop a bomb. Just thought you ought to have a little warning."

"Thanks, Grandpa. I owe you one."

"Dr. Tavera to Admin."

"I heard that," Steven said. "Just one more thing. Your mama wants you to bring the old family herbal with you. Wants to look up something. Love you. See you tomorrow, Doctor T."

"I love you, Grandpa."

Lenor Tavera stood outside Carl Bowder's office wondering whether to storm in and demand to know why she'd been summoned or to knock and enter as an innocent who'd been called before the pope. She thought she knew what the hospital administrator wanted to talk about—rave about. One of two things, really. Either he had some new problem with her "story-time" experiment on Ward Two, or he'd heard about what he'd probably call the medically unorthodox, medically unsocial—no, antisocial—diagnosis she'd made in front of a New York City newspaper journalist, who understood Spanish and whose speaking voice could be heard all the way to the east end of Long Island.

She smoothed her already smooth hair, made sure any loose strands were tucked back safely into the heavy knot at the base of her skull. White coat buttoned? Check. Her still-controversial attire of blue work shirt, cowboy boots, and jeans was camouflaged as well as possible. As an extra precaution against reminders of past arguments about dress codes, Lenor lifted her heavy silver and turquoise cross by its silver chain and dropped it inside the collar of her shirt. Briefly she considered taking off the three large Indian silver and turquoise rings she was wearing, then decided against it. The kids loved her elaborate southwestern jewelry.

Dr. Carl Bowder had never been against his hospital getting publicity, as long as it was favorable, and Lenor Tavera had garnered plenty of beneficial publicity and, as a result, money. Even before she'd graduated from Columbia, she'd been recognized as having extraordinary skills as a diagnostician. While Columbia University took the credit, proclaiming its superior teaching methods, Lenor privately attributed many of her diagnostic successes to intuition fostered, since childhood, through her *desarrollo,* her apprenticeship to her mother, a *curandera* with extraordinary gifts and the power to work in any and all of the three levels of *curanderismo,* the Mexican-American folk healing system. Plus Lenor had a direct link with certain parts of the "other world," a heightened awareness that would have to stay her own private secret. Whatever the reason for Lenor's brilliance, Foley Hospital had prospered and been able to become even more high-tech because of it.

Now a diagnosis and treatment may peg me as the witch of Endor. Well, divination notwithstanding . . . a good offense is the best defense.

Without knocking, Lenor pushed the door open and walked purposefully to the front of Carl Bowder's desk. He wore his usual navy three-piece suit with the obligatory male power symbol, a red tie. His fingernails gleamed from a recent coating of clear polish. "You look startled, Carl. I thought you were expecting me."

He was immediately on guard. "A knock would have . . ." He gave it up and relaxed back into his cushioned chair. "How's Steven?" he asked.

"Grandpa's fine. Better than fine, actually. I just talked to him. Says he doesn't feel a day over thirty."

"And he'll be . . . ?"

"Eighty-nine on Saturday."

"Amazing."

Not really.

"Sit down, Dr. Tavera."

Lenor remained standing. Carl's small talk was just a ruse to lull her into a more passive state. "I presume you want to know whether my article for the *New England Journal of Medicine* is ready to be submitted," Lenor said, trying to keep the morning's emergency-room event off the agenda. "It is, and I don't have time for a visit."

"Then I'll be brief."

That'll be a switch, Lenor thought, but she remained standing, just in case his prefacing didn't take longer than the usual half hour.

"Neither I nor any of the staff physicians here at Foley have ever seen diagnostic powers such as you have, Lenor," Bowder began sweetly. "That reporter who gave you the nickname Sherlock unknowingly did us all a favor."

To the tune of about twenty-seven million dollars in donations, Lenor wanted to say, but she let it go.

"The sobriquet—" a female voice began.

Lenor turned quickly toward the open door, then back to Bowder. "Public Relations?" Lenor asked.

"A last-minute decision. I asked Violet to attend."

Violet Rodriquez, dressed in her usual—yet another shade of purple—propelled herself across the room and sat down in one of the two chairs in front of Bowder's desk. "If I may continue . . . the nickname increased your journalistic potential to even greater proportions when you admitted to being more than a little interested in the deductive techniques used by the famed detective."

And you and the administrator haven't missed any opportunity letting the media know what's going on in this hospital, Lenor thought. "I see you have a new boyfriend, Violet," she said.

"What has that got to do with—" Violet's eyes opened a little wider. "How do you know—?"

"Nail polish," Lenor said. "New shade."

Violet's cheeks turned a color almost matching her damson blouse. "My private life is not the topic of discussion here, Dr. Tavera," she said huffily.

Lenor gave her a brief but knowing smile, then sat down. It was going to be a longer session than she had time for, which was usual for Bowder and his public relations crew. Nothing was ever simple for them since hospitals and physicians had started taking incoming bad-rap rounds from the public for skyrocketing costs. *And lately I seem to be their main target for needling.*

Violet continued with a vengeance. "Have you given up deductive reasoning altogether with the Perez case . . . or just taken temporary leave of your senses?"

Lenor bristled. "So now my interest in healing the spirit as well as the body threatens to undo all the good my previous fame has accomplished," she said directly to Bowder.

Bowder leaned forward. "You have to understand, New Yorkers take their heroes quite seriously."

"And *you* have to understand that being a mother is the hardest job on earth, especially if her child is ill, and I'm not about to make it any harder. Mrs. Perez needed a talisman. The child needed an appetite stimulant. I gave them *both* what they required *and* what they could afford," Lenor said.

"But a diagnosis of *mal de ojo*? The evil eye?" Bowder asked, seemingly more bewildered than angry.

"Preposterous," Violet sneered. "Even down in Texas—"

"That's what Mrs. Perez believed . . . and could understand," Lenor interrupted calmly.

Violet reached for the afternoon newspaper on Bowder's desk and tossed it into Lenor's lap, front-page headline facing up.

MD THUMBS NOSE AT DRUG COMPANIES, PRESCRIBES TREES

The opinion piece on page two went on to say, *". . . the well-known 'Sherlock' Tavera, a resident at the high-tech Foley Hospital, has slapped modern technology and orthodox medicine in the face by diagnosing 'bad magic' and prescribing branches, berries, and smoke. Please tell me, just what do juniper trees and bright green leaves have to do with . . ."*

Lenor had already seen it. She tossed it back into Violet's lap. "This is right up your alley, Violet. A little scandal, a little controversy."

"And the next time you're called to diagnose for the mayor's children what will it be? *Susto?*"

Lenor had to smile. "I didn't realize you might put any stock in witch fright. Congratulations, Ms. Rodriquez."

"And I didn't know you put any stock in the *curanderismo*, Dr. Tavera," Violet said sarcastically.

"You'd be surprised what I value. I'd be glad to tell you sometime."

"Ladies, please. This is getting us nowhere." Bowder stood up. "We have a lobby full of reporters."

"Let Violet handle them," Lenor suggested.

"I don't think it's going to be that simple," Bowder said, then pushed a button on his telephone.

"Yes, Dr. Bowder?" a feminine voice asked.

"Bring that other newspaper to Dr. Tavera, please."

"Yes, sir."

When the secretary handed her the opened paper, Lenor stared down at the questioning title of the editorial.

BOWDER BOOTS *BRUJA*?

What else can the administrator of Foley Hospital do when one of his doctors begins taking the science out of the diagnosis? When that same doctor takes the medicine out of the treatment? Dr. Carl Bowder has to decide: is there a *bruja* (pronounced brew-ha), a witch, amongst us?

Has mysticism taken the place of lab tests? Will supernatural possession take the place of measles as the number-one childhood disease? Can we inoculate for *mal de ojo* (pronounced mahl-day-oh-ho)? Can Foley's myriad computer terminals handle magical etiology?

Dr. Lenor Tavera . . .

She didn't read any more. She didn't care to know what this obviously unenlightened journalistic twit had to say about anything.

"I'm in a difficult position, Dr. Tavera," Bowder said.

Lenor squared her shoulders and tossed the offending newspaper to the floor, sending pages sliding across the gray carpet. "More difficult than when that intern began making love to half the female senior citizens in geriatrics, and CNN got hold of the story?" she asked.

Bowder looked at Violet. "She has a point."

"*There,* we were dealing with a man who was obviously mentally ill," Violet said. "*Here,* if we give our renowned pediatric cardiologist the benefit of the doubt—"

"And assume I'm sane?" Lenor asked sweetly.

Violet nodded. "—then we're dealing with an entirely different kettle of worms."

"Do I understand that if I'm *not* crazy, we have a big problem?"

"Insurmountable, perhaps," Violet said.

"Do you mean to tell me that the New York populace is so

unsophisticated, so dense, so tuned in to pills and scalpels that it can't understand and accept the validity of thousands of years of the overlapping, triangulated, validated results of traditional folk medicine? What kind of skeptical twitching is this, anyway?"

"It's called objectivity," Violet said.

"For disease, perhaps. But what about dis-*ease*?"

"A placebo?" Bowder suggested.

"At twenty-nine ninety-five a bottle?" Lenor said. "Be serious, Carl."

"This is not a charity hospital, Dr. Tavera," Violet said.

Lenor's anger flared, but, instead of a swift uppercut, only a scathing glance shot toward Violet's pretty face. "Carl, you used to practice medicine, and you know what I'm talking about. In your field, what percentage of impotence cases ever turned out to be organically caused?"

Carl shrugged. "A few," he said.

"And the rest?" Lenor asked.

"Psychological."

"We're off the subject again, people," Violet said.

"And just what *is* the subject, Ms. Rodriquez? A correct diagnosis? A proper treatment? Or bad publicity for the hospital?"

"My job is to see that we get good publicity," Violet said.

"You think Foley will fold under the weight of bad publicity?" Lenor asked. "I think you're jousting at windmills, Violet."

Violet continued unflustered. "And that's exactly what *you're* doing when you start treating 'bad vibes.' "

"There's just no way to get through to you, is there," Lenor said, her frustration finally showing through her usual calm. "I'm going to explain this as simply as I can, just one more time, then I want you to adjourn this meeting." She stood up to her almost-six-foot height and looked down at the woman still seated in the chair.

"Many, *many* illnesses are caused by the intellect being at cross-purposes with the body. You treat yourself badly in some way and you get sick. We orthodox physicians are poorly equipped to handle most of what walks through our office doors. To many physicians, it seems to be sacrilege to simply tell a patient, 'If you'll quit doing *this,* then *that* will go away.' Instead," she went on, "we poke and medicate and cut, and sometimes end up adding more insults to the first. The patient leaves us with more problems than the one he originally presented because we're afraid to tell him the truth. 'You *don't* need a doctor, sir, you need some self-restraint.' He wants a magic bullet. We give it to him in the form of an expensive pill. Unless someone is broken, bleeding, or otherwise obviously out of kilter, there's really very little we can do except act as a supportive friend and suggest life-style changes that few patients want to adopt. How about you, Violet?" Lenor asked.

"Me?"

"Have you quit smoking yet? Have you quit eating those jelly doughnuts the hospital cafeteria so charmingly advertises as having no cholesterol? One of these days you'll be tearing in here demanding good health from some poor sap who'll have to send you to respiratory therapy to be fitted for one of those portable oxygen machines—that's right after they do a quadruple coronary artery bypass, of course, and you spend six weeks in intensive care with tubes stuck in holes you didn't even know you had."

"I don't have to listen—"

"But eventually you're going to have to *pay*. You could start right now by making those life-style changes and maybe sipping a little tisane made from the root of the inmortal plant. If you don't, the price to you and yours will be much higher later on. Think about it."

"So you're going to persist?" Violet asked, as if she hadn't heard anything Lenor had said.

"You can *bet* on it. You both know this isn't the first time I've prescribed something unorthodox . . . and it won't be the last," Lenor said. "This is just the first time it's gotten any publicity. It may not be the last time *that* happens, either. Especially if my research on pediatric heart patients yields the data I'm expecting it will."

"Then we'll just have to go with what we have," Violet said.

"Which is?" Lenor asked.

Violet sat up straight. "We'll back up your decision to treat the Perez case with juniper berries by citing your previous successes."

"That's very kind," Lenor said stiffly.

Violet seemed uncomfortable. "You must realize, we weren't suggesting that you publicly renounce anything you believe in."

"Except . . ."

"Except what, Dr. Bowder?" Lenor asked.

His round, pink face winced as he leaned forward and said, "Witchcraft," very softly.

Lenor sighed. *Are these two as hopeless as they seem?* "I've studied all kinds of occult phenomena, Carl. Wicca, shamanism, you name it. Contrary to popular Christian belief, the rest of the world does not worship devils. Western science just doesn't explain everything. What about acupuncture? What about the data gathered from the Australian aborigines? There's so much to learn. Remember Dr. Fry?"

"Wasn't he the psychiatrist who did research on the physiological effects of laughter in the sixties?" Carl asked.

"And he took a lot of flak for a long time. In his medical education, Dr. Fry had been taught that if a patient said something funny, the doctor's response should be silence, followed by the question, 'Why do you think you made that joke at this time?' "

" 'Neuroendocrine and Stress Hormone Changes During Mirthful Laughter' was in the *American Journal of Medical Sciences*. I remember it," Carl said. "Decrease in stress hormones, blood pressure. Muscle relaxation. I can't remember the rest."

"You remember the essentials—"

"Look, Dr. Tavera," Violet interrupted. "As much as Fry and Ornish and others of their ilk would like it, body-mind theories and life-style changes are not yet scientifically proven. The fields are well-known, but . . ."

"You know very well that Dr. Ornish's heart disease reversal research with adults and subsequent studies were scientifically valid! Maybe you're just jealous the publicity wasn't yours to broadcast."

"We need more studies," Bowder chimed in.

"Thank you, Dr. Bowder. The one out of four children who have a high cholesterol level, and I, are glad to have your support," Lenor said.

"Well . . . I wasn't exactly . . . I'm just trying to say . . ." He cleared his throat and shifted in his chair. "We . . . ah . . . physicians in general need more time to get comfortable with the concept of prevention and reversal."

"And the possibility of making less money?" Lenor asked in an innocent tone.

"Well . . ."

"It cost us all about seventy-eight billion dollars last year to treat heart disease. Insurance companies pay thirty thousand for a bypass, seventy-five hundred for a balloon angioplasty, but if I teach a patient to prevent or reverse the diseases that cost all of us billions every year, I get a big fat ZERO for my time. I see something deadly wrong with this system, folks."

"But Foley gets a good-sized chunk of all those insurance dollars," Violet piped in.

"So we finally get to the real issue. Right, Violet? The almighty dollar."

"The almighty dollar pays your salary, Doctor."

"I didn't go into medicine for the money," Lenor said. "And the Hippocratic Oath says, 'Do no harm.' Do you think causing financial ruin is doing no harm? Why do you think the Hemlock Society is signing up new members every day? Why do you think the suicide how-to, *Final Exit,* was on the best-seller list for so long? Why do you think magazines like *Prevention* and *American Health* and all manner of health newsletters are attracting more and more subscribers? It's because we orthodox medical Caesars have been making too much money by prescribing too many tests, too many procedures, and too many drugs. The American people are getting smart, and I, for one, say it's about damn time!"

Bowder leaned forward. "These drastic changes take time. We have to be absolutely sure . . ."

"And we'll all just prescribe Valium and the scalpel in the interim," Lenor said. "Well, no thank you, Doctor. Not when a warm cup of evening primrose tea and a prayer will do the trick just as well—or better. Not when a very low-fat diet and exercise will rule out bypass surgery. Not when a daily session of yoga will protect against high blood pressure and stroke."

Bowder looked increasingly uncomfortable. "Can we talk about your article, Lenor? You said it was finished."

"And you're thinking of trying to suppress it," Lenor said flatly.

"Well . . . maybe I should see it before you submit it."

Lenor's article was on the subject of the lack of funds available for studying preventive medicine. What she called "the criminal lack of financial support" from insurance companies, Medicare, and Medicaid for preventive prescriptions instead of the invasive procedures and mind-numbing drugs that cost premium-payers and taxpayers billions of dollars was going to raise a ruckus. Bowder seemed to be afraid that, in the event of publication, they at Foley Hospital could all become targets—or worse, victims—of disenchanted supporters.

In a week I may have my grant, and the article can be put away and forgotten. "Compromise. I'll delay submission for two weeks," she said. "During that time you can decide how you're going to get comfortable sitting on the fence."

"Well . . ."

"I have to go now," Lenor said abruptly as she stood up, then started for the door.

"You can't just leave. We haven't finished," Violet said.

"You'll have to go ahead without me. I'm needed upstairs."

"But—"

"Have fun with the reporters, Violet," Lenor said over her shoulder as she left the room.

The telephone clicked, and the secretary said, "Dr. Bowder. Dr. Tavera's needed in Ward Two, stat."

Bowder looked at Violet. "How the hell does she *do* that?"

Three

PANTING AFTER RUNNING UP FIVE FLIGHTS, LENOR stopped at the nurses' station and leaned heavily against the tall counter. For a moment she felt dizzy. *I've got to get more sleep.* But the unusual dizziness passed quickly. "Sable?" Lenor asked the nurse at the counter.

The nurse nodded. "Are you all right, Dr. Tavera?" she asked, but got no answer.

Lenor flew down the hall, white coattails flapping, then pushed through the door to the ward. Ella Wygent, in a petite white pantsuit and looking more like one of the children than the head nurse, stood at the side of the bed at the far end of the long room. Her pixie face was calm. Her slight body, which belied the fact that she could move a three-hundred-pound man from bed to gurney single-handedly, was tense.

Five of the eight beds were alive with restless young bodies and animated conversation. The children in two of the other beds were no less excited, but, restrained by casts and traction, their activities were limited to interjection and laughter. The one thing all the children had in common was rheumatic heart disease. Sable was in the last bed on the right.

"I pushed the call button, Dr. T," Jackie said as Lenor passed her bed.

"Good girl, Jackie. Very quick thinking." She grabbed the curtain and pulled it around Sable's bed as she approached Ella's side. "What's up?"

"I don't know. Jackie said that Sable was just sitting on the side of the bed—they were talking—then Sable just seemed to 'wink out.' "

"Wink out?"

"That's the way Jackie described it, Doctor."

Lenor bent down and looked at the child more closely. There was a sheen of moisture on her forehead. She could feel the presence of at least two "others" in the room but decided against interfering, even though one of them gave off familiar vibes. "What did Jackie say, exactly?"

"Apparently Jackie was out of bed, standing in front of Sable, when it happened. She said that Sable closed her eyes and started to breathe very deeply. Then her body seemed to 'go all heavy or something' and her head fell forward with her chin touching her chest. 'She just winked out.' That's what Jackie said—as near as I can remember."

Sable's forearms rested on her lap. Her hands, palms up and fingers gently curling, lay on her knees. Dr. Bowder and Ms. Rodriquez were going to have a fit, but it couldn't be helped. Lenor turned to speak to Ella and saw a look of horror on the nurse's face. Mouth open, she pointed a finger at the child. Lenor looked back.

Now Sable was sitting bolt upright, eyes still closed but with a wide smile, almost a grimace, on her face. Teeth gleaming in the dim light, her mouth began to slowly open and shut, with the smile seemingly frozen in place.

"What's happening?" Ella whispered frantically.

"Stand back," Lenor commanded instead of explaining, then squared herself in front of the child and lifted her cross out of its hiding place. She spread her feet slightly apart, lifted her arms out from her sides, and turned her palms toward Sable.

"Sable, I'm here to help you," she said. *"Corrientes espirituales* will protect you. Do you understand? The spirits flowing around you will help."

"My jaws hurt." The words were mangled but understandable.

"In time you will be able to speak . . . in the name of the Father, the Son . . ."

Sable's body sagged forward, and Ella moved toward her.

"Stay back," Lenor ordered. Just as quickly, the girl's body straightened again. This time she had a deep scowl on her face. She began to rock impatiently from side to side. Lenor reached out, holding her hand near Sable's head, then moving it in an arc. When she lifted her hand straight up, Sable stopped rocking. "In the name of the Father, the Son, and the Holy Spirit . . . Sable? Will you come back now?" Lenor asked quietly.

The thin body crumpled forward once again. Then, with a sigh, Sable sat up and opened her eyes. "Is it story time yet?"

Lenor smiled. *Amazing child.* "Do you have a protector?" she whispered.

"Of course. Two, actually. But one's crippled. I don't mind. She's always waiting for me."

"I'd like to talk to you later about being more careful, Sable," Lenor said.

"I had to show Jackie," Sable said simply.

"Your gift is not for parlor tricks," Lenor said. "And you must always work *en lo bueno*—in the good."

"I understand. Can we hear the rest of the story you started last night?"

"I'm not off duty yet, Sable. I'll be back later, after you've had your dinner. Okay?"

"Okay."

Ella pulled the curtain back to cheers and applause—and questions.

"What happened?"

"Jackie said Sable died. Did she?"

"I did not say that!"

"Sable? Are you okay?"

Sable sat up in her bed, crossed her legs Indian-fashion, then raised her right hand high above her head for silence. "I'm fine. Dr. T said she'd finish her story later, so you all just calm down and get some rest."

Lenor looked around the room. Happily, everyone was doing as Sable had asked. "Can anybody tell me where I left off?"

"Hail Guardians of the East!"

"It's 'Hail Guardians of the Watchtower.' You gotta say it right or it won't work," Sable said with twelve-year-old authority.

"Wanna bet? Wanna bet?" Jackie turned to face the nurse. "Sable thinks she knows everything about witches."

"I do," Sable said. "All kinds of witches!"

Ella Wygent started walking toward the door. "Calm down, girls. Let's not stretch any stitches here."

"Witch's stitches," a high-pitched voice piped, then giggled.

"But Jackie's got it wrong, Ms. Wygent," Sable protested. "The spirits won't listen unless . . ."

"Uh-uh," Jackie disagreed. "Dr. T said witches just make up their chants sometimes. Didn't you, Dr. Tavera? So I'm making up my own. So there." Jackie stuck out her tongue.

Ella shook her head. It was the same every time Lenor decided to spell the volunteers for story-telling duty. It didn't matter that the turnover of patients in Ward Two occurred regularly and frequently. At least one, sometimes two, were left to pass on the word about Lenor's story time to the next group.

"I'll just *show* you what I know, Miss Jackie," Sable said as Ella reached for the door. "Then you'll see who knows what about witches."

Lenor gave Sable a warning look, then said, "Thanks for catching me up, guys. See you later."

Ella caught the movement out of the corner of her eye. Someone who had been sitting in the chair at the head of the bed nearest the door jumped up, spilled her newspaper under the bed, and was moving quickly toward Dr. Tavera, who was looking the other way. "Lenor!"

The doctor turned just in time to take the hand that was about to land on her shoulder. "Mrs. Hess. I didn't realize you were here. Alicia is doing especially well—"

"I want my daughter out of here right this minute," Mrs. Hess whispered. "Do you hear me? This minute!"

"May we talk about this in the hallway, Mrs. Hess?" Lenor started forward, still holding the woman's hand. She glanced toward the bed Alicia Hess occupied. The child was reading a magazine, oblivious to what was going on around her. *Thank goodness!* "We don't want to upset the other patients, now do we?"

Ella held the door as Lenor ushered the distraught woman out of the room.

"Upset the others?" Mrs. Hess exploded, jerking her hand away from Lenor's as soon as the door closed behind them. "As if you haven't done that already, with your quackery and your crazy stories! What in God's name are you doing to those innocent children? I can't imagine how you—"

"Mrs. Hess, let's go into the staff lounge and talk this over. You're upset, but your daughter is doing very well. I'm sure we can straighten this out and you'll understand if—"

"I understand too much already. I don't want Alicia to spend another minute here. I'm going to call my husband."

And the woman hurried away.

"What was that all about?" Ella asked.

"Could she have overheard what was going on with Sable?"

Ella shook her head. "I don't see how. We were at the opposite end of the room."

"I don't understand it. Her daughter is recovering even better than I expected, but I certainly don't want her moved. She's been out of isolation only a week. Acute rheumatic fever is nothing to play around with. I'm going to check on Alicia. I don't want her upset, too."

"Want me to go after Mrs. Hess?" Ella asked.

Lenor thought a moment. "I guess not. I think she's too upset to be reasonable right now. Just make sure everybody knows to find me the instant Mrs. Hess comes back."

"Will do."

The ward was fairly quiet. An aide filled water pitchers. Pages rustled. The patients' reading materials varied from comic books to a heavy hardcover volume on dolphins. No one watched the softly droning soap opera on the TV at the far end of the room. Busy with a crossword puzzle, Alicia didn't see Lenor come in or even hear her when she spoke.

"Alicia?" Lenor bent closer to get a better look at the puzzle. "Mmm, that's a hard one."

"Just about the hardest one I ever tried," Alicia said, looking up. "Wanna help?"

"Oh, I'm not very good at crosswords. I just wanted to talk to you for a minute. Okay?"

"Sure." Alicia slid over and tapped the bed with her pencil. "Have a seat."

"Are you feeling pretty good?"

"Yeah." Alicia's eyes drifted back to the puzzle.

"Getting tired of staying in bed?"

"Yeah."

"How about the knees? Pain just about all gone?"

Alicia bent both knees up, let them fall down, drew them up again. Using her uplifted thighs as support, she quickly filled in a five-letter word.

"Very good. That was a tricky one. Any more problems with your stomach?"

Alicia shook her head.

"I'll bet your parents are pretty proud of how well you're doing," Lenor said.

"Yeah . . . I guess."

"Your mother's feeling all right?" Lenor asked casually.

"She has a headache, but that's nothing unusual," Alicia said.

"She has headaches often?"

"Lots of them. My dad says she was born with a headache."

"That's too bad."

"Yeah." Alicia finally looked away from her puzzle. "You gonna finish the story about the twin witches tonight?"

"Sure am."

"Good."

It was almost a dismissal. Alicia's attention turned immediately back to the magazine, and Lenor decided it would be prudent to take her leave. The child obviously didn't know what her mother intended or why.

Back at the nurses' station, Ella was just closing a patient's chart and returning it to the hanging file. "Find out anything?"

"Alicia didn't see or hear anything that went on. She did say that her mother has headaches all the time, though."

"Pain makes people do some strange things sometimes."

"Uh-huh." Tapping her finger on the counter, Lenor thought for a moment. "Maybe she objects to stories about witches."

"I guess some people might," Ella said. "Remember Bowder's initial reaction to story time?"

"Don't remind me," Lenor said.

The success of "story time" was now a legend, not only around Foley but at other hospitals in the area. After Lenor had completed three years of residency in internal medicine, four months into her cardiology residency, and after years of pleading and proposals, Carl Bowder had put her idea on trial. Even after hearing her assurances that it would not disturb the hospital's daily routines, he'd still been somewhat opposed.

Both Ella and Lenor were convinced that he hadn't been truthful about his reasons for opposing the idea. Hospital procedures being disrupted had had nothing to do with his initial resistance. They were sure of it. His objections were both political and personal and were directly tied to another article Lenor was writing about the now two-year-old program, after completing a year of follow-up studies. To many physicians, Carl Bowder included, who'd been schooled exclusively in the science of medicine, the mysterious power of the individual's mind to heal the body was unsettling. Advances in that area made them fear for their careers and subconsciously question the legitimacy of their own approach of using solely mechanical and chemical intervention in a multitude of illnesses. Stories were not high tech.

"And speaking of witch stories . . . could you please tell me what I saw in there with Sable?" Ella said.

"Sure. Let's grab something to drink and get off our feet for a few minutes."

The narrow little pantry room was busy. Two aides were filling pitchers with ice and water; a nurse squatted on the floor searching through a small freezer. "What happened to all the orange sherbet?" she asked.

Lenor looked at Ella and shrugged. "I suspect Dr. Simeon," Ella said, reaching around one of the aides for paper cups.

"She does have a sweet tooth," Lenor agreed. She'd often seen Dr. Simeon with a sack full of cookies she called her "bribing bag."

"Uh-oh." Ella nodded toward the doorway as she poured herself some coffee. "It's Jablonski. If he comes in, we'll never get out."

Lenor finished pouring water over ice and turned to look just as the entry filled with three hundred twenty pounds of the tallest, widest, gentlest man she'd ever met. Even at Lenor's near-six-foot height, Nurse Willie J. towered another foot and a half above her, from the bottom of his Nike soles to the bright red headband he wore as protection from doorjambs. Beside him, blond and petite, little Ella looked positively childlike as he backed up to let her out the door.

"Thanks," Ella said as she skirted around him and headed across the hall to the staff lounge. "The place is all yours."

"Good to see you, Willie," Lenor said, sidestepping into the hallway. "How's that knee?"

"Those exercises you showed me did the trick, Dr. T. Thanks."

"*De nada*. For nothing, Willy."

Ella pushed open the door of the staff lounge. "Oh, good, we have the room all to ourselves. You want the early Salvation Army couch or the Louis the Thirty-second recliner?"

Lenor headed for the sagging Lazy-Boy. "You have to promise me now, you won't say a word to anyone about Sable and what you saw this afternoon . . . at least not yet," she said, perching gingerly on the edge of the ancient recliner seat as Ella sank down into the worn cushions of the old couch.

"No problem. You have my word." She squirmed. "My God, this thing is uncomfortable."

"This won't take long to explain. Sable is adept at statuvolence."

"Self-hypnotism," Ella said.

"Yes. She was in a self-induced trance."

"A trance? You're kidding. What kind of trance?"

"Now that's a little harder to explain," Lenor said. "This is only conjecture at this point, you understand. Until I talk to her, ask her some questions, I won't know for sure exactly what or why she's doing what she's doing."

"But you already have some idea, don't you?"

"I think Sable is apprenticed to what we call back home a *curandera,* a healer. In this case an individual who's probably a spiritualist, and may or may not be a practicing healer. It could be that Aunt Judith she talks about."

"You mean she's actually learning how to go into a trance?"

"And contact spirits," Lenor said, nodding.

Ella was shaking her head. "This is *too much!* How in the world did you know what was happening to her? And how did you know what to do for her?"

"That's easy to explain. My mother's a *curandera,* and I went through the same *desarrollo,* the same kind of apprenticeship that I suspect Sable is going through."

"Your mother's a spiritual healer?" Ella asked.

"Actually, my mother has all three gifts. She can heal on the material level, which she prefers, using herbs and foods and objects, as well as on the mental level, using only her mind to diagnose and treat. When a problem calls for some extra help, she can use the spiritual level, *nivel espiritual,* for summoning a particular spirit to participate in the healing process. The combination of talents is quite rare."

"This is fascinating. Tell me more."

"Everyone has the ability to perceive far more than what's going in their immediate physical world. Some people just don't choose to use it, and most choose to deny the talent exists. Women are usually best at it—it's a right-brain activity. As far as Sable is concerned, the only dangers—"

The door opened, and Willie ducked his head in. "Phone call for you, Dr. T, on line two." He pointed to the phone on the table at the end of the couch. "You can take it in here if you want."

"Thanks, Willie. Trade places?" Lenor said to Ella, who was already struggling out of her seat. "Dr. Tavera here," she said into the receiver.

"I can't believe I got you on the first try!"

"Apple Hardy! How the hell's the sheriffing business these days?"

"Big crime wave here in Toya County. John Garcia's old rooster died. Mrs. Sikes's cat got stuck on top of our new telephone pole. Old Woosey, the mountain lion, has been after the calves again."

"Very suspicious stuff," Lenor said. "So what else is happening?"

"Same old thing. The camp kids have been driving Lucielle crazy for two weeks, and she loves it. Junior Garcia's driving his father crazy, and Roy is driving us all crazy, taking notes on everything we say and do. My beehive's still missing."

Lenor smiled. *Same old thing.* "So greater downtown Toya's got a new telephone pole," Lenor said. "I can't wait to see it."

"And we can't wait to see you, either. Grandpa's about set for his party. Has everybody hopping. Seems like Steven's everywhere at once, making sure nobody puts lard in anything he's gonna eat."

"Smart man." Ella had finished her coffee and signaled that she was leaving. Lenor pressed her hand over the receiver. "I'll be out in a minute," she whispered.

"Did I catch you at a bad time?" Apple asked.

"You picked exactly the right time. Ella Wygent and I were just sitting here having a cup of coffee."

"Then let me tell you about . . ."

Ella reached for Sable's chart, which was hanging in a rack alongside the computer terminal in the nurses' station, flipped open the aluminum cover, scanned the printouts, then read Dr. Tavera's unusual-for-a-doctor prose-style notes from morning rounds.

> Incredible recuperative abilities. This patient might still be in isolation for strep, but exhibits remarkable mind-over-matter techniques, even in the aftermath of severe complications from glomerulonephritis. Physical therapy is now at maximum, but the patient persists, doing double—triple—the amount of acceptable prescribed exertion. No ill effects noted. Patient "meditates" four times a day. Unusual behavior in a child of twelve.

No mention of trances or spirits—yet. Ella closed the cover and returned the chart to the proper slot. Just like Dr. Tavera, giving all the credit to the patient, she thought. But something still bothered her about Sable. Something Dr. Bowder might be bothered about, too. She'd have to ask Dr. Tavera if her fears should be a real cause for concern.

"Mrs. Wygent?"

Ella turned to see the aide who worked the yellow hall where Ward Two was located. "Yes?"

"I found this under Alicia's bed. I know how you like to keep up with the news, and nobody else claimed it." She handed Ella a neatly folded afternoon newspaper.

"Well, thank you. I appreciate your thinking of me." From day one on the job the young woman had been something of a bootlicker, but since she performed her duties well and was good with the children, Ella tolerated her occasional fawning. She tucked the paper under her arm and was about to turn back around when she saw Mrs. Hess push through the swinging doors at the end of the hall.

"Dr. T!"

Lenor put her hand over the phone again. "What is it, Willie?"

"Mrs. Hess is back."

Lenor nodded to him, then spoke into the receiver. "Gotta go. I'm really glad you could spend a little time with Carmela. Tell her I'll come over and check the children while I'm there."

"Will do. See you soon."

Lenor stood up. "Where is she, Willie?"

"Ella's talking to her in the yellow hall."

"Thanks." Lenor hurried out of the lounge, past the nurses' station. As she entered the yellow hall, she realized that Willie J. was following her. Briefly she worried what a hysterical woman might do if she were confronted by a seven-foot-six man wearing a bright red headband. But Mrs. Hess and Ella were talking quietly outside the door to Ward Two. Just in case, Lenor signaled for Willie J. to wait at a distance.

"Don't get me wrong," Mrs. Hess was saying. "I'm still upset, but my husband disagrees with me, and I've always found it's easier to defer to his wishes—at least for a time."

"Thank you for changing your mind, Mrs. Hess," Lenor said, stopping beside her.

"What?" Mrs. Hess asked.

"I said, thank you for changing your mind. Moving Alicia at this time in her treatment could have been disastrous. She's been on complete bed rest for only four weeks now."

"And she's doing so very well," Ella interjected.

"It won't be long now. You'll have your daughter home again," Lenor said.

"But what will she bring with her?" Mrs. Hess said quietly.

"Excuse me?" Ella said.

"Nothing. It's nothing," Mrs. Hess said, shaking her head.

"I can assure you, Alicia will come home healthy, Mrs. Hess," Ella said. "We're very careful here at Foley to keep—"

"I told you, it's nothing," Mrs. Hess said again, this time a little more forcefully. "I want to see my daughter now."

Lenor put a hand on the woman's shoulder. "I'm not sure it's—"

"I promise I won't upset her, if that's what you're worried about."

"It is," Lenor said firmly.

"You have my word, Dr. Tavera. You don't have anything to worry about on my account. My daughter's welfare is my uppermost concern."

"And ours also," Lenor said. "Go ahead. I'm sure Alicia is wondering where you are."

"I doubt it," Mrs. Hess whispered as she turned toward the door.

Lenor was sure the woman hadn't intended that her comment be heard. Instead of feeling that the crisis was past, Lenor had the distinct impression it was just beginning. She turned to Ella. "I almost wish I wasn't leaving town this weekend," she said.

"But you've never missed your grandfather's birthday party. Why—"

Lenor glanced toward the doorway Mrs. Hess had just entered.

"You don't think she'll—"

"I really don't know what she might do. That's a very unhappy woman. But there's something else about her . . . can't put my finger on it. . . . There's something wrong, something I'm missing. If I could just spend a little time with her, talk to her."

"About her headaches?" Ella asked.

"Among other things." A message was trying to get through all of Mrs. Hess's denial, but her hysteria kept blocking the signals from Lenor. There was definitely something wrong with the woman.

A woman's voice spoke over the intercom. "Dr. Tavera to ER."

"See you later."

Ella watched as Lenor hurried away. As the doctor rounded the corner and disappeared from her view, Ella glanced down at the newspaper she was holding.

BOWDER BOOTS *BRUJA*?

Four

"GOD, I LOVE THIS STUFF!"

Lenor felt like shuddering every time she saw George Murphy put another bite of the gravy-laden chicken-fried steak into his mouth. She assumed that the hospital cafeteria did a good job preparing it, but she would never know. She had more respect for her arteries than that. And he, a cardiac surgeon, should too. But once again George had passed up the newest additions to the hospital cafeteria line, steamed vegetables and crisp salads, low-fat rice pilafs, pasta and bean dishes, in favor of the smothered hunk and fries. *No arguments tonight,* she reminded herself.

"As a born and bred New Yorker, how did you ever get started eating that southern dish?" she asked.

"My . . . grandmother . . ." he managed between chews, ". . . rest her soul."

She no doubt died of a massive coronary or stroke. Don't ask!

He swallowed, took a sip of his coffee, and swiped at his mouth with a napkin. "Lived all her life in Tennessee. Outside Chattanooga. My father, her youngest son, brought the recipe with him when he came to New York at the age of seventeen. Told me he used to fry it up in an old iron skillet on a hot plate. It wasn't easy, but he craved a taste of home now and again."

"I know how he felt. Sometimes I think I'll go crazy if I can't have a big bowl of green chile stew."

"Won't be long now. We'll be in New Mexico tomorrow by about noon."

"You have the tickets?" Lenor asked.

George smiled. "Everything's set, plus a surprise or two. You don't have to worry about any of it. Just pack your clothes, put Watson in his little traveling cat box, and prime your taste buds."

"You are a darling, George."

"And brave, too. Except for a convention here and there, I've managed to stay in New York City all my life. This will be my first time ever in a foreign country!" There was a horrified look on his face. "Oh no!"

"What?"

"I forgot my visa!" George said, faking anguish.

"Now cut that out. Just because New Mexico's west of the Hudson doesn't mean it's outside the United States."

"West of the Hudson, hell! New Mexico is west of Texas!"

"So is California, George."

He jabbed his fork into the gooey steak and sawed at it with his knife. "So your geography is better than mine . . . you don't have to rub it in. At least I know where to get the perfect bagel."

"Touché." She watched him with her usual pleasure. He was taller than her by four inches, with big strong hands and long fingers much like her father's, and an angular face with enough character to be the model for one of Michael Martino's carvings of saints. Except for the glasses, of course. None of Martino's *santos* wore wire rims. But the gold–wire–rim spectacles served to make George look saintly in a way, intelligent, down to business, down to earth. And he was all those things.

"I'm going to make evening rounds. Want to come along?" George asked.

"I want to, but I can't. I promised the kids on Ward Two I'd finish a story."

"Guess I'm stuck with Rickter." George pointed his fork at Lenor, leaned forward, and lowered his voice. "You know, that man makes me feel sort of uncomfortable. I probably shouldn't say this, but I don't think he likes any of his patients."

Rickter was one of the arrogant ones Lenor could barely tolerate. "Full of himself," she said.

"Huh?"

"Something my mother would say. He seems to be quite taken with his own wonderfulness."

"That's exactly it," George said. "Smart woman, your mother. I can't wait to meet her."

"And all the rest?" Lenor asked.

"Tell me again. Besides your grandfather Steven, who all will be there for this annual event?"

"Well, let's see. My mother and father, Magdalena and Rafael, Grandma Jovita, Aunt Isabel. Of course, the Seña family, Nemesia and Rudolfo, Rudolfo's sister Angelina, and probably all four of their kids: Lita, Arthur, Gilberto, and Eloy. Rudolfo Seña is my dad's ranch foreman. Lucielle, the woman who helps my mother with our summer camp . . . the camp kids will be there, too. Miller Baldwin will come if he's not busy. He's the doctor over in Mora, and his son, Roy, will be there for sure. There'll be a lot of people from Toya . . . and Apple Hardy, my best friend since grade school."

"And she's the sheriff?" George asked.

"Of Toya County," Lenor said nodding. "But sometimes she pulls double duty to help out if Mora's sheriff is busy. There's a lot of country to cover out there."

"Now let me get this straight. Mora is the county seat of Mora County and Toya is the county seat of Toya County. Right?"

"You're a quick study, Dr. Murphy."

George reached across the table and took her hand. "And you're a beautiful and fascinating woman, Dr. Tavera." He gave her hand a squeeze. "I can't tell you how excited I am to be taking this trip with you. It's all so . . . so . . ."

"Exotic?" Lenor offered.

"And mysterious."

And poor. But she'd let him see that for himself. "I'd better get upstairs now," she said. "The kids don't like to be kept waiting."

George extracted a roll of antacid tablets from the pocket in his white coat and began opening it. "I'll call you early."

She knew it would be exactly four A.M. George didn't trust alarm clocks and had taught himself to wake up precisely when he wanted to. Tonight he would tap his forehead four times just before he drifted off to sleep. He was living proof the mind could be a powerful ally—if one knew how to use it. He was going to need her help, though, to get rid of his need for antacids.

"Hail, Guardians of the Watchtowers of the East," Sable said.

Lenor couldn't believe her ears as Sable went on with the chant. She could have sworn Sable had been sound asleep before the point in last night's story where the twins had first seen and heard the witch's chant.

> "Hail, Guardians of the Watchtowers of the East,
> Powers of Air!
> We invoke you and call you,
> Golden Eagle of the Dawn,
> Star-seeker,
> Whirlwind,
> Rising Sun,
> Come!
> By the air that is Her breath,
> Send forth your light,
> Be here now!"

Lenor was astounded. "Where did you learn that, Sable?"

"I don't know."

"Sable can say lots of poems, Dr. T," someone said.

"I told her the first part, Dr. T," Jackie said.

"Yeah, but you told me wrong. You said, 'Hail, Guardians of the East.' "

"How did *you* know it was wrong?" Jackie asked. "You were

asleep during that part of the story last night. You were even snoring out loud."

"Was not."

"Were, too."

"Ladies, please. Maybe Sable was just *almost* asleep last night." Lenor looked at Sable and knew for certain that that had not been the case. She changed the subject. "Let's see now . . . The mysterious lady, sometimes mistakenly called *La Llorona*—that's another story—was just about to turn around and find Mary and Anna hiding behind a tree, and the twin girls were so scared that they were shaking the leaves off the branches."

"A silly old witch wouldn't scare me," Jackie said.

"Bet she would," someone argued.

"I've seen a witch before," Sable said.

"Bet you haven't."

"My Aunt Judith's a witch," Sable said calmly.

"Dr. T! Sable's lying again," Jackie said.

Lenor thought for a moment. Both girls were acting exactly in character, and Lenor didn't want to discount or contradict either girl's beliefs. She decided to be philosophical and address the interchange instead of the validity of either opinion. "It's impossible to know another person or another person's reality completely," Lenor said. "The kindest thing to do, when someone tells you something you don't quite believe, is to just let it pass and reserve your own judgment until you have all the facts about the matter."

"But what if you already know for sure that . . ."

"It's really hard to know everything exactly for sure," Lenor said. "Mary and Anna thought they knew everything about their woods—but they didn't . . ."

After their initial argument, Jackie and Sable settled down and listened. Lenor always encouraged interjection, so everyone had the opportunity to participate. The only voice she wasn't hearing this evening was Alicia's. The child seemed tired, which wasn't unusual for her condition, but it *was* unusual for her not to ask at least one question during a story. *I'll check her over again before I go home.*

". . . so Mary and Anna drove their pony cart away from the witch's house and decided that very night, before they went to sleep, that doing their family chores and taking care of their baby brother wasn't nearly as boring as they'd thought."

"I still think doing dishes is boring," Jackie said.

"Not if you put too much soap in the water," someone said with a giggle.

"Dr. Tavera to five-four-six," the intercom paged.

"Gotta go, ladies. See you all Tuesday morning."

"Have a good trip, Dr. T."

"Say Happy Birthday to your grandpa for us."

"Bring us back some birthday cake."

"I need a *bulto*," Sable said quietly. "My protector—the crippled one—told me about this special kind of statue made of wood. She said it would help me stay well."

"The Virgin Mary?" Lenor asked.

"No. Saint Michael."

"The guardian of small children," Lenor said, then silently questioned Sable's choice. Did she really need the opponent of the devil and all evil, the patron of soldiers? But the request for the carved wooden statue was plainly in Sable's mind. "I'll talk to Mr. Martino."

Sable pulled a ring from her finger and pressed it into Lenor's palm. "This is for payment."

"I understand," Lenor said. "But tell me. Why Saint Michael?"

"I don't know," Sable said.

"Dr. T?"

It was Alicia, and Lenor felt a sense of relief at finally hearing her voice.

"You forgot to tell us Mary and Anna's last name."

"Barela," Sable said immediately, before Lenor had time to make one up. "It's Barela."

Keeping the surprise off her face, Lenor turned. "That's a very pretty name. Do you know someone named Barela?"

"No." Sable shrugged. "I just know that's their last name."

Jackie piped up again. "Sable, you're so full of—"

Lenor raised her hand for silence. "Good night, ladies."

Barela.

The name had no meaning, though it sounded familiar. Lenor couldn't remember if or where or by whom she'd heard it mentioned. Neither in New York nor in New Mexico could she remember anyone called Barela. But there had to be some reason Sable had thought of it. Lenor tried to remember if her father or mother had ever mentioned anyone named Barela, but couldn't, and hoped she wasn't blocking something she needed to know.

Barela.

It was well past eleven before Lenor was ready to leave the hospital. At this time of night the underground tunnel that would take her beneath the street and to within half a block of her apartment building was completely deserted. Even though she loved her big-city life, the poorly lighted, enclosed space always made her long for the open reaches of her home in New Mexico. Some day she might take the time for an extended vacation back in her "Land of Enchantment," but not while her conscience plagued her with almost unbearable guilt for not practicing medicine in Toya County. Since she'd left home for school, there had been only brief, unsatisfying visits and uncomfortable, sad goodbyes.

Barela.

The name kept popping into her mind. Without knowing why or what, Sable had been trying to tell her something—or warn her. Could the name have anything to do with the carved saint Sable had asked for? she wondered, or with the *santero,* Michael Martino, who would carve the *bulto* from the cottonwood root? She had intended to talk to Sable after checking on Alicia, but then Sable had been sound asleep, and Lenor hadn't had the heart to wake her. She was sure Sable would have been able to tell her at least something about the way she came to know the name.

"Barela."

The sound of her own voice startled her, and she looked quickly around to see if anyone had heard her speak aloud. To her surprise she had already exited the tunnel, climbed the stairs to the street level, and was standing on the sidewalk. None of the people around her was paying any attention. Typical New Yorkers.

The trip to quiet New Mexico would be a welcome interlude, especially now that Lenor knew Alicia Hess was still on the progressive road to recovery. She sighed and realized just how tired she was, how good her bed was going to feel, how nice it was to have a place to come home to—even if it was a studio so narrow you had to lift the bed up into the wall to walk across the blessedly ample depth of the room.

Dishes from last night's late-night snack were still on the coffee table, the pull-down bed was unmade and rumpled, and the makeshift bookshelves, floor to ceiling, that occupied all the available wall space needed dusting. But the clutter was all but unnoticeable. Lenor stood in the opened doorway and took a deep and satisfying breath.

The first impression anyone had when entering the room was the almost overwhelming fragrance of both living and drying herbs. Little pots balanced precariously on shelf edges, green-laden baskets and tawny, crisp bundles hung from the ceiling, small trees sprang from terra-cotta earthenware. The narrow glass shelves in three greenhouse windows groaned with the burden of tangles and shoots and blossoms. Those three kitchenette windows had been Lenor's reason for choosing this apartment over all the others she'd looked at.

Everywhere else there was evidence of handmade, homemade personal comforts with a New Mexico flair. Coiled and woven Indian baskets of various sizes and a variety of small clay pots lined the bookshelves in front of the unbroken rows of books and served as handy containers for everything from herbs to jewelry to computer disks. Red Navajo sashes hung from ceiling hooks in one corner. Rumpled, along with sheets striped in desert hues, was a colorful quilt Lenor's mother had sent her. The quilt had been hand sewn by a woman named Juanita, who now worked for Michael Martino as his housekeeper. Surrounded by her plants and her treasures from home, Lenor automatically relaxed. The Taj Mahal couldn't have looked more inviting.

On the counter of the pass-through beside the entry to the tiny kitchen, Lenor had left her open suitcase. She could see two furry black points sticking up over the edge. *I should have closed that thing!*

"Watson! Get off those clean shirts!" The ears disappeared and four white paws rolled slowly into view. "Watson!" This time he reacted as if he'd been attacked. An enormous streak of black and white shot up and out of the open case, leaped the considerable distance from the counter to the bed, then stopped short. He slowly stretched then, as if trying to show off the elegant white socks on his front feet to their best advantage. His languid yawn was accompanied by a lazy, high-pitched greeting.

"Eee?"

She dropped her purse onto the coffee table that was wedged between the couch and the end of the bed, then knelt on the edge of the mattress. "I see you didn't do any cleaning up around here while I was at work." Purring loudly enough to be heard in the next apartment, Watson rubbed his nicked and slightly shredded right ear against her belt buckle. "I suppose you have no excuse for your laziness this time, either." More purring. "Let's see what we can find to eat." She lifted him, tucked and rolled to the other side of the bed, then stood. Watson was nonplussed by their loop-the-loop, but as soon as Lenor stepped closer to the suitcase, Watson pushed and struggled against her shoulder.

"I don't want you on those clean clothes again," she warned. But the shirt on top of the stack was now spotted with black hair—and something else.

Watson stepped into the case and batted at a smooth black stone.

Lenor looked up. Sure enough, her good-luck piece, given to her by her father, was missing from its usual place on the edge of the bookcase above the counter. She reached into the suitcase.

"Ssss!" Teeth bared in warning, Watson swiped at her, but his claws calculatedly missed their mark.

"Okay! I got the message! Why didn't you just tell me you wanted to take that rock on the trip?" She lifted all twenty-one pounds of the now-docile cat from the suitcase and lowered him to the floor.

"Eee."

"Flying is safer than crossing a street, Watson. But if you think we'll need a little extra good luck, I won't argue." Lenor bent down and patted his head. "Now why don't you do something useful and help me find my old herbal. Hmm. Let's see . . ." She scanned each bookcase, then walked all the way around the room, touching a book here and there, moving a knickknack this way and that, while Watson made his own search, balancing precariously on shelf edges. Neither found what they were looking for.

"I'm almost sure it's at home," Lenor told Watson. "We'll find it when we get there."

By a little after midnight, both Lenor and Watson were ready. For her usual bedtime ritual, Lenor steeped catnip tea in a saucer-covered cup, and Watson paced the length of the bed waiting impatiently for his pinch of fresh catnip leaves. The apartment had been straightened, clothes packed, cat carrier retrieved from the top shelf of the closet. Watson's precious black rock was tucked safely inside. He chomped ecstatically at the end of the bed as Lenor settled back on her pillows and dialed a long-distance number.

"Ten o'clock and all's well," a familiar voice answered. "How's the tea tonight?"

"Delicious."

"And the cookies?"

Though the man on the other end of the line couldn't see her, Lenor felt a flush of embarrassment. "I'm only having one," she said defensively. "How did you know, anyhow?"

"I was with Lucielle while she was making them. And I dropped the package off at the post office for her. Don't worry. Your little secret indulgence is safe with me."

"Have you been cooking all day?" Lenor asked.

"All week's more like it."

"So Grandpa has you jumping through hoops, too?"

"About like usual. Maybe a little less than usual. I don't think Grandpa's feeling all that well."

Lenor's stomach tensed. "What do you mean?"

"I don't know. Just a feeling I had. Nothing specific. Maybe Mr. Vigil's death . . ."

Lenor relaxed a bit. That had to be it, of course. This morning she'd felt her grandfather's sadness, but he'd also said he didn't feel a day over thirty. "Daniel and Grandpa were good friends," she said.

"What time will you be here tomorrow?"

"Late afternoon. I'm not sure exactly. George made all the arrangements," Lenor said.

"George Murphy's coming with you?"

"Uh-huh." Lenor caught the displeasure in his voice. "You'll like him, Roy."

"We'll see."

"Just like in high school. You're still disapproving of my boyfriends," Lenor said.

"Is he a boyfriend . . . or a lover?"

"He's a friend, Roy. That's all right now. You know how cautious I am—everyone should be."

"You should be too busy for such nonsense."

"Having George for a friend isn't nonsense, Roy. It makes perfect sense if you think about it. We work together every day."

"And play together every night?"

"Hardly! Working sixteen-hour days doesn't leave much time for play." *Why am I being defensive? Roy's just being Roy, the inveterate pseudo big brother. After all these years, I should be used to it.* "You're going to like George. Just take my word for it."

"Will it make any difference if I don't?" Roy asked.

"Not a bit."

"I didn't think so."

"Just *kidding,* Roy! Don't take everything so seriously. You know your opinions are important to me."

Roy forced a little laugh. "I knew you were kidding."

Lenor listened while Roy took a deep breath. She knew he was waiting for her to tease him about being overprotective, but she wasn't in the mood for their usual banter.

"I'm glad you're coming home," he said finally.

"I'll see you tomorrow afternoon."

"Not if I see you first."

"Good night, Roy."

Before getting herself ready for bed, Lenor had brushed Watson's long hair until it gleamed and dressed him in his red elastic collar with three dangling metal tags. Now, when she started to snuggle down, he roused a bit and the tags clinked together. Unbelievably, he didn't object to the indignity nor the noisy jingling as he usually did.

First the rock and now this? Something strange is going on. Lenor got up and filled a glass bowl with water from a crystal decanter, then put the bowl on the night table beside the bed. From the drawer in the table she took a rosary and a crucifix and placed them beside the bowl. "I understand. We have to talk," she said aloud. "Let's give it a try while I get some rest, shall we?" she invited as she climbed into bed.

June 1860 ◆ The Territory of New Mexico

The loud banging on the front gate woke Leonora Tavera instantly. "I'm coming," she whispered as loudly as she dared, but she knew her softly spoken words would not carry through the thick adobe walls of the hacienda.

"Señora!"

There was agony in the man's voice, and Leonora hurried to find her other slipper in the darkened room before the children were awakened by the ruckus. It wasn't unusual for her to be awakened in the middle of the night by someone's knocking at the front gate, especially since the soldiers at Fort Union had learned that Señora Tavera could heal their wounds and keep her mouth shut about where and how they'd gotten hurt. "I'm coming," she whispered again.

"Mama?"

"Go back to sleep, Dorio. You have much work to do in the morning."

"Yes, Mama."

But Leonora heard her son's movements and knew the boy would follow her out into the courtyard, then crouch behind the stone well to watch. Leonora smiled to herself as she stepped through the bedroom doorway. Dorio was going to make an excellent *curandero* . . . and he'd already learned a lot of English.

The northern New Mexico sky was perfectly clear; the stars above the open courtyard sparkled and laughed as if nothing were amiss, even though the mare in the corral at the back of the hacienda was stamping her heavy hooves and grumbling in distress. Leonora offered a silent prayer for a steady hand and a clear mind as she hurried toward the wagon-wide entryway on the east side of the house.

"Amen," Leonora breathed, crossing herself as she stepped between the thick adobe walls that flanked the entrance. The clatter against the heavy double gate continued, but the plaintive "Señora," had given way to anguished weeping in a different voice. Leonora slid the timber latch back through its metal guides and pulled open the smaller door within the gate. Two men stood outside, one barely able to stand, the other supporting him.

"¿Qué pasa?"

"It's Harold," the man said anxiously. Then, in halting Spanish, "Captain Wright caught him coming back from Loma Parda and thought he should have been on the night watch. The captain was wrong, but that didn't keep him from beating Harold sense-less."

Loma Parda again, Leonora thought. So much trouble in such a little town. Everyone called it Sodom on the Mora, for it tempted the wild young soldiers at Fort Union with every con-ceivable sin of the flesh. Leonora had treated many of the young men, because they dared not present themselves to the doctor at the fort after visiting the off-limits village. "Your name?" she asked.

"Private Roger Colby, ma'am."

"Come in. Hurry."

Harold's feet stuttered over the timber that framed the bottom of the small doorway as his friend all but dragged him inside. Roger knew exactly where to go; he headed for the kitchen in the middle of the northern wing of the hacienda.

Leonora closed the door, slid the locking timber back in place, and hurried toward the well. "Dorio, come with me," she whis-pered as she lifted a half-full bucket of water from the stone well casing. Without looking back, she knew the child was padding quietly behind her.

"Open the door, child, light the candles," she said to Dorio. "Put Harold on the floor in front of the fireplace," to Roger. "Fetch two blankets and a pillow," to Dorio. Pointing to a large willow basket beside the massive corner fireplace, she told Roger, "More wood on the fire, stir it to life, get this water to boiling," and handed him the bucket. Her orders were obeyed swiftly without a single question.

Dorio came back with the blankets and pillow, took a large key from his mother's hand, and unlocked the *dispensa*. "What do you need from the storage room, Mama?"

As Leonora covered her patient and tried to make him more comfortable, she continued to speak crisply. "Bring the liniment, *potentilla, calabazilla, contra yerba* . . ."

"*Contra yerba* alone?"

"No. The powdered mixture with *yerba buena, mastranzo, and oshá*." Harold's left arm lay outstretched in a pool of blood. *Holy*

Mother of God. "Cayenne!" she shouted toward the *dispensa* door-way, then lowered her head, pressing her ear to his chest. She listened for a moment. "Hurry! He'll be in shock soon." Then to Roger, "More light here."

Without being told what to do, Dorio brought the herbs and medicaments back into the kitchen and began to dip the heated water into smaller metal pots, adding a handful of this and a pinch of that, then sitting the pots in the fireplace to boil or steep or simmer.

Leonora worked in silence for a time, her motions guiding the others'. She lifted Harold's feet onto the pillow; Roger knelt beside her and helped undress his friend as Leonora made a thorough inspection of his wounds. She offered Harold a smooth, black stone. "Hold it very tightly, señor. It will help relieve your pain," she said. Then she sprinkled the precious capsicum-cayenne on every gash and tear in his tender flesh to stop the profuse flow of blood. Dorio brought strips of white cloth and dipped some of them into the liniment he'd warmed, then damp-ened others and used them to cleanse the skin around Harold's many wounds.

After several minutes of silence and frantic labor, Leonora looked up with fear in her eyes. *"Susto!"* she whispered, then said in English, "He's in shock. His blood is not circulating properly, and his heart is beating too fast. His body has taken too much abuse."

Roger's mournful eyes closed over hot tears, and his body seemed to crumple under the weight of Leonora's words. His head lowered, both hands covered his face, and his slight shoul-ders shook with weeping. "He's . . . my . . . friend."

Leonora stripped back the blankets and pressed a hand to Harold's stomach. Side to side her sensitive fingers moved, searching for a sign. "Ah . . ." The swelling was an infinitesimal rise just below the rib cage on the left side of his abdomen.

"Canutillo del Llano! Quickly!"

Dorio knew what to do. When the herb had steeped, he poured the infusion from one of the small pots into a tin cup, motioned for Roger to raise Harold's head, then offered the warm liquid to Harold's dry lips.

Leonora breathed a silent prayer. *Let no friendship as great as theirs be ended this night.* Pointing toward a table in the corner of the room, she said to Roger, "Please fetch that crystal bowl filled with water."

Dorio backed away, stopped trying to get Harold to drink from the cup. The herb was of little use now, and *el don,* the gift his mother had for working on the *nivel espiritual,* spiritual level, would have to be used. He went into the storeroom and brought back a small, stoppered bottle, then took the *bulto* of San Miguel from the *nicho* beside the fireplace.

When Roger had brought the crystal bowl to Leonora, she knelt beside her patient, dipped her fingers into the water, and touched her forehead and the base of her skull. With her face just inches above the bowl of water, she began to chant: "In the name of the Father, the Son, and the Holy Spirit, God the Father, God the Son, God the Holy Spirit, dear brother, Saint Michael the Archangel, give this child your spiritual strength and protection."

"Aceite preparado," Dorio whispered, handing the small bottle to his mother.

With a drop of the oil on her finger, Leonora made the sign of the cross on Harold's forehead, across her own body, then took his hand. She closed her eyes and for several long minutes said nothing.

When Roger didn't think he could stand the tense silence any longer, Leonora opened her eyes.

"Saint Michael will intervene," she said quietly as she lay the *bulto* beside the motionless body.

Roger nodded.

"Now we must give the medicines and San Miguel time to work. Sleep, Dorio. Señor Colby, you may stay if you wish. Lie by the fireplace and you will be warm enough."

Cleansed of the caking blood, his wounds treated and bound, his soul released to the care of his summoned protector, Saint Michael, and his Maker, Harold Whisner slept.

Leonora sat beside him for the rest of the night, monitoring his pulse, his breathing, systematically checking his bandages for renewed bleeding and his abdomen for the swelling signs of further internal hemorrhage. Near dawn, the *curandera* finally slept, also.

Though the objects she'd put on the nightstand were supposed to keep her from being frightened by her dreams, Lenor awoke trembling. But nothing about the dream had been frightening.

Maybe it was the fact that she hadn't dreamt of her father's great-great-grandmother since her grandfather had been desperately ill ten years ago. Though Roy had thought Grandpa wasn't feeling well, Apple had told Lenor that everything was fine back home. Odd that Leonora, her namesake, wanted to speak to her now. And strangely, there had been no mention of Barela, as she'd expected there might be.

There were some dream clues to be investigated. The black river rock Leonora had given to her patient was the same stone Rafael had given Lenor as a good-luck piece, the same rock Watson had defended so ferociously. The *bulto* carved of cottonwood that Leonora kept in her kitchen had been of Saint Michael, the same kind Sable had requested last night. Which reminded Lenor that she would have to get in touch with Michael Martino while she was home.

Michael. The *santero,* carver of saints. The Martinos had been the Tavera family's neighbors since the year of Lenor's birth. That year Ramon Martino had bought the little log cabin and several hundred acres of land at the far edge of the Tavera property from Lenor's father, Rafael. Young Michael had gone to school in Mora, so Lenor and her friends from Toya had seen him infrequently, mostly at sporting events and school activities. But oh, how those brief glimpses of him set all the young ladies' hearts to beating—including her own.

Michael.

The thought of Michael Martino made her tremble again. *Why now?* She hadn't thought about her teenage obsession for a very long time. And she hadn't had this quaking schoolgirl reaction since . . . how long had it been? Maybe fifteen years? *Yes.* A rodeo at the state fair in Albuquerque. Michael had brought some quarter horses to show and compete. And he'd escorted Lenor and Apple around the midway, bought them dinner at the Laguna Indian booth, shopped for jewelry at all the Indian village stalls. She and Apple both had been blithering idiots by the time their devastatingly handsome neighbor had said good-bye.

"I've *got* to marry that man," Apple had said.

"Me, too," Lenor had confessed.

"We're being totally unrealistic. He's in college and he's eons older than we are," Apple had said.

"I know, but . . ." Lenor had swooned.

The girls had talked of little else for months afterward. And being the envy of every other girl in school wasn't such a bad thing. They'd played it for all it was worth. "I wonder if Apple remembers," Lenor said aloud, and Watson opened an eye to see if he was being summoned. "Just thinking out loud, boy. Go back to sleep."

The digital clock glowed 3:59. Watson slept again, this morning curled comfortably inside his traveling case on the end of the bed. Lenor propped herself up on the pillows and smiled. The phone would ring in precisely thirty-five seconds.

"Caught you napping, didn't I?" George said in his cheery morning voice.

"I've been up for hours," Lenor lied.

"Did you pack your best dress like I asked you to?"

"Yes, but I still don't understand why—"

"You'll understand soon enough. Will you be ready when I get there?" he asked.

"With bells on. Just come on up. The door will be unlocked."

"Damn it, Lenor! I've told you over and over again to keep your door locked! This is New York, for God's sake."

"I planned to unlock it when I heard you coming up the

stairs, George," she lied again. "But I'll leave it locked, and you can use your key. Will that be all right?"

"Much better. See you soon . . . and thanks."

"For what?"

"Keeping yourself safe."

"You're welcome."

Her shower was quicker than usual, her hairstyle easy, one long, loose braid down her back. Over scant wisps of lacy underwear she put on Levi's, a man's dress shirt of crisp white cotton, dark brown leather boots, then wrapped one of the red Navajo sashes around her waist for a belt. Putting on her jewelry and the beige suede vest decorated with silver conchos would have to wait. Wearing metal objects during a trance could be dangerous. She looked at the clock. Still plenty of time to contact Leonora.

Watson fed and watered, suitcase by the door, bed lifted and behind closed double doors, Lenor moved the wooden chair from her corner desk to the center of the tan-and-black Indian rug that once belonged to Leonora Tavera, and sat down. The small tape machine on the coffee table recorded with a quiet whir. She closed her eyes and cautioned her own spirit to stay close by.

Within seconds Lenor's body slumped forward. A moment later she sat bolt upright. That part of her mind remaining as an observer and a watchdog prevented complete possession and afforded her the opportunity for conversation.

"You are unprotected." The voice was high-pitched but mellow.

"No time," Lenor said. "You wanted to speak to me?"

"To the son of my son's son. You'll see him soon."

"My grandfather. I understand," Lenor said.

"Michael will give you something for your grandfather."

"Michael Martino?" Lenor asked.

"Yes. See that your grandfather keeps it."

"I will give Michael's gift to my grandfather," Lenor said.

George was about to knock on the door when he heard Lenor's voice. *Uh-oh, she's on the phone. Please don't let it be an emergency at the hospital.* He inserted his key, turned it, then touched the knob and heard another sound, high-pitched, a stranger's voice.

"Lenor?" he called out. No answer.

He opened the door and froze.

The only person in the room was *not* Lenor Tavera.

Five

June ◆ Northern New Mexico, County of Toya

MICHAEL MARTINO DEALT BLOW AFTER SAVAGE BLOW to the red-hot curve of iron on the anvil. The tongs that held the victim of his agitation vibrated against his gloved hand with every loud clang of the hammer, and sizzling sparks flew toward him. Since before dawn he'd been working, without pause, on the new horseshoes intended for Oñique, his new stallion.

Michael's night had been sleepless again, and he didn't know why. The disquiet of both mind and body that had been plaguing him for the past few days had increased just after dinner yesterday, when Eloy Seña had asked him when he wanted to ride Oñique. Michael had gotten angry at his foreman for being impatient, lashed out at him with no provocation at all. And he was still angry and apprehensive for no good reason he could think of. He stopped hammering, stabbed the iron back into the coals, and began working the bellows again. It was going to be a long day.

"Cool morning."

"Not in here." Michael looked up from the brick forge, acknowledged Eloy's entrance with a frown, then returned his attention to the glowing coke that concealed his workpiece.

"Got the jump on me this morning."

Michael could feel the tension in Eloy's voice, the lilt that made the simple statement of fact sound almost like a question. Eloy had been inside the smithing shed for only a minute and already he was perspiring as if he'd been working over the forge for hours. *Let it be,* Michael cautioned himself. "I couldn't sleep," he said.

Eloy swiped at a droplet on his brow that threatened to slip into his eye. "Don't blame you," he said, almost casually. "I had some trouble myself. New horse. Always makes for an exciting day."

"Like any other," Michael said, releasing the pull-strap that operated the overhead bellows. He reached for the cross-peen hammer he'd put down on the nearby anvil. The cooler air, away from the hot blast of the coals, made the dark hair on his arm prickle, the sensation reminding him that he'd been holding the bellows strap for a long time.

Eloy pulled on a pair of heavy gloves while his boss drew the tongs that held one of the new stallion's steel training plates from the fire, then automatically reached for a punch and pliers. Neither man spoke while Eloy placed, and Michael drove, the square-tipped punch through the yellow-hot curve of iron.

"Drift," Michael said.

But Eloy already had the tapering metal tool in his hand. The eight small holes were shaped and rounded perfectly with a quick succession of hammer blows. Just as quickly, Michael plunged the shoe into the quench tub.

"Shoe looks pretty good," Eloy said over the hissing sound.

Michael didn't respond. What was the use? Thanks to his own inexplicable anger he couldn't be civil, and his foreman didn't need the aggravation.

"Almost as good as I could have done," Eloy quipped.

"You were still in bed. I didn't want to wait."

"Guess you didn't get your painting done last night," Eloy said.

"What the hell does *that* have to do with anything?"

Eloy picked up the thirty-pound sledge that was leaning against the forge. "When a man has more to do than he can handle, it gets to him sometimes."

For a moment Michael thought the foreman might be right. There *did* seem to be something nagging at him. He just didn't know what it was.

Eloy struck the hardened face of the anvil a sharp blow that sent the heavy hammer rebounding like a golf ball off concrete. "I'm still the best blacksmith in all of New Mexico," Eloy said, bringing up an old joke between them. "I could have done this without your help, you know."

"You're as good a farrier as you ever were, no better, no worse," Michael said, still looking at the shoe.

"I won't be treated like a common ranch hand, Miguel! I don't care how bad a mood you're in."

Michael laid the finished shoe on the edge of the brick forge beside the other three, then looked up. "The best thing you can do right now is to leave me the hell alone." Even to Michael's own ears it sounded like an apology.

"Well, then, that's exactly what you're gonna get—a damn good leavin' alone." Eloy threw the sledge on the ground, turned, and walked out.

Michael was surprised . . . and disappointed. He'd actually been looking forward to tangling with his foreman, to getting rid of some of the anxiety he'd been feeling. A little shouting, maybe a little shoving, could be good for the soul sometimes. Michael's surprise and disappointment turned to puzzlement.

It wasn't unusual for Eloy to be angry, even when he didn't have a reason. He was quite capable of being vexed by almost anything, from a small cut on his finger to a misunderstood word or gesture from a friend. He was especially good at misunderstanding.

It *was* unusual, though, for Eloy to walk out before a disagreement became a full-fledged duel. What could have snuffed his usual enthusiasm for conflict? Michael wondered. What had happened to the man's pride in his usually successful struggles for power? As disrupting as it was, it was just this fierce personal pride that made Eloy Seña an excellent ranch foreman. As long as everyone could put up with his occasional tirades, the ranch, under the benevolent tyrant, ran as smoothly as a roadrunner on a windless desert.

Michael picked up the sledge Eloy had thrown down and gave the anvil another good wallop. It didn't make him feel any better at all.

Juanita fluffed the feather pillows, smoothed the quilted coverlet up over the soft mounds, then stood back to take a look at her work. Headboard, wide dresser, massive highboy, all the heavy, hand-crafted pine furniture shone with the gloss of a thousand polishings, and she nodded with satisfaction at her skill as a house-keeper. She was especially proud of the bright, colorful quilt she'd sewn for her new employer. It was similar to the one she'd made for Magdalena Tavera, but with a difference. In the very center of the quilt she'd sewn a special love charm with a blue thread tied with seven knots.

Juanita leaned over the bed and breathed lightly on the center circle of red cloth. When she inhaled, she could smell the fragrance of rose and lavender. Ground to a fine powder, the flower petals were imperceptible to anyone who didn't know they were there. But if someone with sensitive fingers were to touch the circle in just the right place, they might be able to discern the presence of the fragile ring, fashioned of fine copper wire, that the quilt maker had placed inside. Someday, *after* Mr. Martino had quit seeing his present lady friend from Santa Fe and fallen desperately in love with her, Juanita would tell him about what she'd done, and why his quilt with the square patches had one red circle in the center.

She'd even stitched a piece of *cachana* root into one of the squares to keep him safe from *mal de ojo,* the evil eye, but he could *never* be told about that. Michael Martino didn't believe in such things.

Not that he didn't have a bit of the devil in his soul. Just let something go wrong with one of his precious horses, and he'd go around scowling and silent for days. Still, sometimes that was better than some of his other moods, like the one he'd been in for the past several days.

Juanita sighed in exasperation. "I wish *something* would happen to get him out of the doldrums," she said aloud. No one at the ranch had been able to please the man for a week.

The sound of loud voices drifted through the room. Favoring her right foot, which hurt on cool mornings, she walked across the wide upstairs bedroom. Leaning out the open window, Juanita watched as Eloy came out of the shed that was attached to the barn. Though she was some distance away, and a few widely spaced tall pines in the front yard intermittently blocked her view of him, she could tell, by his determined strides and clenched fists, that he was not a happy man. "Now what?" She sighed, automatically shifting her weight to her left foot and nervously smoothing the front of her apron.

The new stallion lifted his head and pricked his ears forward as Eloy approached the small corral on the north side of the barn. Today Eloy was supposed to put new shoes on the ranch owner's latest purchase. Later in the day Mr. Martino would ride the great black beast.

"I have no use for black horses . . . for black animals of any kind, for that matter," Juanita said aloud. It had been a frisky black mare named Cebellina, her father's prized possession, that had crushed the bones in her right foot when she was a child.

At Eloy's approach Oñique flared his nostrils, pawed the ground, then reared. Juanita heard a loud clang. Seconds later Michael appeared in the doorway of the smithing shed. There would probably be more arguing. Juanita stepped to the side of the open window. In case either one of them looked up toward the house, she didn't want to appear to be eavesdropping or spying. But she kept listening and watching.

Michael Martino was so devastatingly beautiful to look at! He was thirty-four, a year younger than she, but he seemed much older. She'd seen him almost every day for the past five months

and decided that it must be his enormous devotion to his art that
made him seem more mature. For the past eight years Juanita had
been living in Mora, clerking at the general store. But when she'd
seen the ad for a housekeeper at El Rancho de Torbellino, then
been given the job by Mr. Martino himself, she thought she'd
died and gone to heaven. In all her thirty-five years she could
never remember being more infatuated with anyone. She simply
couldn't get enough of the sight of him.

He wore only a pair of Levi's and boots, his heavy arms
glistening with perspiration, the raven hair on his chest all the
more black and silken from the dampness of hard work. The
sheen on his high cheekbones radiated the glow of the embers in
the firepot, and ringlets of coarse black hair caressed his ears and
neck. But there was a fire in his eyes, two arrow-straight lines
between his eyebrows, an uncharacteristic tautness to his lips. He
and Eloy were about to go at it again.

A slight movement at the other side of the window caught her
eye. Eloy was watching her! He was watching her while she
watched Michael. She stepped back out of sight, bowed her head,
and raised clasped hands to her lips. "No," she breathed softly.
"*Madre mía,* Mother of God, please don't let Eloy tell that I was
spying on Mr. Martino."

Juanita leaned back against the wall, well out of sight of the
two men. Something very bad was bothering her boss, and she
wished she could figure out what it was. She stared at the quilt on
the bed. Her eyes went first to the red circle in the center, then
fell to the bottom edge, to the blue square. Inside that blue square
was a blue circle, two pieces of cloth stitched together to hold the
cachana root, which had been cleaved in half. Inside, a tiny crucifix had been carved. She began to feel a little better. Michael was
protected as best she knew how.

She pushed herself away from the wall and sighed. So they'd
all be miserable for a few days. It had happened before. Michael
with his brooding silence, Eloy with his screaming fits that everyone on the entire ranch would be able to hear, and Juanita
. . . *I will be the most miserable of all.*

"This time I won't let any of it bother me," she vowed aloud. But she knew she was lying to herself—again. She shook her head. "And I was wishing for something to happen to get Miguel *out* of the doldrums. This settles it. I'm going to clean the *sala* today . . . no matter what mood anyone is in."

The living room was rarely used except by Michael, and then only when he was painting his beautiful horses and landscapes or carving his *bultos*. And he never seemed to care how dusty or cluttered it got. He had a peculiar mania, an unfathomable anxiety, about anyone touching his tools, his paints and brushes. "Oh, well, I'm not here to understand," Juanita said as she left the bedroom. "I'm here because there is work to do." *And other, more important reasons.* "You will fall in love with me, Michael Martino, if it takes me the rest of my life and yours," she whispered, then tiptoed down the circular wooden staircase and peeked into the *sala*.

Luckily Michael had not come into the house, nor was he sitting before the large easel in the far corner of the living room, as he did so often when he was brooding about something. The morning sun lighted the canvas he'd been working on in the middle of the night. From her bedroom, just under his, Juanita had heard him get up, come downstairs, then begin opening his boxes of oils and brushes and knives.

When she'd first moved in, she'd thought that Michael might be a sleepwalker like her father had been. As a child she herself had been afflicted, but adolescence had been the cure for her. She'd asked Rosa about it, but Rosa had assured her that her new boss was simply a person who required little sleep, that he liked to work on his art during his wee-hour bouts with wakefulness. Still, she thought the man might need more rest. Juanita stepped closer to the doorway for a better look, then caught her breath.

Another portrait of Lenor! How could any man be so obsessed, even if she did happen to be a very beautiful woman? This time he'd painted her in a white doctor's coat, but no matter what she was wearing, Lenor had always reminded Juanita of a Spanish dancer. A reed-slender body was softened by generous breasts and rounded hips. Shining black hair, pulled back from an oval face, gave Lenor a severe look that contrasted sharply with wide-set black eyes that were large and luminous with compassion and caring. Her features, taken separately, would not have added up to classic good looks, but the unusual combination was startlingly beautiful. Juanita knew Lenor had a mind that was just as exquisitely elegant as her body.

But Juanita also knew that Michael hadn't even seen the woman for many years. His fixation didn't make any sense, especially if you took into consideration all the lovely women he'd been associated with in the past.

"He's haunted."

The quiet voice of Rosa startled Juanita. "Don't sneak up on me like that," Juanita scolded in a whisper.

The corners of Rosa's mouth turned up, transforming her wide, full face with a benevolent, cherubic smile. "You mean like you're always sneaking up on Don Miguel?" she asked.

"I don't do any such thing." But Juanita's denial of the truth turned her cheeks a lively pink, because Rosa knew the truth and had obviously just seen her tiptoe down the stairs and creep up to the living room doorway.

Both women looked back into the *sala;* then Rosa motioned for Juanita to step away from the door. "I've been cooking here for nine years. This is the sixth canvas he's done of that woman, the three you've seen and three more," she said quietly when they were several paces down the hallway. "This one he's going to give to Lenor's grandfather on his birthday."

"He's actually going to Steven Tavera's birthday party?" Juanita asked.

"That's what I hear." Rosa thought a minute. "Maybe he'll just have Eloy take it."

"Has Don Miguel always been so . . . reclusive, where the Taveras are concerned?"

"As long as I've known him."

"I hate to admit it, but Lenor Tavera is very beautiful," Juanita said.

"You also have to admit, he seems . . . *obsesivo*." Rosa nodded, as if confirming her own suspicion. "It's been years since he's seen her, yet every portrait he does changes a bit, makes her look a little older, as if he were following her progress."

"He is. He reads about her in the *New York Times*," Juanita said.

"Well, I'm anxious to see if she's changed in the past year," Rosa said.

"And just how do you imagine you might be able to do that?" Juanita asked.

"She'll be here tomorrow."

Juanita's eyes widened in disbelief. "Here? In this house?"

"Shh." Rosa drew her through the swinging kitchen door. "Steven Tavera's birthday party is this weekend. Lenor comes home for it every year."

"Oh, I forgot it was so soon. So that's probably why Don Miguel's so upset," Juanita said sadly.

"Maybe. But that isn't all. Eloy's mother, Nemesia, told me that Magdalena was going to ask her daughter to stay in New Mexico."

"You're kidding! I thought you said Lenor wanted to live in New York so she could keep learning new things all the time."

"Maybe what I heard was just gossip. But then maybe what I told you was what you wanted to hear."

Juanita frowned. "And what is *that* supposed to mean?"

"Only *you* know what it means for sure, pretty one. I keep telling you, you must learn to listen to your heart."

Rosa turned away and crossed the kitchen to the massive stove where a perpetually simmering kettle steamed. "I'll just turn up the fire a bit. Let me fix you some tea." She adjusted the gas flame under the blue enamel kettle, then moved to the cabinet next to the stove and took down two china cups and saucers.

"I really should get into the *sala*. Mr. Martino is outside right now, in the smithing shed. I should clean . . ."

"Michael is outside?" Rosa asked.

Juanita nodded.

"He must have finished the painting last night." Rosa put the cups down on the long pine table that dominated the center of the large kitchen. "The way you were tiptoing around, I thought he was in the living room." She smiled, remembering Juanita's pink cheeks when Rosa had suggested the younger woman had been sneaking up on her boss. "He was in there most of the night, you know?"

"I know. I was surprised when I saw him outside this morning," Juanita said.

"In the smithing shed, you say?"

Juanita sighed. "Yes. And Eloy is angry." Juanita told her about what she'd seen from the bedroom window.

Rosa turned away again and busied herself with the teapot, one of her many copper canisters of tea leaves, and the boiling water. She could tell from the way Juanita talked about her boss that she fancied herself falling in love with the man. *Good luck.*

"What?" Juanita asked.

The spoon Rosa was holding clattered to the countertop, and she carefully placed the lid back on the teapot as she spoke. "I didn't say anything, Juanita."

"Oh. I thought I heard you say something about good luck."

Rosa spun around, surprise in her eyes.

Juanita shrugged. "It happens sometimes."

"You hear what people are thinking?" Rosa brought the teapot to the table and sat down.

"Not too often. Here, let me pour the tea."

"Sorry we're out of honey. Sugar?" Rosa pushed the sugar bowl toward her companion.

Juanita nodded, then began spooning the white granules into her steaming cup. One, two, three teaspoons heaped full. She stirred, sipped, then added another half teaspoon and stirred again. Rosa was watching her as she put her cup back down in the saucer.

The poor woman needs to eat more.

"I don't want to get fat," Juanita said, then looked apologetically at the older woman. Rosa's lips hadn't moved. Rosa had not spoken. "I hope I'm not upsetting you. It's not something I seem to be able to control."

Rosa smiled at her. "Don't try to control it. And don't fight it. You have *el don,* the gift."

"I suppose. But it's never helped me. Not *really,* anyway."

Rosa put a reassuring hand on the younger woman's shoulder. "Give it time. Never resist or fight against the gift you've been given. I promise, it will help you and the people you love. It is also *beneficioso* and is enhanced by this magical place where you live."

Juanita looked into Rosa's steady hazel eyes for a long moment, then nodded. "I believe you," she said quietly.

There was a knock on the back door. "Come in, it's open." Rosa looked around. "Oh, hi, Roy. Cup of tea?"

"Sounds real good." The tall young man put a large sack on the table. "Brought you the flour and honey and stuff you wanted for your cake, Rosa."

"You didn't have to make the trip all the way up here, Roy."

"Just wanted to help out," Roy said. He took a small notebook out of his shirt pocket, scribbled a few notes, then fetched a cup out of the cabinet and sat down at the table. "Hi, Juanita."

"Hello." Roy had been her boss at the general store and he'd been pretty upset when she'd left, so Juanita couldn't help but feel a little uncomfortable. Sometimes she thought she might be the only person in two counties who didn't like the man. "Business good?" she asked.

"I try not to ask," he said. "Now that Adela has the hang of things, I work in the greenhouse as much as I can."

"Oh."

"Yeah . . . Adela has cleaned up the store quite a bit. Looks real nice. And she's starting to stock some new things, too. She's trying to keep up with Salazar's in Toya. You know they got a new freezer unit? I didn't realize it, but I guess we really needed . . ."

Juanita didn't hear anything else he was saying. She didn't care what he and Adela did to that big dusty hulk of a dilapidated old building in Mora. She'd been miserable working there and Roy had been little help, always gone, usually out back in his greenhouse talking to his plants and reading his books and peering into his microscope. And then there was the incident behind the canned-goods shelves . . .

"Well, we'll just have to come on down and see," Rosa was saying. "Won't we, Juanita?"

"No!" In a fraction of a second, Juanita was on her feet and running out of the kitchen.

"What in the world?" Roy said.

"I don't know." Rosa started after her.

"Eloy! Miguel!" The muted thudding of the swinging kitchen door punctuated Juanita's cries. "Eloy! Miguel!" Then she was on the wide wooden porch, across it, and flying down the gradual slope that descended toward the corral without a thought for the pain in her foot. Oñique, wildly agitated, reared and shrieked and whirled as if the Devil himself were after him.

"Get a rope on that horse," Michael ordered, and Eloy threw a wide loop that just missed the massive black head.

Juanita stopped, breathless, at the gate of the corral and watched the rope fall uselessly into the far corner. Her eyes followed it as Eloy pulled it back. Then a slight motion to the left caused her to start. "No!" There was a young boy cowering against the rough rails of the fence, his eyes filled with fear, his thin body frozen with terror.

Without considering the danger, Juanita mounted the fence, dropped into the enclosure, and ran toward the frightened child.

"Wait!"

"Stop her!"

" 'Nita! Get out of there!"

Juanita heard nothing but the loud beating of her heart and the faint, panting cries of the boy. In one smooth motion she knelt, scooped her hands under his arms, and helped him to stand. "Take him," she said as she pushed him to the topmost rail. In seconds the boy dropped over, into Michael's waiting arms.

"Look out!"

Juanita whirled in time to see Oñique lunge toward her, stop, then rear. The horse's giant body blocked out the sun, his shadow slashing through the bright morning to darken the dry air. The beast was so near, Juanita could feel the radiating heat of his body, the pulsing hot breath that coursed from his flaring nostrils. She raised her arms, spread her fingers wide, and opened her mouth to cry out. *Cebellina!* But no sound escaped her lips. There was no need. In Oñique's eyes she saw not anger, but fear.

The stallion's front hooves hit the ground with a heavy thud, and he stood stock-still in the center of the small corral, chest heaving, breath hurling out in short gasps. Complete silence descended on the little group of people who had gathered to help. For a moment Juanita had the urge to walk up to the frightened animal and touch him, comfort him.

Touch him? Comfort him? The thought appalled her, but unbelievably she wasn't the least bit frightened.

"Juanita! Get out of there!" It was Eloy's voice. But it was Michael's hand that took hers.

"Wait," she said, then turned and knelt near the fence where the boy had been. Soft mounds of trampled earth moved easily as she spread her fingers through the dirt, searching. In seconds her hand closed over an object. She rose, pushed the lump of wood into one of the wide, deep pockets of her apron, and obediently followed Michael out through the partially open corral gate. Eloy quickly closed it behind them.

Rosa stood with the boy, one arm around his waist to steady him.

"Is he all right?" Juanita asked.

"Still a bit shaken. He'll be fine." Rosa looked at Michael. "Take the boy to the house. We'll be along." Without a word Michael obeyed her. When the two were well on their way, Rosa took Juanita's hand and pulled her closer. "I want to see what you found." They started walking slowly toward the house.

Juanita pulled the wood from her pocket.

"It's a piece of cottonwood root," Rosa said.

"I don't even know why I looked for it . . . except maybe I

thought I could find what Oñique had been so upset about." She handed it to Rosa.

The older woman turned it over, over again, then held it for a moment in her palm. "Have you ever seen this before?" she asked.

"No."

"Think back."

"I've seen others like it. It's just like the ones Michael uses for his *bultos*." She looked at Rosa, horrified. "You don't think I *took* one of his—"

"Of course not! It probably got baled up with some hay they brought in from the valley." Rosa handed the wood back to Juanita. "At least it will be put to a better use now."

Michael and the boy were waiting for them in the kitchen. An untouched glass of milk and a saucer of cookies sat on the table in front of the child. He looked frightened, but otherwise unhurt.

"I asked him his name, but he won't tell me," Michael said.

"You're from Campamento de Tavera, aren't you?" Rosa said.

The boy bowed his head, lowered his eyes to the table, and nodded slightly.

"You're a very lucky young man today."

The boy's head quickly lifted, wide eyes questioning Rosa's statement.

Rosa smiled. "You got to see Señor Martino's brand-new stallion, Oñique. Did you know that no one else from Magdalena's summer camp has gotten to do that?"

Just the slightest hint of a smile shone in the young eyes.

"You were very brave, sir, to go into that corral with such a powerful horse." She winked at him. "What a grand story you have to tell the others now!"

What had been only a glimmer in the eyes turned into a full-fledged smile. "Yeah," he said enthusiastically.

Rosa offered her hand, and the boy took it. "My name is Rosa Flores." She shook his hand. "I'm very proud to meet you . . . ?"

He stood up, now very much the gentleman. "Name's Thomas. Thomas Newman. Call me Tom."

"Well, Tom, shall we all sit down and enjoy some cookies together?"

"Sure."

By the time Rosa had brewed fresh tea and all four were comfortably seated at the table, Thomas Newman seemed to feel right at home.

"Our camp's the greatest! I love it! We each have our own horse, and we have to do everything for it, feeding, brushing, exercising, everything. My horse's name is Gabber, she's a filly, and she talks all the time. Like this." Tom made several guttural sounds deep in his throat. "She talks to me more than anyone else," he said proudly.

"How old are you, Tom?" Juanita asked.

"Thirteen . . . almost. I'll be thirteen in August."

"How did you find your way up here?" Rosa asked. "This place is quite a long way from the ranch in the valley."

"I didn't exactly find it. I mean, I wasn't looking for it or anything like that. More like I was sort of exploring and just stumbled on to it." Tom looked at Michael. "We were on a hike," he said. "I just kind of . . . sort of decided to . . . to go a different way by myself."

"The Sangre de Cristos can be very dangerous," Rosa said. "Does Señora Tavera allow you to go your own way in the mountains alone, Thomas?"

Thomas thought for a moment, decided on the truth. "No, ma'am."

"You left the other hikers looking for a little excitement?" Michael asked. Tom nodded, and the look on his face told Michael that the boy was grateful for his understanding. "And you went into the corral with Oñique for the same reason?"

"Oh, no, sir. I thought there was something wrong with his foot. He was acting real funny, holding one hoof up higher than the other. He'd kind of prance around, then paw at the ground, then jump back from where he was digging . . . real strange-like. There was nobody else around and I wanted to help him."

"So you went in and . . . ?"

"And he wouldn't let me near him, so I went over to where he'd been pawing and tried to see if there was something sharp stuck in the ground that might have hurt his foot."

"Did you find something sharp in the ground?"

"No, sir. But he wouldn't let me get a good look. He kept jumping at me, like he was trying to scare me away." Tom picked up another cookie from the plate and pointed it at Juanita. "He scared me plenty good, too." He looked back at Michael. "But, no sir, I didn't find anything in the ground."

Juanita reached into her pocket. "I did," she said quietly, and laid the cottonwood root on the table.

The color drained from Michael's face as he looked at it. He knew instantly what he had to do, and for some reason he knew it had to be done tonight. The wood was about five inches across at its widest point and almost eight inches long, the perfect shape and size for a *bulto* of San Miguel. He smiled at Juanita. "Thank you for finding this. It's just what I need."

Almost embarrassed, Juanita whispered, "You're welcome," then looked around the kitchen. "Where's Roy?" she asked, more to direct attention away from herself than to get an answer.

Michael stood up. "He drove that old hearse of his around front to get Eloy to take a look at the engine." Michael turned to Thomas. "He said he'd give you a lift back down the mountain as soon as they're finished."

Thomas was ecstatic. "Wow! All this and a ride in a real hearse, too!"

Six

"MY GOD, LENOR! YOU SCARED ME TO DEATH!"

"I'm sorry, George, I didn't mean to. And I thank you for not interfering. That took quite a lot of restraint on your part."

"Restraint, hell! I couldn't even move my feet or get my mind in gear enough to interfere. You really had me going there for a minute. Those two voices . . . the way your whole body changed when that other . . ." At a loss for words, George ran his fingers through his perfectly combed blond hair, leaving it, unbelievably, perfectly combed. "You looked as if you were being controlled by strings . . . like a puppet!"

"It does sort of look like that," Lenor said thoughtfully, then, "You're looking especially handsome this morning." Despite her advice, he'd not opted for casual dress. Reaching inside his light gray summer suit coat, she put her arms around his waist. "To what spirit do we owe the honor of the bolo tie?"

"The spirit of adventure, of course."

"I was beginning to wonder if you'd ever wear my Christmas gift outside your apartment," Lenor said.

"Wonder no more, my lady. I feel just like this silver eagle today, flying off into the western sky, ready for anything . . . even trances and talking to spirits."

Lenor smiled, gave him a soft kiss on the cheek, and stepped back. As she switched off the little tape recorder, she wondered, *Does he really mean that?* "Would you mind putting the chair back at my desk while I finish getting dressed? Just take a minute—my rings and things."

Two in one twenty-four-hour period! First Ella Wygent and now George Murphy! Two too many uninitiated! Why wasn't I more careful?
She hadn't intended to explain any of what he'd seen this

morning quite yet—maybe not ever. At this stage of their relationship they were still busy catching up on each others' families
and friends, likes and dislikes. Until today they'd been progressing
along a pretty normal route for a friendship that had the promise
of something more. Now she didn't know but what that "something more" might be altogether out of the question.

They had common interests in medicine, in the theater, in
music. Both had a love for children that was second only to their
love for making sick children well. Until now Lenor had thought
the only point of disagreement that might sever their ties was their
diametrically opposed views on the effects of life-style and attitude on health, and she had intended to gently prove her point
over time. This incident might have changed everything.

But George surprised her. "Lenor, that was the most incredible thing I've ever experienced. I'll tell you right now, I never
would have believed it unless I'd seen it happen. Talking to
spirits!" He shook his head. "How in hell can you be so calm
about it?"

"Pretty much the same way you can stay calm when you're
cutting someone's chest open," Lenor said as she fastened the
chain of the heavy cross around her neck. "I'll bet the first time
you exposed a living, beating heart you were a little nervous."

"Nervous! I was almost a basket case."

"But the more times you did it, the less nervous you were.
Right?"

He nodded in agreement, then raised an eyebrow. "So you've
done this many times?" he asked, his expression changing to
something like a mixture of disbelief and disapproval.

"Yes, but only when I have to. You understand, this has to
be our little secret." George nodded. She picked up the small tape
recorder again, then dropped it into her purse. "I'm ready."

"I don't supposed you want to talk about it some more—like
who you were contacting, and why?"

"I can tell you a little, but shouldn't we be on our way? You
said you had a taxi waiting."

"Oh, yeah . . . I did, didn't I? The cab driver will probably be in a fine snit by now." George picked up the suitcase, then Watson's cat carrier. "Good heavens! Has this guy been gaining weight?"

Lenor smiled. "He's taking along a toy. Wouldn't leave without it."

"Egad!" George feigned an exaggerated stagger out the door. "What is it? A rock?"

"That's exactly what it is."

June ◆ New Mexico

"This is your pilot speaking. As a point of interest, folks, in just a few minutes those on the right side of the plane will be able to look out and see the Sandias. The Manzano mountains will be on the left. Beautiful sight. We'll be landing shortly, so fasten your seat belts and take a good look at the Land of Enchantment."

Lenor opened tired eyes and rolled her head to the right. In the distance, the eastern slope of the Sandia Mountains rose from the dry Estancia Valley, the lush fir, aspen, and pine forest a dark green surprise, patchworked with light green meadows. She could see the paths of the ski area, carved out of tall ponderosa. Leaning down she peered through one of the little mesh holes in Watson's kitty camper. "Almost home," she whispered, but he was sound asleep, as she had been for most of the trip. It took Lenor a moment to remember that this time she wasn't traveling alone.

"Your neck's going to get all bent out of shape," she said to George.

He was craning to see out the opposite window. "Magnificent."

The man across the aisle was looking at George. "I live here in Albuquerque and I never get enough of that sight." He pointed. "It's such a surprise. East side of the mountains, tall pines, lush forest; west side, nothing but rocky crags and cactus and desert sand." He sighed. "It's beautiful, isn't it?"

"It's amazing," George said.

Lenor had to agree. The contrast was startling as they crossed the peak, and the alchemy of bright sun and desert seemed magical. She turned back to the man. "Have you lived in New Mexico long?"

He glanced at her, then looked out the window again. "Moved here from St. Louis seventeen years ago." He smiled. "And I'll never move back!"

She could understand his feelings. In her many trips back and forth between New York and New Mexico, she'd seen the sun shining only once in St. Louis.

"Enchanted," George said quietly as he leaned back in his seat for the descent into Albuquerque. "I take back anything I ever said about this place."

The new airport had to be one of the best parts of flying into Albuquerque. Though the expansion and renovation had been extensive, they'd managed to preserve the southwestern ambience. Spanish, Indian, Anglo, ancient, and modern images mixed, as did the colors of the desert, mountains, and clear sky, in the art, the architecture, and the furnishings. Even the main lobby featured carved beams and decorated tiles. The crowds were a similar, pleasing mix as well. As Lenor, George, and Watson made their way to the baggage claim, they passed lovely, dark-skinned women in richly colored Indian velvet blouses. They passed cowboys of every description, Stetsons atop blond hair or black shining hair plaited into long, heavy braids. Enchanting, indeed.

And the enchantment continued to surround them as they flew north, the ride in the chartered plane a surprise from George. Lenor usually drove a rented car, but, being a staunch New Yorker, George hated to drive anywhere. Comfortable in the single-engine four-seater they glided above the gold and shadow of the desert valley, past the rolling hills surrounding Santa Fe, then over the southern end of the Sangre de Cristos and northeast to Las Vegas.

"I'd expected a much bigger place," George said, clearly disappointed, as they flew over Las Vegas.

"Distances out here in the west can be deceiving. It's a lot bigger than you think. In fact, Las Vegas is the largest town in the northeast quadrant of New Mexico."

The landing on the small strip of the Las Vegas Municipal Airport five miles northeast of the town was smooth. When they rolled to a stop near the aluminum-sided building that housed the FAA flight service station, George started to say something. "I'm sure I'm about to . . ." He trailed off, unsure of himself.

"Excuse me?" Lenor said.

George turned around in a full circle, took in the vast expanse of uninhabited land that surrounded the airport, considered their lone aircraft on the otherwise deserted taxiway, then shook his head. "Nothing. We're in your territory now. Lead the way, Doctor."

"Just a year ago, we wouldn't have been able to rent a car here," Lenor said as George signed the paperwork.

"Somehow that doesn't surprise me."

As soon as Lenor was behind the wheel of their rented car, George became quiet. She glanced at him expectantly once or twice, but remained silent herself. They were all the way through and out of town, approaching Storrie Lake, before he spoke.

"Would you mind if we pull over to the side of the road?" he asked softly.

"Are you all right, George?" Lenor asked, as she pulled onto the shoulder and came to a stop. "You're not getting carsick, are you?"

"No. No, nothing like that." He looked out his window.

Silence. "George! Talk to me." He seemed to be trembling. *"George!"*

Finally he couldn't contain himself any longer and burst out laughing. "You're . . . not going . . . to believe this." Tears streamed down his cheeks.

"What? Believe what?"

"I expected . . ." He pulled a handkerchief from his back

pocket, pushed his glasses up on his forehead, and pressed the folded square first to one eye, then the other. "I thought . . . this would be . . . at least something like . . . *the* Las Vegas."

"*The* Las Vegas?" Lenor smiled, then chuckled. "Las Vegas, Nevada?"

"Like sister cities, maybe. Like dinner, dancing . . . you know, like Caesars *Palace*!" The last word came out on a burst of uncontrollable laughter of such force that his glasses fell back down into place.

And now Lenor was out of control. "Caesars Palace! Oh, George! That's why—my *best* dress! What a . . . *sweet* . . . thing to do!"

For a time, neither could speak. Breathing was catch-as-catch-can. Lenor crossed her arms over the top of the steering wheel, rested her forehead on her arms, and gasped for air between giggles. George had opened the car door and was sitting sideways, feet on the ground, bent over, his elbows resting on his knees for support.

"My God!" he said finally. "I haven't laughed like this since . . . since I don't know when." He took a deep breath.

"Need some help, folks?"

Startled, George looked up at the man who was standing only two feet away from him. Starting with dusty brown cowboy boots, his gaze took in an exceptionally long length of blue threadbare denim-clad legs, a gold and turquoise belt buckle the size of a man's fist, and a tattered pink shirt of a material washed so thin George could read the Camel cigarette pack through the pocket. A large black Stetson shaded the man's thin, tanned face.

Lenor leaned down so she could see who was talking. "Eloy!"

The man swiped his hat from his head, bent at the waist, and looked past George. "Lenor Tavera! Is that you?" He shaded his eyes against the afternoon sun. "Well, I'll be damned! It *is* you. What the hell you doin' parked on the side of the road?"

Eloy squatted down so he could see inside the car more easily, and George felt he should move out of the way. It seemed as if the man were looking right through him.

"I guess I could ask you the same thing," Lenor said. "What are you doing clear down here? Don't they keep you busy enough out on the ranch these days?"

"Busy? Hell, Michael *lives* to find more work for me to do. Sent me to Las Vegas on a goose chase to find some special kind of paintbrush. He was up all night again last night. Son of a bitch's got some kinda burr under his saddle lately. Can't do anything right for 'im." Eloy shook his head and sighed. "Maybe the party will do him some good, get him to unwind."

"Mr. Martino is coming to Grandpa's party?" Lenor asked.

"*Mister* Martino? Well, aren't you formal all of a sudden! Why, I remember a time—"

Lenor glanced quickly at George, but George was still looking at Eloy. Eloy, however, got her message.

"—I remember a time when *I* used to call him mister, too. *Long* time ago." Eloy shoved his hand at George. "Didn't mean to ignore you, fella. Name's Eloy Seña. Known Lenor since the day she was born—some thirty years ago now. Pretty good kid she was, too. At least most of the time. I guess it was back in—"

"This is George Murphy," Lenor said, interrupting. "We work together at Foley Hospital."

"Good to know you, George. Any friend of Lenor's . . . as the saying goes."

Eloy Seña. George hoped his surprise didn't show. This oldest son of Rudolfo and Nemesia Seña, whose thin powerful hand he was still shaking, looked a lot older than his forty-seven years. "I've heard a lot about you and your family, Mr. Seña. All good, of course. Lenor's told me—"

"All about how I had a hell of a time keepin' her and her teenage friends out of a hell of a lot of trouble?" Eloy interrupted.

"Well . . . yes. That too."

Eloy let George's hand go. "Bunch of crazy kids, they were. Always into something. Gave us all a scare, time to time."

"I'll bet they did."

Eloy shifted his weight and got a little more comfortable in his crouch. "I remember this one time—"

"Eloy!" Lenor warned.

He smiled at her. "I'll just save that one for the party. Maybe some other folks would like to hear about it. Well, hey. You haven't told me why you're stopped on the side of the road here."

Over George's protests, and through Eloy's high-pitched merry giggles, Lenor embellished the story of George's misconceptions about Las Vegas—with a few minor excursions from the truth for effect.

"Well now, maybe *that's* the story I'll want to tell at Grandpa's party."

George wasn't sure just how to react. Knowing that he'd come from a very small family, Lenor had prepared him somewhat for meeting a large group of people who were either related or close friends and who all took great pleasure in teasing each other unmercifully. He looked at her with one eyebrow raised. "I guess this is just the beginning of my trials," he said.

"That's right. Can you handle it?" Lenor asked.

George smiled. "With pleasure . . . and maybe a good stiff drink."

"No problem, amigo," Eloy said. "Rafael makes some of the best plum wine you've ever tasted." He stood up and slapped his hat back on his head. "You drive careful now. I'll see you tomorrow."

George watched the man walk back to his vintage pickup truck before he swung his feet into the car and closed the door. "So that's Eloy Seña."

Lenor started the car and pulled out onto the road. "Rudolfo's son," she said.

"What did he mean, a bunch of crazy kids?" George asked. "Was he your baby-sitter or something?"

"Not really. But he kept an eye on us from time to time. Now that I think about it, he had his hands full *most* of the time. What with working all day as a ranch hand for Ramon Martino."

"I thought it was *Michael* Martino."

"Michael is Ramon's son."

"But Eloy implied that Michael was his boss," George said.

"He is, now. Eloy went to work for Ramon the year Eloy graduated from high school."

"You said that was the year you were born?"

"That's right. Ramon died eleven years later, when his son Michael was fifteen. Celsa, Michael's mother, died two years after her husband."

George thought a moment. "Leaving Michael to run the ranch all by himself at age seventeen?"

"With Eloy's help," Lenor said. "Eloy was thirty then. After working there for thirteen years, he could have run the whole operation without Michael's help . . . and did, all the time Michael was away at college."

George reached out and took Lenor's right hand off the steering wheel. He held it for a long time as she continued to drive north. Finally he said, "I wish I'd known you as long as Eloy has."

"Be careful what you wish for, Dr. Murphy. After you hear some of his stories you may change your mind." She gave his hand a squeeze. "I imagine he remembers some things I've conveniently forgotten."

"Like who all your boyfriends were?" George asked, feeling a little disadvantaged.

"Hardly. My dad didn't believe in dating. He said, 'Anything you can do on a date you can do in the living room.' "

"I'm really starting to like this father of yours. I can't wait to meet him."

"Won't be long now; we've crossed the Mora County line. But I warn you, Rafael will keep you on your toes."

"I'll try to keep my balance," George said, then changed the subject. "And knowing New Mexico like I do, I'd say we're just about twenty miles from the Toya County line," George said with mock authority.

"Thanks, Doctor. I'm going to sleep better tonight just knowing—"

"Eee." It was the first time they'd heard from Watson since his brief outing at the airport.

"We're coming up on the turnoff to Mora," Lenor explained, pointing to her left, but keeping to the right. "He wants to look outside now."

George twisted around and unzipped the top of the nylon-covered carrier. Before he could face forward again, Watson was perched on the back of George's seat staring out the front window with intense concentration. "Homing device?" George asked.

"Dinner bell," Lenor said.

George gave her a questioning look.

"You'll see. But first you'll have to experience Toya." In another few minutes she said, "That's Toya's gas station just up ahead there." They passed a road sign: TOYA, POPULATION 287.

"Are those bullet holes in that sign?" George asked as they passed it.

"Probably." She glanced back. "Yeah. Bullet holes."

On the barbed wire fence along the road, George saw another sign. ABSOLUTELY NO HUNTING had been handwritten on a white-painted board. That one was full of little round holes also.

The traffic increased. Two pickup trucks passed them leaving town. George twisted around to get a good look at the rifles in the gun racks framed in the rear windows. A 1953 Chevrolet, still painted turquoise and white, pulled out of a side street just ahead of them. Half a dozen cars were parked in front of the stores. Two men stood in front of a feed store. One of them was wearing a beautifully tooled leather holster. The pearl handle of a six-shooter jutted up from the dark leather.

"Is that legal?" George asked.

"Is what legal?"

"Wearing a gun in plain sight of God and everybody?"

"It's legal," Lenor said.

"Saints above us." George sighed and shook his head.

Lenor took his head-shaking as reproof. "You'd rather people carry concealed weapons?"

He gave a little laugh. "It's the only civilization I know."

Much smaller than Mora and sometimes facetiously called its

twin city, Toya consisted of a four-block-long paved main street which was actually a section of the highway. Two unpaved streets paralleled the highway, one on either side. The three north-south "thoroughfares" were connected by narrow but neat dirt roads that divided the town into small squares not quite large enough to be considered city blocks. A variety of houses dotted the blocks.

Lenor slowed almost to a stop behind a barely moving, battered old pickup loaded to the groaning stage with bales of hay. She explained that most of the houses were neatly painted or freshly stuccoed thanks to a recent community drive to attract tourists. Part of each small yard was taken up with a well-kept vegetable garden.

The blond stranger riding in the unfamiliar car turned a few heads as they drove slowly north. But the head-craning and neck-turning wasn't reserved for the natives. George had so many questions, he didn't know where to start. "Why are all the door and window frames of the houses painted blue?"

"To keep evil spirits away."

Bullet holes . . . six-guns . . . evil spirits. He decided to ask the rest of his questions some other time.

The main street, Toya Boulevard, offered a variety of shopping opportunities: a drugstore that also sold sporting goods and tires and fishing tackle and worms, a clothing store that stocked small kitchen appliances next to the men's underwear. A sign hand-painted on the window glass of the Salazar Grocery proudly announced the arrival of a new piece of equipment. NOW A FREEZER SECTION! NOW A WIDE SELECTION!

Across Toya Boulevard from the sixties-modern cinder-block Toya High School, Toya's tourist attraction rose to three stories. On the south side of the only brick building in town, a sign painted black on a background of white claimed it to be DESCARADA EULALIA'S BURDEL. A smaller wooden sign hanging over the front door denied that the imposing structure was the infamous madam's brothel: FRANCISCA'S BED AND BREAKFAST. Another, yet-smaller sign in the window advertised, OFFICE SPACE FOR RENT.

"Francisca's has a ghost."

"I probably could have guessed that," George said as they rolled by the front door. "So this is the famous Dr. Tavera's hometown." He sighed. "Somehow I pictured it a little differently."

"Oh? How was that?" Lenor asked.

George was almost embarrassed to say, "Bigger?"

"Bigger isn't always better," Lenor said.

"I didn't mean—"

"I know what you meant," she said, smiling at his worried look. "It sort of shocks me, too, sometimes. Living in New York makes it easy to forget what a quiet little town is really like."

"So where's your house?" George asked.

"We live a little further out of town."

"Will you look at that!" George said, ducking down so he could see out Lenor's window. "I saw a church just like that in a magazine once. Beautiful!"

"A fortress church. It really wasn't designed or used for defense, but it looks like it could be, doesn't it?" With large wooden double doors facing east, the plastered adobe building and twin spires gleamed white in the afternoon sun, its smooth sculptural quality heightened by a striking massiveness.

Lenor pointed to her right at another one-story cinder-block structure as they came to the edge of town. "And we have a post office and a courthouse with a sheriff's office. Oh, look! There's the new telephone pole I told you about."

"Well then, what else could anyone possibly want?" George said lightly.

"A doctor's office with a doctor in it," Lenor said quietly. Suddenly she felt that peculiar dizziness again. She gripped the steering wheel tighter, took a deep breath, and it was gone.

"You're not thinking about coming back, are you?" George asked.

"I *think* about it every day." Then, "After we check in at

home, maybe we can come back to town for the tour. Nothing as exciting as Las Vegas, you understand."

"Sounds good to me," George said, sorry he'd brought up the subject of Lenor's returning to New Mexico, glad to be past it. He settled back in his seat.

After leaving Toya there were few signs of human habitation. They passed a small gathering of old trailer houses in yards of bare dirt, where mongrel dogs lazed in the shade of rusted-out, wheel-less cars. Here and there tiny tin-roofed adobe homes baked in the afternoon heat. Unclad, the mud bricks looked as if a good rain might melt them to the ground. A few children played near their homes, but Lenor knew that the luckier ones were splashing about in a nearby creek. *I should be here for them.*

George sighed. "The isolation . . . I can't get over the isolation."

"Almost inspirational," Lenor said quietly.

"And the poverty. I never imagined."

"It almost makes me ashamed to show you my home," she said.

"But your people worked hard for everything they have," George said.

"Harder than you can imagine," she said quietly.

Forested in a shimmering ponderosa and aspen mosaic of light and dark, the Sangre de Cristo Mountains rose in the west to almost twelve thousand feet. The road had gained altitude since Las Vegas, and here the foothills of the Rincon Mountains sported stands of densely packed tall pines. Occasionally the trees would abruptly stop and give way to a breathtakingly beautiful valley, some with a small cluster of grazing cattle.

Lenor had begun feeling a little guilty for not being a better tour guide as they'd started their ascent into the foothills many miles back. There were lovely sights, if one knew where to look. Silently chiding herself for not taking the left turn just before La Cueva's historic Romero gristmill and driving into the pictur-esque little town of Mora, she realized she'd made the decision to press on for purely selfish reasons. She'd apologize later. Now she couldn't wait to get home.

"Here we are," she said finally, and George leaned forward for a better look.

"I thought you said a little way out of town," he said.

"In New Mexico, this *is* a little way."

On the left side of the road, two massive adobe pillars marked the turnoff onto the dusty, undulating road that curved its way through hilly Tavera property and led west to her home. Curving over a wrought-iron arch connecting the top of the two pillars, six iron letters proclaimed TAVERA. As they clattered over the cattle guard Lenor rolled her window all the way down, and the fragrance of pine filled the car, the vibrantly scented air bringing with it memories of idyllic summer afternoons at the foot of the Sangre de Cristos.

"Eee."

"You're right, Watson. There's only one way to get the full benefit of this sight, George." Lenor pulled off to the side of the driveway and cut the engine. "See that hill right there in front of us? We're going to walk to the top and have a good long look. You up to it?"

"You bet!"

"Now you'll see what I mean by Watson's dinner bell," she said.

"You're going to just let him out?"

"He's home. Knows his way around better than I do. He'll be fine."

As soon as she'd stepped out of the car and watched Watson take off north for parts unknown, a feeling of total belonging made her deliriously happy, and she couldn't help but anticipate, with great pleasure, her first glimpse of the adobe hacienda where she'd spent her childhood. She took George's hand. "The altitude might make us feel a little shaky at first. We'll just take it slow."

"I feel like I could walk all afternoon!"

The climb was steep, the walk exhilarating. They could hear birds flapping wildly to their right, as Watson shopped for his supper. Lenor pointed, then whispered. "See what I mean about the dinner bell?"

George stopped for a moment to listen, nodded with a smile, and took a deep breath. "How must it feel . . . to be free?" he said softly.

Huffing slightly from exertion at the unaccustomed altitude, they approached the ridge of the the hill, George ahead, Lenor lagging a little behind so he'd be first to the top.

"Oh, my," he breathed when he looked down. He wanted to stop Lenor, to shield her from the sight of the hearse in the circular driveway below. "Lenor, I don't think . . ."

"Pretty special, isn't it?" she said, coming up beside him. The view was just as rewarding as she'd expected it to be, as it always had been.

He put his arm around her. "I'm here for you," he said. "No matter what's happened down there."

"What are you talking about, George?" she asked.

"Don't you see it?"

"What?"

"The hearse."

"It's just Roy, an old friend of mine. I haven't told you much about him."

"You went to high school with him, didn't you?" George asked.

"Right. He's been a regular visitor here since we were both about five years old, and he lived with us for a while."

"Well, thank heaven anyway," George said on a long sigh. "For a minute there—" He didn't say any more, just looked. And it was even more than Lenor had promised.

Isolated, almost dreamlike in its pristine setting among mountain fir and juniper, Rancho de Tavera sprawled below them. Three-foot-thick adobe walls were roughly plastered, and the sand color of the exterior seemed to melt into the ground to join with the earth, as if it were a naturally occurring extension of the planet, like a mountain or a boulder or a tree. The low, one-story dwelling had grown from a simple one-room shelter, built in

1872 by Dorio Tavera, into an enormous four-sided, red-tile-roofed structure built around a lushly planted interior patio, a *placita*.

To the left, south and west of the hacienda, two long bunk-houses, constructed from pine logs taken from the nearby Sangre de Cristo Mountains, sat in a little valley among juniper and scrub oak. Farther west, Rudolfo's sister Angelina, "the spinster," as everyone called her, lived in a sturdy log cabin. At the end of the curving road that continued from the driveway, past the bunk-houses and Angelina's home, stood the little chapel Dorio had built at about the same time he'd been working on the main house. The stained-glass windows in the north and south walls were a more recent addition to the stuccoed adobe church, a fancy of Lenor's great-grandmother, Ada. The two windows had cost fifty head of cattle each, but Ada had died a happy woman.

A large, two-story barn sat to the north and west of the house, with a spacious pine-log corral attached to its south side. Lenor could see several teenaged children currying their horses in the dusty pen.

Lenor pointed, northward, at a log home with a long porch. "That's the Señas' place," she said.

"Rudolfo and Nemesia, Eloy's mother and father, right?" George asked.

"Congratulations. You'll have this crew straight in no time."

"The place is just like you told me it would be, but I wouldn't have believed it unless I'd seen it. Like a picture you'd see in a magazine."

"*New Mexico* magazine did a spread once, when my mother opened the camp. But she's tried to avoid publicity since then. She had to turn down over two hundred applications the second year."

George got a gleam in his eye. "Does she take older kids?"

"You'd have to lose some of your city ways, George. You can get lost in these mountains before you know it—and there aren't any taxis to call."

"I'd study my hardest! Learn how to use a compass and tell

poisonous mushrooms from the edible kind. What a blast!" He looked off into the distance. "George Murphy, seasoned cowboy . . . a mountain man and his trusty steed, alone against the elements of nature . . . with only his wits to keep him alive." He sighed. "A little secret dream of mine."

"No problem. Manny can have you on a horse first thing in the morning." It was all Lenor could do to keep from chuckling, but she didn't want to discourage him. She was sure the closest he'd ever been to a horse was on the sidewalks around Central Park where the hansom cabs waited for fares. "Of course, that fine suit of yours might take it pretty tough."

George rubbed his hands together in anticipation. "I can't wait." Then he turned to her. "There's just one thing."

"What's that?"

"I've never been on a horse before."

All the confidence and aplomb that being a top surgeon in his field had ingrained in him couldn't withstand the fish-out-of-water feeling George developed the minute he and Lenor walked through the Taveras' front door. Lenor had warned him about the teasing, the joking, the constant but kindly bickering, but nothing had prepared him for total immersion in a family world so completely different from his own experience. Both he and Lenor were only children, but while he'd lived alone with his father, Lenor had lived with several generations of two families closely intertwined and unequivocally interconnected.

His first impression was of the huge room he'd entered, a living room wider than it was deep, the ceiling sloping upward from the double doors to a height of about two stories. A stone fireplace across the room dominated the west wall, its hearth extending into the next room.

But the chance to take it all in lasted only seconds. Perched on a high ladder to his left, Rafael Tavera finished taping a crepe paper streamer to a pine log ceiling beam. "Catch!" he said, and tossed a plastic tape holder down to George. "Lenor's here," Rafael called out. "She's brought reinforcements."

George knew that Rafael was fifty-eight, but the burly man came down the ladder like a teenager, taking the last three steps in one bound. Rafael glanced down at the hand George offered for shaking, then grinned widely and had George in a bear hug in the blink of an eye.

Rafael drew back, took George's hand then, and held it with both of his. "*Bienvenido, mi amigo.* Welcome. Welcome."

If mischief could take on any form, it would definitely choose the sparkle in Rafael's eyes. A large but not unattractive nose hovered over a thick black mustache that could not hide a smile of real happiness. *Welcome, indeed.* George shook Rafael's hand. "I'm so glad to meet you, sir."

Rafael's expression changed to a scowl. "But you've stolen my tape, señor."

Startled for a second, George had to think fast. He raised his left hand holding the tape holder up to his ear. "Thought I might listen to it later."

Surprise registered, then, "I like this one, Lenor."

The rising, then falling note of a loud wolf whistle pierced the air. George heard a woman's voice say, "He's a hunk, all right! Maggie, get out here!" The woman coming toward him had to be Apple Hardy. Honey-blond hair combed straight back and braided, green eyes that flashed merriment, an angular face that meant business, and a solid body honed for endurance all combined into a sturdy package of female strength and startling beauty. She wore no makeup and needed none.

There was so much going on, George hardly knew where to turn. Up on another ladder to his right, a man holding a monstrous, many-colored paper burro fit the description of Rudolfo Seña, slight and wiry, dark-skinned, with a perfectly trimmed full beard. Lenor had described his wife, too, so George instantly recognized Nemesia, dressed head to toe in a bright red jumpsuit and red sneakers, who steadied her husband's ladder with strong hands and considerable weight. George wasn't sure about the stately woman who dusted the coffee table in front of the fireplace. She could be either Angelina, Rudolfo's sister, or Jovita,

Grandpa Steven's wife. Before he could do his wondering out loud, Apple Hardy had her arm around his shoulders and was guiding him toward an archway on the left side of the fireplace, where a tall woman—Magdalena—wearing bright yellow rubber gloves stood waiting. Everyone seemed to be moving in the same direction.

"Oh, sure. You catch me in the middle of skinning chickens and decide to have a party without me," Magdalena said, looking from one wet yellow glove to the other. "Get in this kitchen and get to work right now. All of you." She looked George up and down as he neared. "I'll deal with that suit in a minute," she said, then lifted her arms and accepted a hands-off hug from Lenor.

George looked down to see if something was amiss with what he was wearing. From behind him he heard Magdalena's voice. "Lucielle, get this man out of his clothes. He can't work like that." He felt Apple's arm lift from his shoulders; then a tug at the back of his collar had his suit coat slipping down and off his arms. George turned around and found himself facing a woman who reminded him of his own grandmother, whom he'd seen only in pictures. A mound of thick, silky white hair was piled on top of her head and held in place with silver combs decorated with raw turquoise nuggets; cheeks, rosy and full, underlined light blue eyes that were on the same level as his. With a hand the size you might expect to find on a mature milkmaid, Lucielle patted his cheek.

"Nice tie, George. That can stay. Just roll up your sleeves and we'll fetch you an apron."

George did as he was told, shaking hands and returning warm greetings between taking turns on the cuffs of his white shirt. Among hugs and handshakes, he met almost all the people Lenor had told him about; Rudolfo Seña and his wife Nemesia; Rudolfo's sister Angelina, who'd been standing near the fireplace; and the angelic and athletic-looking Jovita, Steven Tavera's wife of fifty-nine years. Jovita didn't look a day over fifty.

Aunt Isabel, Rafael's sister, kept up a running commentary explaining that Steven had gone to the garden to pick the lettuce for dinner. Arthur, a man who could never be taken for anyone but Rudolfo's son, was Eloy's youngest brother. Lita, a small and fragile replica of Nemesia, was three years younger than Arthur. George guessed that the slender man with the beautiful fine-boned face, who watched the introductions from a position at the far end of the room, was Roy Baldwin, the driver of the hearse still parked outside.

Even with over a dozen people in the kitchen, there was still a feeling of spaciousness, and George discovered why as he looked around. At least twenty feet across and double that in length, the room's long west wall was all glass windows and doors that opened out onto the interior patio. Well over one hundred feet square, bordered on all sides by a covered, red-tiled walkway and the interior walls of the hacienda, the open court offered a lush green garden of many plant varieties, with a giant cottonwood as its centerpiece. Feeling a little overwhelmed, George decided that his entire apartment could probably fit into the confines of the kitchen space alone. He sighed, then felt a familiar arm around his shoulders.

"Still gets to me too sometimes," Apple said. "There aren't many of these haciendas left, you know. You're standing in what used to be the entire three-room house. Rafael's great-grandfather, Dorio, started all of this."

"Lenor described it to me, but I couldn't imagine—"

"How's this for appropriate?" Lita was holding up a white chef's apron with bold, hand-painted red letters, *Nueva York*. The petite young woman with coal-black eyes and very short black hair he'd greeted earlier didn't hesitate to reach around him and tie the apron around his waist. "Grandma Jovita painted this for you," she said. She stood back. "Magdalena? What do you think?"

Magdalena moved away from the stove and gave him a stern appraisal. "Much better. A proper greeting, and you'll be ready to get to work." With that, she gave him a gentle hug. "You're very welcome here," she said. "I hope we don't drive you a little crazy."

It was easy to see where Lenor got her classic Spanish good looks. Magdalena had to be one of the most beautiful women George had ever seen. Though she wore none of the trappings of conventional female attire—makeup, nail polish, parlor-styled hairdo, jewelry—her presence and demeanor, in simple tan slacks, plain beige shirt, and bibbed white apron, were more feminine than the most glamorous actress he could think of. He was sorry when she turned away. "Roy, give this poor man something to do."

His attention again drawn to Roy, George was startled to see Lenor in his embrace. He also saw Roy's disappointment at having to discontinue what was obviously a totally pleasurable experience. It took Roy a moment to say "Yes, ma'am," to Magdalena.

The two of them were soon working together at a thick cutting board Roy had brought from the cabinet to the long dining table situated in the curve of a bay window that looked out on the *placita*. Their small talk centered mostly around what George thought of New Mexico and Toya in general, and the Tavera home and family in particular. Roy lost no time in making up for his earlier aloofness with an exaggerated friendliness. George was relieved when Apple joined their conversation after overhearing George confess that he'd never ridden a horse.

"George, my man," she said, draping her arm around his shoulders again, "you can't let a little thing like a lack of experience discourage you. We'll have you poking cows and roping bulls in no time."

George didn't know quite how to take Apple Hardy yet. She was just about his size and surely about ten times stronger than he was. The hug he'd gotten when they'd walked into the kitchen had caught him completely off guard. "You're just as good looking as Lenor said you were, George," she'd told him. And he hadn't known how to react. Had she been teasing? What all had Lenor told her about him? Should he feel flattered or embarrassed by the attention she was showing him?

Roy seemed to sense George's unease. He glanced in the

direction of the stove, where Lenor was helping her mother, then back at George and Apple. "You two make a nice-looking couple," he said. "Too bad you don't live around here, George."

The inappropriate remark didn't bother Apple in the least. "He's always trying to fix me up," she told George, then pointed to Roy's left hand. "But you'll notice he's not hitched yet either. Couple of thirty-year-old misfits, we are, huh, Roy?"

"Speak for yourself, Sheriff." Roy tried to smile, but didn't quite make it.

"If anybody's a misfit around here, I want to meet him," a deep baritone voice boomed out. "You're certainly not talking about this young man, are you, Apple?"

George turned just in time to take a huge basket of vegetables from the tall, white-haired man behind him.

"You look like you can handle that, son," Steven Tavera said, his black eyes twinkling, his berry-brown skin glowing.

"You're Steven . . . Steven Tavera." George quickly put the basket on the table and took the man's hand. "It's an honor to meet you, sir. A real honor. Lenor's told me so much—"

"All lies. The kid never did learn how to tell the truth." To make his point, he looked away. "Hey, Lenor. I thought you said this guy would be a real dud. He's not so bad."

"Grandpa! Will you stop? At least wait till you get to know him a little better before you start abusing him." *Roy must have been mistaken. Grandpa looks great.*

"He looks like he can take it." When Steven looked back at him, George was surprised at his changed expression. "We're glad to have you in our home, Dr. Murphy," he said. "You'll always be welcome here." Then, from warmhearted sincerity to gaiety in the blink of an eye, "Roy! Didn't I ever show you how to make radishes into flowers? Sit down here, son, and take a lesson."

As it turned out, most of the food being prepared was for the birthday party the next day. Supper was a simple affair—if feeding fourteen people at a sit-down dinner could be called simple. But

Magdalena and Lucielle were used to large crowds, especially during summer-camp time.

Overwhelmed by the amount of food on the long kitchen table, George hardly knew where to start. Baking dishes of red chile enchiladas; fresh peas with green chile; tamales with and without meat; hot and mild tomato picantes and salsas; *quelites*—a dish made with pinto beans, spinach, onions, and chile—made pass after pass, family-style, around the table. Without Rafael's icy cold home-brewed beer, George was sure his mouth would have burned to a cinder. And he was completely surprised that everything he tasted, he enjoyed.

Conversation centered around the party, scheduled to start at three the next afternoon. Magdalena expected about two hundred to attend, though the invitation was open to everyone in Toya and the surrounding area. As always it would be a come-when-you-want and leave-when-you-want affair. A potluck dish wasn't expected or required, but most would bring food. Bringing your children was mandatory. All the youngsters, including the kids from the Tavera camp, rejoiced in listening to stories and beating the colorful paper burro and the other piñatas with sticks until they broke through the fragile skin and the hidden candy came pouring out. No birthday gifts were allowed.

Apprehensive at first, George finally relaxed when he realized that the subject of his being a surgeon was not going to come up. With Steven's adverse feelings about the radical invasion of the human body, George could only be relieved that no one mentioned his daily practice of cutting, repairing, and stitching. He told Lenor as much after dessert.

"Oh, we don't allow such unpleasant discussions at the dinner table," she told him. "Interferes with the digestion."

He didn't know whether to thank her or be offended. But he'd also noticed that neither Daniel Vigil's death nor funeral had been mentioned either. Too bad he and his father hadn't had the same dedication to peace or his own digestion might be more efficient. Amazingly, though, despite the hot chilies, he hadn't yet reached for his antacid tablets.

After supper Lenor played tour guide, and George finally got a good look at the room they'd first entered. The east wing was the oldest part of the hacienda. The main entrance, facing the rising sun, opened into the beam-ceilinged living room with a stone fireplace on the far wall that connected with the kitchen and could be lit from either room. Lenor pointed out that it was one of only three rooms in the house with windows to the outside; the other rooms opened their windows and doors onto the interior patio. Veering from the traditional solid outside protective wall had been a concession to Magdalena's wishes during the expansion.

Three overstuffed couches grouped around a heavy pine coffee table in front of the wide hearth made a large but cozy conversation area. A game table and six chairs in one corner was where Miller Baldwin and his poker-playing cronies met when it was Rafael's turn to host. And the antiques . . .

"Incredible," George whispered, running his hand across the back of a uniquely designed wooden chair. Obviously handmade, the back slanted forward to form one wide front leg; the two back legs curved forward and supported the seat. All was held together with wooden pegs.

"What's incredible?" Lenor asked.

"These things should be in a museum."

"Not yet, please! We're still using them."

George gingerly sat down in one of the odd-looking chairs, then settled back, reassured by the sturdiness of the construction. He looked around the room again. "The integrity of this structure absolutely enthralls me," he said. "It's environmentally sound, nonpolluting, and extraordinarily beautiful, not only artistically, but because it will survive for hundreds of years. And it's comfortable."

"Except for the roof tiles, the building materials all came from this site." Lenor sat down across the table from him. "It's labor-intensive, though. If you've ever helped mix adobe mud and straw for bricks you know what I mean."

"I'm afraid I haven't had the pleasure." George said.

Lenor smiled. "Pleasure isn't exactly the word I choose to describe spending hours in the sun, stomping around a gigantic mud hole until your legs feel like cooked noodles and your whole body turns into one huge aching mass of exhaustion. I helped build my own bedroom."

"Really."

"I can't begin to describe all the work that's gone into this place. We've built every building, leveled every road, always grown and raised our own food."

"And you said your grandpa made his friend's casket?"

Lenor nodded.

"He's an amazing man. You realize you have my head in a turmoil over this whole thing."

"What whole thing?"

"Ten years ago Steven Tavera is on his deathbed, needs a bypass, can't stay on his feet long enough to get to the bathroom and back. He refuses both drugs and surgery and has his son construct his coffin. He says he doesn't mind dying because he's had a good time. You're a premed junior in college with a penchant for extracurricular studying. You come across some obscure articles and books with information substantiated only by testimonials, extrapolate an unproved theory from what you've read, then put a bit of your own spin and twist on it."

"Not such obscure stuff, but you're right so far," Lenor said.

"So you come home during spring break with a stack of papers you've typed out for him and explain what you want him to do. Steven literally takes one step at a time, one added step a day, gradually eliminates all fats from his diet, and miraculously walks and eats his way back to health."

"You forgot the prayers," Lenor said.

"And the magic," George said. "Is there something you're not telling me about that?"

"No."

"No, you're not telling me? Or no, there was no magic involved?"

"Just mind magic, George. Grandpa bought it, the whole

idea. It wasn't invasive. It had enough modern theory and enough spiritual ritual to feel comfortable to him. That and his fear of surgery propelled him in the right direction. As soon as he saw the least little bit of progress, he was on his way."

"But how did you know it would work?"

"I didn't. But I'd already bought into the idea that the body does what the mind wants it to do. The *curanderismo* teaches that magic is empirical, and I grew up watching it happen. Besides, there wasn't an alternative."

"Empirical magic isn't exactly science," George said.

"But it can be perceived, recorded, and tested. You might say that the *curandera*'s magic is real, as opposed to theatrical magic, because people believe in it."

"So if someone behaves as if the magic is real, it is?" George asked.

"What the patient perceives and believes is the immediate reality. The ultimate magic, if you will."

"And ultimately psychologically satisfying."

"Hence the prayers," Lenor said. "A very satisfying form of meditation for the believer. And we both know what meditation does, physiologically speaking."

"René Descartes be damned," George said.

"At least discounted. Too bad Descartes couldn't have known Steven Tavera."

"Or come to visit this place," George said. "Earthen homes, made from the very stuff they stand on. It's almost primeval." He shook his head. "I can't believe there's not one air conditioner in the whole place."

"Don't need any," Lenor said. "No furnaces, either."

"You're kidding."

"Come on, I'll show you."

Though already large, all the rooms George saw were expanded further by the use of white plaster on every interior wall. Bedrooms and connecting baths took up most of the north and south extensions, with the exception of a room used as a library in the northwest corner. The master bedroom was at the northeast corner. Lenor's bedroom sat diagonally opposite at the south-west corner. The most recent addition, the west wing, had been started around 1910 and finished with the completion of Lenor's bedroom seventeen years ago. As promised, no furnaces. Each room had its own gently undulating, Mexican-style plastered fireplace blending perfectly into a rounded corner.

"The sleeping arrangements may seem a little Victorian," Lenor said, "but Papa hasn't changed." She opened a door in the west wing. "This will be your room."

George leaned back, looked to his left, then pointed. "That's your room, isn't it?" he asked.

"We'll be next-door neighbors," Lenor said.

"From what you told me about your dad, I thought I might be sleeping on one of the couches in the living room . . . and feeling lucky to be in the same house."

"He's mellowed some," Lenor said.

George grinned and couldn't help leering a bit.

"Not that much," Lenor warned.

George pretended to pout. "Then I guess I'll go get our luggage," he said, and turned just in time to see a blur of black and white streak down the massive trunk of the cottonwood in the center of the *placita*. Watson maneuvered among the myriad plantings, covered the distance to the tiled floor of the surrounding walkway, and positioned himself between Lenor and the door to her bedroom.

Lenor picked him up. "Need a nap, Watson?" she asked, and seemed to wait for an answer. "Okay, okay. Let's see what's going on."

"Are you listening to that cat?" George asked.

"Not in the sense you're talking about." She reached for the doorknob. "He just—"

"Sss," Watson interrupted.

The door swung open to reveal a startled man. Roy stood at the end of Lenor's bed, her suitcase opened in front of him. "Thought I'd help you guys out, hang up a few things," he said.

"I brought your stuff in, too, George." He pointed. "Right there by the door."

George managed a weak "Thanks." There was a tension in the air that heightened when Watson pushed away from Lenor and raced across the room. In seconds he was standing in the center of the opened suitcase, back arched, hissing.

Roy reached toward the cat and got a bloody swipe from razor claws. "What's the matter with this guy, Lenor?" he asked, holding his injured hand with the other. "We used to be best buddies."

The easy repartee the two childhood friends had exchanged at dinner didn't continue. "Maybe he knows you weren't invited into my room," Lenor said sternly.

"Since when do I need an invitation? Besides, I wasn't disturbing anyone . . . or interrupting anything." Roy gave George a knowing look.

It was the first dissension George had heard among the gathered friends and family since he'd arrived. The unexpected turn made him uncomfortable and somehow protective of Lenor and her feelings. He stepped forward into the room.

Roy took a step back from the suitcase. "I guess things have changed." He looked down at Watson, who was still threatening, then up at George. "Anyhow, I left you a little welcoming present. Nothing much. It's in your suitcase."

George shrugged at Lenor after Roy passed between them and left the room, and she just shook her head in answer. He didn't want to ask but couldn't help being curious about both what had happened and what Roy had said about "things" having changed. What things? Had these two old school chums been lovers? Had they shared more than homework, games, and dreams? Though Roy was a handsome man in every way, almost modelesque, with slender body and finely chiseled face, George had gotten the impression that he and Lenor had never been more than good friends.

Lenor could see the confusion. "You're probably wondering

why Roy seems to have the run of the house," she said when Roy was out of earshot.

"The question crossed my mind," George said, watching as Lenor began hanging up her clothes.

"Roy was sixteen when his mother died."

"Poor kid," George said.

"Everyone thought Roy was taking it well—as well as could be expected, after he'd found Gloria's nude body in the bathtub—but Grandpa could see that he wasn't. His father works day and night. The poor man really didn't have time to give his son the care he needed. We've always had room for one more, so Steven brought Roy out here and saw to it that he felt like he was a part of the family."

"And Roy was happy with that arrangement?"

"Roy and his father have never gotten along very well. Miller is a perfectionist of sorts, very rigid in his thinking. Roy is more of a free spirit. Did I tell you he's a certifiable genius?"

"High IQs can make compatibility difficult sometimes. Is Roy impatient, too?"

"He was, but Grandpa kept him busy, teaching him carpentry and gardening. Mama taught him about herbs and cooking. Grandma taught him how to paint and got him interested in poetry. Rafael worked his skinny little behind off on the ranch. He calmed down pretty fast. I'd say he was a well-adjusted kid by the time we left for college."

"Did well in college, did he?" George asked.

"Premed, yes. But med school did him in. He had some sort of breakdown at the end of his first year."

"That's the hardest one," George conceded. "I guess his father wasn't too happy about it."

"I don't know. Miller loaned him the money to buy the general store in Mora. He's been running it ever since."

"That's quite a change of focus for someone who wanted to be a doctor. Had to be a rough transition," George said.

"He won't talk about it."

"Do you think you might have been a little hard on him just now?" George asked, kneeling down and opening his suitcase.

Lenor thought for a moment. "Maybe. It's just . . . I felt like my privacy had been invaded. Like he was taking something that didn't belong to him."

"More like giving something," George said, holding up a glass jar labeled *Honey of an Apple* and filled with a golden liquid. "This must be Roy's welcoming present."

Seven

WHAT IN HELL HAS GOTTEN INTO LENOR? WHAT THE hell is going wrong with my life?

The padlock on the greenhouse door was giving him trouble. The dogs next door were barking again. Adela had left the wrong lights on in the store when she'd closed up. Nothing seemed to be going right.

Roy put the black rock he'd taken from Watson's cat carrier into his pocket, renewed his efforts, and finally the padlock surrendered. He breathed a sigh of relief and vowed to get a new lock as soon as he had the time. All manner of stupid thoughts had been racing through his mind since he'd left Lenor's bedroom. The dumbest of all was that he'd lost the key to the greenhouse lock. Impossible, of course. With superior intelligence, nothing like that could happen to him. To an ordinary man, perhaps. To George Murphy, a *very* ordinary man, something as stupid as losing a key could easily happen. But not to the "brain," not to Roy Baldwin, ever vigilant against such ordinary occurrences.

Of course all the important decisions he was making these days put a little strain on him from time to time. But he didn't mind making decisions. Like right now—he had to decide what to do about Lenor's attitude.

There had been other instances of her hostility toward him. During high school, when Lenor and Apple were together, both of them sometimes had acted as if his presence were unwelcome. That was back when he fancied himself one of their in group. Part of the time it hadn't mattered that they didn't want him around, but frequently their insensitivity had hurt badly. When he saw women act as Lenor had acted tonight, he wondered why his mother had wanted a girl instead of a boy. He could only give her the benefit of the doubt, that a girl-child would have brought her more happiness. But he didn't know how a girl could have survived what Gloria had had in store for her offspring. Lenor could never have survived it.

But that wasn't his problem now. Gloria was dead and he liked his mother much better that way. It was Lenor's attitude that was the problem, and there had to be some way to fix it. Of course, there was the gift he'd given to George. That would eliminate one problem. *After George is out of the way, Lenor might get back to treating me the way I deserve to be treated.* "I'm sure I'm a better friend to Lenor than George Murphy could ever be," he said aloud, now that he was behind the closed door of the greenhouse.

He slowly turned around in a complete circle, took a full breath of the moist, cool air, and enjoyed a deep sigh. No place else on earth had he ever felt so comfortable or so peaceful as right here, with his plants surrounding him, here where all his brilliant and difficult work was done. The contrast with the outside air always struck him as a miracle. One moment he would be in a furnace of dry breezes, the next moment he would be breathing a rarefied mixture of water vapor and the superoxygenated atmosphere from the exhalations of hundreds of lovingly cared-for plants. His babies, as Roy fondly thought of them, took good care of him because he took such good care of them.

But that same philosophy didn't seem to work with people . . . even though he tried to care for them, even brought them sweet gifts. People breathed out poison that Roy couldn't use and could barely tolerate. He suffered from osmodysphoria, an intense and abnormal dislike of certain odors. People tried to suffocate him, with their carbon dioxide exhaust spewing everywhere. And that was just for starters. He'd be as nice to them as he knew how to be, and none of them reciprocated in kind. He had to congratulate himself on his behavior. He'd trained himself until, now, he could stand within two feet of other people and not be completely revulsed by their nearness or the smell of their breath.

To ease the unrest that always caught him by the throat and threatened to strangle him when he thought about being near other people, Roy unlocked and opened the file cabinet near the door. He took out one of the seven clipboards he kept there and started taking notes. It was the only way to control the stampede of symptoms. After several moments of writing, he congratulated himself for coming up with a solution to everything. Junior Garcia, who was drugged and well hidden in Roy's apartment above the general store pharmacy, would be the perfect vehicle for executing revenge for Lenor's behavior.

As soon as Roy had figured out that the cause of his panic was his dreams of Lenor, and not the memories of his mother leaning over him while he slept, he'd been able to design the training plan. The act of writing down what was going on around him released the initial paralysis of his limbs, took his mind off the terror of being smothered, and quelled the pounding arousal. Sometimes.

The nausea was another matter altogether. Somewhere in the back of his mind he was sure he knew what was causing the nausea, but he couldn't seem to dredge it up from the dark recesses where it was hiding. However, that problem wouldn't be hopeless forever. Steven Tavera had once told him he could accomplish anything he wanted to, and he believed that with all his heart.

"Just look what I've accomplished already," he said aloud as he stood in front of a small potted tree. "How many people could get the *Jatropha curcas* to grow in New Mexico?" With its pleasant-tasting seeds, it could be a most useful plant. After the violent purgative effect, the jatrophin poison would inhibit protein synthesis in the cells of the intestinal wall, with death as the inexorable outcome. "Are you all right, my love?" he asked, caressing one of the thick branches.

"What did you say?"

The voice came from behind him, and he spun around, his heart racing. "Juanita!" He scowled at her. "What are you doing in here?"

"The door was open," she said calmly. "Besides, I didn't know the greenhouse was off limits. Is that something new?"

His training took effect. "Of course not! I should put a welcome mat out front. I was just a little startled, that's all. How can I help you?"

"Rosa sent me. Her rheumatism is acting up again. She's out of *yerba del peco* and doesn't have time to get up into the mountains to gather some."

"Ah. The baneberry. An excellent *remedio*." He started toward the back of the greenhouse. "Please give Rosa my sympathies for her pain. I hope this won't keep her from coming to Steven Tavera's party tomorrow."

"Not at all," Juanita said, following behind him. "She's even planning to be there early to help with the preparations."

"And you?" Roy asked, as he opened a back door and entered a small, dark room. "Will you be there, too?" He expected a no, but got a very different response. Juanita's smile transformed her entire face.

"Michael has asked me to go with him."

Roy flipped on the overhead light, a single bulb in an inverted cone-shaped receptacle. "Michael Martino is going to the party?"

Juanita nodded. "He has a gift for Steven."

"His latest portrait of Lenor." Roy inserted and turned a small key, then tugged at a round porcelain drawer-knob in a very large wooden chest full of small, deep drawers.

"How did you know about the painting?" Juanita asked.

"A lucky guess." But it wasn't a guess. Roy had been listening at the kitchen door yesterday morning while Rosa and Juanita had been whispering in the hallway. He'd barely managed to get out the back door before they'd entered the kitchen. Eavesdropping was his latest adventure, his latest diversion. Even geniuses had to have some fun sometimes; and he was getting pretty good at his new pastime. Roy stopped congratulating himself, handed Juanita a small dried root, and said, "You know this is highly toxic, don't you?"

She hesitated. "No. I didn't."

He gave a short laugh. "Only if you eat it. Here, let me wrap it for you. It can cause a skin rash if you handle it too much." He pulled paper towels from a holder on the wall beside the chest of drawers and folded several sheets around the root. "There, that shouldn't give you any trouble. Anything else?"

Juanita hesitated. "A drink of water, if it's no trouble."

"No trouble at all. I brought that old refrigerator from the office out here. Come on up front." He snapped the light off as Juanita exited to the greenhouse. "So Michael is going to Steven's party. Who could have guessed that would ever happen?"

"From what Rosa said, it should be a surprise to everyone," Juanita said.

Especially to Steven Tavera.

"Yes. But I think it will be a *pleasant* surprise to Señor Tavera," Juanita said.

Roy stopped walking. *Did I say that out loud? No. She heard what I was thinking! This woman worked in my store for eight years and never let me know that she could read my mind!* Roy willed himself to stop thinking. Only spoken words could divert her attention.

"Well, I hope Michael has a good time," he said.

Juanita stopped and turned around. "Why wouldn't he?"

Roy didn't expect the question. "Well . . . I've heard he has a temper."

Juanita huffed and shook her head. "I imagine you've heard a lot of nonsense about Mr. Martino. He's really quite a nice man . . . just private, that's all. No sin in that. He works hard." She sighed. "I imagine there are some who are jealous of his success."

"It's not as if he started out with nothing," Roy reminded her as he took a large glass bottle from the refrigerator and reached for a paper cup from a dispenser on the wall.

So you're one of the jealous ones. A son who's had everything handed to him. "How true," Juanita said without conviction. "He started out at the age of seventeen with a funeral for his mother and a mortgage that would have had a lesser man begging for a handout."

"Touché," Roy said, handing her the cup. "I never thought about it quite like that."

"Well . . ." Juanita gulped the water down quickly, crushed the cup, and tossed it into a nearby wastebasket. She held up her small package. "Thank you for helping me." She opened the front door. "See you tomorrow."

"Three o'clock," Roy said. But he'd already planned on being early. There were a couple of things he had to do in the Tavera kitchen.

Apple's arm was draped around his shoulder again, and George really couldn't complain, since Lenor, on his other side, had her arm curled around his waist. *Maybe everyone was right about this being the Land of Enchantment!*

They walked as a threesome toward Lenor's bedroom after a pleasant evening excursion into Toya. They'd had margaritas at Eulalia's bar, a tour of the sheriff's office and the church, and a quick side trip to Salman's Raspberry Ranch store, where George bought a handsome gift box full of raspberry preserves for his chief operating room nurse.

Watson had left the premises, so the three had a choice of seats. Apple flopped down on the bed. Lenor curled up on a deeply recessed and cushioned window seat. George pulled out the chair from the desk and straddled it.

"I can't remember when I've been so relaxed," he said, leaning his forearms on the back of the chair. "Why didn't you tell me how enjoyable this trip would be, Lenor?"

Lenor looked at Apple. "I did tell him," she said. "He just didn't believe me."

"Who can describe New Mexico?" Apple asked, not really expecting an answer.

"Tony Hillerman," Lenor said.

"The mystery writer?" George asked.

"He writes nonfiction, too," Lenor said. She got up, crossed the room to one of several bookcases along the walls, and pulled out a large hardbound book. She brought it back to George. "I'll let you borrow this on one condition."

"What's that?"

"That you give it back to me before we leave." He gave her a that's-impossible look. "It's an autographed copy," she said.

George opened the book, which was titled simply, *New Mexico,* and saw that it was mostly beautiful captioned photographs. "Thank you," he said. "I'll have it back in the morning. And I'll take good care of it."

"Bet you'd like to see some pictures of Lenor," Apple said, rolling to her back, then getting up. From the same bookcase she extracted a well-worn volume with an imitation leather cover, then plopped it down on the corner of the bed nearest George. He pulled his chair closer as she knelt on the floor and opened it.

"Senior year?" George asked.

"Forty-two kids in our graduating class," Apple said. "Lenor and I wanted our pictures to be together, but they put us in alphabetical order." She started to turn the page.

"Wait! That's you, isn't it?" He pointed to a blond girl with two long pigtails.

Apple's hand shot over the page to cover the picture. "Hey, I thought you wanted to see Lenor. She's on the next—"

George ran his finger along the caption. "Basketball, field hockey, track, and . . . garden club?"

"Grandpa Steven's idea," Apple said, flushing slightly. "And a damn good idea, too. Learned how to keep bees, you know. Pretty profitable business, now that I build my own African hives."

"That was Apple's honey Roy brought you, George," Lenor said. She looked at Apple. "I still can't imagine why anyone would steal one of your homemade topbars when they could have taken one of the more expensive Langstroth hives."

Apple shrugged. "I can't either."

"Someone stole a beehive?" George asked.

"Almost two years ago now. 'Course I built another one to replace it, but it's still a puzzle. Kind of a local joke between Lenor and me. We like to call the theft 'the most recent crime wave in Toya County.' "

"I take it it's kind of quiet around here, police-work-wise," George said.

"Most exciting thing I do is deliver babies who can't wait till they get to the clinic at Mora."

"Or those who can't afford the clinic," Lenor said.

"Let's see . . . that would make you a *partera*?" George asked Apple.

"Oh, hell no! I don't have that kind of talent." Apple looked at Lenor. "You teaching him Spanish?"

Lenor shook her head. "He took Latin in school, so he picks up on my Spanish. He's a fast learner."

Apple chanted, "Latin is a dead language, lying in the dust—"

Lenor picked it up. "First it killed the Romans, and now it's killing us."

George laughed at their singsong recital. "*Latina est mors.* I'd forgotten that one." Then, "So nothing much happens around here."

"Not much," Lenor said.

"Junior Garcia ran away again," Apple said.

"What is it now, three or four times this year?" Lenor asked.

"It's the fourth time the little bugger's slipped away. And it's only June!" Apple said.

"John must be worried sick," Lenor said.

"John Garcia is the sheriff of Mora County?" George asked.

"Right. And he's *plenty* worried. Thinks Junior might be into drugs this time," Apple said. "We have people in four counties keeping an eye out for him, but I wouldn't be surprised if he hightailed it to Santa Fe or Albuquerque. The police are watching for him there, too."

The three were silent for a moment, thinking their own thoughts, all pondering the sad situation of a missing child. Finally Apple turned the page in the old high school yearbook.

Lenor had worn her hair in two pigtails just like Apple had. "Well, weren't you cute. Basketball, field hockey, track, and garden club. Is it safe to say that you two were inseparable?" George asked.

Lenor looked at Apple. Both smiled. Both giggled a little. Then they nodded in unison. "Inseparable tomboys," they said together.

George curled the page over so he could see them together. "I can see how that might be a dangerous combination. Mischief here. Mischief there."

"We studied hard, too. You didn't finish the captions."

"National Honor Society, Girls' State. Double dangerous." George smiled. "Apple, you'll be glad to know that your buddy is carrying on the tradition at Foley Hospital."

Apple sank to the floor, then turned so she could lean back against the foot of the bed. With her knees hugged up close to her body, she said, "Tell me more."

"I already tell you everything!" Lenor protested.

"I want firsthand, on-the-scene information, lady. Go on, George."

Warming to the task, George grinned down at Apple. "She's turning the whole hospital upside down. She started out changing the way the cafeteria cooked. We're now plagued with nonfat and low-fat vegetarian dishes."

"Very low fat," Lenor corrected.

"As you probably already know," George went on with a roll of his eyes, "Foley has spent millions on computer and diagnostic equipment. It could easily be the most modern hospital in the world. You can walk in there with almost anything, and, within a matter of hours, sometimes minutes, your malady can be diagnosed and your treatment started."

"How, uh . . . efficient," Apple said.

George nodded. "Feed the symptoms into a computer, read out the possibilities, write a prescription."

"And send the poor slob on his way," Apple said.

"After you clean out his wallet," Lenor added.

"I get the picture," Apple said. "Not exactly a pretty one."

"But it's beautiful in so many ways," Lenor said unexpectedly. "For someone doing research, the data manipulation is absolutely essential. The labs are indispensable. The time saved can save thousands of lives, no matter what field you're in. A physician couldn't ask for a better set of circumstances."

George looked at Lenor. "Then what's Carl Bowder's beef with you all about? Is it that you insist on diagnosing before the data is in the computer?" George looked at Apple. "She's disgustingly right most of the time," he said.

"Yes, there's that," Lenor said. "Several things, really, but I think it's mainly my style. Spending too much time with patients, prescribing an herb tea instead of an expensive sedative . . . That sort of thing doesn't exactly fit Foley's high-tech image or Carl's high-volume goals."

"It's a business," George said. "Carl has to think of the bottom line. It's his job to keep the hospital financially healthy."

"And my job is to keep the patient well."

"So there's the rub," Apple said. "Sounds like Carl Bowder doesn't consider the patient's financial well-being as part of the patient's health."

"George and I were just talking about that earlier today," Lenor said. "René Descartes, of the body-is-separate-from-the-mind school of thought, is alive and well in the form of Carl Bowder."

"And ninety-five percent of all the doctors at Foley," George added.

"That's a shame," Apple said.

"But a handful of physicians are taking a new road," George said.

"For instance?" Apple asked.

"I order massage therapy after surgery—Lenor's idea. Damn good one, too. I was skeptical at first, then amazed at vital-signs response to hands-on treatment. It took Lenor two years, but we now have a chiropractic department. Neither Foley's Pediatric Heart and Lung Center, nor I, could do without the high-tech equipment. But, even though it's considered low tech, the caring human hand is probably in an even higher echelon than the profusionist's heart-lung machine."

Lenor winked at Apple. "He's coming around."

"So integrating modern medicine with folk healing has promise," Apple said.

"More than promise," Lenor said. "I think it's the key to medicine's future. Where the patient sees the doctor as a friend and the doctor sees the patient as an equal."

"Ye gods, you mean there'll be no more demigods?" Apple said.

"That should take a good long time," George said.

"And in the meantime, I'll stay at Foley and fight with Carl Bowder," Lenor said.

"Not if your mama has anything to say about it," Apple said. "Has she asked you to come home yet?"

"I guess she's saving it for tomorrow. Probably choose the perfect time, when we're surrounded by people, so I can't refuse without sounding like a callous lowlife."

"I hope I'm close enough to see the fireworks," Apple said.

"There won't be any fireworks," Lenor said. "With a good forty percent of children between the ages of five and eight already manifesting at least one heart-disease risk factor, my research can't be done anywhere else. I think she'll appreciate that when I explain it."

"That's assuming you live long enough to elaborate after you say no," Apple said.

"No problem. I plan to run like hell."

"Like we used to." Apple giggled.

George chuckled. "I can just see that. You two, I mean. But somehow I can't picture Magdalena running after you."

"She *didn't!*" Apple said on a burst of laughter. "That was Arthur's job."

"Or Eloy's, if he was around," Lenor added.

George's chuckling turned into laughter. All three laughed themselves breathless and teary-eyed.

"Oh, well," Lenor finally managed on a long sigh, "I'll think of some way to wear her down. Mama's a lot less combative when she's tired."

"And speaking of tired . . . I don't want this little party to end, but either I'm going to have to get some sleep or I'll never make my dawn appointment with Tossa," George said.

"He's going to ride your horse tomorrow?" Apple asked Lenor.

"I introduced them. Tossa said he wasn't too bad . . . for a dude."

"Well, the dude has to say good night," George said.

"Me, too," Apple said as she propelled herself up from the floor. She moved to the door, then held it open for George, who seemed to be debating a good-night kiss or an immediate exit.

Apple was right about George's debate, but a glance at the family photo on Lenor's desk helped him decide. "See you in the morning." Watson scooted in as George walked out. "Sweet dreams, you two."

But Watson wasn't ready for dreams. He had a fight to pick with everyone who'd touched his cat carrier. His rock was missing, he'd been out looking for it, unsuccessfully, and he was irritated to the point of yowling.

"If you'll just calm down, I promise I'll help you find it tomorrow," Lenor argued with him. "Right now I have to look for the herbal." She fingered through the books on the shelves.

"Yeow!"

"No, tomorrow won't be too late, and I'm too tired to look for it tonight. Either take my offer or sleep outside."

"Yee ah?"

"That's better," she said as she continued her search. But in the back of her mind Lenor knew he was at least partially right about the smooth river stone. It was much more than just a good-luck charm. *I must be too tired to remember.* And the herbal Leonora Tavera had started, over a hundred years ago, was missing also. *Is there a connection?* "Maybe I need to talk to Leonora again," she said.

"Eee!"

"You realize even spirits can't be everywhere at once, Watson. Leonora is probably very busy with someone else. Okay, okay. We'll see."

August 1860 ◆ The Territory of New Mexico

"Leonora Tavera, resident of the county of Mora, Territory of New Mexico, citizen of the United States of America by your own choice, you were bound over to await this term of the district court for trial. Do you understand the charges that Patricia Wright has brought against you?"

Leonora sat perfectly still in her chair and faced the judge with quiet assurance. "No, señor. I am a healer, a *curandera*. I am not a *bruja*, a witch. I do not understand why Señora Wright would accuse me of anything. I have never seen her husband, nor have I seen the señora until today."

"But you knew of Captain Wright?"

"I have heard the name."

"How so?"

"I was told that Captain Wright was the man who caused Private Whisner's injuries."

"Private Harold Whisner?" Leonora nodded. "When was this?"

"In the month of May."

"So you say that you have not met or seen Captain Wright on any occasion?"

"That is correct," Leonora said.

"Nevertheless, you have been accused of practicing witch-craft and also accused of the murder of Captain Timothy Wright, whose death, allegedly, was a direct result of a spell you cast upon him with a witch's doll. The punishment for murder is hanging. Do you understand?"

"*Sí.*"

"How do you plead?"

Leonora consulted with her son, Dorio, in hushed tones, then said, "I do not practice witchcraft. I have never used *el monito* for any purpose. I have murdered no one, señor."

"But you believe in witchcraft, don't you?"

"Of course. All of our people believe in things of the super-natural. But I do not know how to practice such, nor would I ever consider it."

"Then what is your explanation for Captain Wright's sudden illness?"

"I have no explanation, señor."

The man behind the long wooden table flashed an evil smile. "But you call yourself a healer, don't you?"

"I am a *curandera,* señor." Dorio started to stand, but Leonora took his hand and gave it a reassuring squeeze. "Do not harm yourself on my account, son," she whispered.

"Have you no defense, then?"

A man stood up. "I am Rubén Barela. I will speak for Doña Leonora. She is my neighbor."

The judge nodded. "You may speak."

Dorio was on his feet before Rubén could utter the first word. "No! He will lie!"

"Order!"

Leonora was tugging at her son's sleeve. "Please, sit down," she pleaded. "Señor Barela will not harm us. I have made his children well many times. That is what he will tell the court."

Dorio sat down, still protesting, but now in whispers to his mother. "He is an evil man. I can feel his cruelty, and I have seen him strike his wife."

The judge's wooden gavel came down on the table with a

loud crack. "Order in this courtroom!" He gave everyone the benefit of his fierce scowl, then, "Please proceed, Señor Barela."

"It is as she has said. The widow Tavera is a *curandera*. And even though we cannot comprehend most of the magic she uses—"

"Magic?"

"*Sí,* señor. We who do not understand the healing ways sometimes call the wonders of it magic."

"I knew he would do something like this," Dorio hissed in his mother's ear. "His truth is wrapped in dark clouds."

"Please go on, Mr. Barela."

"I have heard that the Anglos do not officially recognize witchcraft. Just last year, a man from Taos was arrested and bound over by an *alcalde,* a mayor, to be tried by the district court for witchcraft. The charge was dismissed because the prosecutor understood that no such offense existed under the Anglos' laws." Rubén's tiny black eyes shifted toward Leonora, then back to the judge. He continued quickly, "But that trial has nothing to do with this matter. I probably shouldn't have . . ."

"He is putting deadly ideas into the judge's head," Dorio whispered.

"You are right, Mr. Barela. What happened before has nothing to do with the decision of this court." The judge pointed to the black stone that lay on the table. "Can you tell us anything about the witch's doll?"

"*El monito* is just a river stone, nothing more. I have seen it in Señora Tavera's kitchen on many occasions. Sometimes such a stone is heated and put at the foot of the bed to warm a sleeper's feet, but it can have many other uses, also . . . especially if it is the *piedra imán.*"

"*Piedra imán?*"

"A fury stone, sir. Some call it a *monito,* a witch's doll. In the possession of an *ambularia,* a witch, such a stone can make her all-powerful. She can transform into any shape. She can know the unknowable. She can—"

"Enough about the rock. Do you know why it was in the possession of the soldier, Harold Whisner?"

"I can only guess. As a talisman, perhaps?"

"Against what?"

"I haven't a clue."

Dorio could stand it no longer and jumped to his feet. "The stone is *not* a magical charm! My mother gave it to the soldier so he could squeeze it tightly against his pain, while she was trying to heal his wounds."

"Like biting the bullet," the judge said with a sneering laugh.

"I do not know this Anglo saying, señor, but the soldier is in fine health today because of my mother's healing powers."

"Sit down, child. If you interrupt again, I'll send you outside. Please continue, Mr. Barela. If you know, please tell us, how did the rock come to be buried beneath the front stoop of the captain's quarters at Fort Union?"

"I can tell you only what I have heard." When the judge nodded, Rubén went on. "After Harold Whisner got well, he and his friend, Roger Colby, started asking questions about a *bruja* who lives in Loma Parda. No one would answer their questions, so they went to Señora Tavera's house. Some people saw them enter late at night, and the candles burned in the kitchen until the early hours of the morning. When they came out, they were . . . ah . . . *embrujado.*"

"Em-brew-hado?" the judge asked.

"Bewitched, señor. It is said that Harold Whisner himself did not steal the stone, and, I suppose, no one knows for sure who did this. Nor did Whisner bury the stone before the captain's door, but no one knows for sure who did this either." Barela paused.

"Go on."

"At the time of Señor Wright's illness, it is said that, because there was no real doctor at the fort, the soldier was sent to fetch Señora Tavera so she could tend to the captain's illness, but she refused to return with him, so the captain died. Perhaps this is the reason Señor Whisner is in the jail right now. I do not know.

Again, I can only tell you what I have heard, and there are many stories."

"Is there anything else you want to say?"

"Only one more thing. I heard that the *curandera* was seen entering the captain's quarters in the middle of the night just before he died, ah—" Barela glanced at Leonora, then quickly averted his eyes "—in the form of a cat. And even though one man saw the door slam on the cat's right leg, and Señora Tavera now walks with a limp, I am *sure* this story is not true, señor."

Dorio almost exploded in another angry outburst. His mother's ankle had been injured by a rock thrown by Rubén's oldest son, Tilano. Leonora stopped Dorio just in time.

"Is anything in this matter known *for sure,* Mr. Barela?" the judge asked.

"Oh, *sí.* That the soldier hated the good captain because the officer had punished him for not following his military orders. And, at this moment, Whisner is in the Fort Union *cárcel* for some reason, but I do not know the cause of his detainment."

"Señora Tavera, were you summoned to the fort to treat Captain Wright's illness, and did you refuse to come to him?" the judge asked.

"No. I was not called to treat the captain, and I have never refused help to anyone who is ill."

"Are there any more witnesses, Mr. Prosecutor?"

"No, Your Honor."

"Do you have anything to say on your own behalf, Mrs. Tavera?"

"No, señor."

"Leonora Tavera, widow of Juan Tavera, please stand. I've made my decision."

Dorio stood with his mother.

"The testimony given against you here today has been circumstantial, hearsay, and rumors, all of it. The charges are hereby dismissed. The cost for the use of the wagon from your home to Fort Union will be twenty-five cents, *dos reales.*" The judge struck the table with his gavel.

Leonora remained standing, not moving, still facing the judge even as he stood, turned away from her, and hurried through the door at the side of the room.

"It's over, Mama," Dorio said quietly.

"No it isn't," Leonora said.

"Yes, Mama. We're free to go."

"But we haven't heard the end of this. I know it."

"Come, Mama. Let's go home."

"I don't have *dos reales*."

A smiling Rubén Barela turned toward her. "Here," he said, as he dug deeply into his pocket. "Take this." He handed her two coins.

"No." Leonora turned from him and started to walk away.

"Wait. Take it as payment for delivering my last son, my little Mauro. Please."

"No. Neighbors do not pay one another for such things."

"Mama. We have to pay the debt before we can go home."

Leonora looked first at Barela, then at her son. "It will be a debt I cannot repay."

"Why do you say such a thing, Mama? It will be harvest time soon. We will have corn and apples and chile pods to sell."

"Yes, but for a very low price," Leonora said, then turned her back on the two people.

"You don't have to pay it back . . . if you don't want to," Rubén said.

Dorio cringed. Rubén was still using his harmful-sweet words to influence those who were within the sound of his voice. "Mama, you go on. Wait for me outside."

When Leonora had left, Dorio took the coins from Rubén. "Thank you," he managed to say, though he almost choked on the words. The thought of being publicly indebted to this man was almost more than Dorio could bear, especially since he knew that Rubén was in debt to his mother a hundredfold for all the services she'd rendered to the family Barela.

Dorio paid the court clerk, put the black river stone in his pocket, and followed Rubén out the door. *I will pay you back, Rubén Barela—then I will punish you.*

September 1860

Captain James Start sat at his desk, carefully squaring the corners of one pile of papers, then putting the finishing touches on the perfect arrangement of the four stacks in front of him. When he was satisfied that all was as neatly situated as possible and that the office reflected nothing but absolute authority, he called out, "You may send Mr. Barela in now."

Rubén entered the sparely furnished room, crossed to the straight-back chair in front of the desk, and offered his hand.

Captain Start didn't make a move toward the greeting for two reasons. He wanted to intimidate and he wanted to keep his own personal fear from revealing itself through the dampness of his palm. "Sit down, Mr. Barela. We have much to discuss."

Hat in hand, Rubén sat down. "Yes, sir."

"Have you thought about my proposition?" Captain Start asked.

"I have, sir."

"Your decision?"

"To lose my business with Fort Union would bring financial ruin to my family. You've given me no choice, señor. I will do what you have asked . . . in exchange for an exclusive five-year contract with Fort Union to supply corn and hay and other essential food items for the men and the stock."

"Very well. And you will get rid of Señora Tavera?"

"Of course." His plan would bring him much power in the community and, with luck, add to his properties the strip of fertile land that the Tavera family owned. "I have a plan that—"

"Keep it to yourself, Barela." Relieved that Barela had agreed to rid the territory of an alleged murderess and a powerful witch, but repelled by his presence, Captain Start drew back from the little man with the malevolent sneer on his thin lips. "What assurances do you give that I—ah—that the fort and my soldiers will be safe from the evil sorceries of this woman?"

"Only I, or members of my immediate family, will make deliveries to the fort. Everything we bring will be inspected before it is put into the wagon. You don't have to worry about anything."

Captain Start stood up. "But *you* do, Mr. Barela. The penalty for failure to perform according to the letter of our contract, for committing treason, is death by hanging."

One Month Later

The short northern New Mexico summer had slipped by like a warm breeze, but had left the mark of a cruel winter. The humiliation of the trial still burned in Leonora's heart even though she and her five children were busy with a bountiful fall harvest. In the mountains to the west, the aspen dotted the dark green pine forests with vivid yellow patterns, and leaves of gold, orange, and rust decorated the valleys below. Crisp red apples waited in bright clusters; the plum trees were heavy with green and purple fruit that promised luscious *empanadas,* the little fruit-filled turnovers Dorio loved so much. After two days of curing in the sun, mounds of red peppers lay in the Tavera courtyard, ready to be plaited into strings by a roomful of helpful neighbors. There were enough, both red and green chiles, to sell and to last the family all winter long, and there was plenty of green corn for drying.

Leonora was glad the Barelas had not shown up to help make the red chile *ristras,* especially since she planned to use one of the strings to pay a part of her debt to them. From the day of the trial, she'd carefully avoided anyone who was a member of the Barela family. The gossip was that they had not been so lucky as she with their harvest. She knew it was mostly because of laziness. All she would say, when others voiced the same opinion out loud, was, *"De lo dicho a lo hecho, hay mucho trecho."* "From talk to reality, there is a great distance."

Leonora had been silent since the conversation among her guests had taken a turn in the Barelas' direction.

"My harvest of corn has been better this year than ever before, but the fort will buy none of it," Don José said.

"They will only buy from Barela," his wife added. Then the discussion flowed around the room as busy hands tied red chile pods together.

"My goat herding used to be profitable, too, but now the only market for my milk and meat is Barela."

"He wants to give me a penny for two dozen tortillas."

"My *empanadas* must now be delivered by his son, and Tilano doesn't care if they get there cold and all broken up from a bumpy ride in the back of his wagon."

"We can bring nothing into the fort ourselves anymore."

"Barela says his business is good for the community, but he pays us almost nothing for our crops and our goods."

"I've heard that his contract with Fort Union will last for five years."

"At his prices, I'll be a pauper in two."

Everyone nodded in agreement.

"How do you suppose he got this five-year contract?"

"It's the Devil's work!"

"I say it's witchcraft!"

"Señor Barela is a great talker. I'm sure he persuaded them with fine words and grand promises."

Even at twelve, Dorio Tavera knew the ways of the braggart and couldn't help doing a bit of showing off in front of a crowd of friendly neighbors. "Oh, Señor Barela's a great talker, all right. With his mouth, he'll dig his own grave."

"Or mine," Leonora said quietly. Everyone was laughing at Dorio, so no one heard what she'd said except Carolina.

"Why do you say such things, Mama?"

"Señor Barela tira la piedra, y esconde la mano." He throws the first rock, and hides the hand.

"No!"

Lenor's head snapped forward at the sound of her own voice. Her heart pounded with fear at the vision of horror held steady before her open eyes. The slightly swaying rope creaked softly against the branch of the cottonwood tree. Tears streamed down Dorio's cheeks. Rubén Barela smiled. Leonora, her body thin and frail, her face contorted with agony, swung in the hangman's noose.

Willing her heart to slow, her rapid breathing to surrender to reason, Lenor closed her eyes and summoned reality with a long sigh. The image of the hanging woman began to fade, and the nightmare's terror trickled away to hide in the corners of the darkened room. She twisted the switch on the bedside lamp and looked around. Her empty suitcase lay open on the floor. Dr. Watson was curled at her feet, not bothered in the least by her sudden shout or movements. Though she was completely awake now, Lenor still couldn't be sure whether she'd been dreaming or remembering.

Leonora, Lenor's great-great-great-grandmother, had been the subject of so many stories during Lenor's youth, it was impossible to tell if the tale that had just unfolded before her closed eyes had been told to her in its entirety or if she had constructed it from the bits and pieces she'd heard about Leonora Tavera's life. When hearing the stories back then, Lenor had never thought of "Granora" as a living, breathing, suffering human being, but rather as a character in an old-fashioned play.

Barela.

Now, after her dream, she could put an identity with the name, and remember the rest of the story. Rubén Barela had, indeed, been the downfall of Leonora Tavera. He had carefully and viciously aroused the suspicion that she was a *bruja,* practicing *en lo malo,* for the bad. She was blamed for the failure of her community's crops and the illnesses of its children and animals in

1861 and 1862. Rubén Barela had been stoned to death by enraged neighbors in 1862, the same year that Leonora had been hung for practicing witchcraft. Dorio Tavera, Leonora's fourteen-year-old son, had been able to prove Rubén's collusion with Captain Start by sneaking into Fort Union and stealing the signed five-year contract.

Quite by chance one day, Dorio had caught Tilano, Rubén's oldest son, in the act of "poisoning" the wells, and thereby the people, with an unknown, fuzzy yellow root. He hadn't realized the significance of what he'd seen until it was too late to save his mother's life, but the information later helped to clear Leonora's name. The other evidence against Rubén was just as damning.

After Leonora's death, Dorio befriended a laundress who occasionally washed the Fort Union hospital linen. Through this young woman Dorio found out that Captain Wright had died of a combination of dysentery, syphilis, and a disease she'd never heard of, scurvy. In the land of peppers and onions, the illness caused by lack of vitamin C was all but unknown among the natives. More importantly, Dorio learned that the captain had been seen in Loma Parda, in the company of a prostitute, by the young private, Harold Whisner. Captain Wright had committed the most damning and destructive of military sins—being seen by subordinates while behaving in less than gentlemanly fashion.

"You could have taught him a thing or two about gentlemanly behavior, couldn't you, Watson." Lenor leaned forward, lifted the heavy, limp body into her lap, and stroked his back while she remembered more.

While Barela's plan had worked perfectly for a while, he hadn't counted on the tenacity or ingenuity of the Tavera family. As a result of Dorio's efforts and the hard work and dedication of the other four of Leonora's children, not only did the land and the ranch stay in the possession of the Taveras, the family actually prospered, while the Barelas were shamed, shunned, and finally driven from the valley. Disparate rumors abounded—the Barelas had moved to Arizona, to California, to Colorado—but one report remained consistent. In 1863, a fire had consumed both house and remaining family, bringing to an end, for all time, the Barela lineage.

The story had several additions that Rafael Tavera had loved to tell. Two of Leonora's daughters had kept diaries, and Carolina's differed from Juana's in several details. According to Carolina, Private Whisner had been having an affair with Captain Wright's daughter and had enlisted the help of a *bruja* in Loma Parda to get rid of the captain before he found out about it.

Juana wrote of a scandal involving Captain Wright and several Loma Parda prostitutes, and of his subsequent death by poisoning at the hand of his wife, Patricia. No one might ever know the truth.

Still, whatever had taken place, it was hard to see how something that had happened over a hundred and thirty years ago had anything to do with what was happening in northeastern New Mexico today. Lenor's home had always been a peaceful place, a quiet expanse of fertile fields in narrow mountain valleys, pastures for grazing cattle, hills and mountains for collecting herbs.

Why all this uproar over a rock? In this dream, Rubén Barela had referred to the stone both as a *monito* and a *piedra imán*. In New Mexican Spanish both words were used to describe a rock used by witches. The *monito* could be used in much the same fashion as a voodoo doll, to bring pain and suffering to the witch's target. As far as Lenor could remember, the *piedra imán* was more of a powerful good-luck charm for the witch. With possession of such a stone, the witch could know everything and also transform herself into anything she desired. *Not likely.*

"Is your rock more than a simple river stone, Dr. Watson?" Lenor asked.

He opened one eye just a slit. Closed it. Without leaving her lap, the cat stretched out to his full length and began to purr.

Granora, I need to talk to you in person. Soon!

Eight

THE NAME ON THE MAILBOX SAID VIGIL IN LARGE black letters. "Carmela Vih-jull?" George asked.

"Vee-hill," Lenor corrected him.

"I'll remember," George said. "Nine children. No husband. What will she do?" He surveyed the pitiful unplastered ramble of adobe brick walls, the rusty corrugated tin roof, the swayed split logs of the small corral enclosures.

Lenor turned the car into the rutted dust of the driveway. "If the kids stay healthy and keep helping, they might be able to make ends meet." She pointed right. "Those fields belong to them."

"You said you and your grandfather got them started on organic farming. Is there something especially profitable about that?"

"People are getting more and more concerned about environmental poisons all the time. DDT was outlawed in the seventies, and we're only now seeing the positive results. But other pesticides and chemicals still in use are just as dangerous. The demand for organically grown produce increases every day, but the Vigils, and the others around here who decided to give it a try, have problems getting their vegetables and fruits to the buyers. The closest large market is Santa Fe, and that's about two hours away."

George looked at the vintage '58 Ford step-side pickup truck parked close to the house. "I see what you mean. Are any of the kids old enough to drive?"

"Juan will be sixteen in July. If he can stay out of trouble, he'll be the designated delivery boy, just what the family needs to keep them going."

"What do you mean, 'if he can stay out of trouble'?"

"Teenage trouble. Drinking, hanging out instead of helping out. It's the same everywhere. No exception here." Lenor opened her car door. "Come on, let's go see how Carmela's doing," she said, reaching for her black medical bag.

George stood for a moment by the side of the car while Lenor went up to the door and knocked. The contrast between the fields across the road and the Vigils' was striking. One was a smooth stretch of alfalfa with nothing to break up the sameness, the other was lush and vibrant with a variety of healthy vegetables and herbs. Human food versus animal food, he remembered Lenor saying. But would the fickle ways of human nature bring ruin to the Vigils? How long would people be interested in clean, untainted food? As long as something tasted good, what else *was* there to think about?

"George?" Lenor was calling to him.

Once inside the small front room, George had to wait for his eyes to adjust to the darkness, but the cool air was immediately evident. When he could see, he looked around for the air-conditioning vent he was obviously standing in front of. He saw none. The breeze was coming through an open window set well back in the thick adobe wall.

At the other side of the small room, Lenor had her arms around a woman who he'd have guessed was well into her forties. But he knew that Carmela Vigil was only thirty-three.

All the children were present, three younger ones seated on an old couch, four more in an odd assortment of wooden chairs. One defiant-looking boy, about fifteen, reclined nonchalantly in what had probably been his father's favorite overstuffed chair. The oldest son, Juan, leaned against the wall, head down and eyes averted.

George helped Lenor with the simple physicals as each child took turns coming into the kitchen for the exam. Lenor kept up a running banter with them, asking questions about friends, about school, praising them for everything, no matter how seemingly insignificant. She seemed to know all about each one, even though the oldest boy had been only four when she had left for

college. Every child left the kitchen smiling or giggling or laughing outright—except for the sullen one who'd been sitting in his
father's chair. He came in last and obviously under protest.

"Peter, you seem troubled about something. Can you tell me
what it is?" Lenor asked after she'd finished with his exam.

"Nothing."

"A death in the family is very traumatic. You can talk about
it if you want to."

He turned away from her. "Why would I want to talk about
that? It's over. He's dead. He wanted to die and he did. Big
fucking deal."

Lenor put a hand on his shoulder, but he jerked away from
her. "Peter, why do you say your father wanted to die?"

He turned and glared at her. "Look around. Take a *good* look.
If this was yours, wouldn't *you* want to get the hell out?"

George looked around, but Lenor didn't. She kept her eyes
steadily on Peter. "You're saying Daniel was so unhappy that he
would rather die than go on?"

"You catch on quick, Doc. You in your big fancy house,
with your expensive education, your high-paying job in New
York. What do you know about the way we live? And what the
hell do you care?"

Lenor held up her hand when George took a step forward.
"You're right, Peter. We do have a nice house. I'm well educated, and I have a good job."

Peter sneered. "And you'll walk out of here and go back to
your Grandpa's fancy birthday party and forget all about us."

"Right again . . . on two counts, anyway. I'll leave and go to
Grandpa's party. But I won't forget about any of you."

"Yeah, sure."

"Sounds like you're the one who's forgetting," Lenor said.

"Fat chance. I'm the one who's stuck here."

"Being right two out of three times isn't bad, Peter, but
you're wrong about being stuck," Lenor said.

"Oh yeah? That's easy for you to say. I might as well have my
ankle chained to the table here. You don't know *shit*—" he gave

the wooden leg a violent kick "—about being *me* or being *poor*."

Lenor grabbed his arm as he took his first step away and swung him around to face her. "I want to tell you one thing before you get back to feeling sorry for yourself. My parents didn't spend one penny on my education. Not any of it."

"Liar!"

"Check it out for yourself. Ask my parents. Ask my teachers. You'll see them this afternoon. And while you're at it, ask them how you can do the same thing. You're in good health. You've got what it takes up here"—Lenor tapped his temple—"where it counts. I told your friend, Junior Garcia, the same thing. You can do anything you want to—if you have the guts." She let go of his arm.

For the first time since he'd entered the kitchen, Peter didn't retaliate. He looked at George, who was nodding, then back at Lenor. The muted sounds of the younger children playing outside filtered into the room. Peter shook his head in denial, then said, "Are you trying to tell me that I could . . . that I could get from here"—his finger stabbed toward the floor—"to there?" He pointed at George.

"That's exactly what I'm trying to tell you, Peter. I'm telling you that scholarships and grants go begging every year for lack of someone interested enough to find out what it takes to get them and go after them. I'm telling you that you can do it. You can have anything you want, do anything you want."

Peter sneered again, but this time it wasn't as malicious. "Just like that." He snapped his fingers.

Lenor snapped her fingers. "Just like that."

"I wouldn't know how to start."

"Just takes one question. Tell your principal that you want a full scholarship to college, then ask him what you have to do to get it."

"That's it? That's all I have to do?"

"You'll have to do what he tells you to do," Lenor said. "But that won't be any problem for a kid like you. Do the work and people will bend over backward to help. Try it. What have you got to lose? If I'm wrong, you can tell me to go to hell. If I'm right, you and your whole family will be the winners."

Peter looked at George. "She's messin' with my head, isn't she?"

George smiled. "In the best kind of way. She's trying to show you the future."

"Well . . ." Peter took a step backward, then shrugged. "I don't know. I'll think about it."

"That's a good first step," Lenor said. "See you at the party."

George's body started seizing up about noon.

"Just lie still. Try to relax."

That wasn't too hard to do—not now. Rosa Flores had drawn a hot bath and added to the water some magical herbal elixir she'd called *escoba de la víbora*. He'd asked for aspirin, but both Lenor and Rosa had refused his request, giving him instead a mug of tea made from the same herb. They instructed him to drink the *yerba* in the cup while he soaked in it in the bath.

Skepticism about weeds versus pills had kept him tense for a time, but after a few minutes and a few sips of the tea he'd begun to feel the palliative effects. While everyone else scurried around getting ready for the party, George lazed in the tub, drifting in and out of a soothing doze and dreaming of his early-morning visit with Tossa.

Riding a horse had used muscles he hadn't thought about since his college days, some he swore he'd never learned about in medical school. But Lenor's horse had been patient with his bumbling, and he'd learned a great deal from the experienced cowboy and able teacher, Manny. In fact, George reckoned that he would be able to ride again—as soon as he could walk again.

The camp kids had been terrific companions, proud of what they'd already learned and willing to help him when he got into trouble. Thomas Newman, the youngest of the campers, had been especially kind. He and his friend Shirley had gotten George through the basics of cleaning hooves, brushing, leading, and the proper way to saddle, mount, and sit.

Sitting turned out to be the problem. Too many things to remember. Too many muscles involved. George would never again think of sitting as a leisure-time activity. His thighs ached from pressing in against Tossa's sides, his ankles and knees ached from the flexing—up, down, up, down—to keep the sorest muscle of all off the saddle. The gluteus maximus was never meant to take the pounding delivered by a trotting horse, and George had managed to cruelly punish the back of his front—down, up, down, up—when things got out of sync.

But the kinks were easing from his calves, and his backside was beginning to feel less and less like a piece of tenderized rump roast. Half an hour of soaking and sipping had him ready for the massage, the *sobadita,* a treat Lenor promised he would never forget. And she was right.

As he lay on the bed, hot from his steaming bath, cozy under a soft flannel bedsheet, Rosa Flores performed her magic manipulations, the *sobadita.*

"It's sort of a speciality of mine," Rosa said. "Comes in handy up at Michael's place. Something strange about cowboys . . . they fall off, and fall off, and get pitched off, and just keep getting back on. Takes a toll after while."

"I can imagine." But he really couldn't. After the punishment he had taken just riding around the corral and a couple of miles up a mountain trail, he couldn't fathom the wish to suffer further. "Will you tell me more about your specialty, Rosa?" he asked, genuinely curious and interested.

"Only if you'll promise to stop talking."

"I promise."

"I learned the techniques from my mother, who started teaching me when I was about nine years old," Rosa began, talking in a slow, even cadence that matched the movements of her hands. "She was part Navajo and part Hispanic and stressed the importance of the bonding of life's textures, day and night, humans and animals and plants and the elements. Nothing is separate, and any kind of medicine must harmonize and never exclude the concept of wholeness and balance. It's the exclusion that causes the illness or makes it worse."

I wish Carl Bowder could hear this.

"There are two main types of treatment the *sobadores* use, the *mesaje* and the *sobadita*. A *mesaje* is a type of massage for headaches, nervous tension, such as that. A *sobadita* is for a specific muscle problem, sprains, cramps—"

"Like—"

"Ssh," she reminded. "Of course, we have to be sure nothing is broken before we reduce swelling and manipulate the muscles and joints. Plain Epsom salts in water is good for that. I like to use a tincture of birch bark for a liniment and keep . . ."

George heard no more, drifting away to a sunny meadow high in the Sangre de Cristo Mountains. Just he and his horse. George Murphy, seasoned cowboy, a mountain man and his trusty steed, alone against the elements of nature, with only his wits to keep him alive.

"I thought I'd died and gone to heaven." George was telling Apple about Rosa's *sobadita*.

"It's something you could learn, Dr. Murphy," Rosa said.

"Sort of a new rub on his bedside manner?" Apple said.

Rosa dismissed Apple's remark with a glance. "Put your patients more at ease."

"And probably cure them," George added. "What other miracles do you have up your sleeve, Rosa?"

"Wait till you taste her honey cake," Lenor said.

Steven Tavera's birthday party had started right on time, and by a quarter past three, George decided, probably over a hundred people had already arrived. By three-thirty he'd seen so many new faces he knew he'd never be able to remember the names that went with them. Lenor was the perfect companion. Besides looking especially beautiful in Levi's and western shirt, with her shining black hair left long and loose to flow down her back, she'd been guiding him deftly from group to group, including him in conversations, asking his opinions, explaining situations and relationships.

"Two sheriffs in the same room at the same time," George said. "I feel safer than I've ever felt before."

John Garcia finished shaking George's hand. "We have two pretty quiet little counties here, George. Guess New York's a lot different."

"If you want a murder a minute, it's the place to be," George said.

"No thanks," John said. "I'll take the odd missing beehive any day." He winked at Apple.

Lenor smiled; then her expression became serious. "Have you heard anything from Junior?" she asked.

John shook his head. "Guess I shouldn't expect to. He's never called when he's taken off before. Don't know why this time should be any different."

"But he's always come back safe and sound?" Lenor asked.

"Safe, yes. Sound, I'm not so sure. I just can't figure what's going through the boy's head anymore. Aside from being just about the laziest kid on earth, and that hasn't changed, he's always been easy to get along with, considerate. But not lately."

"Do you think it's drugs?" Lenor asked.

"That's what I'm afraid of," John said. "And as soon as he gets back, we're going to find out. If it is, he's going into treatment the same day."

"Good for you," George said.

They all turned toward a commotion at the front door. It was the Vigil family. George and Lenor looked at each other and brightened. Peter was leading the way into the house, looking around as if inspecting something that he could one day own. "Excuse us," George said, taking Lenor's hand and moving toward the new arrivals.

On the heels of the Vigils, Miller Baldwin came in and stood still, his entrance a quiet counterpoint to the bustle of the nine children in front of him. As soon as Lenor and George had said hello to each member of the Vigil family, the children darted in nine different directions, headed for the many collections of food that occupied every available flat surface. Carmela stayed behind and watched as Lenor introduced Miller to George.

"I've heard a lot about you, sir," George said. "All good, of course," he quickly added.

Miller switched his cane to his left hand and put his arm around Lenor's shoulder. "This is my baby. She'd better say good things about the old geezer who delivered her. Right, Carmela?" His expression changed instantly. He released Lenor and took a step toward Carmela, enfolding the slight woman in his long arms. "We're all here for you, Carmela," he said quietly, then leaned away from her. "Don't go wanting for anything. Just ask."

Carmela nodded slightly.

"I mean it," he said sternly.

"I know you do, Doctor," she said.

"Just ask," he repeated.

"I will. And thank you." Carmela glanced at Lenor. *You came to help us this morning without being asked.*

George looked at Lenor. He hadn't missed Carmela's message. Mrs. Vigil wouldn't be asking anyone for anything. And George didn't miss the guilt that spread over Lenor's face like a sheet over the face of a corpse. He started to say something, anything, to distract her from her thoughts, but Miller interrupted.

"So, your specialty is pediatric cardiac surgery," he said. "Exciting. So many innovations, new techniques. I'm amazed how you fellows keep up with your field."

"No more difficult than general practice," George said as he watched Lenor lead Carmela toward one of the food-laden sideboards.

"Well, I'm glad to see you had time to hook up with such a wonderful lady," Miller said. "She'll make a fine wife . . . if you're thinking that way."

George wasn't sure whether he'd been distracted by Lenor's movements and missed something or he'd really heard the implication. "Lenor's a fine doctor, sir," he said, emphasizing the word doctor.

"Well, of course she is, son. But how long can it last? Her folks need her here, what with Steven and Jovita getting up there, and the camp and such. I can tell you, it's all getting to be too much for Magdalena. Besides, you'd like it here."

Lita walked by with a tray of full wineglasses. "Hey, sawbones, how 'bout a sample of Rafael's best?"

"A woman after my own heart," Miller said, taking a glass, handing it to George, then taking another for himself. He sipped. Made cooing sounds. Kissed the side of the glass. "Perfection, my darling Lita. My compliments to the vintner." He held his glass up slightly toward George as Lita moved past them. "Now this is what owning land is all about. Growing the perfect grape. Making the perfect wine. Too bad Rafael insists on grazing cattle." He took another sip. " 'Course, when you own so many thousands of acres, I guess you can do just about anything you damn well please."

"That sounds a little bit like sour grapes to me, Dr. Baldwin," George said, trying to keep his tone light.

"Now don't get me wrong. The Taveras are a smart bunch, but they've had a hell of a lot of good luck, too. Did you know that Dorio Tavera bought the lower twenty thousand and some acres across the highway for a handful of pennies?"

"No. I didn't know that."

"Back in the late 1800s. Paid up the back taxes."

"Is that a fact?" Out of the corner of his eye George caught sight of two people approaching the open front door. He stepped back just as they stepped inside, effectively putting a wider space between himself and Miller. The added distance felt more comfortable.

"Are my eyes deceiving me?" Miller asked, looking at the tall dark man who'd just entered. "Michael Martino, as I live and breathe. It *is* you." Miller flicked the end of his cane toward George. "Let me introduce you to Lenor's fiancé."

"We're not engaged," George said, but Miller's words rode right over his own.

"This is Dr. Murphy, George Murphy, from New York City."

"Pleasure," Michael said, looking at George, kindly but briefly, then letting his eyes quickly scan the room. His attention came back to George. "This is Juanita Chavez," he said.

Juanita's wide smile seemed out of place for someone who'd just arrived at the festivities. "I can't tell you how happy I am to meet you, Dr. Murphy. We—" she glanced at Michael to include him in the "we"—"we've been out of touch with Lenor and her friends for such a long time."

Whether you know it or not, you've been claimed, Mr. Martino, George thought. "Nice meeting you," he said as Michael scanned the room again.

"There's Steven," Michael said. "I want to talk to him."

Either Miller didn't pick up on the snub or he chose not to hear it. He let Michael and Juanita walk away without another word to either of them. "Handsome couple," he said to George.

"Very handsome," George said. But they were even less a couple than he and Lenor. Though Juanita obviously wished differently, George suspected that the two of them weren't even very good friends.

Miller raised his hand to wave at someone across the room. "Excuse me, George," he said as he moved away.

"Sure."

"I see my boss-man has arrived," a man's voice said.

George turned to see Eloy Seña and a very young version of Rudolfo Seña step through the door. It was good to see a familiar face. "Eloy! And this must be your brother, Gilbert," George said, offering his hand.

"*Little* brother," Eloy said, swiping the hat off his brother's head. "Mind your manners, kid. This is a real New York City doctor."

Gilbert gave Eloy a playful whack on the arm, snatched his hat back, then shook George's hand. "Heard about your trip to Las Vegas," he said with a wide grin.

"Get a rep out here in the West, it follows you around," Eloy warned George. "But the kid here knows how to keep a secret."

"I haven't told but about three or five people," Gilbert said.

"So my reputation is essentially ruined," George said.

"For all practical purposes. But you ain't gonna get rode out of town just yet, partner," Eloy said. "Hey, have you seen my old man, George?"

"I left Rudolfo in the kitchen about an hour ago," George said.

Eloy and Gilbert looked at each other, then said in unison, "Food."

"He'll still be there," Eloy said with confidence.

"Come on, I'll help you find him," George offered.

A trio was playing steel guitar, bass, and acoustical guitar in one corner of the room, and a few people were already dancing to the music. Lenor and Carmela had secluded themselves in another corner and were in deep conversation. Michael was still talking to Steven Tavera. The perfect host and hostess, Rafael and Magdalena hadn't stopped moving from conversation to conversation, greeting to greeting, since the party had started. Everywhere there was happy chatter, except, George thought as he passed by them, between Roy and Juanita. Their conversation looked deadly serious. *I hope nothing's wrong.*

"I'm telling you, they are not engaged," Roy said again.

"But why would Dr. Baldwin introduce him as Lenor's fiancé if it weren't true?" Juanita asked.

"You know my dad. Always stirring things up. How should *I* know why he did it?"

"But he'd have no reason—"

"Since when does Miller need a reason? You remember when you worked in the store? He was always coming in, saying things, telling us what we should be doing."

"He wasn't trying to cause you any trouble, Roy. He just had ideas," Juanita said.

"And if I'd taken his suggestions, I'd probably be out of business now."

"You're not being fair, Roy. I think your father has your best interests at heart."

"Yeah. Like old Michael over there has *your* best interests at heart."

"Leave Michael out of this," Juanita said.

"Why? Isn't that what we're really talking about here? You're jealous of Lenor because you think Michael is interested in her, and you're praying that Lenor is engaged to that city boy so she'll be out of the way."

"That's not true," Juanita said. *Yes it is!*

"I didn't just crawl out of a snake hole, Juanita. You're crazy for Michael. Michael barely knows you exist. You should have stayed with me at the store. Then you wouldn't be in the middle of this mess."

God forgive me! Eight years working for you was eight years too many! "I like my new job," Juanita said defiantly. "And you're wrong about Michael and me. If he never speaks to me again, it won't matter. I enjoy what I'm doing now."

"But the jealousy is eating you alive. I've been watching you, and I can see it. You and Michael came in here, and he started looking around the room. You should have seen your face. You might as well have screamed it—'Don't start looking for Lenor!' "

"He was looking for Steven Tavera," Juanita said.

"Was he?" Roy asked sweetly.

I hate you, Roy Baldwin!

Good!

Surprise opened Juanita's eyes wide.

Two can play at this little game of hearing what hasn't been spoken.

Rudolfo was, indeed, still in the kitchen. He looked as if he'd been allowed into heaven and given free rein to sample every-

thing in sight. His two very spare sons joyfully joined in his
ecstatic pursuit of delicacies.

"How do you stay so thin, Rudolfo?" George asked.

"God sent him here to torment us all," Steven answered from
the doorway into the kitchen. "He's one of God's little jokes.
The kind you might play on your worst enemy. Just ask
Nemesia."

" 'For he could eat no fat, and she could eat no lean.' Is that
how it goes?" George asked.

"For he could eat everything in sight, while the rest of us
writhe in hell and try to survive on a peeled grape," Steven said
as he came further into the room.

"But you're slim and trim, Steven," George said. "And I saw
you put away enough for an army last night."

"My own cooking. Lenor's recipes. Not a speck of fat in any
of it."

"So that's how you do it," George said.

"Do what?" Roy asked, inserting himself into the conversation as he entered the kitchen.

"Steven was just telling me about his diet," George said.

"I can eat everything I want to, as long as it comes from the
list Lenor made for me."

"Tell me more," George said, though he heard it from Lenor
all the time.

"First thing in the morning, usually before sunup, I do a
five-mile run. After that I start eating. Fruit first, any kind, all I
want. Midmorning I stop working to have breakfast, usually hot
cereal, toast, jam, stuff like that. Lunch is soup in the winter, salad
in the summer, home-baked whole-grain bread, nothing too
heavy. Late afternoon, after a twenty-minute nap, I snack on
cookies and a cup of tea. I like something substantial for dinner,
rice, beans, pasta, tortillas, salad. Lots of chile, of course. Couldn't
live without my chile."

George started to comment, but Steven went on.

"At bedtime I always have a bowl of cold cereal with honey
and a splash of nonfat soy milk."

"Whew! And I thought *I* could pack it away," Roy said.

"You do all right in the chow department, son. But you'd better cut out the fat. Mark my words."

Roy glanced down at his slender body, then looked questioningly at George.

"He's probably right, Roy," George said.

"Probably?" Roy asked. "You're a doctor, too. Don't you agree with Lenor on this diet thing?"

It wasn't the time or the place to tell the truth, that he hadn't given it enough study to decide one way or the other. "Lenor knows what she's talking about. You can take my word for that," George said. *Lenor! Why aren't you here to keep me out of trouble?*

Lenor had seen Michael the moment he'd arrived with Juanita. No one had told her to look. No one had pointed out that Michael Martino had just walked in the front door. She'd known without knowing, and glanced toward the doorway at the precise moment he'd entered. And he'd looked exactly as she'd expected him to look.

He hadn't changed all that much over the years. Wiser perhaps than the twenty-year-old she'd known. Though she'd grown some since she was sixteen, Michael would still tower over her. His black hair was unruly, slightly curly, combed by the wind. Wisps of it brushed over the collar of his crisp white shirt. A silver eagle clawed at the braided leather of his bolo tie, the thin dark strings tipped with two dangling silver feathers. His shoulders looked wider, the hard work of raising horses no doubt the cause, but the rest of his body was lean and spare, wrapped snugly in blue denim. He hadn't changed much.

But her reaction to the sight of him had surprised her—it hadn't changed much either. A catch in her breathing. Rapid heartbeat. Trembling. Her appetite had completely disappeared. She'd quickly looked around for Apple, to see if she might be responding the same way. Apple had been having a good old time on the opposite side of the room. All the camp kids, plus nine

Vigils, had been listening to one of her stories. Another scary tale about *La Llorona,* no doubt.

That was when Lenor had propelled Carmela into a corner where they could have a good long talk. But now Carmela had been lured away by Magdalena with the promise of some manzanita cuttings that would produce a good cash crop for the landscape nurseries in Santa Fe and Albuquerque. And Michael Martino was headed straight in Lenor's direction.

I needed to talk to him anyway. I need to ask him about carving the bulto for Sable. I don't want to talk to him. Egad! I feel like I'm back in high school!

"May I sit down?" Michael asked politely.

"Of course." *He seems tense.* "It's good to see you, Michael."

"Good to see you, too, Lenor." He sat down and got right to the point. "I've brought something for your grandfather." He held up his hand. "I realize no gifts are allowed, but Steven and your father have helped me out now and again. You understand."

"Perfectly. You're very thoughtful."

"You don't think he'll take offense?" The vertical lines between beautifully arched black eyebrows furrowed.

Michael's highly stressed. Why? "Not at all," she said, then reassured him further. "I think Grandpa will be very pleased." Even in the cool of the shadowed corner, Lenor could feel the heat of his body. He wore no cologne, but the clean fragrance of him washed through her soul. She remembered it vividly. It hadn't changed either. The fair. Had it been so long ago, or only yesterday?

"I was wondering if you'd help me present the gift to him later," Michael was saying.

"I'd be glad to."

"Well . . . thank you. I appreciate your help." He started to rise from the chair.

"Don't go." *Too abrupt. My God, Lenor, settle down!* "Uh, there's something I need to ask you."

Michael eased back into the chair. "Ask away."

"A patient of mine made a request just before I left New York. Are you still doing your carvings, Michael?"

"Yes."

"She wanted me to see if you'd do a *bulto* of Saint Michael for her."

For the first time in weeks, Michael's anxiety lessened a bit. He leaned back in the chair, his body relaxing, his head tipping back, eyes closing, then opening, as he sighed.

Lenor took his reaction differently. "I know it's an imposition. If you're too busy—"

"No!" He straightened. "Not at all. In fact, by the strangest coincidence, I just finished one yesterday." His expression became serious. "Is this child in some kind of trouble?" he asked.

"She's been very ill," Lenor said.

"Then why not Nuestra Señora del Socorro to bring her freedom from sickness?" Michael asked.

"I asked her the same thing about the Virgin Mary. Sable's situation is kind of difficult to explain . . ."

"I'd like to hear about her, this patient of yours."

He's sincere. "Sable is twelve, a delightful child, with amazing abilities. I believe she's apprenticed to her Aunt Judith, who's apparently a medium."

"A healer?" Michael asked.

"That's the hard part. I don't know. I just found out about Sable's talents Thursday afternoon. When I went back to talk to her that night, she was sound asleep, and I didn't have the heart to wake her and ask her questions about this aunt of hers or her *desarrollo.*"

"The child is only twelve," Michael said. "Is it possible she was mistaken about which figure she wanted?"

"I suppose it's possible. But Sable's wise beyond her years. I'd have to say she knew exactly what she wanted."

Michael nodded slightly. "The opponent of the Devil and all evil, the guardian of small children. This San Miguel Arcángel I've done will do battle for her, then. Shall we go see him?"

"You have it here?" Lenor asked.

"It's in my car. This may sound a bit strange to you, but somehow I knew that I had to come here today and bring it with me."

"I'd love to see it," Lenor said, rising from her chair at the same time Michael did. *Knowing Sable, it doesn't sound strange at all!*

With every sweep of the room, Juanita's gaze always lingered on Michael. While she'd been talking to Roy, Michael had been nearby talking to Steven Tavera. When Roy left for the kitchen, Juanita had joined Michael again. But Nemesia had appeared and drawn her into conversation. Now Michael was nowhere to be seen. Nemesia didn't seem to notice Juanita's distraction as the two women chatted about the similarities in their daily lives.

"Rosa tells me that she and Señor Martino are very pleased with your work," Nemesia said. "Are you happy there?"

"Oh, yes. Very happy."

"The isolation doesn't bother you?"

"I wondered about that when I left the store in Mora, but it's really quite nice," Juanita said. "I don't miss being downtown at all."

Nemesia was thoughtful for a moment. "I sometimes think I could do with a dose of solitude. Away from the constant chaos around here."

"Really?" Juanita couldn't remember ever seeing Nemesia Seña without a jolly smile on her face.

"Oh, don't get me wrong. I love it here. Maybe I just need a vacation. Of course, with the camp season in full swing, it would have to be a mighty short one."

"This is my first time here," Juanita said, then took the opportunity to look about the room again. "I can see what you mean about the chaos. I'm sure it's not like this every day, but . . . maybe you'd like to come visit me some afternoon, for a change of scenery." Just then, the scenery in the room changed. In the far corner she saw Michael's face appear above the heads of the other guests.

"Maybe." Nemesia said. "Is something wrong, Juanita?"

"No. Not at all." But something was very wrong. *Michael and Lenor are leaving together!*

Watson waited outside the hacienda for Lenor and Michael. Being sociable with a couple hundred shuffling feet made him jittery. This morning, without Lenor's help, he'd completed a thorough search of the barn, the corrals, and both bunkhouses. In the bunkhouse where the camp kids stayed, boys in one end, girls in the other, he'd found two weeks' worth of teenage junk, lots of dirty clothes, but no rock. Where Jerry and Manny lived, in the adjacent bunkhouse, he'd found spare furnishings and the fragrance of saddle soap. Now he was on the trail of another odor.

As soon as Michael and Lenor stepped outside, Watson checked for any ominous vibrations from Lenor and sensed none. She felt safe with this tall, dark man, and Watson could see why. Michael Martino radiated a pronounced, if slightly tentative, happiness. No problems here.

The problems lay in a different direction, and Watson bounded for the old black hearse parked in the shade of the carport. He gained entry easily through the driver's-side open window. Once inside, he knew he'd hit pay dirt. The *monito* had definitely taken a ride in the passenger seat. Now all he had to do was convince Lenor to take the time to follow the trail.

Though many of their closer neighbors had walked or ridden horses, the drive and the road around to the south that led to the church were lined with all manner of vehicles. The sun shone in a cloudless sky, but the slight breeze that sang through the pines kept the afternoon heat at bay.

"I had to park over the hill. Do you mind the walk?" Michael asked.

"Not in the least. I've been sitting in that corner too long."

"Too bad about Daniel Vigil," Michael said. "He was so young, only forty-two. I saw you talking to Carmela. Is she going to be all right?"

"It's hard to say, but I'd like to think she will. She's a very strong woman."

"I know Daniel and your grandfather were close friends. I'm amazed, though, that Carmela came out today," Michael said.

"Me, too, and I hope she's having a good time. I may have had something to do with her being here."

"How so?" Michael asked.

"Daniel never missed one of Grandpa's birthday parties, and he always enjoyed them so much. I told Carmela that Daniel would have wanted her to come."

"I believe he would have," Michael said.

They were silent then until they reached the top of the hill. Watson bounded toward them. He skittered and pounced sideways as he approached, then gave Michael a brief inspection and subsequent approval by rubbing against his leg.

Lenor knelt down and lifted him up on her left shoulder, where he draped himself into a comfortable crescent shape. "You're in a playful mood, fella. Was the hunting good?"

"Eee."

"Awfully friendly with a stranger," Michael said.

"Oh, Watson's no stranger. He's mine."

"You brought a cat with you, all the way from New York?" Michael asked.

"He wouldn't have it any other way," she said. "He was born here. He likes to come home." She carried him another few yards down the hill; then he was ready to be on his way again. But not before reminding her about the search for his rock.

"Yee-ooow."

Michael waited while Lenor put Watson down. When she straightened, he turned to face her. "Do *you* like to come home, too?" he asked quietly.

"More than anything," was her instant answer. *Why did I say that? Is it the truth?*

"Then why don't you come back?"

Lenor stalled as long as she could, but he was waiting for a response. "What I meant was, I like to come home for a visit. I don't get to often enough," she said, smiling. "But my work is very important to me. It has to come first right now."

"You're needed here," he said, then immediately knew it had been the wrong thing to say. Her face became a mask of dread, her eyes cloaked in pain. The transformation assaulted his heart. He put his hands on her shoulders. "Lenor, I didn't mean to upset you. I intended a compliment, not an indictment."

"I understand," she said bleakly.

"I'm an idiot sometimes. Used to saying whatever comes into my mind. Too used to talking to Eloy."

Ever since Michael had started toward her in the living room, and up until this moment, she'd retained her calm exterior while catapulting over every jolting emotion. Name it, she'd triumphed over it: joy, anxiety, excitement, fear, delight, doubt, arousal. *Arousal?* With effort Lenor tried a slight smile. "Eloy can do that to a person." Michael's hands were sliding off her shoulders, gripping her arms. At one and the same time his touch seemed to be an overly intimate gesture between almost-strangers and a desperately needed comfort.

"I'm truly sorry if I upset you," he said. "Forgive me?"

Would it be proper to lie and deny her response? She looked into his dark eyes. Would it be possible? *No.* "There's nothing to forgive, Michael. The truth never needs exonerating. I'd be fooling myself if I couldn't admit the guilt I feel."

"Then you've thought about coming back?" he asked.

"Thought about it, yes. Considered it, no." *Is that disappointment in his eyes?* "I need to be in a large hospital. Modern equipment, computer access—my research would be impossible without it."

"I see." His hands dropped to his sides. "I imagine your mother was disappointed," he said, turning away, starting to walk again.

"We haven't discussed it."

"But I heard that she was going to ask you to come home." He pointed to a small black sedan parked in the shade of a tall pine. "Here it is."

Lenor followed him to the rear of the car. "She'll get around to asking me in her own time." She waited for him to open the trunk.

"Will she be able to live with your answer?" he asked, lifting the cover.

"The question is, will I be able to live with her? If I say no, she won't let the matter rest."

He turned to her. "*If* you say no?"

If? She hadn't realized what she'd said. It was the second time in just a few minutes that she'd responded to him without taking her usual careful measure. She smiled. "A slip of the tongue. I meant, when."

"Are you sure it wasn't a slip of the heart?"

Lenor instantly bristled at his impertinence; then one glance at his face told her he was genuinely concerned. "Is my ambivalence so obvious?" she asked.

"It wasn't . . . until I blundered in where I had no right to be." He sat down on the edge of the open trunk and took her hand. "Do you remember the day I met you and Apple at the fair?" he asked.

"Yes."

"I hadn't planned it. I probably would have avoided two teenaged girls if I'd thought about it—especially on that particular day."

"Why *that* particular day?" Lenor asked, wishing he'd let go of her hand, then wishing he wouldn't. *Talk about ambivalence.*

"Our horses hadn't done well in competition. I was in a sour mood. But you smiled your way into my thoughts, then talked your way into my heart." He paused. "I'm almost embarrassed to tell you, and I don't mean to make you uncomfortable. But I could see, even then, that you were going to be an irresistible force in whatever endeavor you chose. Your patients must get well just being near the power of your caring. I have to confess, I was completely mesmerized."

Lenor didn't know quite what to say. Her feelings, at that time, had been so intense, so totally overwhelming, that her behavior and her words had been entirely dictated by her emotions—and her hormones. "I don't remember exactly what I did or said to make you say such a thing. At sixteen I couldn't have been much more than a giddy adolescent with crazy notions and silly ideas."

"Ah, but you underestimate yourself," he said, tugging on her hand, pulling her down beside him. He twisted toward her. "You were concerned about how I felt about my mother's death. She died when you were only thirteen, but you remembered and cared enough to ask about my feelings. You drew everything out of me. Is Eloy doing a good job with the ranch? Is Old Woosey still killing the colts? Is Gilberto turning out to be a good ranch hand? How are you doing with your college studies?" He waited a moment for his words to sink in. "Nobody, for a very long time, had cared how I felt about any of it. Am I making any sense?"

"Yes," Lenor said quietly.

"I've never forgotten that day or the way you made me feel . . . as if what I thought and how I felt were important. It's no wonder you're a success at what you do."

"I think that's the nicest thing anyone has ever said to me, Michael. Thank you." She looked down and saw that he now held her hand in both of his. Her glance sparked a response. He let go.

"I'm overstepping my boundaries. I'm sorry. You're engaged, and—"

"Engaged?" Without thinking, she looked down at her left hand, but saw only the ring Sable had given her as payment for the *santero*. No engagement ring had materialized on her finger. "I'm not engaged."

"But Dr. Baldwin introduced me to your fiancé. George, is it?"

"A misunderstanding, maybe. George Murphy and I are good friends. We work together at Foley."

"Miller's only sixty-nine, but he seems eons older than your grandfather at eighty-nine. Maybe his mind slips a cog every now and then," Michael said.

"My mother thinks so," Lenor said.

"Rosa said Dr. Baldwin's afraid he's going to lose all his patients to the *curanderas* in town."

"Really?"

"There are those who think the old ways are better for some things," Michael said.

"I agree."

"You do?"

"That's what my research is mainly about. Combining some aspects of folk healing with modern medicine."

"You find a lot of dissension among your peers, no doubt," he said.

"How did you know?"

"A guess," Michael said. "The doctors I've known, and there are many at the University of New Mexico, have been an arrogant lot. Generally, they look down on anything that doesn't appear under their scalpels or come in a syringe or a medicine bottle."

"A very astute observation," Lenor said.

"Since Rosa came to us nine years ago, no one has been to a doctor for any reason. She takes good care of us."

"George can attest to that. She gave him one of her rubdowns today." Lenor was sorry she'd mentioned George's name. It had an immediate adverse effect on the relaxed and friendly atmosphere. Michael changed the subject.

"That's an interesting ring you're wearing on your little finger. It's so small. Did one of your young patients give it to you?"

Lenor held up her hand. "Actually, she gave it to you," she said, twisting Sable's ring off and handing it to him.

"To me?" Michael asked, hesitating, then taking it from her.

"Sable's instructions were to give it to you as payment for the carving of San Miguel."

Michael reached behind her, pulled out a newspaper-wrapped package, and unrolled the covering. "Do you think this is something like what she wanted?" he asked.

Lenor took the figure from him and held it up. The devotion

and skill of the *santero* were grandly evident in every detail. Dressed in ancient armor and ready to do battle with the Devil, a winged Saint Michael the Archangel stood atop a fallen mountain lion, the scales of justice clutched in one hand, a sword held high in the other. The watercolors used were subtle and fitting. "Magnificent," she breathed. "I'm sure this is exactly what she wanted. You are truly an artist, Michael."

"It's more important that Sable relate this artifact to the sacred reality than to the artist's concept of it," he said.

"She's quite capable of understanding the tradition. She won't confuse your inclination with the power of the Holy Person."

"And what is my inclination?" Michael asked.

"Honesty. It shows in your work."

"I'm afraid you're doing it again."

"Doing what again?" Lenor asked.

"Caring. You flatter the *santero* and the child." *I wish you'd send George Murphy home and stay right here with me forever.*

"Well, George," Apple said to her partner on the dance floor, "what do you think so far?"

"Extraordinary. Best party I've ever been to," he said.

"I don't mean *just* the party. The whole thing—this place, this family, this whole bunch of assorted crazy people."

George thought through one slow turn. "Let me put it this way. The Land of Enchantment has me enchanted. The beautiful people here delight me to distraction. And the Taveras have me puzzled."

"Puzzled?"

"Completely. I'm no expert. I was an only child in a single-parent home, just my father and me. But I've spent plenty of time with so-called normal families. You probably have too. So tell me. Isn't there supposed to be some fighting going on? Just a little disagreement now and again to keep things interesting?"

Apple smiled. Looked at him. He was completely serious. She burst out laughing. Everyone in the corner of the living room that was being used as the dance floor turned to look at her. She toned it down, but with some difficulty. "You are a precious gem, George. And because of that, I'm going to tell you what's happening here."

Surprised by her sudden laughter and sobered by the unwanted attention of all the dancers on the floor, George guided her toward the west wall for a little more privacy, then whispered, "I'd appreciate that."

Apple leaned against the cool white plaster and said in a low voice, "In the vernacular, this is what's known as putting on a good show."

"The Taveras are putting on a show? For whom?" George asked.

"For Lenor, of course."

"But Lenor knows these people better than anyone. They can't fool her about family matters," George said. "Is something wrong here that Lenor doesn't know about?"

"Nothing's wrong. You know the old saying, 'You can catch more flies with honey than with vinegar.' They're trying to lull her into a mood that will be conducive to her saying yes."

The light dawned. "So she'll say yes when Magdalena asks her to come home."

"You got it."

"Sneaky." George smiled. "But I'm relieved, in a way. I was beginning to think that what I considered normal family behavior was an aberration."

"I didn't think Magdalena would wait this long," Apple said, "but the fireworks are coming. You can bet on it."

At least Steven has warned her!

"And, last but not least, this is Thomas Newman," Steven was saying from his position in front of the fireplace, where he and Jovita had been parading one child at a time up onto the hearth to be introduced. "So now you've met all of our camp kids. They're a fine bunch, don't you think so, folks?"

Everyone applauded.

"Now get on with your partying," Steven said. "Jovita and I want you to have a good time. Enjoy!"

"Not quite yet, folks," Lenor said as she and Michael stepped up on the hearth. One on each side, they held a large, flat, brown-paper-wrapped package between them. Lenor turned toward Steven. "Grandpa, Grandma, I'm not much at speeches, but this occasion calls for a few words. *Amor, salud, y pesetas, y tiempo para gozarlos.*"

Everyone applauded again.

She repeated the *dicho* in English. "Here's to your love, health, and wealth, and time to enjoy each. This is a gift from Michael Martino."

"A gift?" Steven asked, as Jovita frowned and shook her head.

"Not a gift," Michael said. "A thank-you to both you and your wife. *La mano no se gasta, si el corazón es grande.*"

The hand does not waste if the heart is big, Michael had said. Steven's eyes glistened with tears.

"Open it, Grandpa," Lenor said.

Steven tugged at the paper, and it came away easily. Everyone in the room caught their breath at once, and, for a long moment, no one made a sound—including Lenor.

Tears of happiness streamed down Steven's cheeks as he looked at the magnificent portrait of his granddaughter. When she'd been vacillating between going to medical school and returning home to carry on the tradition of the *curanderismo,* he and Jovita had been the ones who'd encouraged her to go on with her medical studies. And now, here she was in white medical coat, captured for all time in Michael Martino's painting. "Oh, my," was all Steven could say.

The room was atitter now. "She's beautiful." "He's a master." "I didn't know Michael and Steven were friends." "If they weren't before, they will be now."

Lenor stared at the piece, unable to take her eyes off it. Aside from doing expert work with the brush and the blade, Michael had captured the essence of the dichotomy they'd just been talking about. He'd put her heart in two places at once, with uncanny accuracy, by dressing her likeness in two fashions. The crisp white coat symbolized her accomplishments, her place in New York, while the dark navy pants over western boots and the heavy Indian silver and turquoise ring on her right ring finger brought her home again. If she'd posed for it in person, he couldn't have been more faithful to reality—or to the two conflicting truths.

She wanted to ask him how he'd known, but couldn't think how to ask. A blatant "How did you know?" might sound like an accusation of intrusion to someone as sensitive as Michael. Like an automaton, she helped him lift the painting onto the mantelpiece.

Steven had recovered slightly, dabbing at his eyes with a big white handkerchief, smiling at those who'd come forward to compliment the artist, praise his subject, and congratulate Steven and Jovita on their good fortune.

Arthur Seña brought up the end of the procession. "That belongs in your own living room, Lenor," he said. "Don't you agree, George?"

"A photograph would be less a likeness than this. It's lovely," George said.

"He's good, isn't he?" Lenor said, then lowered her voice. "Just between you and me, Arthur, I'd love to have it."

"Why don't you ask him?" Arthur whispered. "Grandpa would do anything for you."

Lenor would never have asked such a thing, but the thought reminded her of Leonora's words. *'Michael will give you something for your grandfather. See that your grandfather keeps it.''* "I couldn't do that, Arthur . . . but I would love to have it."

"I heard that," Steven said, smiling at her. "Does this mean I'm going to have to put guards around my painting until you leave?"

"Maybe she won't be leaving this time."

It was Magdalena, and Lenor blanched at the sound of her mother's voice. She thought she'd prepared herself for the moment, but she hadn't. The words hit her like a sledgehammer blow to the gut. Someone put a steadying hand on her back. For a moment that gentle pressure at her waist was the only point of calm she possessed.

"Mama, I—"

"I think you *should* come home," Arthur said. "These people need you, and, God knows, Miller could use some relief."

Lenor looked at Arthur with a question in her eyes. *You, too?*

"It would be great, Lenor," Lita chimed in. "And it would make your mama and papa so happy. Wouldn't it, Rafael?" she asked.

Rafael nodded and smiled. "Very happy."

So everyone is in on the conspiracy!

"It's logical, Lenor," Magdalena said. "You're ready to practice. What better place than here? You know we'd all love to have you back home."

A murmur of assent rippled through the guests near enough to hear their conversation. At least the music had started again and some of the crowd hadn't been listening to them. With this many people around, though, it wasn't the time or place to discuss personal matters. Lenor wanted nothing more than to divert everyone's attention. "What a nice thing to say, Mama. I'm sure I don't deserve such a compliment, but I'll certainly think about your suggestion . . . when the time comes."

Arthur frowned. "Is that it? Is that all you have to say? You'll think about it . . . when the time comes?"

"Arthur . . ." Lenor whispered. *He has no right to put me on the spot in front of so many people, when he himself lives and practices law in another state.* Anger blossomed. "You're in no position to dictate, Arthur dear," she said sweetly. "But if you want to debate who should be coming home, I'd be glad—"

The pressure at the small of her back increased. She glanced back to see who was responsible.

"I think it's time to dance," Michael said. "Will you excuse us, Arthur?"

"This *isn't* the end of the discussion, Lenor," Arthur said.

"We'll continue it in *private*, Arthur," Lenor said sternly.

As Michael propelled her toward the music, Lenor caught a glimpse of Juanita. She stood all alone, staring vacantly into a half-full glass of iced tea, and Lenor felt a tinge of guilt. She turned back. "Come on, you people," she said to her parents and grand-parents. "Let's all dance." She was relieved to see George turn to Juanita.

But her burden returned as the two guitars began the slow and haunting strains of "The River." It was one of her favorites, and she'd listened to Garth Brooks sing the words so many times she practically knew them by heart. Slow dancing with Michael Martino would surely be chancing the rapids. She delayed the inevitable another moment.

"Thank you for helping me out," she said quietly.

"Thank you for confiding in me," he said.

"Thank you for listening."

That quickly, there was nothing more to say. And she couldn't have made any sense anyway, once his arms moved to her waist. She lifted her hands to his shoulders and tried to relax as she and Michael started to move to the hypnotic beat.

The space was small. The dancers filled it. They strained to keep a proper distance between them, both mindful of the dangers. Lenor tried to avoid looking at him at first, glancing around, smiling at one, nodding at another. She hummed to the music. She sang the beautiful words in her mind. But at the end of the second verse, Michael brought her attention back by whispering the words for only her to hear.

"Will you 'dare to dance the tide,' Lenor?"

When she looked into his eyes, there was something burning there. When she thought about what he'd asked, her heart skipped a beat and her cheeks burned with a flush of color. His eyes glittered with a little smile then.

"Will you come home?" he asked.

"Someday," she said, and she wanted to give him a little kiss on the cheek for not making a pass at her in her parents' living room, with George and Juanita looking on. *I'm assuming an awful lot from a few whispered words!* "Someday," she repeated.

The music stopped, and in that quiet moment Michael asked, "Someday soon? Never mind," he amended quickly. "I shouldn't have asked that."

"I'm not upset anymore."

"Maybe you should be," he said and glanced sideways as the music started again.

Lenor looked. Juanita and George had changed partners. Juanita with Gilbert, George with Apple.

"Your two friends look like they enjoy each other's company," Michael said.

"They do."

"That doesn't bother you?" he asked, starting to move to the music again.

"Should it?"

"You tell me."

"No, it doesn't bother me. The only thing that was worrying me is past." But no sooner had she spoken than the couple behind her pressed against her back. The dance floor was now filled to capacity. Her body touched his.

It was too late for apologies, too early for denials. Lenor glanced in George's direction. He and Apple were cheek to cheek. A smiling Juanita had her hands clasped around the back of Gilberto's neck. Gilberto grinned from ear to ear.

Michael was looking, too. "He's wishing with all his heart," he said.

"Gilberto?" Lenor asked.

"He's in love."

"Looks like she might be, too," Lenor said.

"Maybe. I don't know."

"Oh, Michael, what a thoughtless thing for me to say. I'm so sorry. You brought Juanita to the party." He looked down at her. That something was burning in his eyes again. Then he pulled her closer so his lips were almost touching her ear.

"Because Gilberto asked me to," he whispered.

"I'm . . ." She'd started to apologize again, but then his words made sense. The dizziness she felt now wasn't from lack of sleep. "Michael . . ."

"Shh." He pulled her closer and whispered again. "For this moment, just let me hold you."

Nine

"I HAVE TO LEAVE NOW."

"So soon?"

"It's best."

Lenor was reeling from her dance with Michael. Only a minute after he let her go, he had a few words with Gilberto, said his thank-yous, and left the house—alone. Juanita didn't seem to mind. She and Gilberto, wearing wide smiles, told Lenor how much they were enjoying the party, even while Michael was making his exit. And Lenor hadn't even said good-bye.

Inexplicably wishing she could leave with him, Lenor also felt relieved he was gone. *Ambivalence again.* But half an hour with someone who was little more than a stranger could hardly account for her strong desire to accompany him home. That could only be explained as irrational thinking, a mode of emotionalism in which Lenor seldom dared to dwell. But there was something liberating about being illogical. And something deliciously enjoyable.

Without letting George and Apple know where she was going, Lenor made her way through the crowd, out into the center of the *placita,* then sat down on the wooden bench that surrounded the trunk of the old cottonwood. It was a good place to let her mind take a few flights of fancy, at first trying to visualize her grant award and the satisfying work that would follow, then trying to think of George. But her focus kept drifting away to Michael's house, to Michael. It was a long time before the quiet and the cool shade began to calm her thoughts somewhat—until

Watson decided to join her. Then she stopped thinking of Michael altogether.

"So you think you've picked up the trail?"

"Eee." *Without a doubt.*

"Roy Baldwin?"

No question.

"I think you're mistaken, but I'll ask him."

He'll lie.

"Don't be silly. Roy can be strange, but he doesn't lie."

You're wrong about that.

"I've known him longer than you have, Watson."

"Known who?" It was Arthur Seña.

Lenor patted the bench next to her as Watson jumped down and walked away. "Have a seat, Arthur. Watson and I were just taking a breather from the party."

Arthur let his slight body drop down beside her and gave a long sigh. "God, I wish I could set up a law practice here. I don't know how many more times I can come home, then force myself to go back to Phoenix."

"Is that why you were giving me the business about coming home?" Lenor asked.

"I guess. Sorry about the blind-side. Guess I thought if we'd pool our nerve, maybe we could both say good-bye to the rat race."

"And Lita?" Lenor asked.

Arthur nodded. "My sister is just about burned out with California, too. Los Angeles scares her, the crazies drive her to distraction, and she can't find a suitable partner for her overloaded practice. Says she's already interviewed almost a hundred psychologists."

Lenor leaned back against the tree. "Wouldn't it be nice if we could turn the clock back once in a while? We'd be playing together or working together or just doing nothing together, like old times."

"You, me, Apple, and Lita. Those were the days." Arthur turned toward her. "What will you tell your mother?"

"That I can't leave my work right now."

"That's not what Magdalena wants to hear."

"I know—but I have to go back."

On the return trip, Watson wasn't the polite little gentleman he'd been on their way out. He complained and clawed, and made a nuisance of himself. And all because Lenor hadn't been able to find a rock.

George couldn't believe Lenor would put so much stock in what some half-wild cat *allegedly* found important. He'd turned their disagreement into a full-blown battle on the drive to Las Vegas.

"What on God's green earth can be so important about a rock that you'd miss breakfast and leave me to fend for myself? I felt like a sirloin in a lion's den."

"The *monito* belonged to my great-great-great-grand-mother."

"That doesn't explain anything. Not talking to cats. Not running off heaven knows where looking for a chip of stone. Not leaving me—the person with whom you're about to leave home—to make small talk with your aggravated mother and your disappointed grandmother. Magdalena and Jovita, no doubt, hate my guts by now."

"They don't hate anyone, George. Least of all you. You're letting your imagination get the best of you."

"*My* imagination? What about yours? First you're talking to spirits. Then you're following orders from a mongrel cat who's no more than a *pet* by any rational person's standards. If that's not enough, now you're ascribing outlandish significance to a piece of basalt. Next you'll be telling me that the rock has magical powers."

"It does," Lenor said quietly. She debated with herself, then said, "And Watson is my guardian angel." Might as well start the acid test, get it all out in the open, and watch the sparks fly. It hurt, but she couldn't expect George to understand or be com-fortable with her ideas. He'd been immersed too quickly and was just too new to the "other" world. "I'm sorry I left you to fend for yourself this morning. I am really, truly sorry."

George didn't say anything, just stared straight ahead out the windshield. This morning he'd felt abandoned and angry. His muscles were sore, though not as painfully uncomfortable as he'd expected. His mind was still rocking from the volcanic argument Magdalena had started with Lenor after the party. Apple had warned him about the inevitable fireworks, but he hadn't expected to be right in the middle of them.

Grandma Jovita had taken Magdalena's side. Understandably, she wanted Lenor close by to watch after her husband. Rafael and Steven were less adamant about the immediacy of Lenor's return, and agreed that Lenor's research was important. But George could see that the two men wanted their "baby" back in the safety of the Land of Enchantment and away from the dangers of New York.

Lenor had held her own most of the time, explaining the importance of her projects, statistically supporting one outcome against another, and generally making a good case for continuing her work in New York. But while Lenor analyzed numbers and theories and timetables, Magdalena named names. Jimmy Martinez and Maria Jameson and Betty Simms. Real children who suffered without medical care. Lenor knew them all, knew their parents, and each name had stabbed at her like an ice-pick blow to her heart.

While George really couldn't fault any of the family for their sincere beliefs, he'd felt sorry for Lenor. He knew how it all hurt her. He and Lenor had their differences, but their cerebral disagreements weren't the heart-ripping, soul-killing kind. As far as George knew, Lenor hadn't slept or eaten a bite of anything since Saturday afternoon. Unfortunately none of that made him feel any less hurt and angry right now. He knew he'd be sorry for not accepting her apology, but he just couldn't.

Both George and Lenor were frazzled and out of sorts by the time they reached the East Coast. Their taxi ride from the airport was dismal and quiet.

★ ★ ★

Monday, outside the door of Ward Two, he said, "How about lunch after you've finished here?"

"Not today, George. I'm way behind."

"You're not taking your own advice. You need to take a break, eat something."

Lenor didn't think she could stand to sit with him and watch him consume a greasy burger or, God forbid, a chicken-fried steak. Her nausea wouldn't allow it. "I'll catch up with you later. We'll have coffee or something." But even the thought of coffee set her stomach flipping. "Thanks anyway."

He'd been dismissed, and he could fault only himself, after the way he'd acted on their trip back. To renounce everything she believed in had been monumentally stupid.

George watched Lenor disappear behind a slowly closing door. She hadn't stopped since they'd gotten back. Though they'd arrived late the previous night, she'd insisted that the taxi driver wait while she dropped off Watson and her luggage at home, then let her off at the hospital. Something about a delivery to Sable Faraday. By that time George had been so tired from the strain between them he hadn't had the strength to argue with her. Lenor was clearly operating by some personal agenda, and he obviously wasn't included. George was sorry that he'd made such a big deal out of relegating Watson to pet status, but, try as he might, he still couldn't conceive of a cat being the embodiment of Lenor's guardian angel. "I'll just ride out the storm," he said aloud.

"Dr. Tavera's storm?" Ella Wygent asked.

He hadn't realized the nurse had come up beside him. He sighed. "She's a driven woman," he said lightly.

"Worse than that," Ella said. "She told me about the fight with her family. I don't blame her for being upset. How could they ask such an impossible thing of her?"

"It's a long and complicated story," George said and sighed again. *And I've made it worse.*

"I don't give a damn how complicated it is. They had no

right," Ella said. "Excuse me for saying this, but Lenor's the best thing that ever happened to this hospital, and now, between Carl Bowder and her mother, she's being mangled to a pulp."

"What's Carl doing now?" George asked, feeling left out. Lenor had confided in Ella instead of him.

"Dr. T came in last night to see Sable. Bowder was making one of his nighttime inspection forays. He walked into Ward Two in the middle of a discussion of guardian angels and how to summon them while in a trance."

"Bowder came unglued," George said.

"And Dr. T spent half the night in his office."

"On the carpet, no doubt," George said.

"You got it. On top of that, we had a Code Blue in five-eighty-six just as she left Bowder's office. She came running, of course. And that Mrs. Hess is threatening to move her daughter, Alicia, to another hospital again."

"So Lenor was up all night. And she has to give her presentation to Truelex tomorrow evening," George added, then thought to ask, "Did she eat breakfast here with you this morning, Ella?"

"No . . . and I brought in some of my mother's blueberry muffins. Lenor said she didn't have time."

"That's a first," George said. "I hope she's not catching something. She'll be down to skin and teeth if she's not careful."

"She *does* look like she lost some weight over the weekend. And you look worried, Dr. Murphy," Ella said.

"I am."

Thank heaven for small favors! Sable had no idea that the friendly Dr. Bowder who'd visited her last night had caused Lenor so much trouble. Lenor had checked all of her patients on Ward Two before drawing the privacy curtain around Sable's bed.

After her examination, Sable sat up against the headboard and placed the *bulto* of Saint Michael beside her. "Thanks for this," she said, patting his crowned head. "I just love him to pieces."

"Thanks for telling me about your Aunt Judith. I talked to her on the telephone this morning, and I'm glad to know you're in good hands." Lenor smoothed the bed linen and sat down. "Sable? Would you mind if I asked you a few questions?"

"Ask away, Dr. T. I owe you." She patted Saint Michael's head again.

"First, I want to make sure you understand something about your talent. When you use your abilities as a medium, do you realize that the information you receive is for you alone?"

"Aunt Judith told me that. Don't worry, Dr. T. My days of parlor tricks with Jackie or anyone else are over. I got in trouble with my aunt when I told her." She rolled her eyes.

"Good. You can ask me anything, and I'll try to give you an answer. But everything we talk about is strictly private."

"No problem. So what do you want to ask me?"

"Tell me what you know about your spirit friend who limps," Lenor said.

"Well . . . she's nice. She limps because some mean boy threw a big rock at her and hurt her ankle. She was born in 1822 and she died in 1862. I think she was a doctor." Sable smiled. "Hey! Maybe that's why she came to see me in the hospital!"

"I'll bet you're right," Lenor said. "Do you know anything else about her?"

"A funny thing. She kept the rock that mean boy threw at her and used it for . . . hmm . . . I'm not sure. But it was smooth and black."

"I see. Anything else?"

"Well, not really. But I know *I* wouldn't have kept the rock. I'd have thrown it right back!"

"I think I probably would have thrown it back, too," Lenor said. "Listen. I have to go now, Sable, but I'll be back later. Okay?"

"Okay. Sure." Sable wiggled down into the bed, pulling Saint Michael with her.

"Take good care of San Miguel," Lenor said.

"Oh, don't worry, I will. I *have* to."

"Why do you say that?" Lenor asked.

"Because I think the *santero* carved him for somebody else, and I might get to keep him for just a little while."

"Oh."

"Grandpa, I'm glad you called, but I only have a minute." Lenor stared at the written portion of her grant presentation on the computer screen and continued to type as she listened.

"I just wanted to apologize again . . . for all of us. You took it pretty tough this weekend," Steven said.

"Let's not talk about it, okay?"

"Okay." He was silent for a moment. "You'll be glad to hear that Peter Vigil came to talk to us about his schooling this morning. I think he's going to take your advice."

"That's good."

Silence. Then, "Michael Martino called to thank us and tell us he enjoyed the party. He said to say hello if I talked to you."

Lenor stopped typing. She felt suddenly weak, then shook her head in denial. Lack of appetite and not eating were the causes. But she felt something else, too. Euphoria? Hunger? Yes. But not for food.

"Lenor? Honey, are you still there?"

"I'm here." *But I want to dance again and forget about the world for a while.*

"I know you're busy. I just wanted to say one more thing. As much as I love the painting Michael did, I'd be happy for you to have it, if you want it."

He must really feel badly about my argument with Mama, she thought. "You're so sweet, Grandpa. I love you so much. But the painting is yours and you're going to keep it forever." She hated to do it. "I really have to go now. I'll call you tomorrow night after my presentation to Truelex."

"I love you, too, honey. Talk to you tomorrow night."

Lenor looked back at the computer screen after she'd hung

up the phone. All the way across the luminescent white she'd typed

Michael Michael Michael Michael Michael Michael Michael

New York ◆ Tuesday Night

"Dr. Tavera?"

Lenor turned to see a burly brown-haired man with a bright red beard hurrying toward her through the crowded hallway. She waited while he negotiated the last few steps around several people.

"I just wanted to shake your hand. I was in there just now. That was the best damn presentation I've ever heard."

"Well, thank you, Mr. . . . ?"

"Stan Crawford."

"*Dr.* Stan Crawford?" Lenor had heard of him. Truelex had funded years of his research on sleep disorders.

"Right. I'll tell you right now, Dr. Tavera, if they don't give you this grant, they should all be shot at sunrise."

"Thank you again," Lenor said. He seemed anxious, but kind. She smiled at him.

"Ah, I know you must be busy, but I was wondering . . . would you have time for a cup of coffee? I mean, if it wouldn't interfere with your schedule or anything."

Lenor looked at her watch. A quarter to ten. She'd finished earlier than she'd expected to. "I have a little time, if the coffee's close by."

"Right in there," he said, pointing a few feet further down the hall. The name painted on the door was STANLEY R. CRAWFORD, M.D.

"You have an office here?" Lenor asked, following him.

He ushered her through the door, through a reception area,

and into a good-sized office. "And one at Columbia University. It's the old New York empire, patricians and promoters. Coffee or tea? I have both."

"Tea."

"Have a seat." He pointed to a corner seating arrangement complete with coffee table and two small couches, then crossed the room and opened two louvered doors to reveal an efficient arrangement of kitchen essentials. "Guess I'm one of the patricians," he said, with his back to her. "I try to stay as far away from the politics as I can, though."

Lenor liked him already. "But you're one of the high priests," she said.

"God! Don't throw me in with that bunch of Napoleonic little dictators." He turned around with two steaming cups, one saucer in each hand, and came toward her.

"So you don't consider yourself one of the elite defenders of scientific medicine?" she asked, taking the cup he offered.

"Perish the thought." He sat down on the opposite couch. "And that's really why I asked you to have coffee with me."

"I don't understand."

"I've seen the newspapers, read the articles about you. Now I've heard your grant presentation. I'm impressed. I'm aware that you're butting heads with some heavy artillery at Foley, maybe here at Truelex, too. But I also know that programmatic results, promised from several quarters in your hospital, have *not* been forthcoming."

"Money in, nothing out," Lenor said.

"Exactly. Up till now, patricians and promoters alike have been unresponsive to the needs of their constituents. Carl Bowder is on the hot seat because the general public is beginning to demand accountability from their former demigods. People are beginning to ask questions. Patients are beginning to say, 'Hey, wait a minute, Doc, that doesn't sound right.' And the mountain of demand is even higher than the red tape."

"Carl has every administrator's disease. An allergy to red ink," Lenor said.

"So people go wanting. And they're mad as hell about it."

"But how is that pertinent to this conversation?" Lenor asked, sipping tentatively at her tea, waiting for the nausea to hit again.

"Like this." Dr. Crawford leaned forward, placed his cup and saucer on the table, and continued in a lower voice. "Those defenders of scientific medicine you mentioned before have so narrowly defined 'scientific' that people like you and me may be forced to go to . . . herbal tea companies for research money." He leaned forward and whispered the last.

"Explain," Lenor said softly.

"My specialty is sleep disorders. Subspecialty, sleepwalking. In the past year, my lab studies of night terrors have led me to consider some very unscientific possibilities."

"Such as?"

"Possession," he whispered, then waited for her response.

The word didn't faze her. Arthur Seña had been a preteen sleepwalker and sufferer of night terrors. She and everyone else involved had considered possession a logical possibility. "Go on," she said.

His look of surprise faded quickly. "I *knew* you'd understand. But, for now, this can't go beyond my office door. Okay?"

"Okay."

"In a handful of cases who suffer both sleepwalking and night terrors, I've ruled out heredity, parent-induced disturbances, chemicals, logical triggers, psychopathology, both personality disorders and psychosis, physical problems, family problems. During transcription of the brain's electrical activity, all have the characteristic blips during stage-four sleep."

"An elite group," Lenor said, then asked, "None respond to hypnosis?"

"Not one. So here's my question to you. Would it be possible for you to help me follow some of these special cases?"

He looked so eager for her to say yes, she hated to turn him down. But with the load she was already carrying, and the possibility of a research venture of her own on the horizon, there was really nothing else to do. "I'm flattered that you think I could be of help, Dr. Crawford, but I don't see how I can take on another project right now. Besides, this is completely out of my field."

He was crestfallen, but didn't give up. "Not really out of your field, when you think about it. You said yourself that you were apprenticed to your mother. You made a very good case for all three levels of the *curanderismo*. No one nodded off." He smiled. "Sorry. But you *did* convincingly tie aspects of folk healing and modern medicine together in a compatible knot. These studies I'm talking about might even complement your own. And most importantly of all, as a fellow on a study, albeit one with a secret agenda, you'd have a foot in the door here at Truelex."

"Interesting," Lenor said.

"And I can pay you," Stan added hopefully.

"It's tempting . . . but I really can't. Isn't there someone else?"

"No one I feel I could trust. Even though I have a pretty free rein, I don't think the Truelex bean counters would go for my hiring a parapsychologist at this point."

"But you say nothing else explains the phenomena. Simple logic would—"

He interrupted. "Remember the newspaper article last week where the writer said you'd prescribed 'branches, berries, and smoke'? Well, somewhere in that piece he described Truelex's philosophy to a T. 'Such ideas are unsuitable to scientific discipline.' End of report."

"End of study. Here, anyway, I guess." Lenor stood up. "I'm sorry, I just can't manage it. I am truly sorry, Dr. Crawford."

"Dr. Tavera, please just think about it. That's all I'm asking." He rose and hurried to his desk. Retrieving a file folder from its shiny surface, he hurried back to her. "Let me give you this patient file. Just look it over. Take your time."

She took it from him reluctantly. "I don't know when I can get to this. I can't promise you I'll have any time at all."

"I understand. Just let me hear from you." He pressed a business card into her hand. "Even if the news is bad."

★   ★   ★

During the taxi ride back to Foley, Lenor ruminated on the events of the past seventy-two hours. She'd allowed her family to turn a request into a threat to her personal health. Neither George nor Watson was happy with her. She'd been called on the carpet by Bowder. Mrs. Hess considered her a mortal enemy. Dr. Crawford probably thought her daft to turn down a chance to get into the Truelex menagerie. And she'd learned that her namesake, Leonora Tavera, was in contact with one of her patients. To top it all, Michael Martino had been on her mind almost every minute since Saturday afternoon.

Michael will give you something for your grandfather. See that your grandfather keeps it.

Oddly, Leonora's words kept popping up from her subconscious every time she thought consciously of Michael Martino. Why?

Her detective's heart couldn't let it go.

Michael. Okay, I know who he is.

Will. No problem with that part of the verb.

Give. Yes, he did! She shivered. *No! Get back to the problem!*

You. Okay, that's me.

Something. The painting.

For your grandfather. All understandable.

See that he keeps it. Michael's painting was still in New Mexico, still with her grandfather. No problem with any of that.

Michael will give you something for your grandfather. See that your grandfather keeps it.

Michael. Martino, no doubt.

Will. He did.

Give. He did that, too.

You—

You? No!

Michael had given the painting to her grandparents, not to Lenor. He'd given her the *bulto!*

Lenor slid to her right so the driver couldn't see her in the rearview mirror and closed her eyes. A deep breath and a silent plea got her through almost immediately. *Granora? Am I right about the bulto being for Grandpa?*

You are.

Lenor opened her eyes and leaned forward. "I'm in a hurry."

The driver grinned.

New York ◆ Tuesday ◆ 11:10 P.M.

Urgency pushed her, and Lenor might have taken the stairs two at a time, but she wasn't feeling up to her usual sprint. At a walk, one step at a time was almost too much. Probably delayed fright from the frantic ride after she'd told the cabbie she was in a hurry, she decided. But she'd felt this way before the ride. Something was definitely going wrong. Maybe a trip to the lab to draw some blood and order a few tests would be the wise thing to do. *Just as soon as I call Grandpa and get this package sent.*

No messages waited for her at the nurses' station. Lenor glanced at the clock on the wall of the staff lounge. It was only nine-fifteen in New Mexico. Though her meeting with Dr. Crawford had lasted longer than she'd expected, it still wasn't too late to call and check on things at home. When Steven answered the phone, a wave of relief curled her into a comfortable tendril in the corner of the sagging couch.

"How's everything? Everyone?" Lenor asked.

"Spry as ever. A little tired, maybe, especially Magdalena, but she did most of the work. Even with everybody helping to clean up after, the party was still a lot of work."

"Worth every bit of it, too," Lenor said. "Grandma's okay?"

"Giving me hell about the phone bill. Trying to get me into letter writing. She's in great form, as usual. How'd it go with Truelex?' he asked.

She didn't want to tell him that Truelex might be opposed to her mystical bent. "One of the doctors who heard my presentation said it was the best one he'd ever heard," Lenor said.

"Oh, honey, that's terrific! When will you know?"

"Within a couple of weeks, I guess. They have a lot more to review, and I hear they take their time. Could be longer, I guess."

"You're not going to worry for two weeks, now are you?" he asked.

"No, Grandpa. I've been through this before."

"I know. But every time some corporation turns you down, it gets a little tougher, doesn't it?"

"Good question." Lenor pulled off one black pump, then the other, and let them drop to the floor. Her lightweight black knit dress stretched easily as she pulled her knees up on the cushion. "I think it gets easier, actually. Gives me a chance to tune up the material, pare it down, make it more presentable." Lenor looked up to see George standing just inside the door.

"You look *very* presentable," George whispered.

Instead of acknowledging what he'd said, Lenor spoke into the phone again. "You'd think my stuff would be pretty sleek by now, but it still took me an hour and forty-five minutes to get through it."

"I don't know how you do it all, honey. I think you're working too hard."

Standing in front of her now, George whispered again. "Is that Steven?"

Lenor nodded. "You know better than that, Grandpa. Work never hurt anyone. You said so yourself."

"Guess I did, at that. But you have to love what you're doing."

"You know I do," Lenor said.

George lifted his hand, thumb to his ear, little finger to his chin.

Lenor nodded at him again. "Grandpa. George just came in. He'd like to say hi." She handed the receiver to George, but didn't listen to their conversation. She was more tuned in to her own thoughts, her own worries. She should have left San Miguel Arcángel with her grandfather instead of bringing it back to Sable.

When Sable had asked for the *bulto,* she'd said she didn't

know why it should be Saint Michael. Even Michael Martino had questioned her choice and suggested a particular statue of the Virgin Mary, Nuestra Señora del Socorro, Our Lady of Help. Last night Sable had told Lenor that she had a feeling the statue actually belonged to someone else. *How could I have missed all this? All these clues?* She looked up. George was holding the receiver toward her.

"So . . . you're feeling all right, Grandpa?" Lenor asked.

"Better than ever, honey, now that I've talked to you."

"And everyone else is okay?"

"Will you stop worrying yourself, Lenor? You've got enough to think about. Now go have some dinner, listen to some Mozart or some Garth Brooks, and get some rest. George tells me you're not taking care of yourself. I won't have that. You hear me?"

"Will you stop worrying yourself, Grandpa?" she said, parroting his own words. She heard him chuckle. "That's better. And yes, I'll go have some dinner now."

"With me?" George whispered.

"I'm going to send you an overnight package tomorrow, Grandpa. Expect it Thursday morning. All right?"

"What is it?" Steven asked.

"A surprise," Lenor said.

"I can't wait."

Lenor hung up the phone, slipped into her shoes, and stood up.

"Did Steven tell you to have dinner with me?" George asked, smiling.

"He told me to go home," Lenor lied.

George's smile disappeared. "Dress looks nice."

"Thanks."

"You should wear dresses more often," he said, trying a little smile again, this time with a flavor of flirtation.

"I'm *already* a woman. A *silly* woman, at that. You want me to handicap myself further by wearing a ridiculously restrictive costume?"

George hung his head. "Lenor . . ."

"You don't have to say anything, George. You didn't deserve that. I'm out of sorts, that's all." *And asking Sable for her precious San Miguel isn't going to be a pleasant task.*

"It's because you're hungry. Maybe you should be taking some of your own medicine. What was it? Juniper berries?"

He was baiting her again, but she didn't feel up to challenging him. "Maybe you're right," she said. *But not for the reason you're thinking. I need a talisman, not an appetite stimulant.*

"Come on. My treat."

"I can't," Lenor said.

"You mean you don't want to."

"I mean I can't. I have to check on Sable."

George looked at his watch. "You're going to disturb a child at eleven-twenty at night? I can't imagine what could be so important that it couldn't wait till morning."

She didn't feel like explaining. He wouldn't understand anyway. She knew that now. "No, George. This can't wait another minute."

Sable was sound asleep, with Saint Michael cuddled in her arms, and Lenor considered taking the *bulto* and leaving a note on her pillow. But she just couldn't do it. The icon was already too precious to the child. Lenor lightly touched her shoulder.

"Sable?" she whispered. "Honey?"

Sable's eyes opened slowly; then she smiled up at Lenor.

"Honey, I'm sorry to wake you at this hour, but I had to talk to you."

" 'Bout what?"

"You were right about Saint Michael. He *was* carved for someone else."

"Who?"

"For Steven Tavera," Lenor said.

"Your grandpa?"

"Yes."

"The *santero* made a mistake?" Sable asked, sitting up.

"No, *I* made the mistake. I'm so sorry, honey. But I promise

I'm going to call the *santero* tonight and ask him to make another, just for you. Okay?"

"Will I have to pay him again?"

"No! Of course not!"

"Well . . . it's okay then. May I talk to Saint Michael for a minute? Say good-bye?"

"Sure."

Lenor waited while Sable relaxed, closed her eyes, breathed deeply. She slumped forward, then straightened, while a fierce look of determination crossed her face. Her expression changed several times before she finally opened her eyes to see Lenor's hand above her head. Sable smiled at Lenor, then looked down. She lifted the statue to her lips and gave it a light kiss. "Take good care of Dr. T's grandpa," she said.

"Thank you, Sable . . . and for understanding, too. See you in the morning." Lenor turned to go.

"Dr. T?" Lenor looked back. "Don't worry so much about making a mistake. *Everybody* makes mistakes."

Lenor smiled. "Thanks, Sable."

Everything Lenor needed to get the *bulto* ready for mailing she found in the office behind the nurses' station—an empty box, a brown paper bag, and a roll of plastic tape. She marked the package OVERNIGHT, then added FRAGILE and EX-TREMELY URGENT in bright red letters on all sides. She wrote ELLA OR WILLY on the front of a business-size envelope and tucked in two twenty-dollar bills, along with a note explaining that the package had to go out first thing. She felt considerably more relaxed as she placed the package on the front counter and told the duty nurse what to do with it.

"I might be a little late in the morning. I have a meeting. See that Ella or Willy look at this as soon as they walk in."

"Sure thing, Dr. Tavera."

Everything would be okay now. Grandpa was in good spirits and feeling fine; he'd just finished telling her so himself. He'd be going to bed soon, and he'd rest well. At last she could go home, too, quit worrying. After a quick visit to the lab, she left the hospital in good spirits.

Most of her plants were drooping when she let herself into her apartment. They looked exactly the way she felt—wilted. She usually watered on Sundays, but this weekend had been a different story, and, what with one thing or another, she'd forgotten all about them. Still, they'd have to wait a little while longer. She had an important phone call to make.

By the time she'd put her purse and briefcase down and crossed to the phone, her hands were trembling. By the time she'd looked up the number in the Toya phone book, she felt like she was wearing her clothes out from the inside out. *Get a grip, woman!* Both Michael and the ranch were listed, under Martino and El Rancho de Torbellino. She chose the Martino number, then checked her watch. Quarter past twelve. Quarter past ten in New Mexico. *Too late? Call in the morning? Don't start with the excuses! You promised Sable you'd call tonight!*

What to say? *"Just called to say hi, and, oh, by the way, the spirit of my long dead great-great-great-grandmother told me that the bulto you made was really supposed to be for my grandfather." "Oh, really? Well, I'll just get right busy and make another one for Sable."*

Oh, please.

Lenor put her hand on the receiver. Took a deep breath. Lifted. Dialed.

"Your number cannot be completed as dialed. Please check the number and try again."

Come on, lady. Watch what you're doing.

The dialing took two more tries. Even Nose-Out-of-Joint Watson got curious about what was going on. He came over to watch her. *Probably hoping to see me make a complete fool of myself!* "Scat!"

"Excuse me?" the voice on the other end of the line said.

"Oh, dear. Not you. I was talking to my cat." Lenor heard a deep chuckle.

"I hope you're not planning to take the same tone with me!"

"Michael?" Lenor asked tentatively. She was hoping it was
Eloy.

"Lenor?"

"Yes."

"Well, now that we've established who we are, this is a very
nice surprise."

"Were you in bed?" *Wrong thing to ask!* "I mean, did I wake
you?"

"No problem."

This was getting off to a very wrong start. She had a simple
request. No ulterior motives. Then why did she have to clench
her teeth together to keep them from chattering?

"I'm really sorry to bother you at this hour."

"You New York folks stay up pretty late," he said.

"I know. And we don't have to get up before sunrise. I'm
really sorry."

"You can stop apologizing, Lenor. I'd be happy to talk to you
at any hour."

She could hear him smiling. She could see him lying in bed.
He was propped up on two pillows. No shirt. Wide shoulders.
Soft black hair—She caught her breath. "I know it's late . . ."

"You said that."

"You're right. And I don't want to keep you. I'll get to the
point."

"No hurry."

Her chance to break the spell. "That's because you're not
paying the phone bill," she quipped.

"Hang up. I'll call you right back," he said.

"No, no. I was just joking," Lenor said.

"I wasn't," he said quietly.

Just say it! "Michael, I'm calling to see if I can commission you
to do another carving of San Miguel Arcángel."

"You don't have to commission me."

"I mean to pay you for your work," Lenor said.

Michael was silent for a moment, then, "How's George? Did

he survive his first visit to New Mexico all right? Did he enjoy the party?"

"He's fine."

"That's a pretty short answer to a pretty long question. You two are still friends, aren't you?" He hoped not.

"I don't know *how* George is. We had a disagreement. I haven't talked to him about the trip . . . or much of anything else."

"Sorry to hear that." He really wasn't. Not that George wasn't a good guy. Michael had talked to him a little at the party, enough to know that the man was a nice fellow. If his own daughter had chosen Dr. George Murphy as a beau, he'd have approved.

My own daughter. Lenor's daughter. Our daughter.

The thought grabbed him like a boa constrictor and wouldn't let him go. He had no control over his body, his racing heart, his torrid thoughts. Unbidden, the passionate arousal was an almost painful reminder of the distance between them. *Damn!*

"Michael?"

"I'm here." *The worse for wear, but here.* He felt as if he had a fever.

"At the party . . . the dancing . . . I didn't mean to . . ."

"Lead me on? Don't worry. You were the perfect lady. Neither George nor Rafael have anything to worry about as far as your behavior is concerned."

Lenor stiffened. He was playing with her. "I'm not sixteen anymore, Michael."

"True," he said, and he could feel her woman's body touching his. He shifted the phone and pulled himself up higher on the pillows. He was trembling, but it wasn't because of the cool mountain air stirring the curtains at the open windows. The wavering breath he exhaled was filled with tension.

"What?" Lenor asked.

Had he made a sound? He wanted to scream. "Just getting more comfortable," he said.

"Well, I'll let you get to sleep. I'm really sorry to have bothered you so late."

"Call anytime." It was all he could do to speak, but he wanted to beg her to stay on the phone. "I mean that. Anytime," he said instead.

"Thank you, Michael." She should hang up the phone, but she couldn't.

"Lenor?"

"Yes."

I want to fly to New York and be with you right now! "When do you want the San Miguel?"

"Soon. As soon as possible. Just send it COD to me at the hospital."

"I understand. Good night, Lenor."

I understand. The magic words. No questions. No accusations. She sat for a moment, her hand on the still-warm receiver. She wanted to see him again. Soon.

Logically, a relationship with Michael Martino was out of the question. She'd never bought the old adage, "Opposites attract." As far as she could see in others' relationships, if two people didn't share like interests, professions, and life-styles, they were doomed to living a nightmare together. But Michael wasn't a nightmare. He was a dream. *Opposites or not, I'm attracted!*

As Lenor fed Watson and watered her plants, she wondered why she'd broken her own rules where George was concerned. Co-workers had always been off limits until he'd come along. He'd seemed to represent everything she valued. He loved children and treated them with the respect they deserved. He was intelligent, devoted to his work, highly skilled. And he was a good friend.

But he had a blind spot. Somewhere, deep down in his subconscious mind, he couldn't accept the mystical part of her world. Could she really expect him to? Women had been misunderstanding men, and men women, forever. Throw in some spooky stuff and forget it. George had tried to cope, but he couldn't. Lenor blamed herself for that. At this early stage, she never should have been so careless as to let him see her "talking" to Leonora.

No matter how it all turned out, Lenor wanted George for a friend. He really did have her best interests at heart. For him, she tried to eat something before going to bed. One bite of her own homemade vegetable soup went into her mouth, the rest into her compost bucket under the sink. She decided instead on a few drops of a tincture of gentian in a cup of warm water. Jovita's special recipe, with orange peel, honey, and cardamom, in brandy, did the trick. Within minutes after her head hit the pillow, Lenor was asleep.

And minutes later the ringing of the phone jarred her awake. She checked the time. Half past one. She'd been dreaming about Michael. They'd been in the barn at her home. The spring day was warm, Michael was about to kiss her. Was Michael calling her back? As tired as she felt, the prospect was rather exciting. She answered with a smile in her voice.

"Hello."

"Lenor?"

As soon as she heard her father's voice, she feared the worst. "Papa, what's wrong?"

"It's your grandma, Lenor. It's Jovita."

Lenor immediately started thinking like a doctor. "What's wrong with her? Tell me everything."

"My mother's dead," Rafael said. "She—"

Lenor heard a sob, a shuffling sound, then Magdalena's voice. "Lenor?"

"Mama. What's going on? For God's sake, tell me what happened!"

"Jovita had a heart attack, Lenor."

"Impossible!"

Magdalena went on. "About ten-fifteen, as far as Dr. Baldwin can tell. She went quickly. Miller says she probably didn't suffer."

"But Mama, Dr. Baldwin just gave both my grandparents a

clean bill of health. He told me that just four days ago. What could have gone wrong?"

Magdalena was crying softly. "I wish I could tell you."

"How's Grandpa?" Lenor asked.

"Devastated."

"I'll be there sometime today," Lenor said. "I don't know what flight I can get, so don't expect me at any specific time. I'll be home as quickly as I can."

Magdalena couldn't say good-bye. Lenor heard a click, then a dial tone. She made an immediate call for an airline ticket.

A weather delay in St. Louis set her back several hours, but by sunset she was skirting Santa Fe in her rented car. She entered Mora County a little before ten and questioned her decision not to call her mother from the airport in Albuquerque. At the time it had seemed like the right thing to do. She'd already called from St. Louis and explained the delay. Since then the trip was going as scheduled. But now she wondered whether she'd made the correct choice. A pickup had been following her for the past five miles, along a road where deer outnumbered automobile traffic by about a hundred to one. He'd made no move to pass her when she slowed, and made a definite effort to stay with her when she speeded up.

"It's just my imagination," she said aloud, glancing in the rearview mirror for the hundredth time. But she wasn't convinced, and all her antennae were tuned to something sinister. An evasive maneuver would take just a few minutes. She turned left toward Mora.

The little village was quiet as she drove through on the main street that was lined with at least half the buildings in the entire town. She considered stopping at Dr. Baldwin's house to call her mother, but there were two cars parked in his dusty front yard. She didn't want to disturb him if he was with patients. There was also the possibility that Roy would be at home and insist that he accompany her the rest of the way to the Tavera ranch. Her family didn't need another person to deal with tonight.

She was doubly glad she hadn't stopped when she saw the truck that had been following her pull into the doctor's yard. Her apprehension disappeared; her cramped fingers eased their death grip on the steering wheel. The lights were on in the high school gym. These summer nights in a small town meant dances, a few smuggled beers, a lot of youthful romantic conquests—or attempts at them.

"Eee."

Lenor opened Watson's carrier, which sat on the passenger seat next to her. He stretched his neck up over the edge, then bounded easily to the back of the driver's seat. "We'll be home pretty soon," she said as she made a U-turn.

About a block from the general store, Watson got as close to the window as he could.

"No, you're not getting out here," Lenor told him.

"Yee-ow!"

"I know we should look for your rock—okay, okay, *my* rock—but Roy doesn't have it. He told me so." Watson continued to yowl. "I can't handle the commotion right now, Watson. Shall I put you back in your box?"

That did it. As they rolled by Roy's general store, headed for the old adobe gristmill at La Cueva, Watson calmed. But Roy Baldwin was still on Lenor's mind.

The Baldwins had always lived in Mora, but Gloria Baldwin had bought a small residence in Toya. She'd sent Roy to school there, ostensibly because of the smaller classes, and he and Lenor had been friends for a long time. There had been a time in her life when she thought she might be enamored of the doctor's model-handsome son. He'd been so unlike most of the boys she'd known during her teen years, a gentle, modest, self-effacing sort who seemed to live only for the pleasure of pleasing her, especially after his mother died. He'd been like a brother; his attentive listening and appreciative caring had been more than welcome.

Had he been a viable choice among suitors? No. But last Saturday night, after the argument with her mother, she would have welcomed his shoulder to cry on. Eight miles north of La

Cueva, Lenor realized she'd started thinking about seeing all of the family she loved so dearly.

All but Jovita.

Ten

JOHN GARCIA SPOKE SOFTLY INTO THE RECEIVER. "What do you mean, *she's* here? Who's here?"

"Lenor Tavera's here," Baldwin said impatiently. "My man just followed her into town."

"Oh? Why would she drive into Mora?"

Miller Baldwin grimaced, shook his head, but couldn't stanch the flow of sarcasm. "Because she wanted some wild excitement before coming out to the ranch!"

"Guess she spotted your guy following her," Sheriff Garcia said in a mild tone. "Wanted to throw him off the trail."

"Sorry, John. I didn't mean to be belligerent. Sloppy job of tailing. Incompetence just gets to me sometimes."

"No offense taken, Doctor." He wanted to ask Dr. Baldwin why he'd had Lenor Tavera followed, but decided the question should be asked in person and in private.

"If Lenor turned around and left town right away, she should have been out there by now. You haven't seen her?" Miller asked.

"No."

"Well, get off your butt and go take a look."

Miller waited what seemed like twenty minutes for the sheriff to check outside the Seña home. *God, please let her be there,* he prayed. He knew Lenor had to be grieving for her grandmother and knew she was in the habit of driving or riding her horse around the Tavera property when she had a problem that needed sorting out. *God, please don't let her find the beehive!*

"Not here yet, Doctor."

"Damn! What the hell is the woman doing, then?"

"I couldn't guess," John said.

You wouldn't even try to guess. You haven't been through the torture I have, you fool. "Just keep a watch out for her, can you do that?" Miller said evenly.

The doctor had been acting strange lately, and John hadn't been able to figure out why. It worried him some. He was used to knowing the whys and wherefores of everybody's business— except his son's. "Sure. Then what?"

"I'm paying you to keep her safe. Don't let anything happen to her. Understand?"

"No problem."

"Is the boy who ran away from the Tavera camp this evening still missing?" Miller asked.

"Yes. Thomas Newman is still missing."

"Well, *find him!*"

"We're trying."

You can say that again! He instantly felt bad about being so abrasive with John Garcia, what with his son, Junior, still missing. But it wasn't as if the boy from the Taveras' camp were an older teen, like Junior, who'd made it a habit of taking off whenever he pleased just for the hell of it. Miller Baldwin slammed down the phone, ran impatient fingers through his thick white hair, then turned away from his cluttered rolltop desk. "You can forget about being paid for tonight," he said to the man seated on the couch across the small room. "I want you and your truck out of town and out of sight until I tell you differently." He turned back to the desk, wrote a few lines on a scrap of paper, then extended it toward the man. "You can stay with this woman in Las Vegas. Here's the name and address."

The man rose, reached for the note. "But, sir, you didn't say anything about—I don't even know this—"

"Just do as you're told." Miller stood up. "Perhaps if you do this right, there'll be some compensation for you later."

188 ◆ MARY ELIZABETH LYNN ◆

A hopeful smile flickered across his face. "I'll go home and pack a few things."

"No. I want you to leave right now." Miller pointed to the note. "This woman will have everything you need."

"But my wife will wonder what—"

Miller vented the anger he'd been feeling toward the sheriff. "For Christ's sake, man! You're only going to be a few miles down the road." He summoned a little more control. "I'll talk to your wife," he continued more gently. "She'll understand."

The man nodded, looked down at the note, then nodded again. "I'll wait for your call."

"You won't regret it. Have a good trip." He slammed the door behind the retreating man, then went back to his desk.

Get a grip on yourself, Doctor. Miller pulled his checkbook off the top shelf of the rolltop, filled in an amount of two hundred dollars to the man's wife, and made a notation: *For use of tractor/ tiller for garden.*

Deception? Yes. A lie? Not exactly. He had borrowed the equipment from them, but they'd never expected payment. It wouldn't have been the neighborly thing to do.

The note he wrote to accompany the check simply said, *"Thank you for the use of your tractor and tiller. Your husband will be helping me with some research for a few days. He will be home very shortly, as soon as his work is finished. Please call me if you have any objections to this or need help with anything."*

"Roy?"

Miller's son opened the door, stepped inside the room, and stood there for a moment, counting a stack of poker chips he held in his hand. When he put the chips down, he took out a notepad and ballpoint, jotted a few words, then returned both to his shirt pocket. Finally he said, "Yeah, Dad?"

"Has everyone left yet?"

"About ten minutes ago. They didn't mind making it an early night . . . decided they were tired enough of losing for one evening."

"Good." Miller held out an envelope. "Will you deliver this, then come back here, please?"

Roy looked down at the address, then up at his father. "It's a little late to catch the mailman, isn't it?" he quipped.

Miller huffed. "Can't anyone do what they're told, when they're told to do it?" Then he settled back in his chair. "She's waiting for it, son," he said sweetly. "Okay?"

Roy shrugged. "Okay."

Eleven holes in the dam, and only ten fingers. Miller stared at the door that closed behind his son and wondered, again, what had happened to their once-comfortable relationship. Roy used to be such an obedient boy, never questioning his father's wishes, always trying to please in any way he could. Even though he hadn't completed medical school, with his genius IQ he'd learned enough so the two of them could discuss unusual cases. Miller had cushioned Roy's disappointment in the medical school failure by encouraging his interest in owning a business and, nine years ago, financing the purchase of the general store.

For the last two years, though, Roy had been slowly changing from an apparently happy and grateful son to a belligerent, hermitlike creature who would rather tend his plants, look through his microscope, drive an old hearse around, and take notes on God-knew-what-all kinds of trivia. Miller's curiosity about the changes in his son had been mild at first. A few innocent questions had gotten him only sullen and unsatisfying answers. Then Juanita had quit working at the store, telling Miller's housekeeper, Inez, that she'd seen Roy masturbating behind the canned-goods shelves when there were customers in the shop. Miller hadn't wanted to believe the hearsay, but Juanita had had no reason to lie to her longtime friend. Then there was Junior Garcia, still missing after almost a week. Not unusual for Junior, or any number of local teenagers, but Miller suspected, at gut level, that Roy had something to do with Junior's disappearance. Now Jovita Tavera was dead.

So many things had changed. If only his son had completed medical school. If only Miller didn't have to question whether he'd been a good father to his motherless child. If only he wasn't starting to doubt his own competence as a doctor. If only his wife, Gloria, hadn't died. Miller felt lonelier now than he had in all the fifteen years since her death. So many changes.

Once an avid collector himself, Roy no longer took any interest in the valuable assortment of antique medical instruments Miller had carefully preserved for him. Tired eyes scanned the mounted array of ancient medical paraphernalia around the walls of his office. There were medicine bottles with glass stoppers, forceps and cauterizing irons, syringes, needles, primitive scalpels and clamps. In the far corner of the room, the old wheelchair, rescued from the tuberculosis sanatorium in Valmora, waited patiently for the doctor's son to give it a reason to exist.

Roy seemed to resent everything his father had ever done for him, everything his elder said to him, everything he was asked to do. Miller wasn't a psychiatrist, but he could tell normal from abnormal, neurotic from psychotic, and his son appeared to be perched on the edge of the latter abyss. Didn't Roy Baldwin realize that everything Miller had ever done was solely for his son's good?

And now Miller suspected the worst. The only doctor in a three-county area, he'd pronounced Jovita Tavera dead. He'd declared the cause of death—and signed his name to the lie. His entire being wanted to deny the truth—that Jovita had been poisoned.

Only days before Steven's eighty-ninth birthday, Miller had given both him and his wife a clean bill of health. His patient for so many years now, Jovita had the constitution of a sixty-year-old, bio-markers a fifty-year-old would envy, and should have lived another twenty good years.

Magdalena had called him at the first signs of Jovita's distress—sweating, vomiting, rapidly increasing heartbeat. By the time Miller had driven out to the Tavera place, Jovita was unconscious, her heart was fibrillating, and the final stages of respiratory paralysis had the once-vital woman at death's door.

He'd asked the usual questions of the family, and the puzzle hadn't been that difficult to put together. The three years Dr. Baldwin had spent in a pathology lab in the early 1960s had heightened his awareness. Both Steven and Jovita lived life by the book according to Lenor Tavera. Their regimen never varied. Grandma's last day on earth had been spent like every other one for the past ten years, even down to the usual bedtime snack, a bowl of cold cereal with honey and soy milk. Nothing that could have caused death. But Steven had unknowingly thrown all the puzzle pieces on the table and put them all together by offering a little more information than the doctor had asked for. *Jovita would have wanted Roy to know. The honey was delicious.* It had been too late for gastric lavage, and the quinidine he'd administered might as well have been water. Jovita died within minutes after Miller's arrival.

For a woman of seventy-nine, a heart attack would be perfectly plausible. But now Miller would have to go back and alter Jovita's medical record, add some unspecific allergy to some unknown allergen to explain the respiratory difficulties. It was the only thing he could think to do until he could prove to himself, with solid evidence, that he was right about Roy. He had to protect his son until he could figure out how to help him. Gloria wouldn't have had it any other way.

At least he had evidence of Roy's past caring to comfort him. From the wide center drawer in his desk Miller took out a large book, which he laid carefully on top of a pile of papers. He rubbed his hands over the old leather cover, relishing, for a moment, the feel and the antique frangrance of perfectly preserved, one-hundred-fifty-year-old cowhide. The thought of so many people taking such loving care of a volume for so long made him smile every time he looked at the priceless possession, the priceless gift from a loving son.

He knew some of the history of the book. It had been brought west over the Santa Fe Trail from Independence, Missouri, by a merchant who had begun trading in the Southwest not too long after the U.S. flag had been run up over the Palace of the Governors in Santa Fe and Juan Bautista Vigil y Alaríd had officially surrendered New Mexico to the United States in August of 1846. The purchase price, when the book had been sold just outside Fort Union, was two red chile *ristras* and one sack of onions. All this was noted on the inside front cover in a bold hand. Its blank pages had been intended for use as a diary, but the first and subsequent owners had written much more than simply daily events.

He hadn't read much of it. Written all in Spanish, it was hard going, but he intended to keep at it until he'd studied it thoroughly. He was sure that it contained the knowledge he needed to treat those patients who couldn't bring themselves to trust a medical doctor, those who still believed in the *curanderismo*. He was positive he'd learn how to help his son.

Miller reached into a bottom drawer and withdrew a hefty flask. The amber liquid burned on the way down, but infused him with a warm, comfortable feeling. Another long pull on the bottle made him sigh. When things got better, he'd try to make some sense of his life, he decided. So many things didn't make *any* sense right now. He still didn't understand why Lenor had given the book to Roy. For taking care of her horse, Tossa, Roy had said. Whatever the reason, Miller was grateful to have it.

If only I'd started studying it sooner.

Eleven

AS LENOR APPROACHED THE HOUSE, SHE COULD SEE A woman walking toward the Señas', where, even at this late hour, lights were on. Magdalena turned, glanced at the car, then kept walking, as if she didn't recognize her daughter. Watson dashed out; Lenor left her luggage in the car and hurried to catch up with her mother. "Mama?"

Magdalena stopped just short of the steps to the Señas' porch. "Lenor!"

"Hello, Mama. I'm sorry I'm so late." She put her arms around her mother and felt a desperate need for comfort in the fierce embrace she got in return. "Are you all right?" she asked quietly when her mother let her go.

"As well as could be expected."

Lenor held her emotions in check, but she was appalled at how her mother looked. Within a few days' time she seemed to have aged ten years. "How's Grandpa?"

"Not well. Miller gave him a sedative. He's staying at Angelina's. Can't bear to sleep in the same house or the same bed."

"That's understandable," Lenor said, then asked the hardest question. "Is Papa okay?"

"No. He's putting up a good front, but under it all . . ."

"Is he here?" Lenor asked, pointing to the Señas'.

Magdalena hesitated. "There's something else going on."

"What is it?"

"One of the boys is missing."

"One of the ranch hands?" Lenor asked.

"One of the boys here at camp. Thomas Newman."

"Oh my," Lenor managed.

"I was on my way over here to see if Sheriff Garcia had heard anything from anyone yet." She took Lenor's hand as they started up the steps, and Lenor could feel her mother trembling. "The last time anyone saw Thomas was after supper. Shirley said 'one minute Thomas was right behind me, the next minute he was gone.' "

Lenor wished she could think of the right thing to say. "It's not the first time one of the kids has wandered off, Mama. He's probably just pulling a teenage prank to get some peer recognition."

"He took off one morning last week, too, during a hike."

"Where did he go?" Lenor asked.

"The Martino place. Roy happened to be there and brought him back." Magdalena knocked on the screen door, then opened it, and the two women walked into the house. The living room was empty; the voices were coming from the kitchen.

"Maybe someone dared Thomas to do it again," Lenor said as they continued toward a door to their left.

"That's what Apple said, but Michael, Eloy, and Gilberto searched around their place for hours after I called them. No luck."

"Is Apple here?" Lenor asked.

"She and Rafael left about two hours ago, riding out to the southeast. Roy's driving the back roads. Rudolfo took Jerry and Manny out on horseback, and John is going to drive through the canyons on the other side of the hills, up past Coyote Creek State Park. Lucille is staying in the bunkhouse with the rest of the kids."

Nemesia and Sheriff Garcia turned as Lenor and Magdalena entered the kitchen. Lenor could tell by their expressions that no one had reported any good news yet. John nodded a greeting from his position near the phone. Nemesia gave Lenor a hug, then wrapped her arms around Magdalena. "It'll be all right," Nemesia said quietly.

The look on John Garcia's face didn't have the confidence of Nemesia's words. Torn between leaving her mother alone and finding Thomas, whose return might alleviate part of her mother's anxiety, Lenor made a difficult decision. "Why don't I change clothes and ride out for a while. Another set of eyes would help, don't you think?"

"No. I don't want you out there at night alone," Magdalena said.

Lenor was puzzled. "But I've gone riding by myself at night many times. You've never objected before."

"I'm objecting now." Magdalena's face was lined with worry, but remained stern and unyielding.

"I don't understand. I'm perfectly capable of riding a horse, no matter what time of day or night it is."

Magdalena slumped forward, and the determination seemed to flow out of her thin body as Nemesia steadied her. "You're right, of course." She glanced at Nemesia, then across the room at John. "I don't know what it is," she whispered, "but I sense danger. Something's going on around us that I can't see and can't figure out." She shook her head. "Maybe I'm just getting foolish in my old age."

Lenor smiled at the beautiful woman standing in front of her. "I wouldn't call fifty-six very old, Mama. Things will get better, I promise you. You'll be feeling yourself again. You'll see." But Lenor wasn't so sure. She'd never seen her mother look so worn out or heard her talk of unseen dangers or of getting old and foolish. "Why don't you try to get some rest, while I'm out looking?"

"No. I'll go with you."

Lenor shook her head, then phrased her refusal carefully to avoid sounding overprotective. "I think you should stay here, in case Thomas comes back."

"But Nemesia will be—"

"If Thomas is frightened or hurt when he shows up, he'll want to see you and no one else, Mama," Lenor said.

"Perhaps."

Nemesia nodded in agreement.

"You know I'm right." Lenor moved to her mother's side. "You've always been everyone's refuge, Mama. I love you." Magdalena's tears streamed freely now. Lenor leaned close and kissed her. "I'm sorry this had to happen, especially just now, but I'm sure everything will turn out all right."

"Don't go near Martino's place," Magdalena said.

"I won't." But she knew she might. "Is Tossa in the barn?"

Her mother nodded. "She'll be glad to see you."

Lenor headed for her own house, her own room. Several small lamps, placed close to the ground, cast circles of dim, amber light to illuminate the winding flagstone paths. The massive cottonwood that the hacienda had been built around stood majestic and still, rising toward the night sky. The only sound Lenor could hear was the quiet splashing of the small waterfall in the far corner, and the peacefulness of the *placita* made her want to sit down on the pine bench that circled the ancient cottonwood and relax for a while.

But the peace wasn't real. Even the graceful arches and pillars that supported the breezeway covering surrounding the center garden seemed to bear the additional weight of great sadness. Lenor knew that all the people who made this the happy refuge it usually was were either away or too devastated to bring any kind of cheer to the place. Though perfectly groomed as always, the safe haven seemed to be in shambles.

One lone kitchen light threw a singular shaft of brilliance a short way into the *placita,* highlighting lush foliage of perfectly trimmed cedar and juniper, tufts of bear grass, and other plants of the high mesa. Lenor made a quick detour to get carrots for her horse, one of Lucielle's cookies for herself, and a few knobs of dried oshá root, then walked along the south breezeway.

Filled with an extended family only two generations earlier, the province of children and parents, aunts, uncles, and grandparents, the dark and silent hacienda now seemed lonely and much too large. It was no wonder that Magdalena surrounded herself with the smiling faces and happy hearts of young teens every summer.

As Lenor passed the doors and windows that lined the open hallway along the south side, she could almost taste the overwhelming sadness her mother must experience every time she thought about having grandchildren who could come to visit and sleep in the vacant rooms that had not been meant to stay dark and empty and quiet.

Lenor opened the heavy pine door of her bedroom, turned on the light, and stood for a moment looking at the familiar sight. The large room, made cozy by low ceilings, deep window seats softened by calico-covered pillows, bookcases full of precious and well-worn books dating as far back as the early 1800s, and congenial groupings of every imaginable kind of stuffed animal, resurrected memories of happier times, like when Apple and George had shared a lively visit there. Watson followed her into the quiet room.

There was no need to retrieve her luggage from the car. Lenor crossed to the tall pine chest between the two windows on the west wall and took jeans and a sweater from a drawer. Three pairs of cowboy boots slouched in one corner of the closet that ran almost the full length of the north wall, but they were left alone in favor of the soft, brown leather squaw boots. As she changed, Lenor eyed the comfortable bed across the room from the closet. It would be so nice to lie down, to sleep for a while, to rest before helping with the funeral arrangements. But that was not to be. Lucielle's cookie and the red clover tea she'd brewed on the plane would have to rejuvenate her for the time being.

When she'd finished dressing, she tied a denim jacket around her waist and gave Watson a pat. "Too bad you never learned to ride a horse, sir. I wouldn't mind having a pair of cat eyes helping me tonight." His response to being disturbed was to quickly rise on all fours, arch his back into a high, tortuous curve, then flop back down on the pillow in a tight ball, facing the opposite direction. "You'll be there when I need you," Lenor said.

Leaving her room, she went directly to the barn. A feeling of déjà vu wrapped itself around her as she entered—the barn's interior was exactly as it had appeared in her brief dream about Michael. She struggled to put the disturbing thought out of her mind. The effort made her feel slightly dizzy, but the sight of the horses helped. In the dream, there had been no animals in the barn.

Stalls lined both sides of the structure. The horses lifted their heads, almost in unison, to greet their unexpected visitor. They shuffled, made soft sounds of welcome, but otherwise seemed undisturbed by her presence. Tossa was in the first stall on the right; the white blaze that extended the full length of her face appeared to flash on and off as she nodded her head and stamped her feet in anticipation. The sturdy little quarter horse had been a gift from her parents when Lenor had graduated from the University of New Mexico, and even though she and the mare hadn't spent very much time together in the ten years since then, they'd become good friends who enjoyed long rides and long conversations during Lenor's vacations home.

Tossa made no fuss about leaving her stall. "Oooh, that's a good girl," Lenor said soothingly as she stroked and petted her sturdy neck and shoulder. Leading her out of the barn was even easier. All Lenor had to do was walk away, and the inviting fragrance of fresh carrots had Tossa following, sniffing and searching every pocket for her surprise, as she had so many times before. Lenor rewarded her efforts, talking all the while in a low, lilting tone that Tossa enjoyed.

"You ready to go, girl?" she asked when Tossa was finished with her carrots. The horse accepted the bridle readily, and Lenor slipped it easily into place. In one smooth motion she grasped the mane, gave a slight jump, and swung her right leg over the horse's bare back. They started off in a northwesterly direction. Lenor gave Tossa her head, the reins swaying loosely in two sagging loops on either side of her neck, and the conversation continued for a short distance.

"If this is Thomas's second excursion, he probably has some idea of the lay of the land. If he left the hiking trail last week, he might have decided to keep to the north of the trail to avoid all the little villages and outlying homes to the south. I wouldn't be surprised if he went to the same places this evening."

Lenor wasn't too worried about Thomas's coming across any dangerous animals. Sometimes stray longhorns visited Coyote Creek, but they were usually timid and would take off in the opposite direction if a stranger approached them. The mountain lions and coyotes kept to the hills, since most of the narrow valleys were dotted with small farms and ranches well peopled with shotgun-toting, two-legged predators. Old Woosey's lair was well to the north near Black Lake. Of more concern were the many barbed-wire fences that surrounded almost every piece of private property in the area. Lenor knew from painful experience that a single strand of barbed wire, invisible at night, could jerk a running person off his feet and leave him sprawled and bleeding. She had a one-inch scar on her left temple to prove it.

Most of the grazing land on the Tavera ranch stretched north and east of the main house in flowing meadows and grassy valleys. West by northwest, the terrain rose from the seventy-five-hun-dred-foot altitude of the high mesa country and began the ascent into the Rincon Mountains, where the highest peak rose to over nine thousand feet. Staying north of the hiking trail, Tossa slowly picked her way through stands of pine and around clusters of aspen. Her ears were in constant motion, listening, searching for interesting sounds. With gentle pressure from her legs, Lenor kept them as high as possible on the slopes of the hillsides for a better view of the surrounding country.

Little had changed over the years since Lenor had left, and she was familiar with every turn, every outcropping of rock or choice herb-collecting spot, every moon-thrown shadow. She felt com-pletely at home, comfortable in her western clothes, at ease with the familiar fragrance of warm horseflesh and pine and the cool mountain air. But unease still curled inside, like a mutant tape-worm that relished her substance and her soul. Denial of the assault wouldn't work much longer.

"But how would a city boy feel right now?" Lenor bent forward and whispered. "Cold and hungry, that's how."

Lenor was already feeling the chill of the night air. Very likely, boys being boys, Thomas hadn't brought a jacket along. Unless he knew of edible mountain plants, he would have had nothing to eat. She looked at her watch and was surprised that they'd already been out for over an hour.

Was Thomas frightened? She could only guess that he was. To the uninitiated, unfamiliar surroundings could be terrifying. After her childhood in New Mexico, her first night in Manhattan had been the scariest six hours she'd ever spent on this earth, what with the crowds of people crushing past her on the sidewalks; the din of a thousand voices, car horns, sirens, street hawkers; lights that never seemed to go out, blazing at her from every direction.

Tossa stopped and pricked her ears forward.

"What is it, girl?" Lenor whispered. The horse remained motionless for a moment, moved forward a step, then stopped again. Lenor listened as hard as she could and heard nothing unusual. "What do you hear?"

Straight ahead, just on the other side of a line of trees and down the hill, Lenor knew there was a small clearing where the kids sometimes camped out under the stars. She urged Tossa forward and to the left until she could see into the open space at the bottom of the steep hillside. Nothing seemed amiss. Not one of the stones in the circle around the large campfire area was out of place. Nothing stirred.

A movement caught her attention. She could see across the top of the next low hill and past it to a road. About three miles away, Lenor could make out a lone car, its lights on low beam flashing this way and that as it took the gentle curves of 434 at a slow speed. As soon as those disappeared behind the hill, another set of headlights popped into view. They were perfectly round.

Lenor gave Tossa a pat. "Looks like those lights might belong to Roy's old hearse," she said. "Well, whoever's down there, I hope they're here to help us."

Roy stayed just far enough behind John Garcia so the sheriff wouldn't see him. He was supposed to have been searching along these back roads earlier, instead of playing poker, and he couldn't let John find out. Funny that his father hadn't insisted he leave the house before.

His hunch had paid off, though. After he'd overheard his father talking about Lenor being in Mora, Roy had quickly delivered Miller's message and followed her. He'd parked out of sight, down the Tavera driveway, then eavesdropped on the conversation in Nemesia's kitchen. It was the perfect situation, the perfect setup for giving Lenor a little taste of her own medicine.

It would be good practice, too. Until he'd stolen the *piedra imán* from Lenor, Gloria's tormented spirit had been giving him trouble, fighting for control. But now, with the power of the fury stone in his possession, he could command his mother's cursed soul at will. Getting revenge for all the suffering she'd caused him was as sweet as her intimate caresses had been—at first.

The black stone felt hot in his pocket. He was used to that now. Since the day he'd taken it, it had grown steadily warmer. Tonight, after he'd ordered Gloria's spirit to stalk Old Woosey, then inhabit the mountain lion's hungry body, the fury stone had almost glowed. Now, with the animal propelled by Gloria's viciousness, Old Woosey and Lenor were on a collision course. *Lenor!*

Roy groaned. "Noooo . . ." His body was on a collision course, too. He took one hand off the steering wheel and pushed against the growing mass of uncontrollable flesh between his legs. "Damn you, Lenor! Not now, not now!" he pleaded to the silence.

But why *not* now? Roy stopped fighting the pressure that inched upward toward his belt. Perhaps there was nothing wrong with doubling his pleasure. He was in control. His plan was in motion. A bit of revenge lurked just over the next few hilltops. Why not sit back and enjoy both? A glance at his watch told him he had plenty of time. He slowed the old hearse to barely a crawl. Why not, indeed?

Roy grinned as he pulled out his handkerchief and laid it on the seat beside him. With his free hand he unbuckled his belt, unbuttoned his fly, and, for the first time, actually welcomed the shaft of fiery flesh out into the open air. Just looking at himself, in the pale light from the dials, set his heart pounding with an overwhelming sensual pleasure.

Roy eased his weight from the seat and pushed his clothing down further. It was difficult working with one hand, but that didn't matter. Nothing but complete freedom, complete exposure, could satisfy him in this new experience. He spread his legs, slipped his hand beneath his testicles, and lifted. The lily shape of his sensitive glans slid up his tensed belly and made him shiver with delight. "See, Lenor? This beautiful phallus will be for you. Just you." He lowered his organ, then lifted and lowered again, then jiggled playfully, so that the soft spheres in his palm rolled and nudged together in gleeful intimacy. "But right now, it's just for me. See, Lenor?" He jiggled again, then squeezed until his fingers throbbed with excitement. "Are you jealous, Lenor?" he asked, as he moved his hand away from the dangling globes and closed it around his still-thickening penis.

"Maybe I'll let you touch me someday." The thought of her hand encircling him sent jolts of throbbing pleasure through the burning flesh he held. *Not yet!* His fingers clamped down tight. He wanted to delay the rapture for as long as he could. After a moment the stricture worked, and he was able to ease his grip. His mother had taught him well.

One long finger gently traced from root to tip and back. He felt proud as he traced again. "Well endowed," Gloria had told him. "Pillar of pleasure," she had called it. Why had he ever hated it? What he'd thought of as the slimy stalk was suddenly a glorious and sacred campanile. On the pornographic stage his mother had set long ago, Roy would now be a willing actor in Lenor's spotlight. "I'll let you look at me first, Lenor," he said. "Not touch! Just look. I'll tease you, like you've teased me."

First he would undress her, rip her clothing off if he had to. Then he would order her down on her knees and stand before her, legs apart, so she could see all of this lovely male weapon. *No more cowering in the corner.* "You'll beg to kiss me here," he said, mockingly, glancing down. He pinched the swollen glans and squeezed a glistening droplet of fluid from the slit. "You'll *beg* to lick me clean," he crooned. As his finger spread the viscous liquid, he could see Lenor's tongue flick out to taste. He brought the hearse to a complete stop.

Yes. He'd control Lenor completely. Though both his hands were moving up and down the length of his penis, Roy imagined them on each side of Lenor's head. Unlike Roy's mother, Lenor would probably have to be coaxed and guided. No matter. Her lips would part, her mouth would open, and she'd draw the length of him inside. She would suckle like a hungry baby at the breast, her tongue a hot propelling pump. She would whimper with desire to continue if he tried to pull himself away. She would drink . . . He was on fire!

The fury stone in his pocket burned his skin, even through

the cloth of his jeans. Breathless and trembling, he let himself go and impatiently pushed the stone away from his leg. It pulsed against his fingers. When he looked down, his erection seemed to grow before his eyes. In seconds, it was twice the size it had been. His heart thundered against his chest, engorging his penis at every beat with lava-hot blood, until his skin felt close to bursting.

Now his long fingers could barely reach around the painfully distended shaft. Now two hands couldn't contain the pulsing mass. Roy thought he was going to faint. Then he was afraid he might not faint, and wanted to—desperately. He flung one last controlling thought toward Old Woosey before the lightning struck, then let out a scream of pleasure as the geyser erupted.

Like graceful projectiles, stream after sizzling stream of molten white ecstasy burst forth in arcing trajectories. He panted and moaned and watched in horrified fascination, unable to control the course of the volcanic gushings. Fleetingly he thought of the pristine white handkerchief. Then he could think no more about anything.

When Roy could focus both mind and eyes again, he looked at his watch. He'd been "out" for five minutes. Had he been hallucinating? Had he imagined it all? Had the massive tower exploding from the root in his loins been a dream? With trembling hand he opened the glove box, pulled out a pen-size flashlight, and directed the circle of bright white light between his legs. Even at rest, his penis hung thick and long and heavy from the hairy plateau of his pubis. He cradled it in his palm. From every angle it now looked normal. But it didn't feel quite normal. As if plumbed directly to his heart, the bullish column visibly pulsed, base to cap, each jarring throb more disconcerting than the next. *Damn you, Lenor!*

Roy flashed the light around the front seat. Everywhere, there were globs and wide streaks and spreading rivulets of whitish ooze on the old brown upholstery. He looked down his dark green shirtfront. There, too, he saw plump domes, distorting now before his eyes, like melting islands of paste. Both hands on the steering wheel, Roy tried to hold on, but his whole body shook so violently that his fingers couldn't grasp tightly enough. He wanted to believe he'd imagined it, but the deluge of flooding, splattering, drenching, soaking ejaculate seemed to be *real!* As damning proof, the dank, dun-white resins clung to him like the Devil's own baptism.

It took several more minutes for the shaking to stop and his frantic breathing to slow. The lone white handkerchief, Roy knew, would not be sufficient to the task of cleaning up. *Damn you, Lenor!* He reached under the seat and brought out an old towel he kept there for wiping the windshield. Dabbing at the creamy splotches on his shirt, he whisked the towel in downward strokes. A corner of the rough terry cloth scuttled down the length of his penis and flicked the tip with a stinging little jab.

Frantically Roy plucked at the offensive bit of material but only managed to stimulate his sensitive nerve endings and tangle the towel further. *Damn you, Lenor!* He picked and grabbed and pulled and swatted, as if attacking some giant invading spider, until the clump of cloth began to rise skyward on a seething shaft. For one horrifying moment he had no control over his hands. He flung the towel aside, and his fingers wrapped themselves around the dauntless reddening probe that climbed up his belly to greet him with one widely distended eye.

Goddamn you, Lenor!

Lenor straightened up and looked around, then started to ease Tossa down the slope. "I don't know what you heard, but we'll go have a look," she said.

The camp clearing revealed nothing unusual except a change in the level of sound. Coyote Creek gurgled softly nearby in its descent toward the Mora River to the south. "You have a drink while I sit on that rock and do some thinking," Lenor said as she swung her right leg over Tossa's neck, then slid to the ground. Absently she dug in her pocket for one of the pellets of oshá root, put it in her mouth, and began to chew. If the nagging nausea and recent headache were viral or bacterial, the herb would make short work of it.

In town, the dance at the high school gym would be in full swing. Back in the bunkhouse, the campers, eleven of them, at least, would be sound asleep, exhausted from another day of riding lessons and ranch work. Here, the oshá began to do its work, and Lenor's chilled body began to warm.

She twisted the silver and turquoise ring on her right index finger, helping it to catch and reflect the moon's light, wondering at the marvel of the artist's conception of a desert sunrise. She looked up at Tossa. "If you were a young boy, where would you go for some excitement?" As soon as she'd spoken, she knew the answer. Aside from the usual precautions—being considerate of the other people's property that surrounded the Tavera ranch and staying off and away from places and things that didn't belong to them—the only caveat for the campers was the avoidance of one spot, designated as out-of-bounds for all visitors because of the wild horses it sometimes harbored. The Martino *rancho*.

"Tossa, I'm sure of it. Not many teenagers can resist at least a peek at the very thing they're forbidden to see. Thomas couldn't. He went to Michael's before. I'll bet he just waited for their search to end tonight, then went back again. Why not double the coup?" The excitement in Lenor's voice caused Tossa to lift her head from the stream and give an enthusiastic snort. "I'm glad you agree, girl. Let's go."

In spite of her mother's warning, Lenor reined the horse due north, still scanning from left to right as they moved closer and closer to their destination near the northwesternmost limit of the Tavera property. The air was getting much cooler. At about eighty-five hundred feet, Lenor put on her jacket and started chewing on another piece of oshá root. She couldn't see more than a few yards to either side of the trail; the low juniper and scrub oak of the valley had completely given way to tall pines that blocked her view and much of the light from the moon. Tossa huffed up an incline and came to a stop on a narrow dirt logging road. Lenor looked around. On a tree to one side, a sign had been nailed marking the Martino property line.

PRIVATE PROPERTY.
DO NOT LEAVE THE
ROADWAY FOR ANY REASON.
VIOLATORS WILL BE
SHOT

Someone had spray-painted through *"prosecuted"* and substituted *"shot."*

Such signs weren't uncommon in the backwoods of New Mexico. Hunters and piñon nut gathers, picnickers and tourists alike seemed to think that any uninhabited land belonged to them to do with as they saw fit. But Lenor shuddered to think about the sign's wording. *"Do not leave the roadway for any reason."* Wouldn't a simple *"No trespassing"* or *"Posted"* have done just as well? There was something ominous about this warning. Even so, she urged Tossa past the sign and back into the woods.

It seemed stranger to her than it ever had before that she knew so little of Michael Martino's life. No one at the Tavera ranch spoke of him very often. There were so many reasons she herself had never pursued the subject—she'd been so busy, he'd been so inaccessible, and most importantly, her mother had convinced her, in so many ways, that Lenor was too enterprising for entanglements.

In the shadows ahead, Lenor thought she spotted a speck of light. "Ho, Tossa. Let's take it slow and easy for a minute." A few feet more, and Lenor got off her horse and led her a little further. The light she'd seen was a spotlight attached to the front of a large barn, straight ahead and about two hundred yards from the trees. Another hundred yards to the west, at the top of a gently sloping hillock, a magnificent, two-story log home stood nestled in the tall ponderosa pine trees that seemed to extend their dark green shadows for miles into the ever-rising mountains behind the house. Two smaller buildings were partially hidden among the trees at the edge of the opposite side of the clearing a little farther to the north. Lenor looked at her watch. Just after midnight. She took one step away from the protection of the trees.

Then her nerve completely failed her. Her hands began to shake, her stomach tied itself in knots, her heart raced ahead of her thoughts, then threatened to beat in reverse. She took several steps back into the safety of the woods. "This is ridiculous!" she whispered breathlessly. "I'm acting like I'm scared to death of my own neighbor." She put her arm under Tossa's neck and gave her a squeeze. "I'm not acting."

It was the truth. The fear was absolutely real. There was danger nearby. She couldn't move into the open space of the clearing even one inch. *This is silly!* And the rationalizing began. *I'm tired and I haven't eaten much since . . .* She couldn't remember her last real meal. She'd been keeping herself going with Lucielle's nutrient-dense cookies and herbal stimulants, like red clover and oshá. *I'm feeling a little weak and this fear is just an aberration. There's no time for this nonsense!*

She leaned against Tossa for support. "If the lost boy came back here, he wouldn't be lost," she said softly. "If Thomas made his presence known, I know Michael would keep him safe, and he wouldn't keep Thomas against his will. He sent the boy back safe and sound before; he'd do it again. Michael would know Magdalena would be worried, and he couldn't possibly play such a thoughtless trick as keeping Thomas's whereabouts a secret. Don't you agree, Tossa?" But—maybe because she'd seen the No Trespassing sign—she couldn't even agree with herself. *He couldn't possibly play such a thoughtless trick?*

Of course he, or someone else here, could do such a thing! Anyone could—under the right circumstances. 'Don't go near Martino's place.'

She led Tossa back into the woods, tied her reins to a slender trunk, and began to walk around the perimeter of the clearing. Determination replaced fear. It was hard to admit, but Michael Martino might be capable of just about anything. Now she wished she'd learned more about him, at one time or another. *Who knows anyone well enough to be sure what they'll do?*

During their childhood, like most children of ranchers, they'd been distant neighbors. The occasional birthday party had brought them together, and she and her closer friends had found

Michael a tolerable playmate—when he wasn't intent on looking for odd pieces of wood to whittle or playing typical bratty-boy practical jokes. The only thing she could remember Michael ever really getting into trouble for was a sketch he'd done that allegedly sent the Mora High School principal into a rage.

According to the secondhand story, the principal had suspended him, but Michael's mother had insisted that he be expelled from school. Luckily, the principal prevailed. However, in Michael's presence, the principal had burned the drawing to a cinder in his ashtray—but not before some enterprising student had made a copy. Lenor and her friends had paid twenty-five cents to get a glimpse of the offending artwork, and she'd been shocked by it herself. But then, at twelve, she knew from her mother's teachings that teenage boys were more than a little interested in girls—especially nude ones.

Who knows him well enough to be sure of what he might do?

She was at the back side of the barn now, still in the trees; the slight breeze continued to come from the north. In just another few feet she would have to circle back to Tossa to avoid getting upwind of the horses in the corral on the other side. Her search of the area would necessarily have to be incomplete, but she'd seen nothing out of the ordinary, no lurking danger as she'd imagined before. If Thomas were anywhere nearby, he hadn't left any traces that she could find. Perhaps she'd been wrong about where a teenager would go for excitement. There was certainly no excitement around this place. Off limits or not, the only thing going on here was the usual shuffling of a few restless horses. If the boy were staying the night here, she felt he would be safe.

In spite of her fears, as far as she knew, Michael had never been a violent person.

Twelve

MICHAEL MOVED RESTLESSLY IN HIS BED. SOMEONE OR something was tugging at the corner of his quilt and wouldn't stop, no matter how tightly he held on. He looked. It was Lenor again, trying to get him out of bed. "Lenor!"

The sound of his own voice woke him, and Michael sat straight up in bed still clutching tightly to the top of the patchwork coverlet. "Damn!" Another dream about Lenor Tavera. Since all he could do was think about her, not see her, the dreams were driving him a little crazy. He reached for the bedside light and snapped it on. Neither human nor beast was in the room with him, but there was something going on outside.

"Now what?"

Reluctantly he left the warm bed, reached for the Levi's he'd draped carelessly over the back of the straight chair next to the bedside table, and crossed the room to the window. Still a little shaky from his abrupt awakening, he swayed from one foot to the other, trying to put on his pants and look outside at the same time. The saddle horses, kept in the corral north of the barn and usually quiet during the night, stirred restlessly near the fence closest to the house.

"Cougar."

Cursing under his breath, Michael half walked, half hopped back toward the bed, finally hiked his pants up around his waist, and sat down. He fished his socks out from under the chair, put them on, stood up, and jammed one foot, then the other, into his boots. Shirt, jacket, and hat he pulled from the wooden pegs at the door as he left the bedroom.

"This whole damned day has been just one aggravation after another," he griped, though he knew no one was listening. Near the front door in the hallway, he flipped on the hall and porch light, lifted a shotgun off the gun rack and a handful of shells out of the drawer below it. Dropping the cartridges into his jacket pocket, he stepped outside. The horses were still upset about something and were starting to make all kinds of racket.

"Go ahead. Might as well wake everybody up."

Restless horses! Up until that moment Lenor hadn't been aware of any particular sound. She hurried back to the other side of the barn just in time to see a light come on in a second-story room of the main house. "Damn," she said under her breath, then turned east and plunged deeper into the woods. The squaw boots she wore allowed her to move almost noiselessly, and she was barely out of sight of the barn when she stopped and turned around to take another look.

The horses were more than restless now. She could hear their shrill whinnies and loud snorts. *Please keep quiet until I get back to you, Tossa.*

The front door of Michael's house opened. Back-lit by the hall light, the dark shadow of a man filled the frame, then stepped out onto the porch. A large-bore shotgun rested in the crook of his right arm.

Michael!

And what had Lenor just told herself?

Michael has never been a violent person.

Lights were coming on in the other two houses. Eloy came out the front door of the foreman's cottage, still trying to get into his clothes. He intercepted Michael halfway down the hill. "What the hell's going on out here?"

"Search me. Could be that beat-up old mountain lion we've been seeing down around the east pasture. Least that's my guess," Michael said.

"Good a guess as any." For the first time Eloy saw the shotgun Michael was carrying. He shouted back over his shoulder. "Gil, bring me that thirty-ought-six off the wall." He looked back at

Michael. "Let's give the old boy something to think about, shall we?" He looked up at the sky. "Good night for a ride."

Michael grimaced at Eloy's eager, smiling face. *All I really want to do is go back to bed and try to get what might be left of a night's sleep.* In the past weeks he hadn't been able to get more than a couple hours' rest at a time, waking up at odd hours of the night in a state of agitation. For the last few days he'd been feeling as skittish as the horses in the corral.

Gilberto ran up beside the two men and matched their stride. "You ridin' out?" he asked as he handed Eloy one of the two rifles he was carrying.

"Gonna try to get Old Woosey," Eloy said.

" 'Bout time. That old cat's been stirrin' up trouble long enough. Want me to come along?"

"The more the merrier," Eloy said.

It was the first time since their argument about Oñique that Michael had seen Eloy happy about something at the ranch. At least one thing was back in order, Michael thought. Now if he could only get himself straightened out, everything could return to normal.

Gilberto ran on ahead, climbed the corral fence, and dropped lightly to the ground inside. "I'll cut one of these ponies and saddle up out here."

Eloy and Michael went on into the barn. As Michael saddled Penny Wise, he wondered what he'd been thinking of when he'd thought about getting back to normal. "Normal" was as far from what he really wanted as New Mexico was distant from Tokyo. And how far was that? When he tried to figure out what was going on in his head, he might as well have been trying to ride a horse across the Pacific. He'd never been so discontented or so completely disenchanted with "normal," with the way things were, since those first two years after college when he'd moved into the cabin that Eloy now called home.

He'd felt only anger back then, and the rage had kept him going, kept him busy. He'd been determined to be a success at ranching and raising quarter horses, to show his parents, once and for all, that he was a decent person who didn't need any advice or help with anything—especially his art. Eleven years of hard work, plenty of sweat, and a hefty dose of fierce dedication had gotten him recognition not only in the sphere of quarter-horse breeding, but also in the world of the western artist. He had paintings hanging in a well-known gallery in Santa Fe. His fame as a *santero* was growing. He'd built a beautiful home, a sturdy barn, a bunkhouse, and had as many as twenty-five cowboys working for him at times. And most importantly of all, he'd made regular payments to the Taveras for the five thousand acres of land his father had bought. Even in the hard years, when horse prices had plummeted, when bitter cold had killed half the spring foals, he'd managed to hang on.

No doubt about it, Michael Martino had made it.

But . . . something was still missing.

The fear returned. Lenor felt physically ill, and her stomach wouldn't settle no matter how many deep breaths she took. Almost certain that she hadn't been the cause of the horses' agitation, she had to believe that Thomas Newman was somewhere nearby. A gun, an agitated man, and a small boy hiding in a dark woods could be a deadly combination.

Willing her weak knees to hold out for just another step, Lenor reached the nearest tree and leaned against it. From her vantage point she could see the front of the house, the two cabins, and the south side of the barn.

Michael took the porch steps three at a time, hurried down the hill, and was met by Eloy Seña. The two men were talking loudly, but she couldn't make out the words. Only their agitation was loud and clear. By the time they'd reached the bottom of the slope, Gilberto Seña had joined them, carrying two rifles. He handed a gun to Eloy. They spoke for a few seconds; then Michael took off his hat and turned directly toward her.

Heart racing, Lenor wanted to duck behind the tree, but kept her head. If she remained still, the shadows would conceal her. The slightest movement or sound might get her shot. She had to take her mother's warning seriously. If she was to be of any help to Thomas, she had to stay alive.

Michael stood still for a moment, so tall, so handsome, so beautiful to look at. But something about his face had changed. In the harsh light coming from the spot on the front of the barn, she could see a hardness to the set of his mouth, a callous look in his eyes. And something else. Sadness?

The tears would not be stayed. All the feelings she'd ever felt for her first teenage puppy love came welling up in one unstoppable flood of emotion. *What might have happened if . . . ?* The question and obvious answer settled her somewhat, along with the realization that she was really crying about her grandmother's death. Lack of food and sleep was making her giddy. Determination interceded long enough to stop the trickle of tears. She started thinking rationally as she saw Michael turn and enter the barn.

There was an immediate problem with which to deal. If Thomas Newman was somewhere nearby, he wasn't safe, not with three armed men riding into the woods. She hurried west, past Tossa, then slanted north when she was well behind Michael's house. From higher up she would be able to see where the men were headed. Then she saw a flash of something moving to her right.

Thomas?

Several miles north of Guadalupita, Roy pulled onto a side road and headed up and east. The old hearse wouldn't make the top of the steep rise, but Roy wanted to drive as far as he could. Still limp and drained from his ordeal, still sore and tender, he sat gingerly tilted to one side. Every bump in the old abandoned logging road was a lesson in pain. Walking would be even worse.

He was now in constant contact with the spirit of his dead mother. Gloria cursed and damned her son for trapping her inside the body of the ravenous old mountain lion, but Roy enjoyed her agony—almost as much as he was going to enjoy Lenor's terror when they met. He realized that it would have been a lot simpler to go into trance, send his spirit out, and watch the meeting from high above the two. Not nearly so thrilling, he'd decided, as being there in person. And it might just give him the chance to be a hero—in everybody's eyes.

The hearse wheezed and slowed. Roy turned the wheel hard right, then parked. Silence surrounded him as he began the climb. At the crest, he tuned in to Lenor. She was moving west by northwest, directly toward him, but still at least a mile away.

Gloria had her orders. Old Woosey stopped heading west and turned south. The coordinates were perfect. In a short while, Lenor would be terrified.

The three men rode out quietly. Gilberto headed east to check on the cattle, and Eloy went straight north toward Black Lake, where Woosey had his lair. After telling Rosa that they were heading out again, Michael had ridden west, toward the logging camp where the old cougar had been spotted on several occasions.

Penny Wise walked easily, taking the steady climb at a leisurely pace. She stepped carefully and quietly, as if sensing the need for stealth. Michael cursed the quiet for giving him more time to think.

All I need is a good horse, a little piece of land, a good goddamned leavin' alone, and I'll be happy for the rest of my life.

That was what he used to think. At nineteen, Michael had been positive about the validity of his philosophy. At thirty-three, it had still been true. Now, at thirty-four, he wasn't sure about anything anymore. Hell, he couldn't even get excited about Christine coming back from Europe in August. His latest girlfriend had been gone for two months, and he hoped now that she decided to stay gone for good. He didn't care if he never saw her again.

Thoughts of Lenor occupied his mind, clouded his thinking. Perhaps illusion would be enough until the infatuation had passed. Such fancies always had before.

Michael shifted in the saddle and let out a long breath of air. In the success columns, totals were way beyond his original expectations. No one, not even his dead father, could call him a failure at anything he'd set his hand and mind to.

That was it, of course. There was no one to appreciate or denounce any of his feats or provoke him to commit further acts of heroic retribution. A sad state of affairs. He'd set himself up for certain failure this time. When dreams ceased to be enough, what would he do? What could he do?

All I need is a good goddamned leavin' alone.

Thirteen

THOMAS COULD FEEL HOT TEARS LURKING BEHIND HIS tired eyes. He'd have liked nothing more than to stop, sit down, and have a good cry. *Boys don't cry!* And he couldn't stop. *La Llorona,* the murderous ghost Apple Hardy had told all the kids about at the party, was still following him.

What a stupid thing I've done, he thought, as he tried to keep up a jogging pace, weaving among the pines. The off-limits Whirlwind Ranch had been too much of a temptation—he'd had to see El Rancho de Torbellino again and explore more thoroughly. Since his short visit before, he could imagine only one *real* reason why the Tavera campers were forbidden to set foot on the place—it had to be a guerrilla camp, where outlaw soldiers trained with deadly automatic weapons for secret foreign wars. Last week he'd seen none of that.

To say he'd been disappointed tonight, after his second look around, to find just another ranch in a country full of ranches, would have been an understatement. Last week, the thrills that had followed his uninvited entry into the corral with the enormous black stallion, Oñique, had been just about as much excitement as one boy could stand.

Now his stupidity was complete. On his first visit the people had been nice to him, hadn't punished him in any way. *They probably should have.* They'd given him milk and cookies, asked him a few questions. Then the strange, but halfway nice, Roy Baldwin had driven him back to the Tavera camp in a real hearse.

Thomas had fully intended to follow the camp rules from then on. But this evening had been so warm. In his selective memory, Oñique had been beautiful and exciting. He'd had to go back and get one more look. On the way, one distraction had led to another. Every unfamiliar draw had to be explored. Every tree with accommodating limbs had to be climbed. Every new vista from the top of every hill had to be surveyed. Time seemed limitless until he'd finally reached the Whirlwind and realized how late it was. The cow ponies had already been put up in the corral, and Oñique was nowhere in sight.

Thomas's third mistake had been to think he could wait until everyone had gone to bed and then sneak into the barn and see Oñique. His fantasy had been grand: he'd saddle the mighty stallion, ride out into the night, and discover gold in the Sangre de Cristo Mountains. Then he'd parade back through the tiny town of Mora as the conquering hero, a very rich and famous conquistador of the modern world.

His father had warned him about grand fantasies. *Not often enough!*

All he'd accomplished was a quick glimpse of the horse through a crack between boards in the back of the building—then he'd had to run for his life when someone had come into the barn.

Thomas stopped jogging. He was so short of breath he didn't think a full day in bed could revive him. He'd never been so tired—or so frightened. Through the hiss of panting breaths, he tried to listen. A new sound had been added to the night, faint, impossible to make out, but it sounded like voices. *Hallelujah!* His heartbeat started to slow.

Then the voices stopped, a twig cracked nearby, and his heart began racing again before his feet could get moving. There was no doubt in his mind about the existence of *La Llorona,* the weeping woman who had drowned her babies and now roamed the earth looking for children to take their place.

I'm a goner!

Damn! Roy stopped and listened. Too much commotion for one lone woman and an old mountain lion. Sounded like there were more than two players on his sporting field. *What the hell is going on up here?*

He hurried forward as quietly as he could. The lion and Lenor were getting closer and closer. In just a few minutes, they would be face to face.

Damn it, Lenor! Keep moving!

Lenor almost called out to the moving figure, but stopped herself before she made any sound. She didn't want to frighten him, nor did she want to alert him or the three men to her presence. It would be better to follow, then approach in a way that wouldn't make him run from her. Keeping behind the trees as best she could, Lenor moved west again, then turned northwest, every few feet catching glimpses of what seemed to be a human form, dressed in something white or light-colored, moving ahead of her.

They'd been traveling almost due west for several minutes when Lenor heard the unmistakable sound of a horse's hooves on bare ground not too far north of where she stood. After diverting her eyes to her right just long enough to be sure the animal wasn't within eyesight, Lenor realized she'd lost her quarry. Nothing moved in that direction. She hoped the sound of the horse had startled the boy, as well, and had caused him to hide until the danger of being seen had passed. She tensed, praying that the next sound she heard *wouldn't* be gunfire.

Silently, cautiously, Lenor moved forward a few steps at a time. It was getting more and more difficult to see; almost all the light from the moon was blocked by foliage. Her eyes strained against the darkness. One more step . . . one more . . . and she was falling. It took all her will to keep from crying out when her ankle struck a large rock at the bottom of the pine-needle-slick incline.

Heaped in the bottom of a shallow ravine, Lenor kept perfectly still for a moment, mentally checking every part of her body for serious injury. A minor scrape here, a little scratch there, nothing really serious. Carefully she began to move, bending her knees and elbows, flexing her wrists, circling one ankle and then the other. She raised her body to a sitting position. No bones were broken, no muscles were sprained, but her left ankle was badly bruised.

As she tried to stand, she caught the flash of light again. It seemed to be on the same ground level as she was, in the arroyo, and several feet to her right. Her first step was a lesson in pain management; her ankle fairly screamed for relief from the weight she put on it. *Get a move on!*

To get a better view of the shallow arroyo and remain concealed, Lenor climbed back up the slippery bank and started north behind the cover of the trees. Within just a few yards she stopped short. In the middle of the ravine, the person she'd been following was now partially in view. Lenor could see the profile of the woman's face, her lovely features and long, dark hair, over the top of a small pine. Lenor couldn't believe her eyes. It was Juanita Chavez.

Lenor crept close enough to see around the obscuring tree, then caught her breath. Except for a pair of soft leather moccasins, Juanita was completely nude.

No excitement here? Lenor pulled back behind the branches and instantly revised her opinion of Michael's place. People roused in the middle of the night, men with guns, a nude woman prancing through the forest in the wee hours of the morning. Off limits, indeed!

What the devil was going on here? Devil? An odd choice of word under the circumstances, but it brought memories of tales told long ago. Bits and pieces of stories about witches rushed back into Lenor's mind. Witches traveling as sparks of fire, witches meeting in the deepest recesses of the forest, witches dancing naked in the light of the full moon. The only thing missing was the goat.

When she peeked around the branches again, Juanita was dancing! No, not dancing in any real sense of the word, Lenor decided, simply moving slowly around an invisible circle and humming softly to herself. *Am I imagining all this?* Transfixed, Lenor watched the surrealistic scene before her. Slender as a young child, but with the flaring curve of hip and breast of a woman, Juanita moved with the grace of a ballerina. She seemed oblivious to the chill in the air, and a light sheen of perspiration glistened on her smooth skin.

Lenor shivered. Perspiration? Impossible. The detective in her began searching for answers, but only for a few seconds. *Footsteps!* In the distance behind her, someone was walking in heavy boots. Was someone coming to join the beautiful Juanita? Michael perhaps?

The sounds were getting nearer. *Get out of here!* Keeping as low to the ground as possible, Lenor limped away from the arroyo and headed south and east again. *Wait for me, Tossa.* When she was several yards from her hiding place, she straightened, then attempted to run. Her injured ankle would not allow it, and she had to walk. If she could get just a little further south, she could turn east and head straight for Tossa. Her ankle throbbed. *Just a little further.* The altitude, the injury, and her weakened condition had her breathing in short gasps. *Just a little bit . . .*

Something clutched at her shoulder. A gloved hand closed over her mouth. In seconds, Lenor was in the grasp of two strong arms, held tightly against the hard body behind her.

Madre mía!

A damn good leavin' alone? Truth be told, Michael was seldom left alone, but the attention he got, he could do without. There was always something. Eloy, Gilberto, Rosa, Juanita, and now this old reprobate mountain cat who'd already signed the death certificate on a fine colt this year.

Juanita? Michael thought back. When he'd left the yard,

Juanita's bedroom light had not been on. Strange. Everyone else had been awakened by the hubbub. Maybe she was just too tired to get up and see what was going on. She'd been looking a bit pale around the edges lately. Terrific. That was all he needed, a sick housekeeper.

Gotta stop worrying and start paying attention. It was time to put the old cat out of his misery; it was too young to die, too old to fend for itself except to kill what couldn't run away. Michael's neighbors had been losing animals too, sheep, goats, chickens. They'd all be glad to hear about Woosey's demise.

"Don't scream. I won't hurt you."

Lenor struggled against her captor's tight hold, but to no avail.

"If you'll calm down and promise to keep quiet, I'll let you go."

Ironic. Years in New York, and she'd never been mugged. A few hours in the backwoods of New Mexico and . . . Lenor nodded her answer.

"Good." He let her go.

"John!" she whispered. At this close range she could see the streaks of gray hair at his temples and identify Sheriff Garcia. Lenor shook her head in disbelief. "Where did you come from?"

"Out of the night." He slashed an imaginary *Z* in the air.

"Still playing at Zorro, I see." Lenor frowned. "Was that you I saw on the road from Mora?"

He nodded.

"How did you find me?"

"Lucky, I guess. Just wandering around looking for Thomas." He shrugged. "Your mother was worried. She'll be glad I did."

Lenor turned and started walking again. Sheriff Garcia followed. "Any word about the boy yet?" Lenor asked.

"No. But I'm sure he'll turn up."

"Oh, really?" She was sure he wasn't as confident as he sounded.

"Kids get a kick out of this sort of prank. We'll probably find him in his bunk, under the covers, when the breakfast bell sounds."

Lenor looked at her watch, then glanced back over her shoulder. "He'll have to be there pretty soon if he wants to make breakfast."

"My car's just over the hill. Shall we go see if I'm right?"

Lenor shook her head. "Thanks, but I want to keep looking for Thomas. Tossa's close by and—"

John interrupted. "Let's just send Tossa home. She'll be glad to head back to her morning feed, and you look too tired to ride. Besides, it isn't safe to be out here right now." John put his hand on Lenor's shoulder. She stopped walking and looked at him. "I'm sorry about giving you that little scare back there. I couldn't let you make any noise."

"Oh? Why was that?"

He gestured in the direction of Michael's house as they started walking again. "You might have seen them. Michael and his boys rode out looking for a mountain lion. Woosey is getting vicious in his old age, and I didn't want you to attract him or scare him away—or get shot doing either one."

"Thanks, John." But the explanation didn't sit quite right with her. His tone of voice didn't match with telling the truth. It was a puzzle. On an intellectual level, his explanation was plausible. On a gut level, Lenor felt Sheriff Garcia had a specific reason to come looking for her. But what? Would her mother really have sent him? Magdalena had been so agitated . . .

"I don't think you should go near Michael's place again," John said. "He hasn't been the friendliest neighbor over the years, and you don't want to worry your mother."

"Enough said."

John stopped, looked at her as if he were seeing her for the first time. "You're limping."

Lenor started to tell him why, then realized . . . *He didn't see me fall!* "I had a little accident earlier," she said.

He put his hand under her elbow for support. "Let me help you."

The puzzle was getting more and more complicated by the minute. Had the sheriff really been looking for Thomas? Could he have been going to see Juanita and found Lenor instead? Might their meeting have been purely chance, as he'd said, and not deliberate, as Lenor had suspected? If he'd been following her, he could hardly have missed her graceless plunge into the arroyo. If he'd been watching her after the fall, he surely would have noticed that she was limping. What odd piece of this intriguing puzzle would show up next?

Even before it happened, Roy knew he was losing his chance to terrorize Lenor. The last few steps to his observation point near the prescribed meeting place had taken all the strength he had left. He leaned heavily against a tree and cursed the night, damned the interfering busybodies, and railed at the excruciating pain between his legs.

His sexual interlude should have been a sacrament. Instead of a communion with pure rapture, Roy had borne witness to the monumental power of the *piedra imán*. He'd known the fury stone's potential, but never imagined the extent of its force. Frightening! But ultimately exciting. The meeting between Lenor and the lion paled in comparison to the new plan he had in store. He had the perfect weapon now. No woman could possibly accommodate his enormous phallus.

The confined mass of tender tissue and hot blood pulsed steadily in his crotch. He could disregard the aftermath of pain. Ecstasy had so far outweighed discomfort that the power of pleasure had quickly and easily corrupted him. He cupped his hand over his throbbing genitals and smiled. He was hungry to try it again.

The moon was bright, but its light wasn't helping much. In another hour or so, the sun would shine on another day. Another routine day. At least then, with a little more light, he'd feel more comfortable about shooting at something. Damned Eloy, always ready for a chase and a fight, no matter what time of day or night. Damned cat, disturbing a man's sleep. Damned—

Woosey! Penny Wise stopped instantly from a feather-light tug on the reins. The cougar crouched at the edge of a gully, upwind, about fifty yards ahead, his scraggly-thin body poised for a leap across the narrow ditch.

Michael clenched his jaw against a sudden impulse to shout a warning to the aging lion, give the decrepit fellow a few beautiful summer days to enjoy. It was a curse to be old and slow and trying to survive in this unforgiving corner of the world. But a quick death would be more humane than the long-term ordeal of starvation. *Get it over with, you softheaded fool.*

Out of the saddle, Michael moved as quietly as he could over the dry ground cover of fallen pine needles. With the slight crunch of each step coming closer and closer, the animal should have been off like a shot out of a cannon, but he didn't move. *Has the cat gone deaf, too?* Approaching from the animal's left side, Michael got as close as he dared, raised the shotgun, and squeezed off the perfect shot.

Old Woosey cartwheeled into the ditch, accompanied by a bloodcurdling scream. *A human scream!*

Lenor reached for the handle of the car door.

Boom!

The sound of a gunshot echoed through the mountains. Lenor let go of the handle as if it were a piece of red-hot iron. "What was that?"

John Garcia frowned. "Guess they finally put Old Woosey out of his misery."

Fourteen

"WHAT THE HELL?"

In one beat of his heart, Michael dropped the shotgun, leapt into the gully, and found himself looking straight down into the bloody face of a young boy. Thomas Newman. *My God, what have I done?* For an instant Michael thought his knees were going to give out on him; then a measure of good sense returned. A quick check of the cougar assured him that the cat no longer posed any kind of threat.

"Don't move, son. For God's sake, don't move." Thomas didn't stir. Eyes open, he seemed to be conscious, but dazed to the point of no response. Michael knelt down and frantically examined the boy's body from one end to the other. Feet okay. Legs okay. Hands okay. There was blood everywhere, and in the dim light, Michael was sure that Thomas must be near death's door. *Get ahold of yourself, man.* From the angle he'd fired, the kid couldn't have taken more that a few pieces of shot. On the other hand, one sphere of lead in the right place could kill. Michael's hands were shaking so badly he couldn't unbutton the boy's shirt. He ripped it off.

"Hang in there, son. I'll have you out of here in just a little bit." Not a scratch on the boy's chest. Michael breathed a sigh of relief, pressed his ear against the smooth white skin, and gave a prayer of thanks that the racing heartbeat was strong and even. *Where's all the blood coming from?* A small hole in Thomas's right shoulder gave Michael a partial answer. The rest of the red deluge poured from a gash in the boy's head. On closer inspection, the wound looked superficial. He couldn't be sure that his hasty examination was complete, but Thomas was beginning to come around. Still kneeling, Michael gently raised the limp young body to a sitting position, supported the weight against his chest, and pressed his handkerchief over the head wound.

"Can you hear me, son?" Michael asked softly. Thomas groaned in response. "Where does it hurt?"

"Nowhere," Thomas said, his voice barely audible. Then he lifted his hands and took a look. They were spattered with blood. He began to shake.

"Take it easy, now. You're going to be just fine." Michael peeked under the handkerchief and flinched. Nothing more bloody than a grazed scalp. He pressed the cloth back into place and hugged the boy a little tighter. "I'm going to carry you out of here in just a minute. Do you understand what I'm saying?"

"Yeah," Thomas breathed.

"If you could hold this bandage in place, we could start riding back right now."

Thomas made a feeble effort to raise his hand, then let it drop uselessly by his side. "Yeah," he said again.

Michael reached for the torn shirt and, with one hand, twisted it as best he could. "Thomas? Bear with me, son, just a minute longer. I'm going to tie this around your head." When he'd finished with the wrapping and tying, he lifted Thomas off the ground.

The boy went limp in his arms as Michael carried him out of the gully, and didn't seem to mind when Michael jostled him as he picked up the shotgun. The ride back was going to be difficult if Thomas couldn't keep his balance in the saddle. Thank goodness he didn't weigh all that much, Michael thought, as he managed to pull himself up behind the saddle with the boy tucked under his left arm. Penny Wise stood perfectly still while Michael lifted Thomas, then lowered him to a sitting position in the saddle. Wrapped in Michael's denim jacket and held snugly against Michael's chest, Thomas relaxed completely as Penny Wise started down the hill.

Please let him be all right!

As soon as Penny Wise had disappeared from sight, Roy shut his eyes and slumped back against the tree. He could feel his heart beat in every cell of his body. When he'd first heard the sounds of the horse, Roy had moved closer so he could intercept Thomas before Old Woosey did. He might have been able to play the hero, too, but Thomas had disappeared, tumbling into the dry ravine.

Roy took out his handkerchief and mopped at his forehead and neck. The chill of the mountain night wasn't helping to cool him down. He knew he should have gone to Thomas and taken care of whatever injuries he'd gotten from the fall. It would have served his purpose even better if the boy trusted him right away. He would have taken Thomas safely home and humbly accepted words of praise. But then Old Woosey had to show up. That was when the profuse sweating had started. When Michael rode up, Roy lost what little composure he had left. He was still shaking uncontrollably.

But the spirits had been on his side. No one knew what he was up to. Magdalena was playing right into his hands by asking Lenor to come home. So far, a brilliant scheme and luck had brought him through the first step in his plan, if not the second. Steven Tavera wasn't dead, but Jovita was. They would all gather for Grandma's funeral. Steven and Rafael would be next. Magdalena had already proved to be an easy target. He hadn't planned on the complications of either George or Michael. *But as soon as George decides to use the honey, he'll be out of the way!* If Michael had to be dealt with, too, so be it.

Roy and Lenor would be married. Then he'd instigate the perfect accident and, finally, be the proud owner of the land that was rightfully his.

But not before he'd introduced his bride to the exquisite torture of intercourse with a beast.

Fifteen

"I TOLD YOU THAT KID WAS TROUBLE. KNEW IT FROM the first time I laid eyes on him."

"He's not a bad boy, Lucielle," Magdalena said.

"I know he's not bad, Mizz T, but he's curious. And he's smart. Dynamite combination, curious and smart." Lucielle turned away from the waist-high countertop that divided the bunkhouse kitchen from the dining area and started stacking dirty dishes into the stainless steel sink full of sudsy water. "My guess is, Thomas Newman won't be found until he wants to be, no matter how many people are looking for him," she continued. "He'll walk in here when he gets good and ready, and he'll be just fine."

Never one to mince words or stand on ceremony, Lucielle liked to get right to the point. After twenty years of having her as a cook, Magdalena was used to her bluntness, and usually enjoyed it. Magdalena continued wiping the long wooden table where eleven of the twelve campers had just finished eating their breakfast. They'd talked nonstop about Thomas Newman's disappearance. "Maybe you're right, Lucielle, but your opinion doesn't make me feel any better."

Lucielle turned from the sink with an apologetic look on her face. "This has got to be really hard on you, what with Jovita's death and you not feeling all that good anyway. I could just kick that Thomas's butt if I could get my hands on him."

"Don't be too hard on him, Lucielle. These kids are of an age when an old person's death doesn't seem like much of an event if it isn't one of their own family."

"Maybe. But . . ."

The door on the opposite side of the room opened, and Lenor and Dr. Watson stepped inside. "Grandpa's going to stay up at

Angelina's today, but he said to let him know if you need any help with the cooking."

"Cooking's the last thing Steven needs to think about on the day before his wife's funeral," Lucielle said.

"I was surprised. He looked a little better when I saw him this morning," Magdalena said.

"He still hasn't gotten out of bed. I'm worried about him," Lenor said. "And about you, too, Mama. You should have taken my advice and gotten some rest last night."

"Look who's dealing out the prescriptions," Lucielle said. "You look like warmed-over death yourself, Lenor. Don't they feed you back there in New York?"

"You do look awfully thin, dear," Magdalena said.

Maybe it's the guilt trip you put me on. "All I needed was a shower and clean clothes. I got both. I'm fine. We were talking about you, Mama."

"How are the kids doing?" Magdalena asked, directing the conversation away from herself.

"Everyone's busy with their horses," Lenor said as she walked across the room to the dividing bar. "Even though he's the youngest one of the group, Thomas Newman is turning into some kind of hero."

"God, don't tell me that. We'll have kids taking off every day if that's the way they feel," Magdalena said.

"Everybody wants to ride out and join in the search as soon as they can get their horses saddled," Lenor said. "Manny told them no, and they're not a happy bunch right now."

Lucielle lifted a long-handled spoon from the soapy water, tried shooing Watson off the counter with a wide, unsuccessful swipe, then pointed it at Magdalena. "I say let them look. Maybe they'll find him in the bottom of an arroyo with a broken leg. That'll change their minds about taking off themselves. I guarantee."

Magdalena frowned. "I thought you said Thomas would be fine."

Lucielle shrugged. "Just a thought."

"Maybe she's right, Mama. If Manny thinks he can keep track of them, the ride might keep them occupied and out of trouble for a while. I could go with him."

"After the scare you gave me last night?" Magdalena crossed to the counter and sat down on the stool next to Lenor. "That horse of yours comes galloping in here at dawn without a rider, and John doesn't bother to let me know he's bringing you home, and with an injured ankle to boot. I'm sitting here worried sick."

"I thought you might have sent the sheriff out to find me," Lenor said.

Magdalena shook her head. "I probably should have. It would have kept me from jittering around that empty house all night." She shook her head again. "Just forget about riding out this morning, young lady. Besides, you don't look up to another ride."

"But I could help Manny keep track of the kids."

"If I decide they can go, Jerry can go along to help."

"I think Lenor's right," Lucielle said. "Let 'em go. Keep those kids busy for a while. Give all those people out there some time to have a good look around, with a little extra help thrown in for good measure. Meantime, we can get some cooking done."

Lenor nodded agreement. Rudolfo and Rafael had started calling again just after five o'clock this morning and had managed to enlist the help of almost all their neighbors on both sides of Coyote Creek. If the boy were anywhere in the area, he'd be found.

Magdalena looked from Lenor to Lucielle, thought a moment, then looked back at Lenor. "Tell Manny it's okay. If they still want to go, tell him to get Jerry to ride with him. One hour out, one hour back, no more."

"I'll tell him," Lenor said and stood up. "How about another cup of coffee when I get back?"

"I'll make fresh," Lucielle said.

The two bunkhouses sat at an angle south and west of the main house. The one with the kitchen in the middle, which was used for the campers in the summer, was closest to the barn and corral. After the spring roundup, only Jerry and Manny lived in the other one. Lenor circled behind the barn to the corral, where the campers were tending to their individual horses. She put one foot on the bottom rail and pulled herself up so she could look down into the enclosure. "Manny, may I talk to you for a minute?"

Manny looked up from the horse's hoof he was inspecting. "Sure thing, ma'am." He let go of the hind leg, straightened his pencil-thin frame, and casually weaved his way past several other horses.

When Lenor told him about her mother's decision, he looked a bit skeptical for a moment, then brightened. "Now that's really not such a bad idea after all," he said, smiling.

Lenor was puzzled. "I thought you were against it."

Manny pushed his crusty, wide-brimmed hat back with a long slim finger. "I was, but I just thought it through." He winked. "Jerry and I won't have to teach these kids how to load a horse into a horse trailer today."

"Good point," Lenor said. She knew what he was talking about. No matter how well-trained horses might be, they could get downright cantankerous when confronted with the yawning maw of a rattling contraption like a horse trailer.

"Thanks, ma'am." He got a little closer to the fence, jerked a thumb toward the kids, and whispered. "Don't tell *them,* but we can ride fence while we're at it. Get two things done at once, if you get my drift."

"Understand." Since Magdalena had started the camp, one of the hardest things for the cowboys to do was to get the summer chores done and still take good care of the campers. Fixing fences was just one of the jobs Jerry and Manny tried to keep up with by using the various groups of teens, with their dubious skills, as extra ranch hands. The kids were sometimes a lot more hindrance than help.

Lenor smiled at him. "You and your cowpokes have a good morning, Manny."

"Thanks, ma'am."

Lucielle's strong black coffee was the perfect tonic after the mere two hours of sleep she'd gotten. Although a few more hours' sleep would have done Lenor more good, she decided it would have to wait as long as she was needed.

"I'm gonna go make a bunk check," Lucielle said, reaching for the doorknob. "Who knows, maybe that little stinker has snuck back and wants to lie low for a while."

"Good idea, Lucielle. Mother? Can we have a little talk while she's gone?"

"Of course, dear. What about?"

They sat down together at the long table, and now that the opportunity was at hand, Lenor didn't quite know how to start. "Mama, I know you're not feeling very well, and I don't mean for this to upset you, but I feel like I have to ask. Do you have any idea why John Garcia might have been following me last night?"

"He was following you?" Magdalena asked.

"I think he was. He sort of implied you'd asked him to."

"I left Nemesia's house right after you did." Magdalena twisted in her chair so she could face Lenor. "I told him I'd see him later. That's all."

"Is there some kind of trouble between Michael Martino and the Mora sheriff?" Lenor asked.

Magdalena shook her head. "Not that I can think of. Just like ours, part of Michael's property is in Mora County, but I've never heard of any problems between the two men." She thought a moment. "I guess Gilberto raises Cain in town now and then. Why do you ask?"

Lenor told her what John had said about Michael's house not being a safe place.

"I warned you against going there last night because I felt you'd be in danger. But I can't imagine why John would say such a thing."

"Neither can I," Lenor said. "I know Gil's been in a few Saturday-night scrapes, some heavy drinking, a fistfight or two.

But nothing serious. He didn't have anything to do with your premonition, did he?"

"No, not Gil, not a person. Whatever it was is gone now. But maybe something funny *is* going on up there," Magdalena said thoughtfully.

"Why do you say that?"

"Michael came to Steven's birthday party," Magdalena said. "I'd call that pretty strange."

A swift debate, then Lenor decided not to tell her mother about the *bulto* and why Michael had decided to come to the party. There was no need to add to Magdalena's already heavy burden.

"If I'm remembering right, Michael hasn't set foot in our home since just before his mother died," Magdalena went on.

Lenor remembered the time well. She and Apple had just gotten off the school bus and were walking up the long driveway to the house. Michael had driven right by the two high school freshmen without even acknowledging their presence, and they'd been crushed by his rebuff. "He came for some herbs for his mother, didn't he?" Lenor asked.

"Against my advice, Celsa refused to see a doctor. Poor woman. I think Miller might have been able to save her if she'd trusted him, but Celsa insisted that Miller had killed her husband," Magdalena said.

"What was wrong with her?"

"Parathyroid deficiency. Eloy finally called Dr. Baldwin in because of the convulsions, but she died that same day."

"You're right. Miller could have cured her," Lenor said. "Poor Michael. Losing his father just two years before, he must have been devastated."

"I'm just sorry I didn't know Celsa better," Magdalena said. "If we'd been good friends, I might have been able to talk her into seeing Miller before it was too late."

"You did everything you could, Mama. The Martinos were always a very private family. There was nothing you could do about that."

"Perhaps . . ."

"No sign of him," Lucielle said as she pushed through the bunkhouse door.

"Oh, that's too bad. I was hoping . . ." Magdalena's voice trailed off and she stood up. "Guess we'd better get busy."

Lenor stood also and reached for a large bowl and a pair of kitchen scissors in the center of the table. "What will you want from the garden, Lucielle?"

Lucielle gave her an up-and-down appraisal. "Hadn't both of you better get a little rest first?" she asked.

"Mama, you really should try to sleep for a little while."

"Too much to do," Magdalena said.

Lucielle shrugged and gave Lenor an I-do-my-best look. "Tomatoes, jalapeños, green onions. And trim some of the larger leaves off the chard."

"You've got it." Watson hurried out the door in front of her. The garden, with its soft, well-tilled earth, was one of his favorite places. "Happy cat," Lenor said. The big green bowl and scissors were a sure sign that he wouldn't get chased out of the broccoli patch. Head down, deep in thought, Lenor kicked a small rock and watched as Watson pursued it just ahead of her. She caught up to it, kicked it again, watched it roll, stop—against the hoof of a horse.

Lenor looked up. Towering above her, Michael Martino sat atop a huge roan mare. A bleeding boy, wrapped round with a denim jacket ten sizes too big for him, was held tightly in Michael's arms.

"Thomas!"

The boys eyes fluttered open. "Call me Tom," he said weakly.

Lenor's shout brought Lucielle and Magdalena running out of the bunkhouse.

"Madre mía!" Magdalena crossed herself.

"Let me have him," Lenor said in her most demanding voice.

Without taking his eyes off her, Michael lifted Thomas's right leg over the saddle horn, then lowered him gently into Lenor's waiting arms. He dismounted quickly, took the boy, and followed her.

When they reached the door to her bedroom, Lenor started giving orders. "Michael, put Thomas on my bed. Lucielle, get some towels from the bathroom. Mama, bring that black bag over here." Michael laid the boy on the bed, stepped out of the way, and Lenor gently removed the makeshift bandage from his head. "Not too bad," she said softly, then lovingly touched Thomas's cheek. "Can you hear me, son? Do you hurt anywhere?"

"My shoulder. When I do this." He tried to lift his right arm and winced in pain.

"Try not to move anymore, Thomas. I'm a doctor. You're going to be just fine now." She untied the silk scarf around her neck and pressed the soft material into Thomas's hand. He immediately began to rub the silken cloth between his fingers. "I want you to relax, think pleasant thoughts," she said, pleased with his quick response to the diversion. While she continued her examination, she began to chant in a low, lilting voice.

> Set sail, set sail,
> Follow the twilight to the West,
> Where you may rest, where you may rest.
> Set sail, set sail,
> Turn your face where the sun grows dim,
> Beyond the rim, beyond the rim.

Magdalena nodded her approval of Lenor's approach, and took up the chant where Lenor left off.

The head wound, still seeping blood, would have to be stitched, but that, and the minor scrapes and scratches, would keep until she'd finished the rest of her examination. Magdalena put the black bag on the bed, then lifted Thomas's head and slipped a clean white towel beneath it. Lucielle went back into the bathroom, returned with damp washcloths, and began cleaning the area around the head wound. Lenor couldn't have asked for a better team in an emergency situation.

And she'd certainly worked enough hours in an emergency room to know a gunshot wound when she saw one. Entry, right shoulder, two centimeters below the right clavicle. Exit? Lenor gently lifted his shoulder. No exit wound! The sheriff's words came back to her in a flash. "The boys rode out looking for a mountain lion."

"Who shot this child?"

From across the room a low, male voice answered, "I did."

Lenor looked in the direction of the voice. Michael Martino had shot this young, helpless boy. She felt as if her heart were going to drop into her boots; then anger took over. "Shotgun?" she asked curtly.

"Yes."

"Load?"

"Double-ought buckshot."

"Thank you." Michael registered the dismissal in her voice.

"We'll have you fixed up good as new in no time," Lenor whispered reassuringly to Thomas.

Michael breathed a long sigh of relief. Thomas was going to be all right.

"Close your eyes . . . rest . . . relax."

Thomas nodded slightly, then obediently closed his eyes.

Dismissed or not, Michael couldn't move from his position in the open doorway. In addition to the stress of the accident and its aftermath, seeing Lenor was taking a devastating toll on his energies, both psychic and physical. He had fully intended to turn Thomas over to Magdalena, explain what had happened, make sure the boy was not critically injured, and leave with all possible haste. Later he would deal with his own feelings. Now, leaving was impossible.

He watched as Lenor worked, and began to feel an unaccustomed pride in another human being's accomplishments. She knelt on one knee beside the bed, and every move she made was a study in skill and economy of motion.

"I can feel the lead here," she said. "I'll have to go in through his back to get it. Lucielle, can you hold him in position while I work?"

"You got it." Lucielle moved to the other side of the bed, smiled at Thomas, then made him as comfortable as possible lying on his left side.

"You're going to feel a little needle stick in back of your shoulder here, Thomas. Try not to move. Okay?"

Michael couldn't take his eyes off Lenor. She was as beautiful as ever, just as he'd painted her. Her black hair was pulled sharply back from her face and caught up off her slender neck with a long comb-clip. The blue denim shirt and jeans that would do nothing for an ordinary figure sculpted womanly curves that made his mind reel.

He gripped the sides of the door until his knuckles screamed for relief from the brute force. *Leave this place, you idiot.* But he didn't. He couldn't. All he could do was watch.

It was as if the three women had been working together for years. Each of their movements seemed to be harmonized to take advantage of time, place, and circumstance. Thomas neither moved nor cried out, and Michael wanted to go to him, take his hand, and tell him what a brave boy he was being. He took one step into the room. Lenor's eyes flashed in his direction. Michael froze. In that split second she'd told him volumes. *Do not interfere. Do not get in the way. You've done quite enough.*

Michael looked down at the floor and thought about shooing away the huge black and white cat that was rubbing against his leg. Watson followed as Michael took one step back with every intention of leaving. Then came the clink of metal against glass. On the bedside table, a bloody double-ought lead sphere sat in the bottom of the tumbler Magdalena had brought from the bathroom.

"Lucky kid. Good place to get it—if you have to get shot," Lenor said.

Magdalena nodded agreement.

"Good job," Lucielle said. "Lot better'n I coulda done with a kitchen knife."

Lenor leaned away from the bed, stretched tired muscles. "You've done this before, Lucielle?" she asked.

"A few times. Long time ago." She smiled. "Had a rowdy old man. Know what I mean?"

"You are a marvel, Lucielle," Lenor said.

The marvel was that he was still here, Michael thought. He was in the same room with the woman who had haunted his dreams and his waking hours. If he hadn't been so worried about the boy, so anxious to see if he would be all right, he never would have dared to allow himself such a dangerous luxury. His was an impossible dream. The boy was fine. Michael still didn't move.

Obsessive behavior. Like the cat who still rubbed against his legs. Michael picked him up and absently started stroking the animal's head. He'd heard about obsessive behavior, wondered, worried, agonized about it. If he believed in such things, he'd say he'd been cursed by a witch. But he didn't believe in such things, though lately he was beginning to wonder. His dreams were getting stranger every night—but those were just dreams. This waking furor was something else. He hadn't been able to admit it seventeen years ago, but now . . . He couldn't pretend or lie to himself any longer. *I should leave.*

Yet he stayed, until Lenor finally stood up, removed her surgical gloves, and looked directly at him. Her expression was severe. Michael cringed inside. Her face changed to register something like surprise when she saw the cat resting comfortably in the crook of his left arm.

"Eee."

The expression on Lenor's face lasted only a split second, but somehow Michael knew he'd been spared a harsh lecture. It was as if the cat had spoken to her, telling her something important.

"Let's move Thomas into the next room," Lenor said. "I can open both bathroom doors and keep an eye on him for a while."

Michael hesitated only a second. Without giving him a direct order, Lenor had implied that he was to carry the boy. He crossed to the bed, put Watson down, and scooped Thomas's thin body into his arms.

"Old Woosey?" Thomas whispered softly.

"Yes. I'm sure you'll feel a little dizzy for a while," Lenor said to the boy.

Thomas shook his head, then looked up into Michael's black eyes. "Old Woosey?" he asked again, this time more plainly.

Michael rejoiced. The boy had heard him talking, heard everything he'd said on the long, tortuous ride down the mountain, and the one-sided conversation had kept him from lapsing into complete unconsciousness. He smiled at the child in his arms. "We got him, son. He can't hurt anybody ever again. I promise," he said, then turned and followed Lucielle through the bathroom into the adjacent bedroom.

Magdalena shook her head and sighed. "He's going to be all right, isn't he?"

"Good as new," Lenor said.

"I have to call his parents," Magdalena said, clearly dreading the anticipated conversation.

"If you wait a little while to call, I'll be glad to talk to them," Lenor said, stepping into the other room.

"I appreciate that. Thanks." Magdalena followed her daughter. Lucielle and Watson were sitting on the side of the bed entertaining Thomas.

"Anything your little old heart desires for lunch. You name it."

"Hamburger," Thomas managed.

"You got it, kiddo. And how 'bout some chocolate cake?" Lucielle looked up. "If it's all right with the doc here."

Lenor smiled. "Anything he wants."

Lucielle winked at Thomas. "I'll just get back to the kitchen and bake that chocolate cake. Okay, kiddo?"

"Yeah."

"Thanks, Lucielle," Lenor said. "I meant it—you're a marvel."

"Ain't it the truth."

Lenor watched Lucielle go, then glanced around the room. Something—someone was missing. *Michael.* She looked at her mother, and Magdalena shrugged. "I don't know where he is," she said.

"Well, Thomas, how do you feel?" Lenor asked as she sat down on the edge of the bed.

"Hurt all over."

Lenor smiled. "I'll bet you do. You're all scratched and bruised. Want to tell me how this happened?"

"Just trying to . . ." His eyes fluttered closed, then opened. "Just trying to get . . ." His eyelids drooped again. "Tired."

"Of course you are." Lenor leaned forward and kissed his cheek. "You get some rest. I'll be right in the next room if you need me. Okay?"

Thomas didn't answer.

"I think you should try to get some rest, too," Magdalena whispered.

"I have a better idea. Since I need to stay close for a while, I'll just straighten up the bedrooms in this wing. We'll need every bed we can get by this evening."

"You're right. That'll be a big help. I haven't had a chance to . . ." Her eyes glistened with tears. "If you need me, I'll be in the kitchen with Lucielle."

"Okay. See you later."

Magdalena left by the door that opened into the *placita,* and Lenor went back to her room through the connecting bathroom. The bed was cluttered with instruments, bandages, and medicines. She carried everything into the bathroom. There would be plenty of time, while the linen washed, to get it all back in order. She started by putting her own sheets in the machine in her bathroom, then systematically began opening doors so rooms could air, dusting where necessary, gathering sheets and towels.

Since Thomas was sleeping soundly, Lenor began at the bedroom nearest the kitchen. Arthur would probably sleep in that one since Rudolfo had people coming in from Las Vegas. Aunt Isabel would return to her own room, and Lita would stay in the next.

More as a delaying tactic than anything else, Lenor looked in on Thomas before going into her grandparents' bedroom. He was resting peacefully. Another load in the washer, one in the dryer, kept the moment at bay a little longer. Finally, necessity overcame the dread, and she pushed open the door, fully expecting to see some evidence of the chaos that must have preceded Jovita's death. But the room was perfectly neat. The fragrance of sandalwood, Grandpa's favorite, filled the room. Lenor opened the drapes at the two large windows that faced the *placita* and flooded the room with reflected sunlight.

Flanking the open bathroom door, the two heavy triple dressers crafted by Steven's father, Fabio, gleamed with polished care. In the center of the nearest one, small bottles of Jovita's self-concocted colognes were perfectly arranged on a handmade strip of lace. On the other, three folded cotton shirts, ironed to perfection, waited to be put into one of the wide drawers. Grandpa's tiny five-inch portable TV sat on its wire stand. His baseball cap, filled to the brim with now-wilted rose blossoms he'd gathered for his wife, rested in the seat of his favorite easy chair.

On the right side of the room, a wide desk sat against the wall. Jovita's cactus-paper thank-you notes were sorted into several neat piles atop the wide desk, she'd probably been writing thank-yous to the families who'd attended Steven's birthday party.

A glass of water held an assortment of the fine watercolor brushes she'd used to paint the notes. The brushes had been cleaned; the water was clear. Above the desk a small oil painting of Rafael and Magdalena hung beside another of Lenor. A watercolor of Isabel, done when she was about seventeen, hung above the other two. In a row along the back of the desk were framed photos, some dating back to the early 1900s. No family member that Lenor could think of was missing from the collection. Open closet doors on either side of the desk revealed neat rows of clothing arranged according to category; Grandpa's shirts, then pants, then jackets, Grandma's blouses, skirts, dresses, ready for someone to make a selection.

On the south wall, two niches held *bultos,* one of Santa Margarita de Cortona, patroness of charity, and one of Saint James the Greater, patron of soldiers, horses, and horsemen. For her failure to keep Jovita safe, Saint Margaret had been turned to face the wall.

Crossing to the right side of the bed, Lenor sat down in Jovita's chair. "Ah, *abuela*, dear friend," she said softly. "I can't believe you're gone." With her mother and father working so hard, she'd spent much of her time with her grandparents. Lenor remembered with great fondness the patient hours Grandma had spent teaching her about everything unscientific—music, art, fragrance, how to give of oneself. "Santa Margarita, you should have been more vigilant with your faithful servant."

With tears in her eyes, Lenor stared at the neatly made bed between the two *nichos* and wondered if she should disturb the perfect order of the room. She sighed and wiped a tear from her cheek. If she didn't do it now, she, or someone else, would have to do it later. The patchwork quilt, similar to her own, came off first and got a good shake outside, in the *placita*. She spread the next thin blanket on the floor, tossed the pillowcases into its center, stripped off the top sheet—and froze. The sight was all too familiar. The stain, now dried, had been a bloody diarrhea.

Lenor had to sit down in Jovita's chair again. Her mind reeled with questions. How had Dr. Baldwin missed the symptom? Or *had* he missed it? How could a medical doctor dismiss such a blatant sign of a problem totally unrelated to cardiac and pulmonary failure? Diarrhea, perhaps. Bloody diarrhea, never.

The symptom pointed to many causes, but a first suspicion would probably have been ulcerative colitis. Weakness, loss of weight, uncontrollable diarrhea, joint pains, and more—but none of these symptoms had been present in Jovita three days ago. Meaning . . . the problem had been of an acute nature. Contaminated water? No. Everyone else in the house was all right. Food poisoning? No. Everyone ate at the same table. Jovita and Steven excluded meat, fish, fowl, eggs, and dairy products from their diet, but consumed everything else that was served. Not food poisoning.

Poisoning?

Jovita was poisoned?

Jovita was murdered?

Guilt struck her like an avalanche of cold mountain snow. Lenor began pacing the room, tears streaming uncontrollably down her face, her body shivering with the chill of doubt. *It's my fault. I should have been here. My mother was right. I never should have left. Even Michael asked me to stay. Even Watson wanted me to stay . . . if only to find his precious rock.*

Stop it!

Lenor went into the bathroom and splashed warm water on her face. It didn't relieve the chill, but it helped her to focus somewhat. Looking in the mirror, she was jarred to see an emaciated shadow of a woman staring back at her. It looked as if she'd lost at least twenty pounds in just a few days. *What is happening to me? Am I doing this to myself?*

Lenor went back into the bedroom and stared down at the stained sheet. If Jovita had been so desperately ill, why hadn't Dr. Baldwin found something during her annual physical just two weeks ago? *Either he's incompetent or there was nothing to find.* Both were possibilities. Assuming Dr. Baldwin had missed something, what could Lenor have done if she'd stayed home? *I would have found the problem!*

Though Rosa and Magdalena both had their doubts about Miller Baldwin, Lenor didn't think he was so incompetent that he would miss a bleeding ulcer or any other patently obvious cause of Jovita's symptoms. She looked at the blood-streaked smear again. *And he couldn't have missed this one!*

Poisoning. It didn't seem possible. Everyone, literally everyone, loved Jovita Tavera. She was kind, moral, ethical, generous to a fault. Lenor's mind began spinning off. Murder was still possible—there were crazy people everywhere. But who? How? Why? And how would she find out the answers to those questions? Jovita's body would be brought from the mortuary late this afternoon. Guests would start arriving this evening. Friends would begin showing up first thing in the morning. Steven wasn't well and neither was Magdalena. Though the search for Thomas had prevented her from talking to her father, except briefly, Lenor knew that he, too, was on the edge of emotional disaster.

Should the funeral go on as planned? Or, even without positive proof of foul play, should she bring in the authorities, begin an investigation right now? Perhaps if she took Apple into her confidence, asked her advice. Yes, that was exactly what she would do. Apple Hardy was a levelheaded woman who was once removed from the emotion of the situation. Together they could decide what was best under the circumstances.

As dreadful as it might be for everyone, the body could be exhumed and examined later. There would have to be a witness. Could Steven possibly stand the strain of that task? Not anytime in the very near future.

Could the whole procedure be done in secret? Midnight excavation, unwitnessed exhumation, lab specimens sent to New York for examination. Was that a possibility? No. Violation of sepulcher leaped immediately to mind. That had to be at least a misdemeanor in common law, not to mention tampering with evidence. An exhumation and autopsy would have to follow strict legal procedures, no matter what traumas it caused. But on what grounds? And what if she were wrong?

Maybe, if she could just think it through, she could figure out what had happened quietly, secretly. If murder were a real possibility, there had to be other evidence, and all Lenor had to do was find it before disrupting the entire family.

Lenor removed the bottom sheet, folded it carefully, then rolled it up with the other linen and took the bundle outside. Leaving it with the other mounds just outside her bedroom door, she hurried into her room, with Watson in hot pursuit, and sat down at her desk. She opened the top right drawer so Watson could sit beside her. Perhaps if she made notes, she could come up with some logical connections.

As she considered the list she was about to make, it was impossible to get her mind off her mother. Maybe Magdalena's ill health was connected to Jovita's death. Magdalena looked fairly well physically. Emotionally, she was stressed. Mentally, she was distressed. *Questions: In what specific way is Magdalena ill?* Last night she'd said, "I sense danger here." *What, specifically, threatens her?*

Illness? The symptoms Lenor had seen were insidious: trembling hands, pale skin, weakness, mild paranoia. Brain chemistry imbalance, tumor, drug side effect, viral infection, bacterial infection, or plain anxiety were just a few of the possibilities. And Lenor couldn't rule out simple sorrow and fear, two of the most devastating emotions known to the observant *curandera*. Jovita's death and Thomas's disappearance could be blamed.

Fear could be induced by . . . "*Brujería en lo malo,* Watson?" she asked her companion. Witchcraft practiced for the bad? Her formal education had taught her that there had to be a reasonable explanation for everything, but her experience in this corner of New Mexico had conditioned her differently. Anything was possible, whether it was possible or not. She reached for a pencil from the coffee mug on the desk, then froze midmotion. Watson arched, fluffed his tail to gigantic proportions, and hissed.

No sound had startled either one of them, but Lenor had the feeling that someone had entered her room. She spun around in her chair to find no one. The door was still closed; nothing stirred. Watson scuttled into the closet. The feeling of another presence was so strong, Lenor shivered with an apprehension that doubled with each second. She stood up, turned toward the bed, and gasped.

Roy was standing in her bathroom, just inside the door. He was smiling. "Your mom said you'd probably appreciate some help doing the beds and straightening up," he said in a whisper. "I'm sorry if I startled you. I didn't mean to."

Lenor let out a sigh of relief. Roy was a cheerful presence, helpful in the most unexpected and pleasant ways. "I didn't hear you come in."

"Well, I didn't know anyone was in the bedroom next door, so I came through there." He jerked his thumb back over his shoulder. "I was trying to be quiet so I wouldn't wake the boy."

"Thank you," Lenor said.

"Did you see the package I put on your bed?" Roy asked.

"No." Lenor looked. It was the *bulto* she'd sent to Steven.

"I thought you might want to deliver it yourself. Or do you want me to take it up to Steven at Angelina's right now?" he asked.

It's too late! "No, I'll give it to him later," Lenor said, fighting a sudden wave of nausea.

Roy turned back into the bathroom and pressed a button on the dryer. It began to whir softly. "Got another load started," he said, then appeared in the door again with his arms full of linen. "Come on. I'll help you make up the beds."

Fearing the worst, Lenor crossed to her bedroom door and opened it. The sheets she'd left outside were gone, no doubt the load Roy had just put in the washer. She turned back into the room and almost bumped into him. He was still smiling.

"Something wrong?" he asked. "You look worried."

"Tired," Lenor managed. Nothing she could do or say would right the situation.

"Your mom said you were out looking for Thomas all night. Why don't you get some rest? I can do this stuff . . . and you don't look so good."

"No. I'm fine. Used to staying up all night. Hospital work kind of gets you into the habit."

"I guess," Roy said. "Shall we get started, then?"

Sixteen

"Where's Lenor?"

The shouted question was punctuated by the loud smashing sound of George Murphy's office door slamming back against the wall. George leaped from his chair. "What the hell?" The familiar face registered. "Oh, it's you."

"Damn right, it's me."

"Dr. Bowder, this is a surprise."

"I can't get a straight answer out of anybody around here."

George sat back down behind his desk. "What's the question you want answered?"

Carl Bowder huffed. "Can't you hear me, mister?" He stomped across the room and struck the top of the desk with a fist. "Where's Lenor?"

"Is there some kind of emergency, Carl?"

"Answer my question, man."

"As soon as you answer mine," George said calmly.

Carl shifted his weight from one foot to the other. "It's Sable Faraday," he said, then lowered his stocky frame into the chair opposite George's.

"Sable Faraday?" George asked, though he knew very well whom Carl was talking about.

Carl leaned forward, an almost desperate look on his face. "I tried to get Lenor on the phone Tuesday night. The nurses said she'd gone home. She hadn't. I tried till midnight."

"I talked to her about eleven-thirty. She was getting ready to go home then." George decided to keep Lenor's late visit to Sable a secret.

"The hell she was! She went to Ward Two."

"I guess that's possible," George admitted. "What's so urgent?"

"You're not going to believe this. You're just, by God, not going to believe what I heard from Phillips this morning." He explained quickly. Phillips, the pediatric orderly, had been restocking the linen shelves and had observed what he'd described as the "possession" of Sable Faraday, then her subsequent "exorcism" by Lenor Tavera. He'd related the story to one of his friends, who told a group of lunching buddies in the cafeteria. "This thing has spread like wildfire!"

"I haven't heard about it," George said.

"Well, everyone *else* has. I've got to find Lenor!"

George wasn't sure why he decided to lie again, except that he'd always delighted in making this particular man squirm. It pleased him to aggravate the person who'd turned the last three years of Lenor's life into a miserable nowhere-to-hide media spree. "I know Lenor left a message for you with Ella Wygent. Have you talked to her?"

"No. She's busy." Carl reached into his jacket pocket. "Take a look at this." He shoved a crumpled newspaper clipping across the desk.

George took a quick look at the headline and read the first sentence.

TAKE YOUR DEMONS TO FOLEY
Exorcism while you wait.

"Do you have any idea what this is going to do to the reputation of this hospital?" Carl shouted.

"It's just trash," George said, but he knew he couldn't really dispute the impact of such a piece.

"This isn't run-of-the-mill trash."

"You mean Foley has never gotten this kind of publicity? Come on now, Carl."

"Of course we have. What hospital can avoid it? But in the last eight days there have been three articles like this. We can't take it! And what about the kid? What if something is organically, medically wrong with her? She comes in here sick and all she gets is . . . depossessed? Jee-sus!"

George picked up the phone and dialed. "Willie, will you bring Sable Faraday's chart to my office, please?"

"I've already looked at it," Carl said.

"We'll, let's have another look."

While George scanned Dr. Tavera's notes and the lab reports, Carl fidgeted in his chair. "Well?"

"Lenor indicates here that the child had a very slight, very brief seizure, not uncommon considering the glomerulonephritis complication. And that was over two weeks ago." George said finally.

Carl shook his head and sighed, almost as if he were suffering a defeat of gigantic proportions. "I didn't see anything unusual either."

"Is something else bothering you?" George asked.

"A Mrs. Hess is taking her daughter, Alicia, to another hospital."

"Why is she doing that?"

"She wouldn't say. Apparently she first wanted to move the child a week ago. According to Ella Wygent, her husband talked her out of it, but she wasn't happy. I think all this talk of witches and exorcism . . ." Carl shook his head. "Can't you just tell me where Lenor went?"

George picked up the square of newsprint. "What can Lenor do at this point?"

"Christ!" Carl snatched the article from George's hand, slammed it down on the desk, then jabbed at it with his finger. "She can, by God, deny this, right this goddamned minute," he shouted. "Now you get her on the phone and tell her to get her buns into my office in the next thirty minutes, or I'll have you both begging for pennies out on the street."

"I'm afraid that's impossible," George said, as calmly as he could. "Lenor is out of town."

"Last chance, Murphy. I can ruin her and you know it."

George took a deep breath, sighed, and hoped he hadn't overindulged his desire to aggravate Bowder. "Lenor's grandmother died Tuesday night. Lenor left early yesterday morning. Jovita's funeral is tomorrow."

Carl Bowder looked stunned. "Jovita Tavera died?" He slumped back in the chair. "I don't get it," he said, shaking his head. "I may give Lenor a hard time about some of her strange ideas, but deep down I know she's right most of the time. My God, her grandparents were her prize patients! She's told me all about them. They were here to visit last year, in better health than you and I! Damn it, man, what went wrong?"

George shook his head and frowned. He'd never seen this caring side of Carl Bowder and was pleasantly surprised. "I wish I could tell you. Her age maybe? She was seventy-nine."

"God. Lenor must feel terrible."

"If you insist on getting in touch with her about this"— George pointed at the newspaper article—"she's going to feel a lot worse."

Carl was silent as he walked to the door. Then, "When will she be back?" he asked.

"I don't know. The funeral's Friday at noon. I guess Monday night."

Carl turned to face George. "If the funeral's tomorrow, why can't she take a flight back Saturday?" He went on without waiting for an answer. "I really don't mean to seem insensitive, but I need her here, George. I mean it."

George picked up the phone as soon as Carl had closed the door. "Ella Wygent, please." He waited. "Ella? George Murphy. I want to follow the Sable Faraday case while Dr. Tavera is gone. Any problem with that?"

"No, sir. No problem at all."

"I want to be informed if there's the slightest change in her condition. The *slightest* change. Clear?"

"Yes, sir."

"And Ella, do you have a patient of Dr. Tavera's by the name of Alicia Hess?" George asked.

"Not anymore. Her mother—"

"Never mind. Thanks, Ella." He hung up and thought for a minute. Maybe Carl *did* have a caring side, but it was clear that he cared more about his hospital than his doctors. Whatever Lenor's emotional state, George was certain of one thing—she was better off not knowing about this latest turn of events.

No, that wasn't right. He had to give her a chance to prepare a defense—no matter how flimsy.

George reached for the phone and dialed the Taveras' number in New Mexico.

"Tavera Guest Ranch. This is Lucielle."

"May I speak to Lenor Tavera, please?"

"Who's calling, sir?"

"This is George Murphy, in New York."

"Ah, Dr. Murphy. How nice to hear your voice again. How are things in the big city?"

"Things are fine, Lucielle. May I speak to Lenor?" There was silence on the other end of the line. "Lucielle?"

"I just buzzed her room and she doesn't answer. Maybe she turned off her phone and went to sleep. She had a busy night."

George tensed. "Is she all right?"

"Oh, sure. Just tired." Lucielle decided not to tell him all the details of the night's ordeal or that Lenor looked like she needed a month in a health spa. "Is it really important? Some kind of emergency?"

"No, there's no emergency."

"Glad to hear it. Can I have her call you back when I find her?"

"When will that be?"

"Couldn't say. I'm armpit-deep in red chile right now. Want me to send you some?"

"Thanks, but . . . just have her call me."

"Soon as I can. Okay?"

George had to smile. Now that he'd met Lucielle, the gregarious sixty-eight-year-old cook and confidante Lenor admired so much, her easy repartee and cordial familiarity made him feel a little better. "I'll just try back later this evening, too," he said.

"I'm sure she'll be glad to hear from you, George. 'Bye now."

George hung up the phone, leaned back in his chair, and tried to relax. He couldn't. Maybe there was more to this than the obvious.

The hospital administrator had always seemed to be one hundred eighty degrees opposed to Lenor's research. Sure, he let her tell stories to the patients in Ward Two, but George knew that was only because it seemed harmless and created no adverse press.

Did Bowder know about the Truelex grant? Part of the research was intended to prove that the sixty or seventy different peptides, or chemical messenger molecules secreted by the brain exchanged information between the brain, the nervous system, *and* the immune system. Lenor hoped to confirm her hypothesis that the immune system, previously thought to be entirely autonomic, was actually in direct communication with the nervous system and the brain. She wanted to prove that the immune system could be directly influenced by hope, pleasure, and other positive emotions, thereby enhancing the body's ability to cure itself. For orthodox medicine, the idea that a patient didn't have to give up complete power and control to the physician was revolutionary—and dangerously controversial. Especially in pediatrics.

Lenor was up against some big guns. The *New England Journal of Medicine* had once called the body-mind connection "folklore." All over the world, powerful and influential scientists doing basic research, denounced psycho-social factors in healing as so much voodoo. George closed his eyes and said a little prayer.

The race was on, and even the winner could lose.

Seventeen

"HEARD ABOUT THE BOY. WONDERED IF YOU'D LIKE ME to take a look at him."

Magdalena stood back from the open door. "Come in, Miller."

Lenor's mood went from anxious to disappointed. She'd been hoping to see Apple, not Miller. Apple had called from her office earlier and found out that Thomas had been found and was all right. After that, she'd had to testify in court, then attend a meeting in Santa Fe. No one knew when she'd return.

Magdalena closed the door behind Miller. "We just made a fresh pot of coffee. Will you join us?" she asked.

"Be my pleasure, thank you." He stopped just inside and turned to Magdalena. "You look lovely, dear. I'd say that shade of blue is your best color."

"How kind of you to say so, Miller," Magdalena said.

Even from across the room, Lenor could see that her mother was uncomfortable with the compliment. She couldn't remember Dr. Baldwin ever being so solicitous.

"And how is my patient tonight?" he asked, taking Magdalena's hand. "Still feeling tired?"

"Some," she said.

"Not to worry." Using his sturdy, silver-topped cane, Miller Baldwin slowly crossed the living room, then sat down opposite Lenor on one of the sofas.

"Coffee won't take me a minute," Magdalena said.

"When you're ready to carry the tray, I'll come help you," Lenor said as her mother started for the kitchen door.

Magdalena glanced at Miller. "Roy can help me," she said.

"Roy's here?" Miller sat forward. "What time did he come out?"

He seemed surprised, and that surprised Lenor. Roy had always been a regular, frequent, and welcome visitor. "Roy helped me get the bedrooms ready," Lenor said. "I'm really not sure what time he got here. Is there a problem?"

"No problem." Clearing his throat, Miller sat back. "So, how long will you be staying?" he asked Lenor.

"I'm flying back Monday."

"Too bad you can't stay longer."

"Too much work," she said.

"Perhaps you should consider asking a colleague to take your cases. Steven might need you after this. I'm concerned about him."

"He's better today, thank heaven. But if Grandpa needs me, I'll stay as long as he wants me to," Lenor said.

"How's your father taking all of this?" Miller asked.

"Not well," Lenor said. "He came in just before dinner. Hardly ate a bite, then went straight to bed."

"It's all so sad." Miller was silent for a moment, then, "Last weekend you said you were making a presentation for a grant. What's your project?"

"Psycho-neuro-immunology, among other things," she said.

"Throw away the medicine, bring on the magic, is that it?"

Lenor was beginning to feel uncomfortable. Miller's attitude was obviously antagonistic. "There's a little more to it than that." She decided to change the subject. "So you came to see Thomas?"

He nodded. "But the boy must be doing all right. You don't seem to be too worried about him."

Magdalena called out from the kitchen, "Thomas is feeling just fine now, Miller. Lenor took good care of him."

Lenor could hear the pride in her mother's voice and was slightly embarrassed when she turned to see her mother's beaming face. "His injuries weren't serious. Lucielle or my mother could have taken care of him." It was the wrong thing to say, Lenor knew immediately by the dejected look on the doctor's face.

"Sometimes I wonder what I'm doing here," Miller said

forlornly. He ran a wide hand through his silver hair, then leaned forward. "You have no idea how it is out here. A patient will come to me with a stomachache, I give him something for it, and the next thing I know, he's going down the street to Mrs. Hurtado."

"Mrs. Hurtado?" Lenor asked.

"Used to be Maria Maldonado. She married again a few years back."

"Yes, I remember Maria," Lenor said. The woman had been practicing *curanderismo* in the town of Mora for the past forty years with excellent results. Many of the people in the area wouldn't even consider going to Miller Baldwin, no matter what was wrong with them. "Are you saying Maria is taking business away from your new clinic?"

He nodded. "She . . . and a few others," he said sadly.

"That surprises me," Lenor said, trying to be polite. But she understood perfectly. As with so many small, rural communities, the population of the valley had always been a closed and suspicious society, and when the first Anglo doctor had moved into town, they were wary of the newfangled gringo ways of the "educated" healers. Their brand of health care had served them for centuries, and they weren't about to give up the tried-and-true for the pretentious. The battle had been, and still was, hard fought.

"Not that I'm not busy. And the clinic is doing fine."

"I'm glad to hear that a few nonbelievers aren't a problem," Lenor said.

He leaned back heavily and sighed. "You, of all people, should know how far superior our modern medicine is to witchcraft."

"Witchcraft?"

"I'm being facetious, of course."

Lenor wasn't convinced. He sounded more bitter than playful, maybe even a little bit envious. Would it be improper to defend the time-honored *curanderismo* that she'd grown up trusting? No. Not as long as the defense was posed as a question. "The

Mexican-American system of healing still has many valid uses, wouldn't you agree, Dr. Baldwin?"

Miller frowned. "Refection for the common cold, perhaps," he said, his tone aloof and condescending.

His statement was a direct assault on her mother, who'd always taken care of most of the medical problems on the ranch. She'd never suspected that he opposed Magdalena and the other practitioners in the area so vehemently. Was the man so insecure in his own discipline that he had to attack the complement? She didn't want to start an argument, but she couldn't resist making a point.

"There's a lot to say for tender loving care."

"Pabulum for the brain. I leave the TLC to mothers."

Magdalena came back into the living room, followed by Roy, who was carrying a large tray and coffee service.

Roy knelt down and slid the tray onto the low table between the two facing couches.

"Black for Lenor and Roy. Cream for me. Miller, cream and two sugars."

"Exactly right, lovely lady. Nothing wrong with your memory, now is there?"

Magdalena smiled at the doctor, and Lenor's antennae went up. Had her mother consulted him about losing her memory? "Dr. Baldwin and I have just been discussing the merits of orthodox medicine versus the *curanderismo,* Mama. You never told me he had such an aversion to the old ways."

"Miller? Against the *curanderismo*?" She looked at the doctor, then back at Lenor. "He must have been pulling your leg, dear. Isn't that right, Miller?"

"Quite right. I was just indulging myself in a little shop talk," he said. "It isn't every day I get to share information with another real doctor."

If his statement hurt or offended her, Magdalena didn't show it. He was lying about his conversation with Lenor, but why? Lenor took the cup and saucer her mother offered, then leaned back. This small talk could prove to be an interesting lesson in evasion—but it didn't. She listened while Magdalena told Miller about Thomas's injuries, about Lenor's skill in taking care of them, about Thomas's remarkable resilience.

Roy was silent. His father was ignoring him, and Roy seemed to prefer it that way.

"You must possess healer's hands," Miller said to Lenor. "It makes me very happy to hear it."

"I do my best."

"I'd like to see the boy, if you don't mind, Dr. Tavera."

His formality surprised her. "Not at all, Dr. Baldwin."

Magdalena was the first to stand up. "I'm sure he's not asleep now," she said. "Lucielle took him dinner a little while ago and he ate like a Trojan." She smiled. "All thanks to my daughter, I might add," she said proudly.

"And thanks to you and Lucielle," Lenor said. "I couldn't have done it without your help."

"She's being modest," Magdalena said to Miller.

"I'm sure she's not," Miller said flatly as he got up and started to follow Magdalena out of the room.

Lenor walked behind the other two. The cane Miller used was something new, acquired sometime since Steven's birthday party last year. She wanted to ask him what made the cane necessary, but decided against it. She wanted the man to leave, and wasn't really keen on letting him see Thomas. Before the doctor had showed up at their front door, Lenor and Magdalena had been conversing pleasantly after talking to Thomas's mother and father on the telephone. The Newmans had been horrified at first, then, after talking to Lenor, thoroughly reassured that he would recover under professional supervision. Thomas had cheerfully related his adventure as well, and his excitement had further calmed his parents.

They were about halfway across the *placita,* when Miller stopped and sat down on the wooden bench that encircled the huge cottonwood. He breathed deeply and leaned back against the trunk.

"Are you feeling all right, Doctor?" Lenor asked.

"This is a holy place, child," he said. "I'm never better than when I'm sitting right here."

Lenor looked at her mother, puzzled. How often did Mora's doctor come to call? she wondered. For some reason, the idea that he visited often was uncomfortable.

"I could die and go to heaven right here on this very spot," Miller continued.

"And you might, if you don't mend your ways," Magdalena said.

An angry look spread across his face, and Miller stood up abruptly. "Enough on *that* subject."

It was hard to contain her curiosity, but Lenor managed. No need to stray into an obvious combat zone without the protective gear of the facts. And "combative" was exactly the right word to describe Miller's tone of voice. Magdalena didn't react to his assault. She simply turned, walked the rest of the way across the interior patio, and knocked on Thomas's door.

"Come in."

Magdalena opened the door. "You've got a visitor, Thomas."

Miller went inside first. "Well, my boy, you look comfortable."

Thomas was propped up on several pillows, smiling, stroking a very happy Watson, surrounded by a clutter of comic books, notepads, and pencils. He wore Lenor's colorful silk scarf around his neck. "I *am* comfortable," Thomas said. "Who are you?"

"I'm Dr. Baldwin. I live down in Mora. Thought I'd come by and have a look at you."

Watson moved from beside the boy to the boy's lap, facing the doctor. Thomas's smile faded, and he pressed his body further back against the pillows. "I'm fine," he said softly.

"I'm sure you are," Miller boomed. "This is just a friendly visit . . . if you don't mind."

"I guess I don't mind."

Lenor sat down on the other side of the bed and took Thomas's hand. "Dr. Baldwin just wants to have a look at your head and your shoulder. It won't take a minute. I need to change your bandages anyway. Okay with you?" she asked.

Thomas nodded, grasped a corner of Lenor's silk scarf between the thumb and forefinger of his left hand, and leaned forward so Lenor could remove the dressing from his back.

"Surgery?" Miller asked, when the wound was exposed. He was obviously surprised.

"Minor surgery, Doctor," Lenor said. "I removed a piece of buckshot." She began to unwrap the gauze that held the bandage on Thomas's head.

"Double-ought buckshot?" Miller asked, when the dressing was gone.

Lenor nodded.

"How long ago did this happen?" Miller asked gruffly.

"Between four and five this morning, as near as we can figure. About fifteen hours ago," Magdalena said.

Miller frowned. "Impossible."

"Excuse me?" Lenor said.

"These wounds look three days old."

Lenor wasn't sure what to say. At this point in her research, she didn't want to mention any of the techniques she'd been experimenting with. She decided to state the obvious and hope that would satisfy the man. "Young boys heal quickly."

"Not this quickly," he said to Lenor, then to the boy, "How did this happen, Thomas?"

"I don't know," Thomas said.

Miller's voice boomed out then. "You got shot and you don't know how it happened?"

Magdalena put a hand on Miller's shoulder. "You're upsetting the boy, Miller."

He brushed her hand away and gave her an imperious look. "Stay out of this." To Lenor he said sarcastically, "He's young, he'll get over it quickly." Leaning down over the bed, his face just inches from Thomas's, Miller fixed him with a penetrating stare. "I want to know how this happened. Right now."

Thomas cringed away from him, looked at Lenor, then at

Magdalena. Lenor took his hand and began rubbing it between both of hers. He relaxed a little. "Mr. Martino shot a mountain lion. I got in the way," he said finally.

Miller straightened, gave Magdalena an astonished look. "Michael Martino?"

Magdalena nodded.

"Who brought you here?" Miller asked.

"Mr. Martino," Thomas said softly.

Again Miller looked at Magdalena, and she confirmed what Thomas had said with a nod of her head. He jabbed a thumb toward the door. "I want to talk to you. Outside."

Lenor began replacing Thomas's dressing as Miller and Magdalena left the room.

"I don't like him," Thomas said as soon as the door was closed.

"He's just upset, Thomas. He doesn't like to see children hurt." But she knew it wasn't the boy's injuries that had angered him.

"I still don't like him. He's loud."

Lenor smiled at him.

"Mr. Martino isn't loud," Thomas said. "I like him. Do you like Mr. Martino?"

It was an innocent question, but it jarred her. "I don't know him very well," she said.

"My friend Shirley said he's a hunk."

"Shirley's right."

"Then how come you don't know him very well?"

So many reasons. "I've been away from home a long time, Thomas," she said. "It takes a lot of years at school to learn how to be a doctor. Understand?"

"I guess." Thomas picked up a comic book, began to look at the pictures, then looked back at Lenor. "Shirley and I saw you guys dancing at your grandpa's party. We think you should marry Mr. Martino."

There was a knock on the door, and Lucielle came in. "Cookie wagon!"

"Just in time," Lenor said, relieved. "I've finished changing his bandages. He's ready for a snack."

"Yeah," Thomas agreed. He'd already forgotten his upsetting visitor.

Lucielle handed Thomas a glass of milk and put the plate of cookies on the bed beside him. "That ought to hold you till breakfast," Lucielle said.

Lenor looked at the huge pile of cookies. "And then some." She looked up at Lucielle. The woman's mouth was smiling, but there was a grimness in her eyes. Lenor got the message. "Shall we leave our patient to his goodies?" she suggested.

"You get a good night's sleep, Thomas," Lucielle said.

"I'll look in on you on my way to bed," Lenor told him, then kissed his cheek. She started for the door, but Lucielle motioned for her to follow her through the bathroom instead.

"What's going on?" Lenor asked in a whisper when they were behind the closed door in her own bedroom.

"You couldn't hear them?" Lucielle asked. Lenor shook her head. "I've never heard Miller Baldwin so angry," Lucielle went on. "They're in the kitchen, and Miller is reading Magdalena the riot act."

"Why?"

"For one thing, because Michael brought the boy here instead of driving him into town to the clinic. As if Magdalena has any control over Michael." Lucielle snuffed.

Lenor thought a moment. "Why did Michael bring Thomas here instead of to Dr. Baldwin?"

"I personally can't stand the pompous old braggart. Maybe Michael can't either. His mother hated him." Lucielle shook her head. "I don't know why Michael came here. You tell me."

"A ride in a car from Michael's place to town wouldn't have been a lot faster, but it would have been more logical," Lenor said.

"And Michael might have found the old goat with a snoot full."

So that's what Magdalena had been referring to when she

suggested Miller should mend his ways. "Drunk? At that hour of the day?" Lenor asked.

"It's happened before," Lucielle said.

"No wonder people are going to Maria Hurtado instead," Lenor said.

"Cried on your shoulder too, did he?" Lucielle asked. Lenor nodded. "The nerve of that rich old bastard. He's got the backbone of a worm. To hear him talk, the whole world plots against his success. Whatever goes wrong, it's always someone else's fault."

"I know the type," Lenor said. "But I don't remember Miller Baldwin being insecure about anything. I've always considered him highly intelligent and extremely efficient."

"I think it's old age," Lucielle said.

"Old age?" Lenor had to smile. The doctor was probably younger than Lucielle.

"Old age and the bottle. A combination of curses," Lucielle said.

"Shall we go rescue my mother?" Lenor asked.

"From the jaws of hell." Lucielle elbowed Lenor's side and winked. "*Jaws* of hell. Get it?"

"You hardly ate a thing. Something wrong with the green chile?" Rosa stood near the table and waited for an answer. When none came, she tapped on his water glass with her spoon. "Michael? Anybody home in there?" She tapped on the glass again.

"I'll get it." Michael pushed his chair back, stood up, and started toward the phone on the kitchen wall.

Rosa shook her head as he lifted the receiver.

"Hello?" He listened, then hung up. "Crank call," he said.

"The phone didn't ring," Rosa said.

Michael walked over to the refrigerator, took out a carton of milk, and reached for a glass in the nearby cupboard. "I'm starved," he said as he poured. "When's dinner?"

"About an hour ago," Rosa said.

He looked at the table as if he were seeing it for the first time that evening. It was cluttered with dirty dishes and the remains of a meal already eaten. He looked at Rosa as if she'd just walked into the room. The situation slowly registered. "I guess I'm a little preoccupied," he said. He put the full glass of milk down on the countertop and started for the door. "I'll be in the tack room if you need my help with anything."

"A lot of help you'd be in this condition," Rosa said, as he disappeared through the swinging door. She cleared the table and started washing the dishes.

Eloy stuck his head in the back door. "Where's Michael?"

"In the tack room."

"No, he isn't; I just came from there."

Rosa shrugged. "All I know is what I'm told."

Eloy shrugged, backed out, then scowled as he made room for Juanita to step inside the kitchen.

"Here are the newspapers you wanted, Michael." Juanita looked around the room. "Where's Michael?"

Rosa snorted. "What am I, his personal secretary? The man said he'd be in the tack room, that's all I know."

"You don't have to take my head off," Juanita said.

"If anybody should know where he is, it should be you, 'Nita."

"Rosa!" Juanita looked quickly toward the doorway where Eloy had been standing, then sighed with relief when she saw that he was gone. "You shouldn't say things like that in front of Eloy. You know how he is."

"Eloy needs a good thrashing," Rosa said. "And I may just be the one who gives it to him." Rosa dried her hands, left the sink, and propelled Juanita toward a chair at the table. "Did he badger you about Gilberto again last night?" she asked when they'd sat down.

"He tried," Juanita said softly. "I told him to get lost."

"The man's a menace."

"I can sort of understand. They're brothers. Eloy thinks I'm leading Gil on. All he wants is for his brother to be happy."

"So he says." Rosa thought a minute. "Tomorrow morning, I'm going to tell Michael what's been going on."

"No! Rosa, please. Gil's a nice person. I don't want to get him or Eloy into any trouble."

Rosa frowned. "Why don't you just tell Gilberto that you don't have any interest in him and be done with it?" she asked.

"Because I like him a little . . . maybe more than a little. He makes me laugh."

"I saw you dancing with him at Steven's party. Looked to me as if you liked him more than a little," Rosa said.

"He's a good dancer," Juanita said.

"Well, I don't see how you can fancy yourself in love with Michael and have such a good time with Gilberto," Rosa said.

"I'm not in love with Michael."

"Who are you trying to kid? Me or yourself?"

Juanita looked down at the table and started drawing circles with her finger. "I'm just . . . confused." She looked up. "I don't know what I feel . . . not for sure. When I saw Michael dancing with Lenor, I was so jealous, I could have strangled both of them. But then Gil started talking to me, saying funny things. Pretty soon, I forgot all about Michael. It was so strange."

Rosa shook her head slowly from side to side. "I give up. You're confused and I'm bewildered, but Eloy has no right to bother you. Just because he and Michael haven't been getting along is no reason for him to take his frustrations out on you. I still think I'll have a word with Michael about him."

"What if Michael fires him?" Juanita asked.

"Or beats the living hell out of him." The horrified look on Juanita's face made Rosa sorry she'd exaggerated. "I'll let it be for the time being. But I'm not going to put up with the craziness around here much longer or I'm going to be a raving maniac. Understood?"

"I understand. And I'm glad you're not going to say anything about Eloy." Juanita raised both eyebrows. "You wouldn't want his mother mad at you."

"I'm not afraid of Nemesia. Let her get as mad as she wants to."

"I've heard she's dangerous when she's angry," Juanita said.

Rosa patted Juanita's hand, then drew her own away. "She's dangerous when she's *not* angry. So what?"

"So, I'm glad you're going to let it go. Nobody needs the kind of trouble Nemesia could cause."

Rosa stood up and went back to the sink. *No one knows that better than me . . . except Michael.*

Lucielle led the way back across the *placita* to the kitchen, but when she and Lenor entered, there was no one in the room. They went into the living room and were surprised to find it empty, too.

"Where could they have gone?" Lucielle asked.

Lenor crossed the room, opened the door to the master bedroom just a crack, and peeked in. Rafael was sound asleep. "I haven't a clue," she said, turning back to Lucielle. "This whole thing between my mother and the doctor is odd. I've never seen her so complacent about aberrant behavior."

"Maybe she doesn't see it," Lucielle said.

"And he's so condescending toward her. She would never put up with that from anyone."

"I know."

"They would have been told to take a long walk in the woods and not come back until their foolishness had been exorcised."

"And they'd have done it, too." Lucielle picked up the coffee tray. "How about another cup?" Lenor nodded. "I'll just refill this pot. Be right back."

As Lucielle left the living room, the phone rang. "I'll get it," Lenor said. "It's probably George." She sat down on the couch and picked up the receiver.

"Hello?"

"Lenor? Is that you?" George asked.

"It's me, George. I tried to get you earlier, but you were busy. Did you get my message about getting in touch with Mrs. Hess?"

"Sure did. And she has your message to see an ear specialist, but I don't know if she'll follow up."

"Thanks, George. What else is going on?"

"Nothing much."

"Come on, George. I've only been gone a little while. You wouldn't have called me unless—"

"Okay, okay. Just let me hear a little news from the frontier first."

"Wild and woolly, as usual." Lenor told him about Thomas.

"Whew! You've had your hands full. You'll be glad to know Sable Faraday is doing beautifully."

"That's wonderful." Lucielle came back carrying the coffee tray. With hand signals, she asked if Lenor wanted her to leave the room. Lenor shook her head, put her hand over the receiver. "Stay here," she said to Lucielle. "Was there something else, George?"

"Bowder came to see me this morning."

"What did he want?" Lenor asked.

"He wanted to know where you were."

"Oh? Why? I left a message for him."

George told her about Phillips, the article, and about Carl's worry that Foley would suffer, irreversibly, from the bad press.

"Let Violet handle it."

"It's beyond Violet's capabilities. And Carl has threatened us both with dismissal."

"You're kidding! That's ludicrous. Didn't you say you both went over my entries in Sable's chart?"

"Sure did."

"Surely, with my notes to back him up and Violet to tell him what to say, Carl could turn this whole thing around."

"You'd think so, but he still wants you back on Saturday." George paused. "Tell you what. I'll call him at home right now, tell him a little white lie, something about your mother being sick or some such. If I can convince him, I won't even bother you again. How's that sound?"

"Like a good plan, George. You're a real friend. Thanks."

"So . . . is everyone all right? I mean, considering . . . ?"

"Not really," she said truthfully.

"If there's anything I can do . . ."

"Handling Bowder is even more than I should ask," Lenor said.

"The least I can do."

"Thanks, George."

"Sure. Talk to you later."

Lenor hung up the phone and took a deep breath. George was a blessing that never would have happened if she hadn't broken her rule of not dating a co-worker. In spite of their disagreements, she didn't regret her folly for one minute. She looked at Lucielle. "*Men!* One minute you think they're sane, the next minute you're sure they've lost complete touch with reality."

"You mean George?" Lucielle asked.

"No, not George. He's about the best friend anyone could ask for. It's Carl Bowder."

Lucielle frowned. "Want to tell me about it?"

"I'd rather you tell me something. Has Mama been feeling all right lately?"

"As well as you could expect, I guess. She works too hard. Worries too much. This idea that you might come home has had her in a tizzy for months. I'd say Magdalena is doing remarkably well for what she puts herself through."

"She doesn't complain about aches and pains of any kind?"

Lucielle shook her head. "Mostly complains about getting senile. I told her she ought to start up her quilting club again, get her mind off the everyday stuff. Get Angelina to come help more often. She doesn't get around as well as she used to, but she's fine with the kids."

"And what does Mama say about that?"

"She says she'd rather spend her free time alone, and that's not like her, not like she used to be. You know how she was. She used to get so excited at spring roundup time when we'd have twenty or thirty cowboys to feed every day. This year, she acted like it was an unwelcome burden she was being forced to carry.

She started this camp after you left home just so she could have people around her. Now she seems tired of it."

"She's too young to be tired."

"You've got that right," Lucielle said.

"And she's too young to be senile. I got the idea that she'd gone to see Dr. Baldwin about losing her memory. Am I right?"

Lucielle nodded. "A cousin of mine has Alzheimer's. It scared Magdalena real bad when I told her about it. She and Juanita went to see him together one day."

"What was Juanita's problem?" Lenor asked, remembering the strange scene she'd witnessed in the woods.

"I couldn't say. I don't talk to Juanita much anymore. Used to see her at Roy's store from time to time, but since she left there, I can't keep track of how she is, not like I used to. I think there's some kind of disagreement going on between her and Rosa." Lucielle shrugged. "Anyhow, I guess Dr. Baldwin did some tests on both of them."

"Do you know what the results of my mother's tests were?" Lenor asked.

"All negative."

"But my mother isn't convinced?"

"I don't know. To be honest with you, Magdalena *does* seem to be a little bit out in left field sometimes lately."

"Lately? Since when?" Lenor asked.

"Since she went to see Dr. Baldwin. But, you have to admit, the old guy doesn't have a dynamite bedside manner. He doesn't exactly instill confidence in his patients, either. He's more like a bedside mangler."

"I noticed." Lenor couldn't help but remember how Thomas had reacted to Miller's visit. "I think I'd better pay a call on the good doctor and ask him a few questions."

"I agree."

The front door opened, and Magdalena walked in.

"There you are. We were wondering where you'd gotten to," Lucielle said.

"I walked Miller to his car," Magdalena said as she came across the room. "He wanted to talk to me in private."

Lucielle looked at Lenor and frowned. Lenor nodded slightly. "So Miller has left?" Lenor asked.

"Yes. Roy left, too."

"Did Miller say anything more about Thomas's condition?" Lenor asked.

Magdalena stared into the empty fireplace. "He still thinks you were lying about when Thomas was shot."

"Why would he think that?" Lenor asked.

"Because of the amount of healing that's taken place."

Miller Baldwin probably wouldn't have believed Lenor even if she'd told him everything about her research. It had happened before, disbelief in the face of proof. Many doctors couldn't bring themselves to credit the power of the patient's mind, so Lenor had decided not to tell Miller about the preop hypnotic trance she'd used on Thomas. The boy's rapid healing was dramatic, but Lenor had seen even more astounding results in burn cases when hypnotism had been used in time. She supposed that Miller Baldwin wouldn't believe those data either.

"I guess he'll just have to live with his doubt about my credibility," Lenor said. "Would you like another cup of coffee, Mama?"

"I'm tired." Magdalena shifted her gaze from the fireplace to Lenor. "I'll see you in the morning."

Lenor wanted to ask her to stay up for a while so they could finish the conversation they'd been having before the doctor's unexpected visit. The drawn look on Magdalena's face made her decide that it wouldn't be wise. "Have a pleasant sleep, Mama."

Lucielle watched Magdalena enter the master bedroom and close the door. "Strange turn of events," she said.

"And I don't like the new course," Lenor added.

Michael had gone into the tack room, turned around and walked out, then gone into the barn to saddle Penny Wise. He'd ridden away in one direction, circled back, and started off in another. He was halfway to the Tavera ranch before he realized where he was going. *I shouldn't be doing this.* But he had to be sure that Thomas was all right.

No one at home would miss him. Juanita was thinking about driving to Las Vegas to see a movie. Eloy had paperwork to finish. He hated it and would probably be in a nasty mood. Rosa always had something to do in the evenings. Michael didn't know what she kept busy with, but she closed herself in her upstairs room at the back of the house, her light burning, sometimes until the wee hours of the morning. Since Gilberto had the evening free, he was probably already in town, meeting his rowdy buddies, and stirring up a little trouble. Michael hoped Gilberto would stay out of Sheriff Garcia's way.

No, Michael thought, no one at home would miss him.

And even if they did, this would be the last place they'd look for the recluse of El Rancho del Torbellino. Michael felt like a spy, hidden among the trees on the hill overlooking the Tavera buildings. He didn't know how long he'd been there. For quite some time the moon had been hidden under the clouds of an approaching storm. All he knew for sure was that he was getting restless being this close to Lenor's home—this close to Lenor.

Except for his concern about Thomas, Michael had thought of little else but Lenor since he'd ridden into the Tavera yard this morning and realized that the woman walking toward him was Lenor. He should have known she'd be there, but Jovita's sudden death still seemed like a horrible nightmare.

But Lenor hadn't been a dream. He'd thought his heart would burst out of his chest when she looked up at him. He'd wanted to hear her speak his name. He could almost feel her beautiful voice caressing him now. *Michael?*

The first sprinkles of a fresh summer rain made tiny popping noises as they hit the ground around where he and Penny Wise stood. Lenor's bedroom light had been out for what seemed like hours. Had she been thinking about him when she was going to sleep? He wanted to watch her while she was sleeping, protect her from the demons of death who might be chasing through her dreams tonight. It would be a vigil of love.

A coil of desire tightened in his loins. *Protect her, hell! Someone would have to protect her from me!* He might be able to watch a sleeping Lenor for about one second. Then he'd have to touch her. Then he'd have to hold her. Then he'd have to . . . *Don't think about it!* But his brain had already given his body the message. *Is it physically possible to live in a permanent state of arousal?* He took a deep breath and willed himself to calm down. *I'm going completely out of my mind.*

And maybe his craziness was making him see things. A shadow seemed to be moving between the barn and the house. Michael was instantly alert, his muscles tense and ready for action. The shadow reached the house. Was the Tavera fortress being stormed? By whom? Michael scanned the area below. Unexpectedly the scene brightened. He looked up. Clouds raced along on their way to the eastern plains beyond the mountains and, intermittently, allowed the moon to peek through. The stealthy form below was nothing more than moonshade. *Simpleton.*

"Good thing only one of us is skittish," Michael whispered to the patient Penny Wise. He couldn't wait any longer. Taking a small penlight out of a tool pouch tied to the horse's saddle, he dismounted, then headed down the hill. The sooner he saw the boy and made sure he was all right, the sooner he could get back to safer ground and less disturbing thoughts.

Both doors were unlocked, and entry was quick and easy. That didn't surprise him. No one out here had ever been much for locking up, day or night. Thomas didn't stir when Michael came into the room, and Michael felt sorry about waking the boy. Still, his trip would have been in vain if he wasn't able to see and hear with his own eyes and ears, that Thomas was getting better.

Silently Michael pushed the bathroom door almost shut, then, shining the small flashlight beam on the wall above the headboard, gently touched Thomas's left shoulder. When the boy's eyes opened, Michael quickly put a finger to his lips. "Shh, it's just me . . . Michael," he whispered, as he sat down on the edge of the bed.

"Hi," Thomas whispered back. His lips curved into a broad, happy smile. "You came to see me?"

"Sure."

"You're not mad at me or anything?" Thomas asked.

"Mad at you?" *How in the world do kids get so mixed up?* he wondered, then backed off the question. He'd been mixed up about a lot of things since he was just about Thomas's age. "Why would I be mad at you?"

"Well . . ." Thomas pulled himself up to a sitting position. "I wasn't exactly where I was supposed to be last night."

"I'm not mad at you, Thomas," Michael said.

"I caused you a whole lot of trouble."

"I don't want to hear any more talk like that. Okay?"

"Okay. Hey, want a cookie?" Thomas reached for the plate on the bedside table. "Lucielle brought me too many. See, I have two left."

Michael took one. "Rosa does the same thing to me," he said. "I don't think I've ever tasted one of Lucielle's cookies."

"Why don't you just come on down and have some sometimes?" Thomas asked, taking the last cookie.

Michael took a bite to avoid the uncomfortable question. "Mmm. Mmm, these are really good. Maybe better than Rosa's."

"Lucielle wouldn't mind if you wanted some of her cookies," Thomas persisted. "She bakes plenty."

"I keep pretty busy," Michael said.

Thomas didn't seem to hear him. "And when you come down for cookies, we could . . . ah . . . talk or something? Maybe we could be friends, you and me."

I shot him, and he wants to be friends! Michael could barely contain the affection he was feeling for this amazing young boy. He took Thomas's left hand. "We'll shake on being friends. Okay, partner?"

Thomas pumped his hand and smiled. "And you'll come down to see me?"

"I don't know about that."

His smile disappeared. "I can't come up to your place any-more. I got a lecture about that."

"Magdalena was pretty tough on you, was she?"

"Not Mrs. Tavera. Dr. Tavera. The lady you were dancing with at the party. She's tough!"

With an effort Michael kept the placid expression on his face. Of course Lenor had to uphold the rules of the camp, but couldn't she have left the enforcement up to someone else? "We all have to follow the rules, Thomas," Michael said.

"Well that's a rule I don't like. Not one little bit."

"If you'd obeyed it, you wouldn't be lying here hurt and feeling bad," Michael said.

"I don't feel so bad. And I don't hurt anyplace." Thomas raised his right arm, bent his elbow, then opened and closed his hand. "See. I'm fine. And Lucielle's going to get me up for breakfast in the morning."

"I can't tell you how glad I am to hear that," Michael said.

"That friend of yours is some awesome doctor, man."

"Yes, she is."

"If *you* ever get hurt, she'll take care of you and make you well in a flash, I bet." Thomas smiled. "Shirley and I think you and the doc should get married. We saw you dancing." Thomas frowned. "You love her, don't you?"

With all my heart. "Listen, son. I've got to be going back home now."

"Did I say something wrong?" Thomas asked plaintively.

"No, no, of course not. It's late. You need to rest. I still have work to do." He couldn't think of any more excuses. "I just have to go, that's all."

"Oh."

Michael didn't know much about twelve-year-old boys. He wanted to give Thomas a hug, but he decided on the more grown-up tack and shook his left hand again instead. "You get some rest now, partner."

"I will . . . friend."

Michael made sure everything was just as he'd found it, the bathroom door open, the cookie plate on the table. Outside, he breathed deeply of rain-scented air and said a silent prayer of thanks for Thomas's apparent good health. What would have happened if Lenor hadn't been here when he'd brought the boy in? He didn't want to think about that.

A dark figure stepped from the corner of the barn just ahead of him. He thought he recognized her, and was sure she'd seen him.

"Nemesia?" he asked.

"Yes?"

Michael turned his small flashlight toward the sound of her voice, then pointed it toward the ground.

"What are you doing here?" she asked.

"I came to see the boy."

"You shouldn't have," Nemesia said.

"I know. Don't worry, I didn't see Lenor."

"That's not what I'm worried about," she said.

"That's good to know." Michael turned and started to walk away.

"You could have saved yourself a lot of frustration if you'd taken the boy into town."

Michael stopped. "I thought you didn't trust Miller Baldwin."

"I don't. Still . . ."

"No preaching. I'm not in the mood," he said.

"You're never in the mood to listen to me, nephew."

"Don't call me that. You have no right."

"So I've been told," she said sternly. But Nemesia was smiling.

Eighteen

NEMESIA STOOD BEFORE A PEDESTAL OF ROCK. THE water in the *copa* glowed in the flickering light of a white candle in an onyx holder. For her altar she had brought the brass crucifix, her rosary beads, a smooth white stone, and a small *bulto* of the Virgin Mary. Her voice whispered at the water.

"In the name of the Father, the Son, and the Holy Spirit; God the Father; God the Son; God the Holy Spirit; dear friend, Jovita, give me your spiritual strength and protection."

She dipped her fingers into the water and made the sign of the cross on her forehead. "Reveal your wisdom to us, so that harmony may reign once again."

She dipped her fingers again and anointed her eyes.

"Bless the goals that I have seen. Light the perfect path for all."

She touched moist fingers to her lips.

"My words must right so many wrongs. My songs must sing good-byes to chaos."

The ritual continued as Nemesia searched for peace by calling upon many individual spirits. Her plea for help was a desperate call for power.

"Master and Mistress of the Blessed Moon and Stars, unlock the whole of our awareness. Expand our vision with our dreams. Show each of us our perfect future."

Nemesia lifted the cross from the altar and pointed it toward the east.

"Take Lenor away into the sunrise and back into your fold. Let her dreams mature so that all can live in joyful peace."

She turned to the south.

"Deliver the child, Juanita, from her obsession."

She turned to the west.

"Restore the vital energies of the universe to my friends, Steven, Magdalena, and Rafael, and release them from the bonds of sadness. Choose their hour of death to suit the fulfillment of the cycle of life."

She turned to the north.

"Protect my sons, Eloy and Gilberto, from the evil that clouds their lives."

From the altar Nemesia picked up the small white rock, dipped her fingers into the water, and sprinkled a few droplets on the river stone.

"Blessed be, thou creature made by Art, celestial Goddess, moon. Your mission is almost completed."

She held the *monito* that Rosa had given her so long ago, and visualized a silver net falling over it. When it was bound by the web, protected by it, she passed it through the candle flame, then held it to her lips and charged it with the power of her breath.

An exhausted Nemesia gathered her things and returned to the woods. The patient black stallion Nahlahn, sire of Oñique, waited for her in the shadows of the ponderosa.

Nineteen

LENOR AWOKE SLOWLY FROM A PEACEFUL SLEEP. THE full moon spilled a mist of soft light through the translucent sheers that hung at all four of the open windows in her room. She stretched languidly, thought of Thomas in the next room, and decided to look in on him.

He slept with tranquil abandon, bedclothes jumbled, one foot sticking out from the rumpled sheets, completely at ease. Nothing battled within his soul or body except the forces of restoration. Lenor stood next to the bed and looked down at the young, untroubled face, automatically taking note of the rhythm and regularity of his breathing, the color of his skin, the neutral position of his body.

He'd enjoyed the story she'd told him at bedtime, the one she loved to tell above any other, the creation myth according to Wicca. *Amazing how, no matter what age they are, most people never tire of hearing stories,* she thought. Amazing, too, how children of all ages loved to hear about the Old Religion, where honor is the guiding principle and life is ecstatic joy, where spirits reside in the sun and the moon, in the soaring birds, the fierce tiger. *There's not enough magic in the world today.*

Lenor wore only a cotton nightshirt, but the air in the room felt too warm. She stepped to the window that opened onto the *placita,* touched the handles on the wooden sash, then stopped, noticing the faint but distinctive fragrance of horseflesh and leather. *Michael!*

The commotion in her mind and the shiver down her spine told her it wasn't her imagination. Who else, besides her mother or Lucille, would come into this room in the middle of the night? *Michael.* Surely she was mistaken. She looked around. The cookie plate, which had been piled high, was empty.

Of course. One of the campers. Lenor chided herself for being so obtuse. What could be more fun than sneaking into the hacienda on a Saturday night and having a secret meeting right under the nose of the camp's director? The midnight visitor had probably been Thomas's best friend, Shirley. Lenor opened the window, then looked around the room for more evidence. The empty cookie plate was the only clue.

"Good night, love," she whispered. *Good night, Michael.*

Lenor and Apple had had a late-night telephone discussion and agreed to wait until after the funeral to open an official investigation. With what little evidence they'd had now washed down the drain, Apple would start looking into Jovita's death secretly. There wasn't a lot she could do in the short time before the funeral, but she could keep her eyes and ears open. Very little happened in Toya County that Apple didn't hear about. If anyone had had it in for Jovita for any reason, someone would be gabbing about it soon enough. Both Lenor and Apple believed that the funeral would provide an emotional closure that would make an investigation somewhat less traumatic for everyone concerned. Lenor wished the mystery could be solved before the sad trip to the little church on the hill behind their home.

Back in her room, Lenor sat in the deeply recessed adobe-walled window seat and looked out on a pristine setting lighted brilliantly by the moon. An earlier shower had left a glittering blessing as far as the eye could see, and seasoned the night with the keen spice of summer. Breathing deeply of the scented air brought a gladness to her heart, a feeling that everything was going to work out all right. Thomas would heal, thrive, and enjoy the rest of his stay at the camp. Magdalena's infirmity could be simply explained and righted. Jovita's death could still turn out to be from natural causes. Lenor would go back to New York, clear her good name, and make a thoroughly convincing case for her research project to Carl Bowder.

"Lenor?"

It was Jovita's voice. "I've been hoping you'd come," Lenor answered.

"I have a message."

"I can hear you, Grandma, I can smell the fragrance of your perfume, but I can't see you."

"In time, Lenor. When my spirit has passed from the earth plane, you will see me."

"We miss you so much, Grandma."

"You must not waste your energies mourning losses, my child. There is much for you to do."

"Tell me, Grandma," Lenor said.

"I did not die of natural causes. The fate of those living on the Tavera ranch has become uncertain. You must protect yourself and your mother. She is neither safe nor well. You must find the one close to her who believes her to be evil. You must protect the legacy. You must find Barela."

"The legacy? What is the legacy?"

"I must go now."

"Grandma, please!" But she was gone. Lenor could no longer feel her presence nor detect the fragrance of jasmine. She hurried to her desk and wrote down Jovita's message before she could forget it.

Barela! Lenor knew, now, where she could find the name. It wasn't only in her dreams, it was also written in a book. "I have to talk to Grandma again, and I know exactly where I can find out how to do it," she whispered, searching again for the ancient herbal Rafael had given her years ago.

As she had before, she touched every book in every bookcase, looked in every shelf and every drawer. The book was nowhere to be found. For years she'd kept it in the bookcase beside her closet. She searched the bookcase again. Not there.

At least now she knew that her poisoning theory was correct. But what was she going to do about the missing book? It was one of her most prized possessions, a gift from her father, an irreplaceable treasure full of long-forgotten secret formulas that could never be duplicated. Tears of loss and frustration stung her eyes. *You must not waste your energies mourning losses.*

Surely the book was somewhere close by. She'd have to search the entire house. But she didn't have the strength to do it tonight.

The comfortable feather mattress beckoned. A dull throbbing made Lenor rub lightly at the scar on her left temple as she got back into bed. If she could get to sleep before a real headache began, the pain would be gone in the morning. With a conscious effort, she diverted her thoughts from the missing book to the sparkling high relief of rain-sculpted art just outside her window. "We will talk again, Grandma." Finally, she slept, and . . .

In the mountain clearing, a blue moon shone down, its voluptuous, white bounty of light restoring the highland's vitality. The wraith fed Lenor's body, the subtle force of its earthly energy restoring her aura with essential strength. Bound to the earth, yet free to make magic, Lenor felt within herself the bud and blossom of the power needed to bend the unseen, to renew the balance of love and life. The rift between spirit and matter existed only if she would allow it.

But Lenor did not know the rituals for such a reawakening. She sat down on the ground to cry, to mourn her own ignorance.

When she finally looked up, she saw the brilliant aura of the laughing God of love. The Spirit Guide of her deepest consciousness approached, took her hands, and helped her to stand. At last she could be as one with her Third Self, communicating with her deepest wisdom and compassion.

"Am I dreaming?" Lenor asked.

"You are beyond the limits of dreaming, near the boundary of knowing," a male voice answered.

"I want to see the astral place. Will you take me?"

"Before you come with me to the stars, I have a warning."

"Tell me," Lenor said.

"I cannot deny my true self."

"I wouldn't ask it," Lenor assured the aura.

"The light will always follow the dark. Life. Death."

"The sun must set, the sun must rise. Both are necessary blessings. Neither light nor dark will frighten me," Lenor said.

"My image has been perverted by those who fear the darkness that is manifest in this cycle of time."

"Death is continuance. Your heart is my concern."

"My heart is yours."

"Then I will count it sacred." Lenor took his offered hand.

"Come. We can weave our wishes into our lives."

They began weaving with satin ribbons. The silken strands spiraled around their bodies, casting a circle, creating a sacred space.

Confused, Lenor fought against the binding, but the threads continued to pull them closer and closer together.

"Why do you resist? Do your wishes frighten you?" he asked.

"Yes," Lenor answered, "where you're concerned."

"I'm a part of you."

"Still . . . we've never been this close before," Lenor said.

"Yes, we have. And closer. I am always with you." He put his hand on her shoulder. "Let me show you."

Lenor turned away. "I don't want to see," she said, then felt his body press against her.

"You will finally know who I really am."

"Will I be unhappy to know?" Lenor asked.

"Only for a moment."

Lenor felt gentle fingers removing the two combs that held her hair up high on her head. When it fell down her back, she heard him sigh with pleasure. His hands were on her hips as she started to turn around to see who he was.

"Wait," he said, and held her tightly against him. "We will enjoy the setting moon together."

Like a child, she obeyed him. The warmth of his body soothed her, as if it radiated an opiate that could calm even the most violent storm.

As his hands moved forward, over her stomach, his breath teasing her ear, the full, white moon seemed to grow and draw closer. Lenor realized she was seeing not the moon, but the reflection of his radiant aura against the dark sky.

"You are beautiful to see," she said.

"Look more closely."

Again she obeyed. And as she gazed into the light, her own reflection appeared, unbound by satin ribbons, a mere shadow at first, then a fully visible woman.

"It is not the real you," he said.

"Then where is the real me?" she asked.

"I will show you."

In the reflection, his hands appeared, dark against the white of her long skirt, then moved up to untie the ribbon at her throat. As the simple camisole fell open, his shadowy fingers brushed across her full breasts. Lenor trembled at the fierce intake of his breath as the white cloth fluttered to the ground.

"You are the inspiration," he said.

Her eyes grew dark with passion, and she pressed her body

back against the warm white light behind her. The fingertips of both his hands touched the center of her throat, then moved down.

"Your heart is the fire."

She trembled; his fingers moved apart, then slowly circled. Her breasts began to feel full and tender, swelling to fill his hands as he cupped, then pressed gently against the sensitive curves. Her arms crossed before her to hide the uncontrollable response of her body. His arms reached around her, giving her strength, his hands guiding hers. Together they moved as one, her own hands circling, her own hands drawing forth the vital essence of her transformation.

"You are the Earth, the nurturing Mother."

From the cradle of her palms, he pulled the flame of life and tied it about her waist. With the rose-colored strands he fashioned a simple bow.

"These are the two linked motes of consciousness, the symbol of the Divine within you, the sign of infinity."

The fragrance of cedar wafted about them, carried on a gentle breeze. Summer's unseen force increased, infusing motion, caressing them with the promise of a storm. Free of its pinnings, Lenor's long black hair whirled like a silken net about her shoulders. Her full skirt whipped and swayed. Outstretched fingers snared the hand-sewn hem, and he pulled the flowing cloth from her body. The wind slowed to a whisper of scent.

She stared at her image in the mirror, disbelieving, joyful, free except for the ribbon tied round her waist.

"You are the Light in the cycle of time, the Power bringing forth all life."

"Am I bound?" she asked, lifting the streamers that hung down from the rose-colored bow.

"Only by love and truth," he said.

"Then I am bound to you by love," she said.

"Tell me why," he said.

"You have shown me the truth."

She let the ribbons fall and watched them curve at her loins.

But she wasn't the only one who watched. A black serpent coiled at her feet, shining eyes intent on the movement of the flickering satin.

"What is this?" she asked.

"That is what you do not know of me. All that frightens you."

Lenor looked at her reflection again and saw untamed, unconstrained freedom in the form of a sexually aroused goddess. "I have never seen this woman before," she said.

"She is what remains after all material needs are satisfied."

"I do not know her," Lenor said.

"Because you hide her away every time you damp the fire in your heart," he said. "But she is always with you, just as I am."

"Then we are one," she said. As if she had issued a command, the brilliant white aura disappeared. She spoke into the darkness. "I am alone again."

"You are not alone." The voice was deep and soft and resonant.

"Why do you hide behind darkness?" she asked.

"I dwell in the darkness within you. Only your heart's flame can bring my image to light."

As he spoke, Lenor felt his hands on her breasts again, slowly circling, gently caressing, tenderly bidding the fire from her heart to rise. Her body grew weak with love and joy, as his strength increased with trembling ferocity. He asked her to lie down.

"No. The serpent frightens me," she said.

"It is only fear. Nothing more," he reassured.

"But you said it is the part of you I don't yet know."

"They are the same."

"Then I must face my fear with courage," she said.

"To conquer fear, you must welcome it."

Standing in the inky blackness, she caught her breath as the snake began to move across her bare feet. Like a wisp of silk on sensitive skin, a smooth helix motion whispered up the back of her leg. Tremors of fear clashed with her determination to confront the unknown. She waited, her mind searching for peace.

Death is an integral part of the cycle of life. For the first time, she knew the meaning of immortality. Still, she did not want to die.

Held fast by his strength, she screamed, but no sound came out. A wedge gently forced itself between the soft flesh of her thighs. She wanted to stop it, stay its progress, protect herself from the sure knowledge of her own terror. But she dared not anger the unseen beast.

The hand at her waist moved lower, found each fold a budding prize, each valley a new treasure of sensation. Charged with the energy of her awakening, he touched a vibrant essence, tasted delicious nectar, probed the beauty he had found. He left no secret untouched; he found every detail, the boundary of every pulsing cell, the shape and height and breadth of every span. Lenor was breathless, trembling, melting, weakening. She could wait no longer.

She whirled around, reaching into the darkness for the presence who had spoken to her.

"Don't leave me." Her hand fell on the shoulder of a man.

"I've been here all along."

"I need you," she whispered.

"I'm yours to command."

"Help me."

The soft fullness of his lips touched hers, staying her plea with a love that brought peace to her mind. The power of the Goddess infused the twins of Dark and Light with perfect freedom. And the serpent that was Lenor's fear coiled into the darkness within her.

Secure in the circle of his arms, his kisses eased her mind.

He whispered, "I love you."

Now, without fear to bind her, free of the loathsome constraint of terror, she spoke the truth. "I have always loved you." And she bade him to lie down beside her on the soft bosom of Mother Earth.

Then the serpent arched, and Lenor cried out while waves of rampant energy forced more and more of its length deep inside her.

"The beast will destroy our love," she cried.

"The beast is gone," he said.

"He inflames me!"

"It was I who set the fire."

Her strong arms wound around him then, pulling him closer. Love, the law of the Goddess, ruled them, guiding them through all her aspects. The gentle love of friends. Fierce maternal love of child. Compassionate love of all beings. Ecstatic love of self. Passionate, sexual love. Divine love.

And at last the darkness disappeared and the Goddess Moon spread a silver veil over her children.

"We are possessed," Lenor said, staring up into the night sky.

"Divine possession," he said.

"Now may I know your name?" she asked.

"Michael."

The dark face of passion gazed at her, and Lenor felt no fear. She took his hand, looked up into the sky again, and whispered his name. *Michael.*

The stars above began to grow, their light spreading until white circle touched circle. The light of truth encompassed her, and the darkness between the stars vanished in a blaze of intense heat. Too hot! She pulled the moon's coverlet from her body and flung it aside—

Lenor opened her eyes. The bright white light remained. She was staring at the sunlit ceiling of her own bedroom. She looked down at her naked body; she was shimmering with the dew of passion, trembling. Her breath still came in short gasps. *Michael!*

Without looking, she felt the other side of the bed, then jerked her hand away from the mound at her side. She looked, saw a rounded form under the jumble of the sheet she'd just thrown off herself. It took every bit of strength she could summon to lift the corner of the white material. Beneath it another sheet. The material seemed to be wrapped about something. What?

With trembling hands, she peeled back a layer of cotton, then another, then another. One eye. One ear. A bloody paw.

Lenor choked back a scream. Her stomach churned, threatened to revolt. None of the grisly scenes she'd witnessed in the emergency room had prepared her for the sight of a mountain lion, half its head blown away, lying beside her in her own bed. She scrambled to the foot of the bed, grabbed the white nightshirt she'd thrown over the end, and tried to stop shaking long enough to put it on. She couldn't. The unruly garment kept flapping toward the mound of horror beside her. She fell to the floor, clutching desperately at the cotton garment.

She finally managed to get into the nightshirt and button it all the way up to her throat. The tile floor felt cold beneath her bare bottom, but she couldn't move. *Think it through,* she told herself, *just think it through.* Her brain felt paralyzed, incapable of making sense. All she could think was that Michael had been in her room and left the cougar's body as a warning to stay away from him. Michael's physical presence might have made her dream of him. She clutched at her throat to hold back a sob. Or had he actually . . . ? A flush of desire, more powerful than she'd ever felt in her life, coursed through her body and left her limp with dread.

"No!"

On hands and knees she scurried away from the bed and pulled herself to a standing position against the wall. *Think!* Call Rudolfo. Check on Thomas. Call Rudolfo. Call Apple. Let Rudolfo call the sheriff. Keep Magdalena from finding out. Keep Magdalena away from—

Lenor's fingers found the edge of the bathroom door. She inched along the wall until she could look into the room. The door at the other side of the bathroom was closed. She looked at the clock on the bedside table. "Thank God." Lucielle had already come to take Thomas to breakfast. After a quick look into Thomas's room to make sure he was gone, she hurried to her phone and dialed.

"Rudolfo?"

"Yes?"

"This is Lenor. Will you come to my room? I need your help."

"I was just about to—"

"I need you now."

"I'll be right there."

While she waited, Lenor looked around her room for signs of entry, for anything that might give her a clue to who had committed this horrifying act of trespass. No footprints appeared on any part of the tile floor, no impressions had been left in the Navajo rugs. The windows were raised, just as she'd left them, their screens intact. She put on her robe, then, with a tissue, carefully opened the bedroom door and stood just outside it.

"Little sister! I wondered when you'd get around to—"

"Don't touch anything," she said, wishing she didn't have to be so abrupt or forgo their usual hug of greeting. "The sheriff might want to dust for fingerprints."

"The sheriff?" Rudolfo asked, stepping inside.

Lenor closed the door and pointed to the bed. "Someone's idea of a practical joke."

Rudolfo crossed the room and looked down at the bloody, partially exposed carcass. "Old Woosey," he said softly, then turned to Lenor and frowned. "Were you here when this . . . happened?"

"Sound asleep. But even as tired as I was, I still don't see how someone could have come in here and put this thing in my bed without my knowing it."

"Do you have any idea who might have done this?" Rudolfo asked.

"Not a clue."

"I'll tell Magdalena," he said. "She has to start locking—"

"I don't want you to tell anyone but the sheriff," Lenor interrupted. "Call Apple. Ask her to come out, but don't tell her why until she arrives. Leave everything just as it is. I'm going to treat this like a threat, and I want her to do the same."

"But Magdalena should—"

"Please, Rudolfo. My mother has enough to worry about right now. I'll tell her later."

He nodded. "I'll get rid of this thing as soon as Apple is finished with her investigation."

"Tell Apple something else for me. The herbal that belonged to Leonora Tavera—remember it?" Rudolfo nodded. "It's missing."

"So you think whoever brought Old Woosey stole the book, too?" he asked.

"I don't know. I looked for it last weekend. It wasn't here then, so I don't know when it disappeared."

"I'll tell her," Rudolfo said.

Lenor gave him a hug. "Thank you," she said softly. "I'll go find my mother now. I'll keep her busy, away from here, until you tell me that this *thing* is gone."

Twenty

IT WASN'T DIFFICULT TO KEEP MAGDALENA, AND EVERYone else, busy and away from Lenor's bedroom. Breakfast for the camp kids at dawn, for the family after that. People started arriving while the family was still at the table, and the steady stream of friends and neighbors continued to come and pay their respects. Steven had kept an all-night vigil in the church with his beloved Jovita, and now, exhausted, he rested at Angelina's.

Later, at the high mass he'd requested, he looked tired and careworn.

"In nomine Patris, et Filii, et Spiritus Sancti. Amen. Introibo ad altare Dei. Ad Deum qui laetificat juventutem meam."

Lenor held Steven's hand throughout the Latin mass he and Jovita had enjoyed so much together. Father Rand, from Las Vegas, had learned the ancient way of worship just for them and taught the choir their Latin chants, though the young priest never celebrated the old liturgy in the other parish. And Peter Vigil, too often absent from the tiny choir of seven voices, sang the Gregorian Chants from memory, as if he'd never missed a practice or a mass.

"I believe she's at peace now," Steven whispered to Lenor after the graveside rosary had been said. They were standing alone, just the two of them, in the small cemetery in the church-yard.

"Father Rand did a beautiful job," Lenor said, looking down at the fresh earth heaped at the foot of the gravestone.

Steven leaned closer. "While I sat with my Jovita last night, I saw a vision of the Goddess," he said. "Seeing the Virgin of Guadalupe was like an epiphany to me. She told me that the Darkness in the Circle of Life is necessary and good. It brings new life."

Lenor couldn't speak for a moment. She had met the Dark-ness last night, and the encounter had left her feeling as if she were a part of something more, a perpetual continuum. Had her grand-father seen her dream as she had experienced it? Did it mean that she would be responsible for bringing "new life"?

"I'm glad the Virgin could comfort you, Grandpa," she said finally. "Your grief will be easier to bear." *Please let that be so!*

"We are old," Steven said. "We were ready to answer God's call. Perhaps I will follow not far behind my love."

"Grandpa, don't say such things."

"I would be content either way," he said, tilting his head to the side. "It's *you* I'm worried about, Lenor. You're not happy. I can see it in your eyes. You're not well. Look how thin you've become in just a few days. It would seem that the serpent has come out from under his rock. What do you fear, child?"

Lenor was shaking her head in denial, but he had seen the truth. How could she begin to tell him? So much had changed since the time when she could reveal her deepest heart to him. But she couldn't lie to him, either. "So many things can go wrong here on earth, Grandpa."

"If we live expecting the unexpected, we can survive,"

Steven said. "You have secrets you don't want to share with me. That isn't wrong, Lenor. It's simply kind. Your concern for me is unselfish, and you'll confide in me when the time is right. Live your life as you must, not as others want it."

"I'll try never to hurt you, Grandpa. You have to believe that," Lenor said.

"I believe you with all my heart," he said. "Now go back to the house and find your father. He needs you right now . . . and I need to be alone with my Jovita. We have much to discuss."

Has she already told him?

After the services, the house filled with Steven and Jovita's friends. The kitchen counters seemed to sag under the weight of all the food people had brought for the wake: *carne con chile verde,* tender meat in fiery green chile sauce; *pozole,* hominylike corn with pork and red chile; *buñuelos,* a sweet bread; *capirotada,* bread pudding with raisins; and *chiles rellenos,* long green chiles stuffed with cheese. As tradition dictated, it was a feast like one served on a wedding day.

By the time Steven had joined them, Lenor had shared a small plate of food and a good long talk with her father. Shared tears, too, had brought them closer, and Lenor felt she knew his heart as she'd never known it before. As usual, Steven had known what had to be done to make things right.

When the last neighbor had finally gone, Aunt Isabel, Arthur, and Lita said their good-byes and left in their rented car for the Albuquerque airport. Except for Rafael, everyone was exhausted. Magdalena disappeared into her bedroom for a much-needed nap. Steven trudged back up the hill to the graveyard. Lucielle returned to the bunkhouse to start the campers' supper.

"I'm going to take a little ride," Rafael said. "Do you remember that place . . . ?"

"Where the maidenhair grows," Lenor said. "I remember. Grandma loved it there."

"I'll be home in time for the family mass." Rafael took Lenor in his arms. "Thank you for talking to me. Thank you for telling me about Steven's visit from Nuestra Señora de Guadalupe. I couldn't have made it through all this in my right mind if it hadn't been for . . ."

"Ssh, Papa. I know. I know. I love you, Papa."

"I love you, daughter. More than you can ever know."

Lenor watched him go. It would be so sad when he learned that Jovita had been murdered. But now wasn't the time to tell him. She felt frantic to get things started. From the phone in her bedroom, where, thankfully, Old Woosey was conspicuously absent, she called Apple.

"Anything yet?" Lenor asked.

"The old mountain lion finally did somebody some good," Apple said. "We got lucky. A halfway decent bloody fingerprint on whatever that was he was wrapped in. No other prints in your room or in Jovita's. We don't have a match on this one yet—it'll be a while—but the computer in Albuquerque is working on it."

"Already?"

"I flew it down there on a charter from Las Vegas. The guy was going anyway, so . . ."

"What about the book?"

"None of my people have seen anything like it anywhere. I remember you were looking for it last weekend. Ask your mother if she's found it. At least then we'd know it's not somewhere in that big house of yours."

"I didn't think of that. Kind of weary-minded, I guess. I'll check the library, then ask Mama, if she's up from her nap."

"If you find it, don't touch it. Leave it right where it is."

"I'm familiar with keeping the chain of evidence intact. You wouldn't believe how many rapes and assaults we see, and all the documentation that goes with that sort of thing. When you work in a New York City hospital like Foley, the police see to it that you learn fast about preserving the evidence."

"Little paranoid, sorry. I haven't arrested anyone, except for being drunk, for a long time. Bear with me, kiddo. I have people watching your house now. They have orders not to let anyone near it."

"But what if—"

"Don't worry. They'll stay out of sight. No one will even know they're there."

"My father just rode out to the east canyon," Lenor said.

"Damn! I knew I should have told you at the funeral. I just couldn't bring myself to disturb you and Steven after the burial. Damn!"

Lenor heard Apple call out to someone, then come back on the line.

"Hold on a sec."

The phone clattered to the desktop. Muffled voices. After a minute, a door slammed.

"I'm back. I've got somebody on his way out there. He'll pick up a horse at the Ortiz place. I told him to stay out of the way and out of sight."

"Thanks, Apple," Lenor said. "Now that everybody's gone, I'd like to check my grandparents' bedroom again. Are you through in there?"

"Got it during the funeral," Apple said.

"If we're looking for poison, I think it might be there."

"Why not the kitchen?" Apple asked.

"Because everyone eats the same thing at the same time. If the poison had been in any of the food, we'd have buried at least three more people today."

"You're right. Okay. We'll wait on the exhumation till you're finished. I can rouse a judge anytime." She was silent, then, "God! I'm *not* looking forward to that."

"I know what you mean," Lenor said. "So let's get busy. Maybe somebody will walk into your office and confess."

"If we're lucky," Apple said. "Don't forget to ask Magdalena about the book."

"I'll do it right now."

> Bright sun, Dark death,
> Lord of winds, Lord of the dance,
> Sun child, Winter-born king

As Magdalena watched, the Holy Spirit traveled through a full cycle of the seasons. Radiantly white, his summer aura brought dazzling warmth to her bed. Then she grew chilled as his brilliance subsided and cooled, as the dark sleep of winter brought him to death in service of the life force. He gladly gave up his life to sustain the spiraling motion of the wheel of the year. Darkness and death were neither evil nor sacrificial, but balanced the cycle so that it could continue in perfect motion and harmony. Magdalena knew Jovita would be reborn as the Sun Child at the winter solstice.

"If only all had been created in your image," Magdalena said.

"Some aspire," was the Spirit's reply.

"I know of none."

"You know of one."

"One who is wild and free, but never cruel? One who is angry, but never violent? A man who loves without coercion?" she asked.

"He aspires to such."

"Who is this man?"

"He will come to you when you need him most. But you must be ready for him."

"I'm ready *now*," she said, and could feel her pulse racing.

"Awake!"

Vibrant energies flowing, Magdalena opened her eyes, sat up with a smile on her face, and looked around the bedroom. She fully expected to see Jovita at the foot of her bed, but there was no one there. Disappointed, she climbed out of bed and went into the bathroom. The malaise that had accompanied her to bed descended again to replace the excitement of her dream.

"So tired," she whispered to her mirror image. "I'm not ready, after all."

Lenor opened the bedroom door a crack. "Mama?" she said quietly. She peeked in. The bed was rumpled but empty. "Mama?"

"In here."

Lenor followed the direction of the voice into the bathroom. Magdalena leaned heavily against the lavatory, looking tired and drained of energy. "Let me help you back to bed, Mama," Lenor said as she wrapped her arm around Magdalena's waist.

"I was going to help Lucielle . . ."

"Get a little more rest first, Mama. I'll go see how Lucielle's doing and get you a cup of tea."

"*Maravilla?* I need something to get me going again."

"Then that's what I'll bring." Lenor helped her mother to sit on the edge of the bed, then softly kissed her cheek. "Just don't worry about helping until you feel better, okay?"

"Okay," Magdalena said, sinking back against the pillows. Her eyes were closed before Lenor reached the doorway.

Lenor headed for the bunkhouse, found Lucielle hard at work, and filled a kettle with water.

"What's your pleasure? Orange Pekoe or something exotic?" Lucielle asked.

"*Maravilla.* It's for Mama."

"Looks like you could use a little stimulant yourself," Lucielle said.

"Good idea." Lenor half turned from the stove. "How's Thomas doing?"

"That kid is unbelievable. He put away enough chow for three at lunch and wouldn't hear of going back to bed. He's up at the barn watching the others. I told Jerry to keep a close eye on him." Lucielle grinned. "His biggest concern was to make sure that I get a lot of cookies baked up this afternoon so he could have them in the bunkhouse tonight."

"He doesn't want to sleep in the house again tonight?" Lenor asked, relieved at her good fortune.

"Are you kidding? That child has got too many stories to tell now, and he can't wait to get started."

"He's one great kid," Lenor said.

Lucielle nodded. "Hey, how 'bout taking some of Thomas's cookies to Magdalena?" She pointed to the end of the long dining table where a tray sat with a plate of cookies and a cup and saucer.

"I was going to make the trip myself, as soon as Nemesia got back."

"Nemesia?"

"I didn't want to bother you. She helped with lunch, and she's coming back to give me a hand with supper. She'll be here any minute."

"Well, what do you know about that?" Lenor said.

"Not a thing. And I'm *not* asking any questions."

"I don't blame you." Lenor poured boiling water into the teapot, set it on the tray, then carefully lifted the tray. "Thanks, Lucielle."

How odd that Nemesia would agree to help cook, Lenor thought as she walked back to the main house. Some years ago, in a fit of anger, Rudolfo's wife had abdicated her position as ruler of the kitchen and vowed never to lift another Tavera spoon in any Tavera kitchen. Lenor, ten at the time, had not seen the conflict. At the time, during a financial crisis, Magdalena had been riding with the hands, working as all the cowboys had to do. Nemesia's tirade and subsequent change of jobs from cooking to housekeeping had been a hardship on everyone. Lenor had never learned the reason for the upheaval, but she suspected that the rift between Nemesia and Magdalena went much deeper than an argument over menus or recipes.

Lenor knocked lightly on the door of the master bedroom.

"Come in."

She stepped inside. "I was half-expecting you to be asleep."

"I should get up," Magdalena said.

"Not to worry. Everything's running smoothly," Lenor said, "and I'd say it's high time you took a little time off." Lenor crossed the room and put the tray on the bed. "Thought you might like something to eat." She lifted the white linen cloth. "*Bizcochitos* with anise. Your favorite."

Magdalena pulled herself up to a sitting position and sighed. "I don't feel very hungry." She looked at the plate of still-warm shortbread sparkling with sugar. "Mmm, those do look good, though."

"Are you comfortable enough?" Lenor asked, taking her mother's wrist to check her pulse.

"I'm comfortable." Magdalena pulled her arm away. "And I'm feeling just fine. I'm just . . . tired." The effort of talking seemed to be too much. Magdalena sagged back.

Lenor put a hand on her forehead. Cool. Perhaps a little too cool. There were dark circles of fatigue under her mother's eyes, and her fingers brushed nervously at a wrinkle in the sheet. "Will you do something for me, Mama?" she asked.

"If you'll stop fussing over me as if I were a sick child."

"I'll stop fussing if you'll promise me you'll stay in bed and rest all day tomorrow."

"Don't be silly. Lucielle needs my help."

"I'll help her," Lenor lied, deciding it would be best not to tell Magdalena about Nemesia's unusual offer. "We'll get along just fine. Right now, I have to look for something in the library. I'll come back and get your tray when I'm finished. We'll have a little visit, and then you can nap some more. Okay?"

"Okay."

In her grandparents' room, Lenor went through every drawer, shelf, and closet. She searched pockets in clothing, beneath cushions and furniture, behind pictures and bottles and baskets. Lenor tested each one, but no alien scent escaped from the several bottles of homemade fragrance on Jovita's dresser. Apple's people hadn't left a clue that they'd been there to search and dust for fingerprints. Nothing appeared to be disturbed or amiss. The library was next.

Lenor intended to ask Magdalena about the herbal if she couldn't find it. The book was nowhere in the library, but when Lenor got back to her mother's room, Magdalena was sound asleep. The tray was still on the bed, its contents untouched. She looked down at the sleeping woman. In repose, Magdalena appeared to be thin and frail and defenseless, the dark circles beneath her eyes an ominous reminder that her once-robust constitution was losing a battle. No more time could be wasted.

★   ★   ★

"Lenor Tavera? Is that you?" Estelle came around the clinic check-in counter, then leaned back for a full-length view. "My God, it *is* you!" The pleasant, chubby young woman rushed forward, arms outstretched.

"Estelle Garcia," Lenor said when they'd finished their hugging. "I haven't seen you since—" She smiled and held her hand at hip level. "Since you were this high."

Estelle wiggled the fingers of her left hand in front of Lenor's face. "It's Estelle Parrish now," she said proudly.

"Little Bobby Parrish? Little Robert Matthew Parrish?"

"Not so little anymore," Estelle said. "You should see him. He's six feet, weighs two hundred and twenty pounds."

"And still cute as a button, I'll bet."

Estelle pushed at the end of her nose. "Pug nose and all."

"Well, congratulations. I didn't know you were a nurse now, either."

"Just finished school in January. Boy, was I lucky, too. I started to work here last month." Estelle frowned, glanced away, then looked back at Lenor. "I guess lucky is the wrong way to put it. You knew about Paula, didn't you?"

"What about Paula?"

"She got real sick, can't work, just has to rest all the time."

"What's wrong with her?"

"Nobody knows. The doctors in Albuquerque can't find a thing."

Magdalena. Lenor could see her mother's face. *So tired.* "That's too bad about Paula," she said. "Maybe it's just something that has to run its course."

"I hope so," Estelle said. "So what brings you to see us today?"

"I'd like to talk to Dr. Baldwin, if he has the time," Lenor said.

"Maybe later. He had to go to Guadalupita. Is someone sick out at your place?"

"My mother's a little under the weather," Lenor said.

"That woman works too hard. Up before five, cooking and

feeding all those kids, giving riding lessons and teaching who knows what all."

"Since Miller isn't here, maybe I could just take a look at my mother's medical record. Would that be all right?" Lenor asked.

"Well, of course. You're a doctor now, aren't you?" Estelle shook her head. "I should have been calling you Dr. Tavera all along! What's the matter with me? Come on back to the record room."

The record room was not much more than a large closet, with just enough space for six four-drawer file cabinets and a table with two chairs. As soon as they entered the room, the phone rang.

"Sorry about the cramped quarters. This is temporary, till they get the new shelves built. Just make yourself at home."

"Thanks."

Patients' folders were in alphabetical order. Lenor pulled open the drawer marked *T-U* and walked her fingers over the name tabs. Tavell. Tavenio. Tavernier. Taves. Maybe Tavera was misfiled. She started at the front of the drawer, Tabaka, Tacker, and went all the way through to the end of the T's, Tuttle. No Tavera. She checked the 'B's' for Barela. No luck.

"Estelle, I hate to bother you, but my mother's file seems to be missing."

Estelle came into the room and repeated Lenor's search. "You're right, it's not here. Let me check Dr. Baldwin's office."

"Look for lab slips, too," Lenor said.

Estelle came back in a couple of minutes. "Not there either. No lab slips. Now that's a puzzle. Magdalena was in here just a few weeks ago." She thought a minute. "Only thing I can think is that he might have taken them home with him. He does that sometimes."

"And he's in Guadalupita."

"But Inez is there. She lives in now, since her husband died."

"Do you think she'd mind if I dropped in?"

Estelle smiled. "She'd love to see you. I'll call her and tell her you're on your way."

"No," Lenor said, too abruptly, then more gently, "I'd rather surprise her. Okay?"

"Sure. Good to see you again, Dr. Tavera." Estelle beamed. "Has such a nice ring to it. *Dr. Tavera.*"

Miller Baldwin's white frame house was set back from the main street. The dusty front yard, cleared of any kind of trees or shrubbery, had been used as a parking area since the days when the doctor saw patients in his home. A picket fence that had probably once been white leaned out toward the street and looked as if it might fall over. It had been tipped that way for as long as Lenor could remember.

When she knocked on the screen door, a small dog began to bark somewhere behind the building, and Inez came huffing toward the front door.

"Lenor Tavera! Get in this house, child. Why didn't you tell me you were coming?" She shook a chubby finger. "I'd have had some *sopaipillas* frying." As Inez talked in rapid-fire Spanish, she pulled Lenor further into the living room, which was filled with the fragrance of something delicious cooking. "How's your mother? How are you? Let me have a look." From her five-foot-two vantage point, she gave Lenor a complete, up-and-down survey. "You're just as beautiful as ever!" She shook her finger. "But too thin. Too thin."

"You're looking fit, Inez," Lenor said finally, when she was able to get a word in.

"Haven't been sick a day since I quit nursing. You better be careful yourself, too, now that you're a doctor. Sick people can give you all kinds of things you don't want. How about a cup of coffee?" Inez started walking toward the kitchen at the back of the house, and Lenor followed her. "I just baked an apple pie for dinner, but you can have a piece right now. Doc B. won't care. Wish he was here to see you."

"So do I. I wanted to talk to him."

"Probably be back pretty soon. Can you stay to dinner? We're having baked heart and dressing, Doc's favorite."

Even growing up on a cattle ranch, where the everyday fare

was some part of a cow, Lenor had never cultivated a taste for beef heart. "I wish I could stay, but I need to get back home," she said.

"Roy will be here," Inez said, as if she were trying to tempt Lenor with her old high school friend's presence. "Have a seat. Why do you need to get back home, anyway?" She stopped. "Oh, dear." Her expression changed to concern. "I'm so sorry, Lenor. Doc B. told me about your grandmother this afternoon. If I'd known sooner, I'd have been at the funeral."

"Thank you, Inez. And now my mother's not feeling well."

"Magdalena's not well?" Inez clucked. "Ranch work. Now that'll wear out a body quicker than anything." She began filling an old, blue enamel coffeepot. "Maybe you ought to stay for dinner so you can talk to Doc B."

"Do you know if he's brought home any medical files lately?"

"Could have. I don't keep track."

"My mother's record isn't at the clinic. Estelle thought he might have brought it home."

"Why don't you have a look in his office, while I get this pot to boiling. Remember where it is? Off the living room."

"I remember," Lenor said. "I'll be right back. Thanks."

The small room was almost exactly as it had been for years. The same rolltop desk was on one side; the same clean, well-worn couch sat against the wall on the opposite side, the same ancient, cane-bottom wheelchair in the corner. A cluttered countertop extended the length of the wall on the far side of the room, with one long shelf, full of books, above it. The three glass-fronted cabinets higher up, where the doctor used to keep medicines, were now stuffed to overflowing with untidy stacks of papers. Miller's mounted collection of antique medical instruments hung in every available space on the walls.

Lenor quickly scanned the contents of the glass-fronted cabinets for the distinctive pink color of the record folder, then went through the shelves below the countertop. It took her only a few minutes to search every easily accessible storage place in the small room. Nothing. There were three locked drawers in the rolltop, three unlocked. She turned to leave the room, decided against asking Inez for the key quite yet, and opened the small top left desk drawer again. A letter opener just might do the trick, and it would be better for all concerned if no one knew she'd opened the doctor's locked files.

Past practice with her mother's jewelry box, when she and Apple would play dress-up, proved valuable, and Lenor had the first drawer open in seconds, revealing two Mason jars full of plum wine, two glasses, and a half-empty bottle of whiskey. She had the second drawer open even quicker. Jackpot! Beneath an old hand-knitted sweater that was stuffed into the drawer she saw several pink folders. The first was Magdalena Tavera's.

Lenor flipped through it from back to front. Major points: three miscarriages; one live birth, a nine-pound baby girl; a broken leg from being kicked by a horse. For a woman her age, except for the pregnancy problems, Magdalena had a remarkably uneventful medical history. The most recent entries were sketchy, with fatigue, minor weight loss, and slight abdominal pain listed as the only symptoms. Estrogen therapy was prescribed. Premarin and Provera. *"Patient was instructed to watch for the recurrence of menstrual bleeding and take naps as often as possible."*

It had been years since Magdalena's menopause had begun, and the estrogen probably should have been started then, but it wasn't like her to see a doctor for a natural event. Dr. Baldwin probably hadn't even known about the cessation of menses until a few weeks ago, and he'd ordered the proper lab tests under the circumstances. There was no mention of depression, senility, Alzheimer's, or anxiety. Lenor didn't know what she had expected to find, but there was nothing unusual about the file— except for the fact that it had been hidden. And so were several others. Lenor Tavera. Rafael, Steven, and Jovita.

Her own record told her nothing she didn't already know. Rafael's contained the straightforward facts: a bout with pneumonia during the record-breaking cold of the 1986 winter; a broken and lacerated finger, compliments of an overstretched strand of barbed wire with a mind of its own; and nothing else, extraordinary or otherwise. Steven's noted the major heart and lung problems later in his life, and commented, *"Patient refuses all treatment."*

There was no history of a heart problem in Jovita's record, only a recent note about an allergy to an unknown substance. *"The patient refused further tests."* A copy of Jovita's death certificate was attached. *"Cause of death: Cardiac arrest due to respiratory paralysis."*

There were three other folders. Curious, Lenor lifted them out and looked at the names. Two were unfamiliar, but the third was Michael Martino. She couldn't help but look. It was the thinnest of all the files. His thirty-four years of living had generated a copy of his birth certificate; a record of his shots and vaccinations; progress reports on the normal course of mumps, measles, chicken pox; and one accident. A very bad accident— January 23, two years ago—a broken arm, broken ribs, collapsed lung, internal bleeding, transfusion, blood type A positive. The notes were fairly extensive. He'd been brought in by Eloy Seña after being kicked repeatedly by a rogue stallion. His hospital stay had been short: *"Patient walked out against physician's advice."*

Lenor shook her head. Michael had told her that no one at his ranch had been to a doctor since Rosa had started working there nine years ago. Why would he have lied about it? And why would Dr. Baldwin have Michael's file here in his home? Lenor closed her eyes, took a deep breath, then leaned against the desk. She felt weak but not hungry, groggy but wide awake. Her mind seemed to be trying to think through a maze of cobwebs. Nothing made any sense. She opened her eyes and looked down.

A small, rectangular pillow lay in the bottom of the drawer. Lenor lifted one corner. There were more pink file folders beneath it. Lenor picked up the top record. Stamped in red on the front: BLOOD DONOR. The name, Nemesia Seña. She flipped through the pages noting illnesses, accidents, five pregnancies, the third child a boy who had been stillborn almost thirty years ago. Little Angel had been buried in the Tavera churchyard. Nothing unusual caught her eye. There were several more records under the pillow, and Lenor reached for the next one. Rudolfo Seña.

302 ◆ MARY ELIZABETH LYNN ◆

"Coffee's ready!"

"Just another minute." Something kept nagging at her brain. Something was missing . . . or, more likely, she was missing something.

Why would Dr. Baldwin keep these records locked up here? Lenor wondered as she hurriedly returned the folders to the drawer. Maybe he preferred seeing his longtime patients in his home. She looked around the room again to make sure she hadn't missed the basic tools and medical instruments needed for examining patients. There were none, not even a thermometer. She opened Magdalena's record again. Her mother had had no difficulty conceiving, but carrying a baby to term had seemed impossible at one point. *"Patient is advised to adopt."*

Not surprisingly, Magdalena had seen Dr. Baldwin many times during her fourth pregnancy, when she was carrying Lenor. Many problems had been noted, among them a fetal heart sound that would indicate a damaged mitral valve. In her hurried scan the first time through, she'd missed the implication. Lenor was born with what should have been a debilitating heart problem. *Impossible!*

Lenor quickly arranged the contents of the drawer just as she'd found them, locked it, then eyed the wide center drawer. Should she open that one, too? No. She went back into the kitchen, wishing she'd had more time. Hot coffee and apple pie were waiting on the table.

"Any luck?" Inez asked.

"I looked everywhere. Didn't find a thing."

"He has a couple of locked drawers in his desk. Want me to get the key for you?"

"What key, Inez?"

Two heads snapped toward the kitchen door.

"Doc B! That was a quick trip."

"Hysterical mother," Roy said from somewhere in the hallway behind his father. "Croup."

"I'm glad it was nothing serious." Inez got up from her chair and pulled two more coffee mugs from the open shelf near the sink. "Now isn't this a nice surprise? Sit yourselves down."

"What key, Inez?" Miller asked again, stepping back and allowing his son to precede him into the room.

"Well now, aren't you the grumpy one?" Inez winked at Lenor. "That old car of his must have given him some more trouble." She looked back at the doctor. "Can't you two just say hello to our guest first?"

"Hello, Dr. Tavera," Miller said flatly.

If smiles could be dangerous, Roy's face would have cracked into a thousand pieces. "Lenor, Lenor, Lenor. Am I dreaming? How long has it been since you've set foot in this house?"

Lenor wondered why the man was being so effusive. "It's been a while, Roy."

"Well, this is just great."

"Calm down, Roy," Inez warned playfully.

Roy pulled another chair from the corner of the room and slid it close to Lenor's. "Grandma's funeral service was lovely," he said. "So sad, but lovely. The Latin was just the right touch, don't you think?"

"Yes," Lenor said.

Roy's smile returned. "Are you staying to dinner?" he asked, then quickly looked at Inez. "You *did* ask her to dinner, didn't you, Inez?"

Inez put her hands on her hips and gave him her you–idiot look.

"You'll stay, won't you, Lenor? Please."

Before she could answer, Miller sat down at the table and cleared his throat for attention. "Now, what's this about a key?" he asked, his tone firm.

Inez told him the reason for Lenor's visit as she poured both of them some coffee. "So I told her I'd get the key to those file drawers in your desk," she finished.

"I see," Miller said to Inez.

He turned to Lenor, and she could have sworn she'd seen a shadow of disgust cross his face when he saw how Roy was looking at her. Roy hadn't taken his eyes off her profile since he'd sat down. His scrutiny was beginning to make her uncomfortable.

Miller cleared his throat again. "I can save you some trouble, Dr. Tavera. There aren't any files here anymore. They're all kept at the clinic now. Estelle probably just overlooked the one you wanted. I'll have to speak to her about her filing."

"I shouldn't have bothered her," Lenor said.

"You couldn't bother anybody," Roy said sweetly.

"I'll be glad to drive you back over there right now," Miller said.

And you won't be able to find the files either, Lenor thought. *Then why has he offered to drive me?* A shiver of fear flashed down her spine. Logically she ought to take him up on his offer, call his bluff, and watch his reaction when his lies were exposed, but an undefined discomfort wouldn't let her. "It's not that important, Miller."

Miller looked relieved, and smiled for the first time since he'd appeared at the door. "Why don't you come in tomorrow? I'd look forward to seeing you."

I'll just bet you would.

Twenty-one

LENOR DROVE BACK HOME IN RECORD TIME, AS IF SHE were being chased by demons. Miller Baldwin had lied to her, but even after looking at the records he kept at home, she couldn't figure out why. She'd seen nothing that would have caused concern, no evidence of malpractice, no evidence of any kind of mistreatment. Of course, she would never know if any of the illnesses had been misdiagnosed—except for her own nonexistent heart problem—but even knowing what might have happened long ago wouldn't help her any now.

There were so many questions to be answered and so little time. Too many things were not as they appeared to be. A woman with no history of heart disease lay buried in the private cemetery near the hacienda's chapel, dead of a sudden heart attack. A woman of unusually robust health lay in bed, exhausted and depleted. Concealed within the massive chest of a man with the physique of a New York Jets' linebacker and the energy of a bulldozer beat the heart of a liar. A young woman danced naked . . .

"Damn!" Her fist came down on the steering wheel. She should have looked for Juanita's medical record when she'd had the chance. Something about the woman had puzzled Lenor ever since her grandfather's birthday party. Juanita wasn't well.

There had to be a logical explanation for everything, and Lenor was determined to find it. As she pulled into the shade of the carport and cut the old pickup truck's engine, Rudolfo came out on his front porch. He motioned to her, and she met him halfway.

"I helped Apple take Old Woosey away," he said in a low voice.

"No one saw you, I hope?"

"No."

"Has Apple talked to you since?" she asked.

"She called while you were gone. Said to ask you about that piece of pink ribbon in the sheet the body was wrapped in. The one with the fingerprint on it. Wanted to know if it meant anything to you."

"Pink ribbon?" Lenor shuddered inside. Michael had tied a rose-colored ribbon about her waist in her dream. "I don't know what that could mean," she managed.

"Didn't make any sense to me either," Rudolfo said.

"Rudolfo, thank you."

"Anytime, little sister." He started to go, then, "May I give you some advice?"

"Of course."

"Trust no one." He turned abruptly and walked away, taking long strides in the direction of the barn.

Her eyes followed him up the hill. Surely he didn't mean her mother and father, her family and friends. If he did, then why?

Belief in the supernatural was a given in this corner of the world, no matter what outsiders like George might think. Lenor had to consider it. Any one of them, Magdalena included, could be under the influence of some kind of evil spell. But who would want to do such an unscrupulous thing?

And what about Magdalena's mysterious illness? Lenor shook her head to force the thought away, but her analytical mind wouldn't let her. Three possibilities: real, supernatural, or sham.

Under what conditions would Magdalena fake an illness to get what she wanted—Lenor's return home? Under great stress, and believing Jovita was murdered, she might be able to do it. *Impossible.* Only Lenor, Apple, and the killer knew that Jovita had been murdered. So why hadn't Magdalena at least mentioned the touchy subject? Straightforward, that's the way she'd always been, no matter what. A charade was not logical—unless, perhaps, the illness was metaphysical. *But what's logical at this point?*

Lenor hurried to the house, went straight to the master bedroom, and knocked on the bedroom door.

"Come in," a singsong voice answered.

Lenor was surprised at what she saw. "Mother! You look wonderful!"

"Well, thank you. I didn't think I'd be up to it, but I was wrong. I'm going to the chapel with your father."

She was dressed in a light gray shirt that enhanced the sprinkling of silver at her temples, slender black gabardine trousers, a black western-style jacket, dark gray boots, and a shiny silver concho around her slim waist. Her hair was parted in the middle and pulled back into a heavy bun at the nape of her neck.

Lenor felt a tremor of fear. The murderer might be among the handful of close friends who were invited to the family mass. Apple would have to keep watch.

"Are you sure you're feeling well enough to go to church, Mama?" Lenor asked.

"You were right about getting some rest," Magdalena said. "I'm feeling much better."

"I'm so glad." Lenor gave her a hug, then stepped back. "I guess we Taveras have pretty sturdy constitutions, don't we?"

"Always have." Magdalena turned to the full-length mirror near the dresser and pressed her hands to the shiny coil of her hair.

"You know, I don't ever remember feeling really sick," Lenor said.

"You had all the usual—measles, chicken pox. But you came through all of them like a champ," Magdalena said.

Lenor didn't want to alarm her mother, but she had more questions. "Have you had time to look for Leonora's herbal since last weekend?" she asked.

"I looked. Couldn't find it anywhere. Why?"

"I wanted to look up something. Could we have put it somewhere and forgotten?"

"No. But I'll help you look for it again."

"Oh, don't bother," Lenor said. "It's not that important right now."

"You'd better get changed for church, hadn't you?" Magdalena said finally.

"I wish I could go, but I promised Lucielle I'd help her, remember?" Lenor said. "Grandma will understand."

Magdalena got a faraway look in her eyes. "Yes . . . Jovita will understand."

Lenor checked her room. The bed was made and everything was in perfect order, just as she'd left it. She called Apple, changed her clothes, and, as she exited, locked her bedroom door for the first time in her life.

In the bunkhouse kitchen, Lucielle confirmed that Nemesia had tidied up a bit. Lucielle shooed Lenor off to get ready for church. Instead of heading for her room, Lenor went to the barn.

She needed answers—and she had to begin her quest at Michael's ranch.

Verbal apologies to Tossa for not having a tasty snack didn't improve the horse's mood and made saddling her a battle of the wills, but the animal finally settled down during their fast ride into the backwoods. There was no sign of Apple's guard. *Congratulations, friend!* This time, Lenor didn't hang back in the trees but rode straight into the clearing and up to the open barn door. She could hear the sounds of someone shoeing a horse in the corral on the other side of the barn.

Lenor suddenly realized that she had no idea how to ask Michael about his lying without telling him why she needed to know. But telling him that she was investigating the murder of her grandmother was out of the question. At this point, as Rudolfo had suggested, no one could be trusted. What tack could she take? *First a diversion, then a trap.* She dismounted, looped Tossa's reins around the hitching rail, and went inside. Just to her left, in the large tack room, a tall figure with his back to the door was polishing a fancy western saddle.

"Excuse me?" Lenor said. The man turned around. Michael. Lenor felt as if her legs would give way as the memory of her dream came flooding back. *Stop it! He can't know what you're thinking!*

He stood perfectly still for a long moment, the shock of seeing her reflected clearly in his questioning eyes. The polishing cloth was still in one hand, the tin of saddle soap in the other, when he finally spoke. "Is Thomas all right?" he asked.

The genuine concern in his tone made Lenor relax a little. "Thomas is fine," she said. "Thank you for asking."

Michael turned back to his work, his mind whirling with questions he wouldn't dare ask. No woman had the right to look so beautiful in a worn pair of old jeans, a simple white peasant blouse, and a pair of scuffed cowboy boots. At least it was easier to begin a conversation if he didn't have to look at her. "What brings you here?" he asked, intent on his polishing.

"A question." She saw the muscles of his back and shoulders

tense. "About the *bulto* of San Miguel," she lied quickly. *A harmless lie. Not like his.* "How's it coming?"

Somehow he knew that wasn't the reason for her visit. He turned around. "Very well. I'll paint it tonight. I would have finished it last night, but I was . . . busy."

Busy doing what? "Good," she said. Nothing was happening in her muddled brain. All kinds of things were happening in her body. *Was he just in my dream, or in my bed, or delivering a mountain lion?* He'd turned to look at her. She looked out the west window that faced the house. "Nice place you've got here," she said, stalling.

"Thanks."

You're going to blow this if you don't start making some sense. Eyes still averted, she said, "You know, the funniest thing happened."

"What was that?" he asked.

"Remember you told me that Rosa had been taking such good care of all of you?"

"I remember." His jaw tightened.

"Well, Miller was telling me about a terrible accident you had a couple of years ago. He said he patched you up."

Of all the subjects in the world! "That's right," he said.

"So you *did* go to a doctor," Lenor said.

Michael studied her face. She was perfectly serious. "Why do you ask?"

Lenor looked around the room as casually as she could. "Oh, I don't know. Somehow I got the idea you wanted us to be friends."

"And you wondered why I'd lie to a friend?" he asked.

"Yes." She paused. "Maybe you had a good reason?"

His reason for the lie made perfect sense, both then and now. The truth would dredge up over thirty years of hate. But now he had no choice. "You probably wonder about other things, too—like why you didn't see more of me when we were kids. Or why neighbors didn't do neighborly things together." Michael took a step back, put the cloth and saddle soap down on a table at the back of the room, then leaned against the wooden edge. He folded his arms across his chest.

Defensive posture. This isn't going to be easy. "Can you tell me why we didn't?" she asked.

He'd dreaded this day for a long time. He'd lain awake nights stringing meaningless words together into meaningful lies. Alone, on a feed run to a distant, snow-covered cattle pasture in midwinter, he'd spoken the truth out loud. He'd been angry, appalled, and ashamed for so long. Could he tell her? He had to.

"My mother and her sister had a disagreement," he said.

Dismayed at his evasion, Lenor frowned. "What are you talking about?" she asked, feeling her anger beginning to flare. She watched as his body slumped heavily back against the table. He closed his eyes for a few seconds, as if readying himself for a monumental task. "I really want to know. It's important to me."

His heart sang and cried at the same time. He'd dreamed of the moment when Lenor Tavera would come to him and tell him she cared. Here she was, standing right beside him, and whatever he did now, he'd still be the loser. The truth would send her away. Another lie wouldn't conceal things for long. He turned to face her. "Nemesia is my mother's sister," he began. "When they were teenagers in Santa Fe, Nemesia supposedly started to dabble in the occult."

"And Celsa disapproved?" Lenor asked.

"Worse than that," Michael said. "My mother was a very strict Catholic, just like her father. She accused her sister of Devil worship and every other vile thing you can imagine. Nemesia ran away from home when she was fourteen."

"Where did she go?" Lenor asked.

Michael shook his head, then shrugged. "This is all secondhand, stories I heard much later. They agreed on most points. Presumably, Nemesia hitchhiked to Placitas, a little town on the northern edge of the Sandia Mountains, where she joined a coven of witches who practiced black magic. She stayed there about four years, then went to Las Vegas, where she met and married Rudolfo Seña."

"Didn't your grandparents try to find her?" Lenor asked.

"My grandmother did for a while, but my grandfather was fanatically religious. He was sure Nemesia was the Devil's child, and that made my grandmother the cohort of the Devil. He made life hell for them for about a year, then walked out on them."

"He left your grandmother to raise Celsa alone?" Lenor asked.

"I guess witchcraft in New Mexico has always been a force to contend with. My grandfather thought he was doing the right thing, punishing the guilty."

They were both silent for a moment, then Lenor said, "I'm beginning to understand why Celsa avoided making friends with anyone from our place, but I don't understand why she would move so close to Nemesia after all that had happened between them."

"That's the sad part. My father bought this place without telling my mother what he was doing. It was supposed to be a surprise, a present for her thirty-fifth birthday. I was only four, but I remember how happy she was at first. And I thought I was in heaven after being cooped up in a little apartment in Albuquerque." Michael smiled, remembering. "A horse of my own, space to play, a boy near my own age who was close enough to visit."

"Arthur Seña?" Lenor asked.

Michael nodded. "My father had told me all about buying the property from a man named Rafael Tavera, whose ranch foreman had a son just my age. I couldn't have been happier."

"So Ramon fully intended to be friends with our families," Lenor said.

Michael nodded again. "For almost a year, I felt like the luckiest kid in the world. I went to birthday parties. I played. Then my mother found out that Nemesia lived on your ranch, and all hell broke loose."

"But how did Ramon keep Nemesia's whereabouts a secret for a whole year?" Lenor asked.

"He didn't. By the time he'd met Celsa, no one talked about

Nemesia anymore. He didn't even know my mother had a sister. The name Seña didn't mean anything to her, so the subject didn't come up."

"Oh, my."

"Nothing was ever the same after that. Of course, my mother couldn't stand having Nemesia's son, Eloy, working here, and my father refused to fire him. My parents' marriage started to go sour. Ramon couldn't understand why Celsa wasn't able to forget the whole thing and start fresh. Nemesia wasn't making any moves to set things straight, though I doubt she could have. Celsa couldn't understand why Ramon was so blind to the evil in Nemesia. Mother made me go to school in Mora instead of Toya. Most of the kids I'd met, Arthur and his friends, were off limits."

"But you still went to birthday parties. I remember some of them," Lenor said. "And I always wondered why none of us were ever invited up here."

"Anyone who had any contact with Nemesia was off limits," Michael said. "Especially Magdalena, who seemed to be Nemesia's best friend."

Lenor shook her head. Estranged sisters. A marriage gone bad. A young boy dragged into the center of an adult quagmire of hatred. It was all terrible, but what did all that have to do with Michael's lie about going to Dr. Baldwin? "Am I missing something, Michael? I still don't understand why you lied to me."

There was no way to avoid it, no way to stop with half a truth. "When I was about fourteen, my mother discovered that I had an interest in girls. She found a nude drawing I'd done. My parents slept in separate bedrooms, and Celsa's opinion of sex, by then, was that it was a filthy sin perpetrated by the Devil. My interest in it proved that I had evil blood coursing through my veins."

"What a horrible thing for a young boy to go through," Lenor said.

"She punished me by telling me a story about my aunt Nemesia, the witch. She said that a little over a year after we'd moved here, Nemesia had had a baby. Celsa claimed she'd seen her sister take the baby into the woods and kill it. I didn't want to believe it, but my life was so strange by then I didn't know what to think."

Lenor started to speak, but Michael held up his hand.

"Let me get through this," he said. "That night, under the cover of darkness, my mother took me to the graveyard in front of your chapel and showed me Angel Seña's grave to prove her story." He grimaced at the memory.

"And seeing Angel's grave convinced you that your aunt had killed her own baby?"

"It's funny how gullible a child can be. Not only did I believe my mother, I was convinced, by the sight of that small gravestone, that I was evil by blood, and that I'd committed a mortal sin by drawing that nude picture. A year later I drove my father to Dr. Baldwin, and he died in Miller's care. Two years later, my mother died, but not before telling me that I'd killed my father by taking him to a friend of my aunt Nemesia's." He took a deep breath and let it out on a long sigh. "And I guess that's the worst of it," he said, "except that since then, I've been ashamed to talk about this with anyone."

"Nemesia's baby, Angel, was stillborn. It's in her medical record," Lenor said.

"I know that now," Michael said.

"And Dr. Baldwin could have saved your mother's life," Lenor said quietly.

"For what? So she could go on hating? So she could continue torturing herself about her sister, the evil witch, and her son, the Devil's handiwork? She's a lot happier dead."

"Maybe. But surely you knew she'd been wrong about everything."

"I grew up," he said, nodding. "But the horrifying part is that, for three years, I had grave doubts about myself, my drives, my passions."

"And all because of a simple drawing," Lenor said, shaking her head.

"It was a drawing of you," Michael said quietly.

Lenor's eyes opened wide. "Michael, I was only ten years old when you were fourteen!"

Michael smiled. "But I'd fallen in love with you, at Apple's birthday party, when you were seven," he said.

"I remember you teased me unmercifully," Lenor said with a smile.

"My mother could never understand the innocence of puppy love. When she found that drawing, all I knew about sex was what any fourteen-year-old knew."

"Which was quite a bit, I'd imagine," Lenor said. "Didn't you try to explain to Celsa?"

"How could I? I'd committed the act, in my mind, hundreds of times," he said simply. He turned to face her, a grim expression on his face. "Those three years of doubt almost drove me crazy. You were growing up right before my eyes. Sometimes I'd see you and Apple in Mora. It seemed you were teasing me just by being there."

"We were silly girls. Playing around," Lenor said.

"You were playing. I was in adolescent agony." His frown mirrored the frustration. "I was almost expelled from school for another drawing I did of you."

Lenor took an unsteady breath.

"Don't worry. No one knew who it was, and you didn't do anything to encourage me. But I'd bring the memory of seeing you home with me."

"I understand," she said softly.

"You tempted me in thousands of ways. Not deliberately, but just seeing you made me want to—"

"Michael, don't—"

"You wanted the truth about me. You might as well hear it." He reached out and took her hand. "Don't tell me you don't remember how it was to be a teenager."

His touch startled her into silence, and she turned her head away so she wouldn't have to look into his eyes. "I remember," she said.

"You might as well know everything. You won't be any more horrified than I was."

She wanted to protest, but instead she tried to put herself in his place, to imagine how difficult it must be to confess such deep and secret feelings. It had to be like opening your own heart and watching your lifeblood drain away.

"Your innocence made it even harder. There was no way I could bring myself to tell you what was going on inside my head and my heart without risking your hatred and your anger. You turned into a woman right before my eyes, and there was no place I could hide from what was happening to your body. And sometimes it even seemed that you had the same feelings I did." He paused, took a breath, then let it out with a long shuddering sound.

"Sometimes it seemed as if you knew what was happening to me. It was almost as if you wanted it to happen."

"It's true," she whispered.

"There were times when I thought you were getting some perverse pleasure out of torturing me. There were times when I thought I was losing my mind."

Lenor looked at him, wanting to say she was sorry. But how do you apologize for childish innocence?

As if he knew what she needed to say and wanted to protect her from the pain of it, he went on. "It wasn't your fault." He lowered his eyes to the floor. "This isn't making any sense, is it?"

"Yes, it is." She almost choked on the words. "Everything you said about me—the way I acted—it's true. I was innocent, yes. But I *used* you, and all the boys I knew, to make myself feel like a woman. Michael, I'm so sorry."

"You shouldn't be. I was old enough to know better. I was the one whose intentions were . . . immoral."

"Don't say that. That was never true."

"I know." He turned his back on her again. "So now that you know the truth, you can be on your merry way, let things get back to the way they were."

"Michael, don't do this," Lenor said.

He turned back around. "I went through some trying times. You were a part of them, though you didn't know it. They were over a long time ago. My life went on in a normal fashion. End of story."

"I understand, but—"

"When my mother told me that I would never be allowed to see or speak to anyone on the Tavera ranch again, it probably triggered what turned out to be a lot of trouble of my own making."

Lenor nodded. How well she knew. If something were forbidden to her, that was exactly what she wanted. Even now, she had to admit that her involvement with George had been partially driven by her caveat against dating a co-worker. Forbidden fruit was always sweeter simply because it was taboo.

"I didn't want to involve you then, and I don't want to now. If you hadn't asked, I probably would never have told you."

"I'm glad I asked," Lenor said. "And it doesn't change anything."

"It changes everything."

"Why?"

"Because . . ." He couldn't say it. He'd told her the truth, and by some magic of fate she hadn't told him to go to hell. But he'd told the truth only up to a point. "Trust me. It's better the way it was."

"I don't agree," she said.

"You don't have to. You can go back to New York and forget any of this ever happened."

"I don't think we should—" The tack room telephone rang and Michael stepped to the corner and picked up the receiver. He listened for a moment, then turned to Lenor.

"I've got to go over to Eloy's house." He started toward the door, almost dismissing her.

"I'd like to talk some more, Michael."

He stopped midway across the room and looked back at her. "Nothing's really settled, is it?"

"No, it isn't," Lenor said.

"Wait for me at the house."

"All right."

Lenor walked up the hill, wondering if she'd made a wise decision in staying. Was there anything more to be said? At this point, all she *hadn't* found out was why he'd left the tiny Mora hospital, two years ago, before Dr. Baldwin had released him. Juanita answered her knock on the door.

"Lenor?" Juanita's eyes were wide with surprise. She took a deep breath and let it out.

"May I come in?"

The screen door creaked open an inch. "I don't know. I . . ." Juanita pushed the door a little wider. "I guess it would be okay," she said tentatively.

Lenor stepped inside. "Michael asked me to wait for him here," she said, looking intently at Juanita. The woman seemed to be struggling to breathe.

"You've talked to him?" Juanita asked.

"Yes."

For a moment Juanita didn't move, just stood staring as her chest rose and fell with each deep inhalation. "You can wait in the *sala,*" she said finally, taking several steps backward down the hall, then pointing to a doorway to Lenor's left. "In here."

Lenor entered the room, then turned to say thank you, but Juanita had silently disappeared. An odd greeting, Lenor thought as she looked around. The living room was comfortably furnished with sturdy pine pieces, the inviting cushions on the couch and several chairs covered in patterned materials of tan, brown, and rust. Colorful Indian rugs dotted the gleaming wood floor, and a massive stone fireplace stood between floor-to-ceiling bookcases on the wall opposite the door. A closer look told her that the room was seldom used as a living room. The tools of the resident artist cluttered cubbyholes and long work tables under the windowsills. A muted evening light shone through the east-facing windows that took up the entire wall to her left, and a tall easel stood in the corner, angled away from the glass panes.

Juanita does a good job of housekeeping, she thought. The two, now three times she'd seen Juanita, Lenor had suspected that the woman wasn't quite well. Again she wondered what Dr. Baldwin had found, if anything. The puzzle kept niggling at her.

Now another curiosity pricked her. Instead of sitting down to wait, Lenor crossed to the easel, lifted the white cotton material that covered the canvas beneath, then dropped it and jumped back, gasping for breath. The split-second glimpse she'd had of the painting had been enough. On a black background, a shining white light haloed the figure of a naked woman. Lenor's entire body flushed the heat of passion radiated into the room as if she'd been set afire. Her heart beat wildly against her chest.

Your heart is the fire.

Someone was trying to play tricks with her mind . . . or she'd only imagined the subject of the painting. With trembling fingers she lifted the cloth again. No mistake. She, Lenor Tavera, was the woman on the canvas. Michael had created the image of her dream.

As if moved by the wind, her long black hair had been swept wildly forward over one shoulder to curl seductively around her right breast, encircling one jutting nipple with dark, silken strands. Her left breast rested in the curve of a hand-shaped shadow. A broad rose-colored ribbon was tied loosely about her waist, the bow just below her navel, the dangling streamers curling seductively into the shadow at her loins.

Lenor dropped the cloth as if it were white-hot, and commanded herself to stop shaking. She paced the full length of the room and back again to look out the windows. No one was coming. Sitting down on the couch might calm her. It did not. Back to the windows. No one was coming. She walked to the other three corners of the room, then looked back at the easel. It beckoned. She approached, saw more canvases leaning against the bookcase.

There were several, each one a likeness of herself. They escaped from her trembling fingers and clattered back against the shelves. So many questions. Would he have hidden his paintings if he'd known she were coming to his home? she wondered, through a jumble of swirling images. Would he be angry with Juanita for letting Lenor wait in a room that could reveal this obsession with a woman he hardly knew? And the most illogical and unanswerable question of them all: How had he painted a picture of something only *she* had seen?

No wonder he'd fought against answering her question. He still felt the same way he had all those years ago. What was even more unsettling was that she was having erotic dreams and fantasies about him. Were they both under some kind of spell?

Maybe her dream hadn't been a dream at all. Or maybe she was losing her mind. Maybe they were all going crazy, slowly, inexorably. She put her hands over her face. *Think rationally.* But all she could see was the vision in her dream—she and Michael together. Had it actually happened? *Get out of here!* But she couldn't.

Eloy's door opened just as she looked out the window for the third time. When Michael came into the house, he would see her sitting on the couch, calmly looking through a copy of the *Thoroughbred Times* she'd seen on the coffee table. She crossed the room, sat down, picked up the paper, and caught her breath. The stack beneath consisted of—not more of the same, but— She counted. Seven consecutive copies of the *New York Times*. Beneath them, a thick scrapbook begged to be opened. It was full of newspaper clippings. "DOCTOR LENOR TAVERA, DIAGNOSTICIAN *Dateline: New York City. In an interview with . . ."*

The screen door creaked. Lenor slammed the album shut, stacked the papers on top, leaned back, and made her eyes focus on the newsprint in the *Thoroughbred Times*. *"Common Hoof Problems. Problem #1: Padding/winging. Solution: Properly balance feet, adjust shoe weight . . . ."*

"Lenor?"

The voice was deep, soft, and resonant, the voice in her dream.

"In here," she said as he walked past the open door. Lenor lowered the paper and sat up straighter, not trusting herself to stand. He took a step back, and she saw him as if for the first time, as if she hadn't really seen him just a few minutes before. He stood in the doorway, almost filling it. Indigo blue denim strained to contain the muscles of his legs. Light blue cotton spread across the wide expanse of his torso, a line of pearl snaps ascending from the silver and turquoise of his belt buckle to the black V of soft hair that spread and curled across his chest. His sleeves were rolled up past his elbows, and there was a long scar, beginning somewhere above the edge of the cuff and extending down his forearm to the side of his wrist. Lenor took a deep, calming breath. He'd had no scar in her dream. Nor had he been frowning.

His frown was from anger. In Michael's home, guests were treated warmly, taken to the kitchen, offered refreshments and cozy conversation. Juanita had brought Lenor into the living room and left her alone—on purpose. Fear followed the anger. Had Lenor seen his painting? He wanted to turn and run, but stepped into the room instead.

"She's just as beautiful as ever, isn't she, Juanita?"

Lenor looked around him and saw Juanita standing in the doorway.

"Yes, Michael," Juanita said softly.

"Ask Rosa to make a fresh pot of coffee, will you please?"

"Yes, Michael."

"Juanita's gone now," Lenor said. "You don't have to pretend anymore."

"Pretend what?"

"That we're old friends," Lenor said.

"I wasn't pretending," he said.

Lenor quickly crossed the room. "Then explain this," she demanded as she threw back the easel covering.

If shame were a solid entity, Michael could have been physically struck down to his knees. As it was, he wished he could trade places with his father. The grave seemed so much more inviting than the prospect of standing in his own living room and explaining, no, *revealing* the most treasured secrets of his life.

"Well?" Lenor prodded.

"I thought . . ." He shrugged. "I didn't think—"

Lenor glared at him. "You didn't think I would ever see this?" She pointed at the stack leaning against the bookcase. "Or those?"

"Those paintings I did for Steven, but I wasn't satisfied with them. They weren't good enough to give to someone who'd been so kind to me in spite of everything that had happened." He looked at the easel. "That one . . ." He paused. "I didn't think you'd ever know about my dream."

His dream? The floor seemed suddenly unsteady, and Lenor put her hand on the edge of the mounted canvas to keep from swaying. Though she felt none of its power present in this room, she was now certain. A spell *had* been cast on the two of them. But by whom, and why? And what part did it play in what was happening to *all* of them? Was there a connection? She was torn between getting on with her investigation and staying long enough to find out more about the mysterious forces that had brought her here. She looked from the painting to Michael—and made her decision.

"This was your dream?" she asked.

Michael closed the door, then crossed the room and stood behind her. "The most beautiful part of it," he said.

"When?" she asked, looking at him steadily.

"Last night." Michael looked down at her, then at his painting again. His long silence stretched the tension between them into a slender, fragile thread of racing memories. His mind reeled. Was his rendering correct? Had his brushes done justice to the woman who stood only inches in front of him? Would he ever know?

Lenor trembled, remembering the hands that had touched her so gently, the hands that had aroused her so completely. She had to ask. "Where were you, when you had this dream?"

"Here," he said. His arms ached to hold her. He wanted to take her upstairs right now. He wanted to undress her before the antique oval mirror that had belonged to his grandmother. He wanted to lure her into his bed.

Lenor felt her cheeks suffuse with color. The anger she'd felt a few moments ago was a long-distant memory. Now all she could think about was the irresistible force behind her. She had to go on. "What do you remember about your dream?"

How could he possibly tell her? He remembered everything about it. Like a play, he'd repeated it again and again, scene after scene, on the stage of his mind. "I saw you standing in a mountain meadow," he began. "We talked for a while . . ."

"About what?"

"A lot of things," he said. "Dark and light. Weaving wishes and dreams into our lives. The blessings of death and life."

The sun must set, the sun must rise. Both are necessary blessings. Lenor shivered, remembering her own words. "Is that all?" she asked.

"No." He couldn't help himself. His hands touched her waist. She didn't resist. He wanted to turn her around and hold her, kiss her, but just touching would have to be enough. "Dreams don't make much sense sometimes," he said.

Lenor put her hands on top of his. "I know," she said softly, looking at his painting again. "But I'd still like to know about this one."

Her touch, so unexpected, struck him silent for a moment. Fighting for control, Michael took a tentative breath, then sighed. "I think I frightened you," he went on. "For a moment, we were bound together with ribbons. You fought to get away."

"And did I get away?" Lenor asked.

"You changed your mind."

"Why?"

"I told you that, if you stayed, you'd find out who I really was."

"But I already know who you are, Michael."

"*Today* you're finding out who I am. Last night . . ." His voice trailed off. Last night he'd seduced her. Last night he'd made passionate love to her. And she'd returned his love.

Lenor leaned back against him and looked up. "I *do* know you better today . . . and I'm glad," she said softly, then looked back at the easel. "Is that what your dream was about? Getting better acquainted?"

He was glad she didn't see the smile he couldn't suppress. "Yes," he said.

Lenor could hear the grin in his voice. It had been a wonderful dream, Lenor thought, and she smiled, too. "Just how well did we get to know each other?" she asked in a playful tone.

Whether she knew it or not, Lenor wasn't making this any easier. "Some things are difficult to talk about," he said.

"More difficult than what you told me a few minutes ago in the tack room?" Lenor asked.

"*Much* more difficult than that," he said.

"Isn't it strange?" Lenor said. "We can talk about hate and deceit and violence so much more easily than—"

"Love," he finished for her.

"Or our dreams," she said. Lenor was beginning to recognize a certain person's special touch in this particular dream, the moon, the woven ribbons. She'd need further details to be sure. "But can't you just tell me a little bit more about this one?"

She was doing it again, asking questions and insisting on answers. Just as she'd done at the fair so long ago. Just as she'd done at Steven's party. Just as she'd done earlier. He could lie to her; he'd done it before. No! The time for lying was past. "No matter what it is . . . do you really want to know?" he asked.

She had no choice. "Yes. I really want to know."

His hands moved further around her and drew her more tightly against him. "In my dream, I held you, just like this," he whispered. His hands moved up until he could feel the weight of her breasts. "I told you that I could show you your true self."

Lenor caught her breath. Her mirrored reflection in the dream wavered before her eyes, and, as if it were happening again, she watched his fingers draw the white cotton aside.

"You are the inspiration," he whispered. "Your heart is the fire."

From his words, she now knew most of what she'd stayed to

find out. She was almost positive about who had cast the spell. It was time to stop him, time to take her leave, time to . . .

"You are the Earth, the nurturing Mother," he said.

Lenor could feel Michael's aroused body straining against hers, sense his trembling, hear the quickening intake of each shallow breath. Her own body waited, moist and ready, for what would come next—but she couldn't let it happen, not now. Grasping his hands, she drew them away, then turned in his arms. "No more," she said breathlessly.

Michael closed his eyes against the pain of rejection and drew her close. She didn't pull away, as he thought she might. Instead, she put her arms around his waist and held him in a gentle embrace. He rejoiced. Whatever her reason for stopping him, it wasn't rejection.

He rested his cheek against the top of her bowed head. In a way, he was relieved that she'd turned in his arms. In his dream, he'd explored her body completely, every hidden place. He'd tasted the sweetness, feasted. And she'd been afraid. A few more moments, and he might not have been able to stop himself—even if she feared him. That was not the way he wanted her. He wanted Lenor's hunger to match his own in every way. *Will that ever happen?*

Lenor knew she should say something. All at once she felt aroused, comforted, penitent, and embarrassed. No sensible words formed in her mind. A knock on the door saved her from making a complete fool of herself.

Reluctantly Michael let her go, crossed to the door, and opened it. "Yes?" he asked.

"Rosa said to tell you the coffee would be ready in a few minutes," Juanita said. Her eyes scanned the room as she backed away from the door.

Lenor was sure Juanita had either sensed or overheard what had just taken place. She'd been frowning when Michael closed the door and turned back to Lenor.

Michael was staring at the floor. When he looked up, there

were tears in his eyes. "I never meant for you to know about that painting, Lenor," he said quietly.

"Did you mean to keep the secret forever?" she asked, finally finding her voice.

"I don't know." He closed his eyes, took a deep breath, then, on a sigh, looked toward the easel. "This morning, it was like someone else was doing the painting. Like I didn't have control over my brushes."

Lenor stood looking at him, asking herself why? There were so many things about him she hadn't noticed today, or yesterday, when he'd brought Thomas to the ranch. She took it all in, the dark eyebrows that dipped so easily into a frown, the slightly crooked nose, the heavy beard that shadowed his broad jaw. All was wrapped exotically in the heady, clean fragrance of cedar.

"I never imagined anything like this would happen," he said. "If I had, I might have been better prepared."

"Would you have hidden your dream?" she asked.

"Probably. Forgive me."

For a moment, neither of them spoke; neither could look away. Then something changed in the depths of Michael's dark eyes. His brows drew together in a fierce scowl. The pain of having her so close and so untouchable at the same time was almost unbearable. "I wish I'd never come to Steven's party," he said.

Lenor was stunned for a moment. "Why?"

"Because, if I'd stayed home, where I belong, you wouldn't have been hurt, and I wouldn't be . . . You'd better leave now," he said quietly. "I had Eloy bring Tossa up to the house for you."

"Thank you." She stood for a moment, looking at the tense muscles of his shoulders, then turned and walked slowly out of his house.

Twenty-two

Our Father, who art in heaven,
Hallowed be thy name.
Thy kingdom come.
Thy will be done . . .

THE EVENING SUN SLANTED DOWN ON THE RED TILE
roof and gleamed brilliantly through stained-glass windows. Inside the chapel's thick adobe walls, it was cool and comfortable
and peaceful. Magdalena held hands with Steven and Rafael during the prayer and gave thanks that the Virgin Mother had calmed
Steven's mind and eased her husband's pain. The Tavera family
took up only the first pew on the left side of the tiny chapel that
Dorio Tavera had built. The children at the camp had all been
invited to this special service, but only Thomas and his friend,
Shirley, had decided to come. Despite her earlier fatigue, Magdalena felt strong. The only thing that could have made her any
more content would have been the presence of her daughter.

Moon Mother,
Bright light of all
Earth, sky,
I call you.

Nemesia and Angelina sat in the last pew of the church and
silently chanted their own prayers. Since Nemesia had come out
of the woods last night, her heart had been weighed down with
an inexplicable sadness, and even the young priest's service,
which she normally enjoyed, couldn't lift the burden she felt. At

one time she'd thought it would be easy to bring balance and order back into the chaotic vibrations that surrounded them all. Now she wasn't so sure. Only one thing was certain. The survival of all the people she loved depended on her ability to harmonize the cycle.

> The sins of the world
> are born in every
> one of us. Suffer the
> little children . . .

Life is a thing of wonder, Nemesia reminded herself as the priest droned on about human suffering and mortal sin. Suffering had no place in the world of the Goddess that Angelina had taught her about. Why couldn't everyone see the simple truth of the Old Religion? Why couldn't everyone understand that being alive should be sheer, intoxicating joy, not guilt and sorrow and shame?

> *Dian y Glas!*
> Spirit Guide!
> I am a servant of
> the life force. I visualize
> my hopes for a new beginning.
> I will taste the sweetness of life.
> Set sail, set sail . . .

Magdalena glanced at the two children sitting behind her. No doubt the wages of sin tempted them with secret whisperings, but the warnings about hellfire and brimstone didn't seem to be tormenting them in the least. With few exceptions, all the youngsters who came to the Tavera camp enjoyed the beautiful little chapel as much as Lenor had when she was a child.

The memories of those times came back to her so easily of late. As they'd come into the church today, she'd been able to see Lenor and the other children on the ranch in front of her. Now the sense of foreboding that had plagued her since before Jovita's death seemed to be lifting, dissolving.

328 ◆ MARY ELIZABETH LYNN ◆

The creak of wood made Magdalena turn her head and look toward the back of the church. Nemesia had stood up and was moving along the short length of her pew toward the narrow center aisle. Odd, Magdalena thought, the priest had barely begun. She'd never seen Nemesia leave the chapel until the service was over.

Miller Baldwin nodded at her from a pew on the opposite side of the church. Roy smiled so broadly that Magdalena thought his face would split into two pieces just below his nose. He'd been so solicitous before, asking after her health, Lenor's whereabouts, Lucielle's good humor, the children's happiness with camp. She couldn't remember Roy being so gregarious since he was a teenager.

Magdalena turned her attention back to the service. Father Rand was a pleasant enough young man, but his sermon was on the evils of the world and the comforts found only in the Church. Magdalena silently gave thanks for the tolerance of her heart, for the prescription of joy that Angelina loved to discuss so fervently. In its philosophy, all other beliefs had a purpose and a right to exist for the needs of the people.

How uncertain, humans, when they do not understand.

The well-meaning Father had certainly captured the attention of two eager young minds. His descriptions of iniquity were vivid, his tone riveting. Didn't he realize that the first thing these impressionable children would want to do after church was begin testing his stringent rules?

Twenty-three

SOMEONE TAPPED LIGHTLY ON THE FRAME OF THE DOOR
to the *sala,* but Michael ignored it.

Rosa entered the room and put a small tray on the coffee table,
then looked around for Michael's guest. Lenor was gone. Just as
well, Rosa thought. It was the first opportunity she'd had all day to
speak to him alone. But something about the tense set of his
shoulders warned her to be careful. Still, he had to know what Eloy
had just done to Juanita. Some kind of peace had to be restored.

"I need to talk to you," she said.

Michael kept his back to her. "Later."

"I have something important to tell you," she said. "It can't
wait."

He sighed. "All right."

When he turned around, she saw the hint of tears in his eyes.
"Miguel? Are you all right?" She came toward him. "What's
wrong?" She'd never seen him cry.

"It's nothing I can talk about," he said shortly. "What is it you
want?"

"Come, sit down. I've brought coffee." Reluctantly he
crossed to the couch, and they sat down together. Rosa poured
a cup full of the strong brew and handed it to him.

"Thank you." He took the cup and held it without drinking.

"Wouldn't it help to talk to me about whatever it is that's
bothering you?" she asked.

"No."

"This is probably not the best time, but I may have already
waited too long to tell you."

"About what?"

"It's Eloy. I don't know any easy way to say this. He's bothering Juanita."

Michael frowned and put his cup on the table. "They argue."

"I'm not talking about arguments. He's upsetting her."

"Eloy takes his role as foreman a little too seriously sometimes, and Juanita rebels."

"It has to stop," she said.

Michael could feel his stomach knot. "Why hasn't Juanita come to me?"

"She thinks she's in love with you," Rosa said.

"What?" Michael could barely contain his impatience. "I think you're mistaken," he said.

"Her feelings are well hidden, even from herself. The woman is confused about both you and Gilberto. You know the pain of heart's confusion."

Indeed, he did know the pain. Too well. How his own heart continued to beat right now, while shattered into a thousand pieces, he couldn't understand. "Tell me about Eloy," he said.

Rosa nodded. "After Juanita saw you with Lenor, she went to Eloy and demanded to know why Lenor had come to see you. Eloy said he didn't know, but Juanita pressed him, and he saw a way to push her in his brother's direction. Eloy told her that you and Lenor were seeing each other."

"You can tell her we're not," Michael said.

"You know that won't help."

Michael sighed. "You're right, of course. It was a stupid thing to say."

"I've talked to Juanita," Rosa said, "but until her head is straight, her heart won't be able to follow. Eloy has been causing trouble with his foul moods for weeks. This turmoil cannot continue."

"I agree. You've done what you can. It's my place to talk to Eloy," Michael said.

But Eloy was nowhere around when Michael walked into the barn.

"He left just a minute ago," Gil told him. "He was in a mighty bad mood. Didn't say where he was going or when he'd be back."

Michael looked at Gilberto and saw qualities that reflected a younger version of himself. The man caused him problems from time to time, but Michael appreciated Gil's easygoing nature, his willingness to work hard, and his almost religious aversion to discord on the ranch. The man deserved more praise and more attention than Michael had been giving him. They all did.

"Thanks," Michael said. "And thanks for spotting the trouble with that colt this morning. You saved us all a lot of trouble."

Gil shrugged. "It's my job, Miguel."

"Tell your brother I want to see him as soon as he gets back."

"Will do, boss."

Lenor got to the house just before Magdalena came back from church. She left Tossa's care to Manny and hurried to the bunkhouse kitchen. Lucielle was busy setting the table for tomorrow morning's breakfast. The fragrance of baking cinnamon rolls made Lenor deliriously hungry, but her stomach had been churning since she'd left Michael's house. As it had for the past several days, eating seemed the least important thing on her list.

"You look peaked, Lenor," Lucielle said. "There's strong coffee on the stove."

"Maybe later. Need any help?" Lenor asked.

"If you brought an appetite, you can sample a sweet roll," Lucielle said. "You didn't have any dinner, did you?"

"A bite," Lenor said, remembering Inez's apple pie. But the memory brought with it the plan she'd conceived in Miller's kitchen. She hoped her questions would seem like natural curiosity. "May I ask you something?"

"Shoot," Lucielle said.

"Was Miller Baldwin here last Sunday?"

Lucielle looked at her and frowned. "Sunday? Let's see . . . Miller doesn't come here for church anymore. I think he and Roy drive to Las Vegas now," she said. "Why do you ask?"

"No reason in particular. Just curious."

Lucielle gave Lenor a peculiar look. "You don't look very good. Are you all right?"

"I'm fine. Maybe a little tired, but I'm used to that."

"Looks like more than tired to me," Lucielle said. "What ever happened to 'Physician, heal thyself'?"

Lenor shook her head to dismiss Lucielle's concern, but her weight loss and cloudy thinking were becoming an alarming handicap. "You're right. I'll have one of those rolls and a cup of yerba santa." Lucielle went into the kitchen.

"Pick-me-up comin' right up."

Lenor slumped forward and leaned on the table. The exhumation of her grandmother seemed inevitable. She rested her forehead on her crossed arms and willed her brain to start working.

On the down side: The herbal was still missing. Magdalena was better, but still not well. Watson's *monito* had not been found. Jovita's spirit had confirmed her suspicions, but Lenor still had no idea what the Tavera legacy might be or how she was supposed to protect it. *If* they could match it, the fingerprint Apple had found might turn up the person who had brought Old Woosey to her bedroom. Was that person also the killer?

On the positive side: Though everyone mourned, the family otherwise seemed in good health. Rafael had left the house and returned safely, so the killer wasn't stalking stray Taveras, at least not now.

So many puzzles remained. Michael had explained his lie to Lenor's satisfaction, but she still didn't know why he'd left the hospital so abruptly. Learning that Nemesia was Michael's aunt had surprised her, but it didn't explain Jovita's death. Though still at the top of her guilty list, Miller Baldwin seemed to have alibis for the questionable times. Most bothersome was Magdalena's illness. Blessed with boundless energy, it just wasn't like her to be so tired. *So tired.* Lenor hadn't connected it before, but Estelle, at Baldwin's clinic, had described Paula's symptoms in the same way.

Lenor sat up. "Lucielle? Do you remember the nurse who used to work at the clinic in Mora? Paula?"

Lucielle brought the sweet roll and a mug of steaming tea to the table. "I know her. She took sick."

Lenor took a bite. "How does Paula feel now?" she asked around a mouthful of pastry.

"Couldn't say. She doesn't get out. I never see her."

Lenor felt a surge of new energy. Paula was so sick from some unknown malady that she could no longer work. It took all Lenor's willpower to stay calm enough to finish the roll and tea and end the conversation without giving something away. "Lucielle, thanks for the snack. Delicious! Just what the doctor ordered." She stood up and stretched. "If you don't need my help, I think I'll go get some rest."

"Smartest thing I've heard you say in days."

Outside, Lenor dug into her back pocket and brought out the piece of paper on which she'd noted what Jovita had told her.

You must not waste your energies with missing me.
There is much for you to do.
I did not die of natural causes.
The fate of those living on the Tavera ranch has become uncertain.
You must protect yourself and your mother.
She is neither safe nor well.
You must find the one close to her who believes her to be evil.
You must protect the Tavera legacy.
You must find Barela.

The late June sunset was still more than an hour away. After the church service, Rafael had changed clothes and gone to the corral to help Manny with the horses. If Lenor hurried, she might catch her mother in her bedroom and talk to her alone.

It wasn't difficult to broach the subject of Miller Baldwin. Magdalena wasn't feeling well again.

"I can't figure out what to do for myself like I used to," Magdalena said. "I'm trying my tonics, but they don't help. Maybe Miller is right."

"About the *curanderismo*?" Lenor asked.

"Yes. But he worries about the right things for the wrong reasons."

"Well, I'm not sure his efforts are doing you any good either," Lenor said. "Do you think Miller's medical practice is in financial jeopardy because of the people who practice the *curanderismo*?"

"No, but he complains. He's always complained about that," Magdalena said. "I don't think he has anything to worry about."

"Has Miller given you any other drugs to take besides the estrogen and progesterone?"

"A few pills for muscle pain. A few for sleeping. Some samples he had."

Lenor chilled with fear. There had been no mention of other drugs in Magdalena's medical record, and the samples left with physicians by drug representatives would not be on any inventory list, even if they were controlled substances. "Do you know what the drugs were?" she asked.

"I still have the bottles."

"Let's go take a look at them," Lenor said.

She silently read the labels. *Tegretol®, Carbamazepine USP, Anticonvulsant, Specific Analgesic for Trigeminal Neuralgia. Halcion®, brand of Triazolam tablets, 0.125 mg.*

Halcion fairly screamed danger in Magdalena's case. Its risks were well known, at least by the physicians Lenor knew. Appalled that such powerful drugs had been given for such minor problems, Lenor searched her memory for the *Physician's Desk Reference* description of Tegretol.

Magdalena turned away from the bathroom mirror. She'd been staring into it ever since she'd taken the two small bottles out of the medicine cabinet and closed the mirrored door. "I look terrible," she said. "I'm going to lie down for a while. Do you mind?"

"Are you feeling all right, Mama?"

"Just tired. I need a nap." She reached for one of the bottles

Lenor was holding. "Maybe I should take one of these. Now, which one was for . . . ?"

"Mama, I don't want you to use any more of these. All right?"

Without looking at her, Magdalena walked past Lenor and into the bedroom. "I'm going to lie down for a while. Do you mind?"

Lenor followed her. "Mama?"

Magdalena pulled back the spread, sat down on the edge of the bed, and reached toward the bottles Lenor was still holding. "Maybe I should take one of these. Now which one . . . ?" Her body sank back on the bed. "Maybe I should take . . ." She pulled the bedspread up over her body. "I'm going to rest for a while. Do you mind?"

Twenty-four

MILLER BALDWIN SWUNG HIS OLD STATION WAGON ON-to an abandoned logging road just north of Chacon, and immediately wished he'd brought Roy's Rover instead of his own wheezing bucket of loose bolts and squeaky springs. He cursed at the ruts and the rocks, railed at the steepness of the grade, and swore at the rising water of the Mora River lapping at the timbers of the condemned bridge. He knew his teacher would be furious if he was late. At last the weatherworn shack, hiding in the tall pines, was in sight. A glance at his watch calmed him. Five minutes to go. But even though he was early, he knew she would be waiting.

With a handkerchief he mopped the perspiration from his neck and forehead, then knocked quietly on the door.

"Enter."

Inside, it was cool and dark, and Miller felt relieved. He

tucked his damp handkerchief into his pocket, sat down at the small table in the middle of the single room, then took off his sunglasses. Rosa lit the two candles on the table and looked at him over the top of the flames.

"This is the last time we'll meet," Rosa said.

Miller stared around the room, noticing the changes now that his eyes had adjusted to the low light in the cabin. Previously decorated with all manner of religious paintings, statues, and icons, the space was now bare, except for the table and chairs. He leaned forward. "But why?"

"I've been helping you with your studies for many years now. I've given you everything I know."

His hands curled into fists. "That can't be possible."

"It is," she said calmly. "All you have to do is practice."

"But you've taught me nothing about the evil realm."

Rosa laughed. "A myth."

"What about black magic?"

"It is the evil of lost souls, nothing more," Rosa said.

"Whose souls? Who are these people?"

"Criminals."

"You mean the witches who work evil spells and make human sacrifice?" he asked.

"You already know about such things." Rosa smiled. "Dr. Baldwin, you amaze me. Surely, when you were in medical school, you had at least one class in abnormal psychology."

"I did. But I didn't learn anything about the witches who practice black magic."

"Those people aren't witches, they're the psychopaths and sociopaths of the world."

"They have great power."

"Without control," she said.

"But power nonetheless."

"I teach the power to heal, not hurt. I teach the power to create, not destroy. I'm surprised you still don't understand after all this time."

"The source of the power still evades me," he said, shaking

his head in frustration. "I assure you, I don't want to do anything evil. I just want to understand. We have to go on."

"I've told you, the source is within you. The power to bend reality, to heal, to influence the fates, is in your soul, in your heart's blood."

"My heart's blood?"

"The same power resides in every entity."

"I think you are lying to me," he said.

"Why would I lie?" Rosa asked.

"I've made you a very rich woman."

"That was your choice. I asked for nothing."

"Nonetheless, I've paid you dearly for the *desarrollo*. But I still fail in most everything I try."

"I told you from the beginning that I didn't think you had the aptitude. You insisted. I instructed. You've done much better than I expected. For some, it happens that way. You mustn't despair. It will come if you keep trying."

Miller scowled at her. "I think you're greedy, and you want to keep the most essential knowledge a secret for as long as you can, so I'll have to keep on paying."

Rosa got up from her chair and blew out the candles. "When you came in, I told you this would be our last meeting. I have nothing more to teach you. If you value your money so much, I'll gladly give it all back to you. I have no need of it."

"You have no need for my money?" Miller squeaked sarcastically. "And why is that, witch? Something else you haven't taught me? Can you spin straw into gold?"

"I have a much simpler way of accumulating wealth," she said calmly. "I weave hard work into reward."

Miller stood up and leaned toward her, his fists on the table. "I'm coming back," he growled.

"I won't be here."

"I'll come get you."

"Is that a threat, Doctor?"

"Take it anyway you like. Our business is *not* finished."

Miller crossed the room and put his hand through the leather pull-strap on the door.

"Have you forgotten about Paula so soon?" Rosa asked.

He whirled around. "You have no proof of malpractice."

"Do you want to stake your reputation on that, *Dr.* Baldwin?"

Twenty-five

LENOR HAD STAYED IN HER MOTHER'S ROOM UNTIL MAGdalena fell into an easy sleep. She'd obviously been confused before she'd gotten into bed, but that wasn't an unusual response to the amount of stress she'd been subjected to. Before Lenor left, she checked her mother's vital signs. Normal.

During the fast drive to Mora, Lenor tried fitting pieces of the puzzle together. Through fuzzy thinking, it wasn't easy. *Keep it simple.*

First: Jovita Tavera had been murdered. The method: probably poison. The obvious suspect: Miller Baldwin. Other possibilities: everyone close enough to Jovita to administer a lethal toxin. Motive: Unknown. The legacy? Perhaps, but also an unknown. The only thing the Taveras had that was worth anything was the land where they lived and worked. A possibility, but Jovita's death wouldn't help anyone acquire the Tavera property. Unless they were all on the killer's list. Lenor had to slow down, try to control her trembling, before she could go on.

Second: Magdalena's illness was probably being caused by one, or a combination, of four things: Tegretol, Halcion, the estrogen replacement, and the tea she'd been making for herself. Lenor had ruled out both Magdalena's and Lucielle's cooking, or the possibility of Lucielle tampering with the food, because so many people ate the same thing at the same time, and Lucielle made everyone serve themselves. Method: Oral ingestion. Motive: Unknown. Possibly none. Possibly the mysterious legacy. Witchcraft and any kind of spell had more or less gone out the window with the discovery of the drugs, but still couldn't be ruled out altogether.

Third: Her own problems. Both the rapid weight loss and violently disturbed thinking processes baffled her. True, she hadn't eaten much in the past few days, but she was used to running on crumbs for long periods of time at the hospital. What she *had* managed to eat lately had been high calorie and nutrient dense. Lenor looked down at her hands on the steering wheel. Every joint in her fingers and wrists protruded sharply, like little stones in a river of skin. Stones. She's almost forgotten about Watson's rock. No wonder he'd been avoiding her like the plague. Probably out searching for it himself.

Fourth: Miller Baldwin had been wrong about Lenor's congenital heart problem. Doctors were sometimes mistaken. Sometimes their mistakes proved fatal. In this case, the outcome had been in the baby's favor. It was an insignificant error in the wake of what had been happening lately. Did that let Miller off the hook for Jovita's murder? No.

Fifth: There might be nothing to it, but Celsa Martino had believed that Dr. Baldwin had killed her husband, Ramon. Michael Martino had gotten up, despite severe injuries, and left Baldwin's clinic. It might be irrelevant, but she wanted to know the reason for Michael's behavior.

The memory of living a part of her dream flashed through Lenor's mind, and brought with it a flood of passion. The dizzying fragrance of leather and cedar and an aroused male body filled the car. Her mirror image wavered into view, then stabilized, reflected in the windshield. The dark hand at her breast moved down between her legs. Fingertips touched her. *Stop it!*

Lenor pressed her knees together and gripped the steering wheel as hard as she could. A rosy flush heated her cheeks, then her whole body, and her breath came in long gasps as she leaned back. For a moment she drove without seeing where she was going. She fought for control until the almost unbearable sensations began to subside. Her heart still beat wildly, then finally began to slow. At last she took a deep breath and continued.

Sixth: Baldwin's nurse, Paula, was ill and might have the same symptoms as Magdalena. Miller was keeping medical records in his home that should be kept at the clinic. Obviously he was hiding something. What and why? Laboratory tests he'd ordered had been proper and routine. The powerful medications he'd given Magdalena hadn't been noted, perhaps because they were just samples containing small quantities. But how many times had he given her samples? Had Paula's record been in the desk, among those she hadn't looked at?

Seventh: Roy Baldwin had complete access to the Tavera home. He'd been acting strangely, but Lenor couldn't conceive of Roy hurting Steven or Jovita, who'd brought him into their home after his mother's death. Still, his uninvited presence in her room on the evening before Steven's party had been decidedly uncomfortable—and unusual.

Eighth: The heirloom, antique herbal was missing.

"I'm missing something," she said aloud. "Damn it! Think!" She made a mental list of all the things that had to be done.

1. *Start exhumation proceedings on Jovita's body.*
2. *Call Estelle and ask if she's found Magdalena's medical record. If she hasn't . . .*
3. *Get back into Baldwin's home and take a closer look.*
4. *Check with the county clerk. People who want to see property records have to sign a log before they can look at the books.*
5. *Talk to Paula.*
6. *Call George: Tell him I might be here for a little longer. Get Dr. Simeon to cover for me until I get back.*

Lenor stopped. A knot of frustration coiled in her stomach and tears burned her eyes. The brilliant Dr. Tavera felt like a quivering heap of bones topped by a useless brain. But there was so much to do.

> 6. *Continued: Tell George to expect a package by overnight mail. Though there was the merest stain left on the sheet Roy washed, it might be enough for sophisticated lab equipment. Include a sample from Magdalena's tea canister, plus the medications, and instructions for chemical analysis. Have Apple send the package from Las Vegas instead of Toya to avoid tampering. Ask George to look in my apartment for the herbal, just in case I missed it.*

Suddenly her thinking cleared completely. *Chemical analysis.* 8-chloro-6-(o-chloro-phenyl)-1-methyl-4H-s-triazolo-[4,3-a][1,4] benzodiazepine. Lenor's eidetic memory focused in on a photographlike image of the *Physician's Desk Reference* pages, and she picked out the salient points.

Halcion®: Chemical name for triazolam, 8-chloro-6-(o-chloro-phenyl)-1-methyl-4H-s-triazolo-[4,3-a][1,4] benzodiazepine. Pediatric use: Not for use in children under 18, no studies. A caution about prescribing for patients with signs or symptoms of depression.

Tegretol®: Pediatric use: Safety and effectiveness not established for children younger than 6 years. Contraindications: . . . possible activation of a latent psychosis . . . Drug interactions: Breakthrough bleeding in patients taking concomitant oral contraceptives.

Breakthrough bleeding! Lenor took a deep breath and pushed her foot down hard on the gas pedal. Miller Baldwin had not been doing his homework on drug interactions. He'd made a note in Magdalena's record about instructing her to watch for recurrent menstrual bleeding—then given her the Tegretol. Practicing ignorance instead of medicine was a valid prosecution for malpractice. She absolutely had to look more closely at the records he kept at home.

★   ★   ★

Mora was no longer the sleepy little town Lenor had seen on the Wednesday night of her arrival. The narrow main street courted a busy, summer-evening assortment of pickup trucks and well-used cars. Loggers rumbled through, their semis trailing long, cumbersome loads, piled high with ponderosa and fir from the Sangre de Cristos, which began their rise to soaring heights where the main street curved north to the tiny town of Cleveland. Since the road to the year-round resort of Angel Fire had been finished, the town now struggled with the burden of extra traffic.

As always, Lenor could feel the magical strangeness of the land where she'd been born, where mystics were as commonplace as grains of desert sand, where miracles, like the healings at Santuario de Chimayó, occurred as regularly as moonrise. It was no wonder that New Mexico was called the Land of Enchantment.

A place of miracles, yes. But the enchanted land knew its devils and demons, also. Ghosts of conquistadors and gun-toting murderers and tortured souls roamed freely, haunting wherever they pleased. Even Salem could not account for more witches, Indian, Spanish, and English. The spirit world knew that New Mexico's doors were always wide open in welcome.

Mrs. Hurtado, the busiest *curandera* in town, was tending her backyard herb garden, the last slanting rays of the sun and the phase of the moon dictating her careful work. Lenor raised her hand in greeting, but Mrs. Hurtado didn't see her. Just as well. It would have been impolite to pass by if an invitation had been offered by sign or signal.

Lenor couldn't believe her good fortune when she saw lights on in the courthouse. Probably a meeting going on, she decided. It would be worth a try to see if she could get in.

Mildred Dizon, tortoise-rimmed glasses on the end of her nose, stood behind the courthouse counter she'd been ruling for the past twenty-plus years. When Lenor told her what she wanted to see, Mildred swung a thick, heavy book around on a wooden pedestal.

"Real estate's been real slow lately," she said as Lenor scanned the book. "Come to think of it, real estate's always been real slow around here." She tapped on the edge of her glasses with a pencil. "Let's see. Last big excitement was when Doc. B. bought the land for the new clinic after the old one burned down. Tax base went up considerably." She pointed to a line in the book. "Here's the volume number you're looking for," she said.

Lenor was amazed that the woman could talk, scan the book upside down, and make out the handwritten scribblings all at the same time. She looked at the line. John Garcia.

"Here it is again." Mildred pointed to another line.

Michael Martino.

"I don't see any more," Mildred said.

"Mildred, do you happen to know if anyone named Barela owns property around here?" Mildred was the only person Lenor had ever heard of who read plat books for entertainment—and remembered what she read.

"Hmm. Barela. 1730-something . . . 1739. A land grant from Governor Gaspar Dominguez de Mendoza. Let me see. Hmm. Did that revert to the state in the early 1860s? Humph! My mind just doesn't work like it used to. Can't remember hardly anything anymore. I could look that up for you."

"There's no need to bother with it. I'm more interested in the present."

"Now? No. No Barelas around here now," Mildred said.

"You are absolutely amazing." Lenor closed the book.

"History used to be my thing, but . . ." She tapped her glasses again. "Just haven't got the memory for it now."

"Mildred, you've been such a big help. Maybe I can get back for a visit before I leave."

"Got some coffee going in the back. Want a cup now?" Mildred asked.

"Can't. Gotta go. But thank you, Mildred. Maybe another time."

Lenor quickly walked the short distance down the main street, turned left onto a narrow side street, and stopped in front of a sagging adobe. The once-bright blue window and door trim was sadly in need of paint, and the corrugated tin of the roof desperately needed attention.

Paula's husband answered Lenor's knock at the front door, and she introduced herself.

"Paula's in bed. I was just on my way out, but I can get her up and dressed if you want me to," he said.

"Thank you, but that won't be necessary. Just ask her if she'll talk to me for a few minutes."

Shortly, he returned, ushered Lenor into the small bedroom at the back of the house, then left the room. Paula lay, pale and thin, in the middle of a rumpled double bed. *The woman should be in a hospital,* Lenor thought as she sat down on the edge of the bed and took Paula's frail, limp hand.

"A little tired this evening, Paula?" Lenor asked, smiling.

"Every day," Paula said weakly, her voice barely audible.

"I'll try not to tire you further. I just want to ask you some questions." Paula nodded her assent. "Do you know who I am?" Lenor asked.

"Lenor."

"That's right. What day is this?"

"Thursday."

"Right again." After a few more correct answers, Lenor was convinced that Paula was completely lucid. "You got sick about a month ago?" Paula nodded her head. "Were you feeling bad before you quit work?"

Paula nodded again, then lifted her hand to the right side of her head. "Depressed, too, since my hysterectomy."

A red flag went up. "Are you taking any medications?"

Paula shook her head. "Just hormones."

"You mean Dr. Baldwin isn't treating *you* with anything?"

"Now now."

"But he gave you something before? What was it?"

"Can't remember."

If she'd been given the same drugs as Magdalena, Paula could be on the road to feeling even worse. Lenor would have to find out. "So what are you doing to get well?" she asked.

"Nothing. No one knows what's wrong."

There was an empty teacup on the bedside table. Lenor began wondering. "I have to leave now, Paula. But I'll come back and see you soon. Will that be all right?"

"I'd like that. We'll have tea," she whispered.

Another tea drinker. Herbal? Lenor wondered as she left the room. She was hoping Paula's husband had returned so she could ask him a question or two, but he didn't seem to be anywhere about. She found the kitchen and Paula's tea canister, then left the house with a sample, wrapped in a paper towel, stuffed into her pocket.

Hurrying back to her car, Lenor puzzled over the two names in Mildred Dizon's book. Both the sheriff of Mora County and Michael Martino had looked at the volume that contained ownership and tax records of the Tavera property. Neither man's interest could be explained, unless they'd been looking at another property listed in that particular volume. Quite possible, and that would bring her no closer to any kind of an answer about who might want the "Tavera Legacy."

Roy Baldwin was standing in the doorway of Mora's general store. He took his attention away from the key he'd pushed into the lock to see who was about to walk past.

"Lenor!" He hurriedly unlocked the door, pushed it open, then turned back to her. "I was just closing up, but . . . Come in, come in! How about a cup of coffee?"

Feeling anxious and rushed, Lenor debated, but only for a second. She didn't dare pass up the chance to find out more about his strange behavior. "I'd love to, Roy."

He flashed his face-breaking grin. "I'll get the pot on right now."

She followed him to the back of the large, one-room, warehouselike store. True to its name, it was stocked with everything from nails, still sold in bulk by the pound, to packaged cake mix to prescription drugs. "Looks like you've turned this into a profitable venture, Roy. Congratulations," she said when she'd sat down beside the cluttered desk near the back entrance.

"Don't mind if I do say so myself. I've brought it back from the brink of bankruptcy. Guess flunking out of medical school was the best thing that could have happened to me."

She was surprised he'd mentioned his failure. Having Roy take his place as the only physician in town had been Miller's one and only dream for his son. "You enjoy the retail business, then?" she asked.

"Oh, it can be touch-and-go sometimes, especially with having to keep so much stock on hand, but I'm starting to really love it. And I'm beginning to make a profit, even with having to make outrageous payments to my dad for all the money he put up."

Patiently making small talk while all her warning signals throbbed for attention was about the most difficult thing she'd ever tried to do. "I'll bet your father is happy with your success," she said.

Roy's smile vanished. "There's no pleasing that man, Lenor. God knows I try. You know how hard I've tried. I do everything he tells me to do, but he's never satisfied. I even try to anticipate what he'll want from me next."

"I'd say bringing this place back to life was nothing short of a miracle. How could Miller expect more than what you've accomplished here?"

Roy shook his head in bewilderment. "I don't know. It's making me crazy, I do know that." Roy reached for the coffeepot and poured two mugs full. "I even went right back to school, after my disastrous semester of med school, and got a degree in pharmacology."

"I'd almost forgotten about that," Lenor said. The thought that Ray Baldwin dispensed the drugs his father prescribed made her shudder.

"Do you think that made him happy?" Roy went on. "Well, it didn't. And the pharmacy is the most profitable part of the business."

Lenor took the mug he offered. "Maybe you should just forget about trying to please your father, Roy. Maybe all the heartache isn't worth it. You've got a degree. You could move away from here, make a life of your own. Pharmacists in larger cities make pretty good money."

"I've thought about that, but cities give me the willies. The traffic alone could turn a guy into a blithering idiot."

"Another small town, then?" she asked.

"I can't leave my home, Lenor." He smiled again. "Besides, I've finally figured it out. What he wants, I mean. I've got plans. And Miller Baldwin is finally going to be proud of his son—if everything turns out like I want it to."

Lenor leaned forward, pretending to be excited. "Tell me."

Roy tipped his chair back against the wall, his smile changing to a sly grin. "Secret," he said. "Can't tell a soul. Especially not you."

Lenor had no idea what she'd expected to learn by talking to him, or where the present conversation would lead, but she had to dig as deeply as she could. He was obviously agitated and she might be able to take advantage of that. "I won't tell anybody, Roy. Don't you remember how it was in high school? We used to share all our secrets. You can trust me."

"Not with this." The front legs of the chair hit the floor with a thud. "You might not approve."

"Is my approval so important to you, Roy?"

He looked away from her with a quick turn of his head. "Not anymore."

"Then why can't you tell me about your plans?"

Without looking at her he stood up and put his coffee mug down on the corner of the desk. "I have to lock up now," he said abruptly. "Maybe we can talk some other time."

Lenor watched him walk away from her. She'd obviously hit a tender nerve. His ingratiating behavior had changed dramatically in just a matter of seconds, and she'd never seen it happen to him before.

Yet another missing piece that doesn't fit, she thought as she left the store. After all her efforts, she was going home without any solid evidence. She hated the thought, but Jovita's body would have to be exhumed as soon as possible.

★   ★   ★

Sometime while Lenor had been gone, Magdalena had changed into a high-necked white nightgown and gotten back in bed. She was sleeping soundly, so Lenor went to her own room. In one motion she turned the knob, stepped forward, and ran straight into the heavy wood. Locked. *Damn!* Locked doors gave her the jitters. The sense of urgency made fumbling for her keys a lesson in frustration, then patience.

Finally she was inside, sitting at her desk, writing down her mental list of tasks. When she was done, she gathered the items she wanted to send to New York, and labeled each carefully. Tea from two sources, sample drugs, stained bed sheet. She put everything in a brown paper sack. Apple would have to take care of the proper package for overnight mailing. Lenor wrote out the instructions for the lab in New York, then picked up the phone and dialed.

"Hello?"

"George? I need a favor. I don't have time to explain right now, but this is an urgent request. First, ask Dr. Simeon to cover for me for a few more days, just in case. Then . . ."

"Whoa! What are you saying? Bowder wants you on your way back here in seventy-two hours. Preferably before that."

"I may not make it," Lenor said.

"Do you realize what you're saying? Are you willing to give up three years of hard work and millions of dollars? You can't be serious?"

"Dead serious, George. There's also the chance I *won't* be late getting back, so you don't have to face him quite yet. I'll let you know."

"He'll be furious. You're not going to believe what's happened."

"What now?" Lenor asked, dreading the answer.

"Ella swears some data she entered on Sable is missing. She thinks Sable can get into the computer with her mind."

At this point, Lenor couldn't discount the possibility. "That's absurd," she said instead. "Even if she could, she wouldn't. Ella must be mistaken."

"That's possible, but if Bowder gets wind of it . . . Never mind. You probably have enough to think about. What's going on there, anyway? Are you playing Sherlock again?"

"Something like that, but I really don't have time to explain. Got a pencil?"

"Shoot."

Lenor told him about the stained sheet, the samples of tea, the pills, and the lab analysis she wanted of each. "Can you stand over them, George? I need the info stat."

"No problem, but—"

"And pull up some lab results on the computer for me. I had some blood drawn Tuesday night. I'd like to know the results of my tests."

George wanted to ask what she suspected her tests would show but decided against it. "I'll call you as soon as I know anything. But, my God, Lenor! Murder?"

"It looks that way," Lenor said.

"I just can't imagine it! Just, by God, *cannot* imagine it! I'll help any way I can."

"I really appreciate it, George," she said. "One other thing. Could you possibly go over to my place and look for something for me? It's a big, old, leather-bound book about four inches thick, maybe fourteen or fifteen inches tall. An herbal, written in Spanish. You'll know it when you see it."

"You want me to call you back tonight?"

"Yes, please. Call from my apartment. And thanks, George. Hear from you soon."

Next she phoned Apple and gave her her instructions, then called Estelle at home, and found out that Magdalena's medical record was still missing. After she hung up, Lenor went to check on her mother again. It was still early, a little before ten, but she knocked softly in case Rafael had joined her. No answer. Lenor peeked inside. Magdalena slept peacefully, but she was looking more pale than she had before. *Not long now, Mama.* Lenor went back to her room to wait for George's call.

But he didn't call. Lenor paged through *New Mexico* again, paced some, tried to rest. George was doing his best. Lenor believed that with all her heart. Even with the irreconcilable differences between them, she still felt a deep affection for the man who'd been her good friend—and still was. She wished she could tell him everything. She wished he could understand and accept.

Finally, to relieve her agitation, she pulled Dr. Crawford's patient file on the sleepwalker from her briefcase and sat down at her desk. It wasn't easy to concentrate. She scanned through the pages once without seeing anything of interest, then started again.

Male Caucasian; thirty-seven years of age; married with three children; architect. Little more than childhood diseases and a torn knee ligament during college made the medical history uncomplicated—until the night terrors and sleepwalking had started. Since that time, the man had been in and out of emergency rooms with a variety of injuries, not the least of which he'd incurred during a high-speed chase with police and a subsequent auto accident. Broken bones and serious lacerations were the result, but the man had no memory of driving his car, the chase, or the crash. His wife reported being often awakened by the sound of his voice, and carrying on a conversation as if they were both wide awake. The man never recalled the discussions. After about six weeks of experiencing both the night terrors and the sleepwalking, the man's fearful wife began sleeping in another room.

The psychological profile was extensive, with no fewer than three psychiatrists reporting. No significant historical findings, but a recent marked tendency toward self-effacement and self-criticism. The man considered himself too wealthy, his modest investments and savings enormous. He'd divested himself of both property and capital. While sleepwalking, the patient had tried twice to hang himself. Finally, the patient's wife had awakened him while he was trying to hang one of their children. She and the children had moved out.

Even though there was no trouble between the man and his parents—both were still living and well—the patient was convinced that one or both of them had something to do with his problem. They frequently appeared in his dreams during REM sleep, but seemingly had nothing to do with the terror that roused him, screaming, almost every night. Unbelievably, his transitions through the stages of sleep were smooth. In Stage IV, deep sleep, he would walk, or drive, to destinations he'd never been, with horrifying results. Often he woke to find himself badly injured. Sometimes the weapon would still be in his hand. Other times he had no idea how his flesh had been cut or his bones broken. He was terrified that he'd soon do harm to someone else.

Lenor felt an overwhelming wave of sadness for this unfortunate man. His symptoms, while rare in the general population, were not unknown among victims of sleepwalking or night terrors, but his desperation had to be monumental. With no help from the orthodox medical establishment, it was no wonder the man was both suicidal and homicidal.

Dr. Crawford's investigation was complete, to a fault, and no conventional treatment had been left untried. To his credit, Dr. Crawford had also delved into alternative treatments: acupuncture, chiropractic, stress reduction, homeopathy, naturopathy, aromatherapy, reflexology, biofeedback, osteopathy, and others. At this point, the patient was ready to give up—but, while understandably frustrated, Dr. Crawford was not. Even if trying "magic" could put his entire career in jeopardy, the doctor was willing to give it a go.

Zombies and demonic possession notwithstanding, Dr. Crawford had bet both his career and this man's life on Lenor Tavera. She couldn't let either of them down.

Shortly after midnight, the phone rang.

"Sorry," George said. "A little emergency held me up at the hospital. I'm here in your apartment now, but I don't see anything like what you described."

"The book's not there?" Lenor asked.

"I've searched the place thoroughly. No book." He paused.

"I *did* find your private little stash of chocolate cookies. Care to explain?" he asked jokingly.

"Not now, George," she said wearily. "What about my tests?"

"Everything you ordered was within normal limits. Cultures all negative. Are you all right, Lenor?"

"I'm fine," she lied, as she looked down at her shaking, skeletal hand. "I wish I had time to explain, George. I promise, I'll tell you everything when I get back. Just hang with me and help me out. Okay?"

"You've got it. I'll expect your package Saturday morning and get right on it."

"There's just one more thing, George. Will you call Dr. Stan Crawford at Truelex and tell him I'll help him?"

George was silent for a second, then, "Stan Crawford? The sleepwalking fellow?"

"Yes."

"I know, I know. You don't have time to explain. See you when you get here. Sweet dreams, Sherlock."

No more dreams, please, Lenor thought, as she left her room with her package and a small flashlight. Next order of business, deliver the package to Apple, then take a better look at the files in Miller Baldwin's home. Inez lived in, but she slept in a cottage behind the house. Dr. Baldwin should be well under the influence by now and deeply asleep. No problem. It wasn't until she'd pulled in behind a building down the street that she realized she had no idea how she was going to get inside Miller's house.

Getting in turned out to be the simple part. The window had been left wide open, and the screen, hinged at the top, pulled easily out of the sash. Since Estelle had said Magdalena's record hadn't been found, Lenor fully expected it to be in the desk's locked file drawer. It wasn't and neither were any of the other folders that had been there earlier. Nor were they anywhere else in the office. Lenor started to leave, then decided to look in the one drawer she hadn't searched earlier. The letter opener worked its magic on the lock, and she pulled the shallow center drawer open. The *Tavera Herbarium*! Her hand went to her mouth to keep the gasp of surprise from erupting into the stillness of the room—but the letter opener clattered to floor.

In seconds Lenor heard the scraping of tiny claws on the polished wooden floor of the hallway. She doused the flashlight. Miraculously the little ball of fur streaked by the open office door and began yapping and scratching at the front door. Not so miraculously, the beam of headlights swept across the office window. Trapped between a barking dog and a nighttime visitor!

She recognized the voice even though it whispered. "Baby, Baby. Stop that noise. Stop it." Miller Baldwin! Where had he come from? Thursday was not ordinarily a poker night, and his battered old station wagon had been in the driveway with a flat tire. He should have been in bed, asleep. Lenor clutched the heavy volume to her chest, debated whether to steal it or leave it where it she'd found it. *Steal it? This is mine!* Miller would never be able to reclaim it. She moved to the window. The front door opened. She touched the wood frame of the window screen.

There were footsteps on the porch, drawing near. Lenor drew away from the window just as the frame slammed in, against the window sash.

"Damn wind," Miller cursed. "Or did you push it open again so you could run in the street? You naughty little dog. I'm going to nail this thing shut once and for all."

Fading footsteps. The front screen door squeaked open. Lenor pushed with all her strength on the jammed window screen. It wouldn't budge. Her heart was nearly beating out of her chest as she ducked down behind the end of the rolltop desk. Miller walked past the door, but Baby stopped, sniffed, and her claws began clicking across the office floor.

"Get out of there, you little pest," Miller said. "I'm going to close that window." He took three steps into the room, then stopped. "No, it'll get too stuffy. Come to Papa, Baby. We'll just close the door. Come to Papa." The door shut.

Too bad he doesn't talk to his patients so sweetly, Lenor thought inanely. *What am I thinking about? Priority one—get the hell out of here!* Lenor began working on the screen. It had wedged crookedly against the sash, but by pressing on opposite corners, she finally got it open. She looked out. Roy's four-wheel-drive was now parked in the driveway beside the station wagon, and she could smell the odor of diesel fuel. A board on the porch creaked when she stepped out, and Baby barked three times. His third attempt was muffled, probably by the doctor's own hand. *Thank you, Dr. Baldwin!*

All was quiet when she got back home. By morning Magdalena should be well rested and perhaps able to stand the thought of the ordeal of exhuming Jovita's body. Lenor was standing under the stream of a hot shower when she realized she hadn't checked any of Miller's cabinets for more sample drugs. *Damn!* When she got out of the shower she eyed her bed, so neatly made with clean sheets, then turned abruptly and went into the next room where Thomas had slept. Behind two locked doors, she got three good hours of dreamless rest.

At four A.M. Lenor let herself into the bunkhouse kitchen, put the coffeepot on the stove, and set up a tray to take to her mother. Magdalena more than deserved coffee and juice in bed after all she'd been through in the past several days. As soon as she was sure her mother was feeling all right, Lenor planned to drive into Toya and be on Apple's doorstep in time to catch a judge just getting out of bed. She'd wait to inform everyone what was going on until she knew what time an officer of the court would show up. Then she would take a good long look at the book she'd "stolen" from Dr. Baldwin's house last night. When Lucielle came in at four-thirty, Lenor asked her to get Nemesia to help with the cooking again.

"Way ahead of you, lady. I asked her last night." Lucielle helped herself to coffee and sat down beside Lenor at the dividing counter. "Hey, this is good stuff. Where did you learn to make coffee?"

"Always digging for a compliment, aren't you?"

"I store 'em up, save 'em till I need 'em."

"I'm probably going to be gone a lot today, Lucielle. Errands and stuff. Will you watch after my mother? I don't want her tiring herself out."

"Do you know what's wrong with her yet?" Lucielle asked.

"Not yet, but I'm a lot closer to the answer than I was this time yesterday."

"We can't have her lazin' around here anymore. This lady-of-leisure bit has gone far enough. I need some help!"

"I know you do. I'll have her back to her old workhorse self before you know it, Lucielle. I promise."

"Today wouldn't be too soon," Lucielle said.

But it wasn't to be today. When Lenor got to her mother's room with coffee and fresh orange juice, Magdalena was ghastly white and her breathing so shallow, Lenor had to put her ear close to tell whether she was breathing at all. Faint pulse. Cold, clammy skin. Lenor threw back the bedclothes.

"God in heaven!" Nothing in her medical career had prepared her to see her own mother in such a condition.

Magdalena lay deathly still in a spreading stain of fresh blood.

Twenty-six

Uterine hemorrhage!

Can I handle this? Can I stop shaking long enough to do the right thing?

"Oh, Mama. I love you so much!" she whispered as she elevated her mother's hips and legs up on a pillow.

Put the fear out of your mind! Get busy! Now!

Lenor called the barn, looking for her father, but Rudolfo told her Rafael had already ridden out with Manny to scatter bulls. She told Rudolfo to get her medical bag from her bedroom and bring it to Magdalena's room as fast as he could. Rudolfo was shocked when he saw Magdalena's condition, but he controlled his fright, gently carried her to Lenor's rented car, then drove to Mora as if the Devil pursued him.

The night light was still on outside the clinic's emergency room door, but Estelle was already inside. "Can you pack a uterus?" Lenor asked her as she and Rudolfo swept through the door.

"Yes, Doctor," Estelle said. "Put her right here, Rudolfo." She was already on the phone. "Inez, get Dr. Baldwin over here immediately."

Lenor began giving orders. "Draw a blood sample. I want a hemoglobin and hematocrit. Type and cross-match. Large needle, leave it in. Get a pressure cuff on her. Sterile gauze?"

"On your right, Doctor, last cabinet, top shelf."

Since Magdalena, Rafael, and Lenor all had type A-positive blood, Lenor decided to take the very slight risk of reaction and use her own blood to transfuse her mother instead of trusting any of the hospital personnel. She wrapped an elastic tourniquet around her arm and left it in place while she lifted the examination table stirrups and placed her mother's bare feet in them.

"Estelle, get an oxygen mask on her. Rudolfo, call Michael Martino."

Rudolfo gave her a puzzled look.

It was a chance she had to take. Michael and Nemesia both had the right blood type, but since Nemesia didn't drive, Rudolfo would have to go back to the ranch to get her. Michael could make the drive to the clinic in less than half the time. "Michael has A-positive blood, Rudolfo. Tell him to get down here as fast as he can."

"Right." He made the call, then said, "I'll be in the waiting room if you need me."

In the next few frantic minutes, Estelle and two others set the standard for Mora's new clinic and soon-to-be-twenty-bed hospital. Lenor was pleased and pleasantly surprised. By the time

Miller walked in, the uterine packing had been completed and Lenor was on a gurney connected to her mother by a lifeline that ran red with vital blood. Ten minutes later Michael arrived and crossed hurriedly to Lenor's side.

"Lenor?" He had to force a rising sob back into the depths of his throat. "What happened?"

"My mother was bleeding internally. I'm not sure why," Lenor said. "Estelle, he's type A-positive. Take a blood sample, get his blood pressure, and cross your fingers." She smiled at Michael. "He looks like he can spare a pint, doesn't he?"

With a hostile look on his face, Miller turned away from the counter where he'd been making notes on a sheet of paper. "How about letting the doctor in charge take over his own operation now, Dr. Tavera?" he said sternly.

It wasn't really a question, it was a demand. Estelle wasn't sure whether to obey Lenor or wait for Dr. Baldwin's orders which, logically, would be exactly the same. She began swabbing Michael's arm with an alcohol sponge.

"That will do, Mrs. Parrish." Miller headed for the door. "A word with you, please? Out here."

When Estelle came back, she told Michael that Dr. Baldwin wanted to talk to him in the hall. "What was that all about?" Lenor asked Estelle when Michael had left.

"Unbelievable. Dr. Baldwin's mad at me because I let you work in the emergency room."

"What?" Lenor asked incredulously.

"He's afraid you're sick." Estelle huffed. "And he said that Michael has had hepatitis and can't give blood."

Impossible! She almost shouted it out, but caught herself in time. "I'm glad to know that about Michael," she said instead. "Saves unnecessary lab time." The question was not whether Michael had had hepatitis, but how Miller would have known about it if he had. Lenor scanned her memory of Michael's record. She saw nothing about his ever having been diagnosed with the debilitating viral infection. There had to be another reason for not allowing him to give blood. But what?

Estelle checked Magdalena's respiration, removed the oxygen mask, then began unhooking Lenor from the transfusion apparatus. "Michael sure doesn't look like he's ever been sick a day in his life, does he?" Estelle said, a dreamy look on her face. "He's so handsome, isn't he?"

"Most beautiful little boy I ever saw," Magdalena said weakly, then let out a long sigh.

"Mrs. Tavera?" Estelle turned to her. Magdalena's eyes were still closed, but there was a smile on her lips. "What did you say?"

"Those eyes . . ." She drifted off again.

Lenor sat up. "Estelle, do you have an off-duty nurse you could call in? I'll pay double time. I want someone with her around the clock until I say otherwise."

"I was off duty fifteen minutes ago, and my 'weekend' starts today. I'd be glad to stay with her."

"You sure you're up to it?" Lenor asked.

Estelle nodded. "Quiet night. This is the first real work I've done in eight hours."

"You're hired. No visitors except Rafael, Michael, Apple Hardy, and me unless I say so," Lenor said as she crossed to the counter where Miller had left his notes. "I'll write the orders for you." She made some more notes on the single piece of paper. "Put this in your pocket. I want all lab slips to come to me first and I don't want Dr. Baldwin, or anyone else, changing anything I've put down here. Understand?"

"Understand, Doctor."

"Understand what?" Miller asked gruffly as he and Michael came back into the room.

"Can we get my mother to a bed now, Miller? I hear three of your new rooms are finished." Lenor's question and comment diverted his attention long enough for Estelle to push the gurney next to the examining table and lock the wheels. "How about a hand with this, Miller?" He had a doctors-don't-do-this look on his face, but he obeyed her.

Magdalena opened her eyes when the jostling was finished. "Miller, you look awful," she said softly.

THE TAVERA LEGACY ◆ 359

He should, Lenor thought. He probably hadn't had much more sleep than she had. "You *do* look a little tired, Miller," Lenor said. Once they had Magdalena in a bed, Miller left Michael, Estelle, and Lenor in the room while he gave Rudolfo an update on Magdalena's condition. Lenor asked Michael to step outside with her.

"What did Dr. Baldwin say to you when he took you out in the hall?" Lenor asked.

"He said Magdalena didn't need any more blood," Michael said.

"That doesn't make sense. Even if she doesn't need any more right now, and he doesn't know that, she should still have a unit in reserve."

"He said that you were hysterical and didn't know what you were talking about."

"Strange. It's just good medical practice to have safe blood these days." Lenor frowned. "He's lying to you."

"That doesn't surprise me," Michael said.

"You don't like him."

"I despise him."

"Mind telling me why?"

Michael looked up to the ceiling and sighed. Here it was again. They were back to his visit with Dr. Baldwin two years ago. He cleared his throat. "Remember the question you asked me about seeing Dr. Baldwin?"

Lenor nodded.

"Eloy brought me in unconscious. When I came to, a couple days later, I wanted to leave, but I was hooked up to one of those IV contraptions, getting blood. And I was strapped down."

Not unusual procedure, under the circumstances, but Lenor could imagine how he must have felt—like a captured animal in the lair of the man who might have killed his father. "What did you do?" she asked.

"I raised a ruckus. The nurse protested. Eloy came in and talked me into being quiet for a minute. I convinced him to undo the restraints. We talked a little longer. That's when I found out about the blood that was going into my arm. Eloy was just trying to calm me down, talking about whatever came into his mind, but when he said that his mother had donated the blood, I came unglued."

Lenor frowned.

"I know. I know. It was perfectly logical. But the fact that Miller knew how my mother felt about Nemesia, and knew none of us ever got along . . . I figured he'd called her in to satisfy his brand of perverse sadistic pleasure. I was furious. I jerked the needle out of my arm and left." He cringed. "It makes me uncomfortable to be here now."

"Do you really think Dr. Baldwin murdered your father?" Lenor asked.

"Just a feeling. Murder may be the wrong word. More like negligent homicide."

"Michael, no matter what there was, or is, between us, I have to ask you to help me. Will Eloy be able to handle things for you while you're here?"

"Eloy stayed in Las Vegas last night, but he's probably back home by now. Even if he isn't Gil can handle things."

"You could stay here, then?" Michael nodded. "Rudolfo will need my car. May I use yours? I need to run some errands."

Michael's expression became grim and suspicious, but he dug into his pocket. "It's the brown truck," he said, handing her a silver ring with three keys. "What are you going to do?" he asked sternly. "Do your *errands* have anything to do with Dr. Baldwin's lying?"

"Yes, but don't ask me any more questions. Please, just help me out. Okay?"

"I don't think you should . . ."

But Lenor was already on her way down the hall. "I'll talk to Rudolfo on my way out. Don't leave Mama's room till I get back." Her words trailed behind her; then she was gone.

Lenor stopped in front of Paula's house. "This won't take a minute," she told Paula's husband, and he led her back to Paula's bedroom.

"I'm back for a little visit, Paula. I can't stay long," Lenor said.

"Tea?" Paula asked.

"Not this morning. I just want to know what drugs Dr. Baldwin gave you when you first started feeling bad."

"I still don't remember," Paula said.

"Let's see if I can help you remember. Aspirin?"

Paula shook her head.

"Tylenol?"

Paula hesitated, then shook her head.

"Tegretol?"

Paula closed her eyes for a moment. "I think so," she said, opening her eyes.

"Halcion?"

Paula nodded right away. "I'm sure about that one."

"I want you to come to the clinic with me, Paula. Is that all right with you?"

"No!" Her scream brought her husband to the door.

"What's wrong?" he asked.

Lenor pleaded with him. "I may be able to help your wife get better. I asked her to come to the clinic with me."

"So Dr. Baldwin can kill her? No. Absolutely not."

Lenor turned back to Paula. "Please, listen to me. I'll be your doctor. I won't let anything happen to you. I promise."

Paula's eyes filled with tears. Lenor Tavera might be her only chance for survival. "I'll go with you," she whispered.

"No!" her husband shouted.

But Paula's mind was made up. Lenor called the clinic. Paula's husband carried her to the truck, propped her up in the center of the seat, and climbed in beside her.

Estelle met them at the front door. Lenor entered the clinic with Paula following, carried in her husband's arms. "She needs a bed. Draw blood. Do a match. I want at least two units standing by. Vitals every hour. No visitors. Can we get a bleeding profile?"

Estelle nodded.

Her husband spoke up. "We have the same type blood and I know we're compatible," he said.

"Double check," Lenor said. Estelle held a wheelchair steady. As soon as Paula was comfortable in the room next to Magdalena's, Lenor debated whether to call Apple or check her mother first. She didn't get to do either. A nurse poked her head out of a door down the hall and yelled.

"Is that Dr. Baldwin?"

A young girl standing in the hall shrugged, then yelled back, "No. Not yet."

"What's going on?" Lenor ask the girl.

"Another emergency." She shrugged again. "Guess this is the second one this morning. Dr. Baldwin went home to get some breakfast after the first one. That's all I know. I just got here."

Lenor raced down the hall, praying that it wasn't Magdalena back in the emergency room. It wasn't.

"Oh, thank God! Dr. Tavera. Sheriff Garcia just brought her in, and Dr. Baldwin's not answering his phone." The young nurse looked terrified as she pointed to the patient on the examination table.

Rosa's pale lips moved as if she were trying to speak when Lenor looked down at her. "What happened?"

John Garcia took a step nearer the table. "Juanita called me about half an hour ago. Said she found Rosa in bed this morning, completely dressed, passed out. She kept drifting in and out of consciousness on the way down here."

"Where's Juanita?"

"Said she had to stay there. Something about Michael and Eloy both being gone. She's still out at the ranch."

Lenor was in charge again. "Get over to Miller's house. Inez should have answered the phone. See if she's all right, then get the doctor back over here," she said to John. "What have you done so far?" she asked the nurse.

"Nothing except cover her up and elevate her feet. I'm sorry, Doctor. John just got here, and I had to call . . ."

"You did just fine," Lenor said in a soothing tone. "Now let's get busy." She started issuing orders. During the flurry of activity that ensued, Lenor almost missed the puncture wound at the site of a small mole over the fifth intercostal space. A pinpoint of coagulated blood darkened the center of the brown spot situated just left of the sternum, between the ribs, on the left side of Rosa's chest. "Get her blood pressure again."

"Still ninety over forty."

Damn! Everything she'd seen so far indicated internal bleeding. Punctured lung? If so, a hole that small would have closed almost immediately. Punctured heart? Lenor pressed her stethoscope to Rosa's chest again and heard a normal rhythm. No aberrant lung sounds. Normal bowel sounds from the abdomen. If her heart had been punctured, it was a miracle she wasn't fibrillating. Lenor shivered at the thought of such a grotesque crime, then started when John Garcia burst through the outside door of the emergency room.

"Inez was out back with her chickens. That's why she didn't hear the phone. She doesn't know where Dr. Baldwin is," he said in a rush.

"Didn't Miller go home for breakfast?" Lenor asked.

"Inez hasn't seen him since about ten after six this morning."

"Does Rosa have any relatives around here?" Lenor asked.

John cracked a fist into his palm and frowned. "Damn! Is it that bad?" He rubbed his hands together nervously and gave the nurse a questioning look. "I don't think she has a living soul close by. Damn," he said again, shaking his head. "I guess the only folks she's got, that she could call family, is the bunch out at Michael's place. Sorry, but I just don't know that much about her. Do you want me to go back out and look for the doc now?"

"Yes, please." Lenor had already started a saline IV in Rosa's arm. "Hurry the lab with that hemoglobin-hematocrit and the type and cross match," she told the nurse. As the woman left the room, Lenor pulled the oxygen mask up out of the way, then leaned down. "Rosa, can you hear me?"

Rosa's eyes fluttered.

"You're in the emergency room now. You're going to be all right. Just relax." No response. "Do you know what happened to you, Rosa?"

Pale lips tried to form words, but no sound came out.

"I can't hear you, Rosa."

"Power . . ." The one word floated on a soft breath of air.

"Power? Is that what you said?"

Rosa's eyelids fluttered again. "Heart's . . . blood . . ." Her head rolled to one side as she slipped into unconsciousness.

"Heart's blood." Lenor repeated the words. Did someone actually insert a needle into the woman's chest and draw blood from her heart? Lenor couldn't imagine a more bizarre atrocity than that. Who would do such a thing? And why? The only explanation she could think of was some kind of black-magic ritual performed by someone who should be locked up in an insane asylum.

Lenor kept talking to Rosa even though the woman was unconscious. All the way to the room, then through the jostling into the safe haven of the bed next to Magdalena's, Lenor talked, but Rosa remained silent and still. There was one bright spot, however. Since the saline had been started, Rosa's condition was steadily improving and her normal skin color was returning.

Magdalena was told only that Rosa had had an accident. It would be enough for a while.

Dr. Baldwin was still missing.

Twenty-seven

SO MANY LOOSE ENDS NAGGED AT THE CORNERS OF Lenor's mind, so many things still needed to be done, but she was afraid to leave her mother or Rosa alone, even for a minute. Paula's husband, Jimmy, had planted himself in a chair next to his wife's bed and was reluctant to move, even when Lenor and Estelle came in to take care of her.

Michael had not left Magdalena's hospital room except to call Juanita, make sure she was all right, and find out if Eloy had returned safely. When she wasn't hovering, Estelle refused to move from the chair between the two beds, until Lenor finally had to insist that she take a breather. She'd come back to her post in less than five minutes.

Lenor couldn't believe how comfortable she felt with Michael. His concern for the three women manifested in total attention to their needs. As for his behavior with Magdalena, it was as if they'd always had a close and loving relationship. When she wasn't asleep, he talked with her about cantankerous horses and hardworking ranch hands and pesky new calves and exuberant children. He filled her water glass and held the straw to her lips. He rubbed her cold hands until they were warm. Why was it, Lenor wondered, that it took disaster or tragedy to bring human beings together?

Before noon, both women were fully conscious. Magdalena was as mentally alert as if nothing had happened to her, but was still too weak to sit up by herself. Rosa remained confused about where she was and how she'd gotten to the clinic. The only other discernible word she'd uttered since leaving the emergency room was "thief." The continuous lab work confirmed that both patients were on their way back from the brink of death. But their steady climb to recovery hadn't taken the edge off the tension that Rosa's "injury" had caused.

Even though neither Magdalena nor Rosa was ready for solid food, Michael went out to get clear broth for the patients and something for everyone else, trusting the longtime cook at Maria's café down the street more than the stranger in the clinic kitchen. Lenor even managed a few bites of a sandwich and a glass of milk.

Apple Hardy dropped in. The package had been sent to New York. A judge would issue an exhumation order as soon as he was out of court. She was on her way to the Tavera ranch to find Rafael, if she could, and talk to Steven.

"This is going to be the hardest thing I've ever done," she

told Lenor. "How do you tell someone that his wife has been murdered and her grave has to be opened up?"

"God, I wish I could go with you," Lenor said. "Do you want me to call him? Try to prepare him?" she asked.

"No. There's no telling what he might do. Somebody should be there when he hears the news. I want to be that someone."

"You're an angel," Lenor said. "I couldn't have gotten through this without you."

"What are best friends for?" Apple said, then hurried away.

John Garcia returned by midafternoon with the report that his search for Miller, like the search for his son, had been fruitless so far. As he'd done when Junior, and later Thomas, was missing, the sheriff had enlisted the help of those townspeople who could get away from their jobs. He was on the way back to his office to call some of the outlying ranches to see if anyone might have some free time to devote to looking around.

Apple phoned later to say that Steven had surprised her speechless. When she'd told him that his wife had been murdered, he said that Jovita had already informed him. Then he'd showed Apple the *bulto* of San Miguel that Lenor had brought to him and said, "I have everything I need to get through this."

"You could have knocked me over with an Apache plume," Apple told Lenor. "He wasn't even worried about Magdalena. Said 'she's in good hands.' Then the man tried to comfort *me!*"

Lenor breathed a sigh of relief. "We must be living right," she said. "Did you find my father?"

"I still have people out looking. No luck yet. Hell of a lot of territory to cover. Steven's waiting at the barn for him, though, and I don't envy Grandpa having to break all the bad news."

"Grandpa will know just what to say and how to say it," Lenor said. "I'll call him right now and tell him Mama's doing just fine so Papa won't worry as much. And Apple . . . thanks again."

"Thank your grandma, kiddo. Jovita did all the *hard* work."

Michael, Lenor, and Estelle continued their watch. It seemed ridiculous for all three of them to stay in the hospital room, but not one of them was willing to leave for more than a few minutes at a time. Lenor had been called to the emergency room once again, this time to prescribe an antibiotic for a young boy's infected throat, but generally the nurses and other staffers were taking care of everything that was going on in the clinic. They considered no request made by Dr. Tavera too great a task to accomplish in record time, and Lenor took advantage of her complete freedom.

First she searched Miller Baldwin's office and found nothing of any significance except a few out-of-date drug samples that should have been thrown away. Next she looked at Ramon Martino's medical record and discovered that he'd died of a Brown-Pierce tumor. The malignant carcinoma on the back of his neck had widely metastasized before he'd sought treatment. In spite of her continuing suspicions about Miller, Lenor was relieved.

About five o'clock, after an eighteen-hour day, Estelle finally agreed to go home. She called in another off-duty nurse, then left to have dinner with her new husband and get a few hours' sleep.

Magdalena was getting more and more uncomfortable with the uterine packing, and Lenor had a nurse remove it around six o'clock in the evening. No new bleeding occurred.

When Rafael called to say he'd be there shortly, he was fairly calm—to a point. For no good reason, he was blaming himself for not knowing that something was wrong with Magdalena before he'd left the bedroom to go to work.

"She's usually up before I am, Lenor. How could I have just left her there sleeping? I should have—"

"You should have been glad she was finally getting some rest, Papa," Lenor said.

"I was," he said bleakly. "But—"

"No more buts. Just get on down here and say hi to this lonesome woman of yours."

By the time Rafael arrived, Magdalena was more than ready for his company. In fact, she was ready to go home and cook dinner. And Rosa surprised them all by smiling at him.

Rosa had needed only one pint of plasma to bring all her lab counts up to normal. She continued to rest comfortably until six-thirty, when Nemesia and Rudolfo came bearing gifts: Lucielle's beef stew, wildflowers in a pottery vase, and the *Tavera Herbarium* that Lenor had asked Rudolfo to bring.

An earlier visit with her mother, when everyone else was out of the room, had confirmed Lenor's suspicions about Nemesia's part in the trouble between Celsa and Ramon Martino. Magdalena and Nemesia had disagreed, then fought about the act of revenge. That was when Nemesia had quit cooking and started housekeeping. It was also when Nemesia decided to leave the Martinos alone, but it was too late to save their marriage. Now Lenor looked forward to talking to Nemesia about the spell she'd cast on Lenor and Michael. But when the Señas walked in, it took all Michael's strength to keep Rosa from coming out of her bed and hitting the floor at a run.

"You've got to stay quiet, Rosa," Lenor told the frantic woman. "If you don't, the bleeding could start again. Do you understand? You've got to lie still."

All Rosa would say was, "Get away . . . get away . . . get away."

Rudolfo and Rafael left the room, but the plea stayed the same. "Get away . . ."

"I don't understand," Nemesia said when she stepped out into the hall with Lenor. "Rosa and I have been friends for years. Why would she want me to get away from her?"

"She's still a little confused," Lenor said. "She's had quite a shock to her system."

"What exactly happened to her?" Nemesia asked.

"We aren't sure yet," Lenor hedged. "She had some internal bleeding. I'll keep you posted. And don't let the way she's acting hurt your feelings. She really doesn't mean what she's saying." *Does she?*

"My feelings aren't hurt, but I don't understand," Nemesia said.

"Neither do I." *Maybe I do.* Two interesting possibilities: One: Rosa is afraid of Nemesia—not likely. Two: Rosa is warning Nemesia. There was only one way to play it safe. "Rudolfo, come here." Lenor lowered her voice. "I want you to take Nemesia home, and don't let her out of your sight. Get out that pearl-handled six-shooter you pack in the Fourth of July parade, load it, keep it with you, and don't take your eyes off your wife all night. Understand?"

Rudolfo had no questions—except one. "What do you want me to do with Watson?"

"Watson?" Lenor asked.

"He's out in the truck. He wouldn't let us leave the ranch without him. Now he's just sitting in the truck bed, waiting for something, I guess."

Lenor went outside with them. Sure enough, Watson sat patiently, at least until he saw Lenor. Then he bounded out of the truck, stopped at the edge of the street, and sat down.

"You want me to catch him and take him home?" Rudolfo asked.

Lenor shook her head. "I think he wants to stay here for a while," she said, but she knew exactly what he wanted. *I can't follow you right now. Wait for me.*

Rosa had calmed completely when Lenor came back in. "She stopped fighting me as soon as Nemesia went out the door," Michael told her. "What's going on?"

"I haven't figured any of it out yet, Michael, but I'm working on it." She sat down and began to page through the *Herbarium* while the others enjoyed Lucielle's beef stew. More than a simple herbal, it had been used as a recipe book, instructional, and diary as well. All the *remedios* were familiar to her. All the recipes called for too much fat. She flipped past what she already knew and concentrated on the diary entries from the summer and fall of 1860.

Her dream about Leonora had been particularly accurate. Leonora had gone to court and been acquitted. The fall harvest had been exceptionally good, but failed to bring a profit because of Rubén Barela's deal with Fort Union. Lenor scanned pages until the writing style changed. Dorio's entries. Then a note in the margin caught her eye.

"Feed needles and water?" she said aloud.

"Piedra imán," Rosa whispered.

"What did you say, Rosa?" Lenor asked.

"The fury stone," Rosa said. *"Piedra imán."*

Lenor's mind was blank. She turned two pages, and the handwriting changed again. The new script was in Carolina's hand. She got up quickly from the chair and handed the book to Michael. "I have another errand to run. I won't be gone but a few minutes. Okay?"

Lenor didn't hear his reply. She was already out the door and hurrying down the hall. In the parking lot she looked for Watson, but didn't see him until he called her.

"Eee."

He was standing on the running board of Michael's old truck. She still had Michael's keys, and was soon headed west into the slanting rays of the simmering sun, with Watson sitting on her shoulder for a perfect all-around view.

Lenor cursed her bleary thinking as they drove along. *I should have guessed.* Her own great-great-grandfather, Dorio, had made a deal with the Devil. Since he'd only been taught the *curanderismo,* he'd probably had to hire a *bruja* to transform the black river rock into a fury stone. Almost any witch who practiced black magic could have done the job, and when she was through, Dorio would have a very powerful weapon to use against the man who'd killed his mother. Barela.

She hadn't taken the time to read further, but Lenor suspected that when Dorio took up black magic, Carolina had assumed the duties of the *curandera* in the family. Lenor looked down at her hands again. They were even thinner than they had been yesterday.

"If the *piedra imán* is lost or stolen from its owner, he or she will lose her mind or dry up like a skeleton," Lenor said. "But you know that already, don't you, Watson?" She thought a moment. "I'm sure there's more to the fury stone than that. I just can't seem to remember. Something about flying? No. Something about infinite knowledge? Maybe. Transformation?" Watson was silent. "A Barela wanted it then . . . but who would want it now?"

"Eee-oow."

"I'm sorry I didn't pay attention to what you've been trying to tell me, but I've been kind of busy," Lenor said.

Watson dug his claws through her shirt and gingerly into her flesh. Lenor pulled over to the curb and stopped—right in front of the general store. It was a dangerous thing to do, but she and Watson got out and went inside. Watson disappeared down one of the aisles.

Adela was busy with a customer, but the slender, gray-haired woman was soon free.

"Lenor Tavera. I haven't seen you in such a long time. I was so sorry to hear about your grandmother."

"Thank you, Adela."

"What can I help you with?"

"I wanted to talk to Roy. Is he here?" Lenor asked.

"He was out back cleaning his car earlier. Want me to go have a look?"

Oh, don't bother. I know my way. I'll just have a look out the back door."

"All right." Just then several people came in. "If he is out there, tell him I could use some help."

"Okay," Lenor said over her shoulder.

Watson was by her side as she stepped outside and immediately ran to the door of the large greenhouse behind the store. Lenor followed, then watched in horror as he scuttled under the padlocked entrance. "Don't do this to me, cat." She tapped lightly on the corrugated plastic material. "You'd better get back out here—" she gave a yank on the heavy padlock "—right now!" The lock slipped down and open. Every cell in her body screamed *Don't do it!* But she had to.

Cool, wet air enveloped her like a sea breeze, tempting her inside, pulling her along the plant-lined, misty aisle into the shadowed interior. Fascinated at first, then horrified, Lenor found herself passing innocent-looking flora that concealed agony and death in their perfectly kept roots, stems, leaves, and beautiful flowers. Daphne, hemlock, monkshood, lily of the valley. And many more. But she could see no evidence of the stone they'd come to find.

She skirted around an old wooden chair and stopped in front of a large pot containing a Jatropha curcas. Ingested, it would be a violent purgative and protein synthesis inhibitor. Prognosis for the victim? Doomed.

"Here, kitty kitty kitty," Lenor whispered softly, then waited. "Watssson!" she hissed. He appeared at the other end of the building and entered a small doorway. "Come here!"

He didn't. Lenor hurried after him, entering the darkened room. "Watson?" To her left she saw a tall, wide wooden chest of drawers with round, white porcelain handles. She pulled at one of the handles, but it wouldn't open. Locked. The rest of the space was full of gardening tools. She saw no black stone. Lenor began to shiver. The skin-and-bones state of her health, the damp air, and pure fear shook her body and rattled her teeth together. "I'm leaving, Watson. I don't care if you stay or—" She froze, hearing the sound of a car outside, the slam of a door, footsteps.

She moved further back into the shadows, frantically looking around for an escape route. There was none. The front door of the greenhouse creaked open, then cracked shut. Footsteps.

"Lenor?"

It was Adela's voice. Lenor realized she'd been holding her breath. "Adela!" The name came out too loudly, on a blast of exhaled air. "I was just looking around this place," she said as she stepped out of the back room. "I'm amazed." She made a display of looking all around. "I didn't know Roy was *this* interested in plants."

Adela looked peeved. "I was hoping Roy was out here with you. We're getting so busy, the customers are starting to park in the back."

"I'm sorry. I haven't seen him," Lenor said. "I'd stay and help you, but I have to run." She felt like literally running, but she waited until Adela had exited, then called Watson. This time he came, and Lenor tucked him tightly under one arm for their walk back to the truck. Her reckless driving back to the clinic had the disappointed cat swaying this way and that, digging his claws into the seat for dear life.

"You look like hell," Estelle said when Lenor walked into Magdalena's room. "Where have you been? Trekking the Amazon?"

"Why aren't *you* still at home?" Lenor asked, to avoid answering Estelle's question.

As soon as Lenor had finished checking the three women in her care, Michael asked if he could speak to her out in the hallway.

He got right to the point. "I want to know what's going on."

"I told you, I don't know yet," Lenor said.

"You obviously don't think any of us are safe. Tell me why." It was a demand.

"We can't talk here," Lenor said.

"How about that empty room across the hall?" Michael asked.

"I don't want to leave them alone."

"Estelle's with them. Jimmy's here. And we'll leave the doors open."

"All right."

"Don't leave anything out," he said as they stepped into the dim light of the unoccupied room.

"I won't." And she didn't—except for the part about Nemesia. In the next fifteen minutes she told him everything, from her grandmother's warnings to her latest bit of information about Roy Baldwin.

Michael listened quietly until she was finished. "Whoa! Now I see why you're confused. I can barely remember half of what you've told me." He took a deep breath and shook his head in disbelief. "Murder. I can't believe—"

"Believe it," Lenor said.

"Before we go any further, I want to tell you right now, the reason I was looking at the real estate records was to find out if I could buy the land north of me. The son of a bitch is subdividing and selling off residential plots, clearing the pines with a damned bulldozer."

"Oh, Michael. That's awful," Lenor said.

"I also have to tell you this. You've taken too many chances without knowing whom you could trust or what might happen to you along the way. Apple's a good sheriff, but she's spread way too thin in a situation like this."

"And what would you have had me do? Ask the law in Mora to help her? After the way he acted Wednesday night, John Garcia could be the man who put Old Woosey in my bed."

"If a man did it."

"Good point. But I found my stolen book in Dr. Baldwin's desk drawer, and you know how tight a trio Miller, Roy, and John have always been."

Michael raised an eyebrow, then nodded.

"So ask yourself this," Lenor said. "How could the Tavera property fall into the hands of someone who desperately wanted it?"

"All the heirs die intestate, and the property is auctioned off by the state," Michael said. "The killer buys it."

"That's one way," Lenor agreed, then thought for a moment. "But in that case, why start with Jovita? When Steven was so sick, ten years ago, he put everything in an inter vivos trust, with Rafael as the trustee, and beneficiaries and successor beneficiaries that go on forever, or until the family dies out all together. Besides, we've all had wills drawn up, too. No Tavera is going to die intestate."

"Maybe the killer doesn't know about the wills or the trust," Michael said.

"Or what if he does?" Lenor shivered in spite of the summer warmth. "Michael, I don't think Jovita was the intended victim."

"Who, then?"

"My grandfather," Lenor said. "Steven is killed. Magdalena is slowly poisoned . . ."

"You think this person will try to kill your whole family?" Michael asked, incredulous.

"It entered my mind," she said grimly. "But there's another way someone could get their hands on the Tavera property."

"What's that?" Michael asked

"Marriage."

"To whom?" Michael asked.

"Me," Lenor said.

Michael's expression was blank for a moment; then the void filled with horror. "You don't think *I* would—"

"You told me I didn't know who to trust," Lenor said.

A sudden jolt of anger propelled him closer to her. "So you naturally supposed I decided to come out of seclusion, sweep you off your feet, kill the Tavera heirs, and marry you? Goddamn it, Lenor!"

"You have to admit, your behavior has been a little . . . unusual."

He couldn't argue with her on that point. In the past few weeks he'd questioned his sanity all too frequently. But during the emergency with Magdalena, Lenor had called on him to help. And she hadn't had to take him into her confidence or tell him any of this. His flare of anger snuffed to an insignificant spark. "Why *did* you decide to trust me?" he asked.

Lenor put her hand on his chest. "Because in here, where it counts, you're a good person. I can feel it." She smiled at him then. "And because Watson likes you."

Michael smiled. "You mean, if I court Watson's favor . . . ?"

Lenor realized she was still touching him. It felt too good. She gave him a playful slap on the chest. It was time to get back to business. "What if the Tavera property *isn't* the key to any of what's been going on?" She went on.

"It's about the only thing that makes a lot of sense. What's one of the most powerful motives for murder, or any other kind of crime?" Michael asked.

"Greed."

"Exactly. I'd say greed outranks envy and jealousy."

"What about revenge?" Lenor asked.

Michael shook his head. "Revenge for what?"

"I'm not sure. Just a thought." But it was much more than that. If the killer were actually a Barela descendant, he or she just might be crazy enough to want accounts settled between the two families, especially since the Tavera family had obviously prospered in the Land of Enchantment, and the Barela family had lost everything—even their dignity.

And there was something else, too. But she couldn't talk to Michael about that just yet. No need to upset him when she desperately needed his help.

"At least now you have an ally. What's next?" Michael asked.

"We get out of here. We'll use the ambulance to—" A bloodcurdling scream pierced the air.

John Garcia was backing out of the doorway across the hall. Michael grabbed him from behind and twisted his arm across his back. Lenor ran into the room and found Estelle trying to hold Rosa down again.

"What happened?" Lenor asked as she pressed her weight onto Rosa's kicking legs.

"John stepped inside the door, said hi to Magdalena, and told us he wanted to report no luck finding Dr. Baldwin. He said the only thing unusual he'd seen all day was a fire in an old abandoned logging shack up north of Chacon. That's when Rosa started yelling."

"He's . . . fouled . . . the sacred . . . space," Rosa hissed between gasping breaths.

"Rosa, please. You're going to have to calm down." Lenor looked up at Estelle. "We've got to get them out of here." She called out to Michael. "You can let John go, but keep him out of Rosa's sight. I'll be out there in just a minute."

When Rosa began to quiet down, Lenor went back into the hall. John was wringing his hands and pacing. "I shouldn't have just walked in like that," he was saying to Michael. "I shouldn't have said—" He saw Lenor and rushed toward her. "I'm so sorry, Lenor. I didn't know . . ."

"It's all right now, John. Rosa's calming down. She'll be fine."

"I just wanted to tell you that I couldn't find Dr. Baldwin, but I ran into somebody else."

"Who?" Michael and Lenor asked in unison.

"On my way back over here, I stopped at the general store to see if Roy had seen his father. He was cleaning his Rover out back. Never mind that. He said he'd be glad to loan you his vehicle, if you need it for any reason."

Michael and Lenor looked at each other. The offer had to be refused.

"Tell Roy thanks, but we can manage," Lenor said.

"Just as well," John said. "He may never get all that hair out of the back end."

"Hair?" Lenor asked.

John nodded and grinned. "He was having a hell of a time trying to vacuum it all up."

Old Woosey!

"John, will you do me a favor?" Lenor asked.

"Sure. Anything."

"Call Rudolfo and tell him we're bringing Paula, Magdalena, and Rosa out to the house. Then tell the nurses I need to use the ambulance and a few supplies. Someone will bring the ambulance right back to the clinic." When she finished telling him what she wanted to take with her, he hurried off down the hall.

"You're going to trust John Garcia?" Michael asked.

"Or trap him," Lenor said. "Either way, we'll accomplish what we've set out to do. Let's go take a look at my book while we're waiting for John. Maybe we can see something in it that someone might be willing to kill for."

But the book Rudolfo had brought was still, mainly, an herbal, written in Spanish, in many different hands. A precious antique, granted, perhaps a priceless piece of memorabilia from the past, but there were older books in the world. There were probably older and more complete volumes on the *curanderismo* to be found in large city libraries and on the bookshelves of some *curanderas* and *curanderos* around the world.

For the material level of healing, *nivel material,* there were remedies for everything from fever and heart disorders to stomachache and sleeplessness. For the spiritual level of healing, *nivel espiritual,* there were nonherbal remedies involving trance states induced to make manipulation of spiritual currents possible. Even instructions for work on the rare mental level, *nivel mental,* had been included, written mostly by Lenor's great-great-grandmother, Ada Tavera, in the years between 1911 and 1949. Aunt Irene, Rafael's other sister, had added a few notes to Ada's entries in the years before her death, 1974. Lenor pointed.

"Look. This is one of the herbs I wanted to look up. Corydalis. I thought my mother might be dosing herself with it, but look here." Michael leaned closer. "It has to be taken with a more specific herb like skullcap or valerian. She'd know better than to take it alone, and she wouldn't have mixed it with her regular tea. Guess I was wrong about this one."

Michael kept turning the pages. Lenor kept shaking her head—until he turned to the last.

"What in the world?" The last page and the inside cover listed, in family-tree form, all the descendants of Juan and Leonora Tavera. From 1827 to the year Lenor was born, all the family births had been written in in a small, fine hand. A tiny cross had been drawn beside each name, with a date underscored by the crosspiece indicating the date of death. "Irene and Jovita. I don't remember these two names being crossed out."

"Did Dr. Baldwin do this?" Michael asked.

"I don't know, but look at this," Lenor said, pointing to the name of Jovita Tavera. "The date of her death has been written in."

"It's correct," Michael said.

"But who wrote it?" Lenor asked.

"Anyone who had access to the book," Michael said. "Could be a lot of people."

"True. Let's see. The book has always been in my home. The

last time I took a good look at it was when Mama asked me to leave it with her when I left for college. I scanned through it then, saying good-bye to something familiar before going off into unknown territory, but I didn't write in it. That handwriting isn't Magdalena's, either."

"What about the names that are circled?" Michael asked.

There were nine circles in all, starting with Leonora Tavera and ending with Lenor. She studied the names for a moment. "If my name wasn't circled, I'd say someone wanted to mark all the people in the family who practiced the *curanderismo* in one form or another."

"But why?"

Lenor shook her head. "Just another puzzle piece that doesn't fit."

The paper backing that was glued to the leather binding had been partially torn loose. Lenor lifted it carefully. From the slit she'd opened, she pulled a folded piece of paper. It was another family tree. Rubén Barela, Tilano, twenty-six names in all, spanning a period from the early 1800s to . . .

Lenor couldn't believe her eyes. Including Gloria Baldwin, all the names but two had been crossed out.

The names remaining were Miller and Roy Baldwin.

Twenty-eight

"Is Estelle there?"

"Dr. Baldwin! I'm so glad you've phoned. We've been worried sick about you. Where have you been?"

"Had an emergency out on the Flora ranch. Let me speak to Estelle."

"Are you all right, Dr. Baldwin? You sound kind of funny."

"Damn it, woman, put Estelle on the phone."

"She's not here, Doctor. She went out to the Tavera place with Lenor and her mother. They left about half an hour ago."

"Is Michael with them?" Miller asked gruffly.

"Michael and Rosa, sir. But Roy is here. Do you want to talk to him?"

"Damn him!" Miller slammed the receiver of the pay phone into its cradle and got back in his station wagon. *Why is Roy doing this? Why is God punishing me?* he wondered as he sat on a dark side street in the little town of Cleveland, just northwest of Mora. "All I ever wanted to do was help people. All I wanted to do was learn how to be the best doctor I could be." His voice bounced off the windshield. He could almost see his words flying back at him, mocking him. *You should have tried to be a better father.*

"God isn't punishing me. It's the Goddess." He pounded the steering wheel with his palm. "Of course. It's the Goddess." He shook his fist at the clouds that were spilling over the mountaintops. "You wouldn't even let me finish my ritual, would you? You made that one candle burn faster than the others."

Just thinking about what had happened in the old logging cabin made him shake with fear. Since there was no longer even a table in the cabin, he'd placed his candles on the floor—carefully, he'd thought. He remembered lighting them before he knelt at his makeshift altar. His trance had been successful, but coming out of it alone, without Rosa to guide and help him, had been more difficult than he'd bargained for. When his eyes had finally focused on the candle burning in front of him, it had been at least three inches shorter than when he started. The next thing he'd become aware of was an intense heat to his right. Now, as he thought of the leaping flames he'd turned to see, he wondered how he'd gotten out alive.

The old Tavera herbal had given him the idea to try to talk to his mother's great-great-grandfather, Rubén Barela, this afternoon. But he'd failed to contact the spirits of Rubén or Tilano Barela. He'd failed in his effort to find out where the *piedra imán* was located. And he'd been so sure he could do it. He desperately needed the magical talisman, the one that Leonora Tavera had used instead of a scalpel to bring a young soldier back from certain death. In his heart, he knew it was the only way he'd be able to help his son. There was only one thing left to do.

"What did my father want?" Roy asked the nurse, who, hand still on the phone, had a peculiar expression on her face.

"He wanted to speak to Estelle."

"Where has he been all day?" Roy asked.

"Out at the Flora place. An emergency of some kind," she said.

"When you asked him if he wanted to speak to me, what did he say?"

The nurse's hand slid from the phone and dropped to her side. "He just said, 'Damn him,' and hung up."

"Oh." Roy turned away. He didn't want the nurse to see his disappointment. When the tears started to burn his eyes, he hurried out the door and headed for the general store. Maybe Lenor had been right. Maybe he should just leave and try to forget his father ever existed. More hot tears ran down his cheeks. He couldn't do it. The feelings he had for the old man were too strong, the ties too secure. There was nothing else to do. He'd have to go on with his plans and pray that they worked.

In fact, he'd have to accelerate them. Of course! Why hadn't he thought about it before? He might never have such a perfect opportunity again. His steps picked up speed until he was running as fast as he could.

Miller got out of his car again, went back to the phone, and dialed the clinic. When he asked the nurse to have Roy wait there, she told him that Roy had already left. *Damn!*

Miller opened his car door, leaned across the seat, and took a full pint of whiskey from the glove compartment. Twisting the top off, he lifted the bottle to his lips—but didn't drink. Instead, he straightened and hurled the bottle at the phone booth. Watching it shatter into a thousand pieces gave him a new feeling of control. He got in the car, started it, and screeched onto the road to Mora in a flurry of flying pebbles. He'd have to hurry if he were going to intercept his son.

The three women were finally settled in the beds that Rudolfo and Rafael had brought into the large north-wing bedroom that Magdalena now used as a library. Several years before, Rafael had built floor-to-ceiling bookcases for her and attached them to every available wall space. Usually the only furniture in the spacious room was one long pine table and four chairs.

Michael and Lenor sat at the table, leafing through books that weren't holding their interest. Estelle had pulled one of the chairs over between two of the beds and was quietly paging through a magazine. Rudolfo and Nemesia were just a phone call away. Steven had visited and returned to Angelina's. Rafael had hovered until Lenor insisted that he go get some rest.

Everyone was comfortable, their appetites satiated by the cookies and milk Lucielle had brought in shortly after they'd arrived. Even Rosa had been able to eat a few bites and take a few sips of milk. Lenor had given all three women a mild herbal sedative. The peaceful room looked like a bedtime story scene in reverse, with the children telling the story and the parents listening—except for the fact that the three women in the twin beds were sound asleep, exhausted by their day of suffering. Lenor and Michael spoke in whispers. Watson sat on the table, listening.

"I want to thank you for staying with us," Lenor said.

Michael closed the book he'd been looking at, rested his hand on the cover, and turned to Lenor. "I wouldn't have had it any other way," he said.

"You know, I don't want to believe it, but I think Dr. Baldwin has been making mistakes for a long time," Lenor said.

"I can believe it, but mistake doesn't sound strong enough to describe what he's done in the name of doctoring," Michael said.

Lenor put her hand on top of Michael's. She knew he was thinking of his father's death. "All doctors make mistakes, Michael. And Miller didn't kill your father. I looked at Ramon's record, and he died of a malignant tumor that had spread to his lungs and his brain before Dr. Baldwin ever saw him."

Surprise registered; then Michael's eyes glistened with tears. He gazed up at the ceiling for a moment, let out a long breath. "All those years," he said, looking at Lenor and shaking his head. "I guess I'll have to revise my opinion of Dr. Baldwin."

"*Maybe.*" Lenor opened the *Tavera Herbarium* to the last page. "Miller started practicing here in his home office in 1965, and he was the attending physician at both the deaths marked in the book, Irene Tavera in 1974, and Jovita. I wonder if he signed both death certificates?"

"I'd like to know the answer to that question, too," Michael said.

"Let's just assume, for a moment, that he's guilty of Jovita's murder and possibly Aunt Irene's. What would his motive have been?" Lenor asked.

Michael shrugged. "The Tavera Legacy?"

"The more I think about it, the less sense it makes. Miller Baldwin could afford to buy all the land anyone would ever want. Why go to the trouble of killing for something you could simply buy?"

"Like you said at the hospital, revenge. The man's a Barela."

"True, but that idea bothers me," Lenor said.

"In this scenario, it makes perfect sense to me," Michael said. "Why does the idea of Miller getting revenge bother you?"

"Because of the circled names and some very strange behavior."

"What strange behavior?" Michael asked.

"You know how, when people are insecure about something they think they lack, they attack the same thing when they see it in others?"

Michael nodded. "Human nature."

"Well, Miller did that to Mama and to me just the other day. He has this idiotic notion that the *curanderas* around here are stealing his business. He raves about how they practice witchcraft. But here's the strange thing. I could hear the envy in his voice all the time he was denouncing their skills as healers. Something tells me that whatever he's up to is directly related to his desire to learn the healing arts of the *curanderismo,* and to those people who practice it. Take Rosa, for example. She's not a member of our family, but she is a practicing *curandera.*"

"Possible. But we don't know for sure that it was Miller who did this to her."

"I'd be willing to bet that that puncture wound was made by a long twenty-two- or twenty-five-gauge needle. Rosa could have easily died if the person who did this didn't have a thorough background in human anatomy. Who else but a physician would be able to do such a thing?"

"Good point, but couldn't a nurse do it?" Michael asked.

"Probably, but as far as I know, there are no nurses involved except Paula, and she's on the receiving end of the equation."

"I still don't understand what Miller could hope to gain by killing," Michael said.

"Maybe he never intended to kill anyone," Lenor said.

"Maybe."

"Let's assume he just wanted to steal their power to heal."

"What?" Michael said incredulously. "You're pulling my leg."

" 'Power' was the first word Rosa said when I asked her what happened to her," Lenor said. "Then she said, 'heart's blood.' I know it sounds absurd, but, gut level, the idea is beginning to make a lot of sense. What if the man is mixed up, maybe a little bit crazy?"

"He can be a real bastard. But insane? I don't know."

"Not really insane, just monumentally frustrated. I think he realized he's spending too much time agonizing over his competition and not enough time keeping up with his medical practice. I'm sure he's aware of his drinking problem. Remember what I told you about my conversation with Jovita's spirit?"

Michael nodded.

"Grandma said I had to protect myself and my mother. Protecting my mother from Dr. Baldwin's drug mistakes was the easy part. Protecting myself directly involves the *piedra imán*. I don't think Miller Baldwin has it or even knows its significance, but it's missing, and look at me." She held up her hands and turned slightly toward him.

Michael shook his head. "You look beautiful to me," he said.

Lenor dropped her hands into her lap and frowned. "I'd say you were prejudiced, Mr. Martino."

"It's possible, but—"

Lenor took a deep breath for courage. It was time to tell him the truth. "Michael, the way you feel about me, the dream . . . it's all an illusion."

"What do you mean, an illusion?"

"You just *think* you're infatuated with me. Your feelings aren't real. They're artificially imposed. You may not be comfortable believing in this sort of thing, but someone has cast a spell on both of us."

"A spell?"

Lenor glanced at Estelle. She was still reading her magazine. "Yes," Lenor said quietly.

"As in magic spell?" Michael said more softly.

"Yes."

Michael shook his head. "I don't believe it. How? Hell. *Who* would do such a thing? Who could?"

"I'm not positive about this, but I think your aunt Nemesia did it," Lenor whispered.

For a moment Michael was stunned into silence. Then, "Why—assuming she could—why would my aunt do such a thing?"

"The way I figure it, Nemesia wanted my mother to have her wish. She wanted to give me a reason to come back to New Mexico, so Magdalena would be happy. What better way to get me to come home? Nemesia knew I was attracted to you. She lived through the months after the state fair, when Apple and I could talk of nothing else but Michael Martino, Miguel Martino, ad nauseam—as Lucielle so eloquently put it back then."

"You talked about our meeting at the fair?" Michael asked.

Lenor smiled. "Until everyone was sick of hearing about the handsome, brilliant, gorgeous, and undeniably perfect Michael Martino."

Michael smiled back. "Handsome, brilliant, gorgeous? If I'd only known."

She hated to do it, but she had to. Lenor took his hand again. "Michael, there's something else."

"What else?" His smile faded to match Lenor's serious look.

"Nemesia may have had something to do with the trouble between your mother and father. Twenty years ago, Nemesia put a curse on Celsa for revenge." She held his hand more tightly. "I'm sorry, Michael." He was silent for a long time, and Lenor suddenly wished she hadn't told him yet, but there was no way she could take back her words. Then he surprised her.

"What my mother did to my aunt was unforgivable. I really can't blame Nemesia for what she did." He thought a moment. "You said it was twenty years ago?" he asked.

"Maybe twenty-one," Lenor said.

"Then Nemesia's curse didn't have anything to do with my parents' problems," he said. "Their marriage started going sour years before that." He took Lenor's hand in both of his and turned it over. It looked painfully thin and fragile. Moments before she'd tried to show him what was happening to her because of the missing fury stone, and he'd made some flip remark. His love for her—and he was convinced his love was real, spell or no spell—had blinded him to what was happening to her right before his eyes. He didn't know if he could help her, but he had to try.

"Let's talk about the past some other time," he said. "Tell me more about the *piedra imán*."

Lenor was relieved. "Remember I told you that I'd dreamed about the black rock?" she asked. "Leonora used it in a ritual way, to help heal a soldier from Fort Union. In the 1860s, the boy should have died from his injuries. Someone reading Leonora's herbal might get the idea that the rock was the catalytic healing factor. Roy Baldwin is always trying to please his father. I'm wondering if Roy borrowed the book, then took the rock to give to Miller, without realizing that Dorio Tavera had it transformed into something altogether different."

"Miller wants the icon?"

"He had my book. He may know about the black rock that Leonora used as a talisman. Maybe he was convinced that it would give him the power to heal. He and Roy might have even talked about it."

"Wait a minute. I'm really confused. In your dream about Leonora Tavera's trial, she denied Barela's suggestion that the rock was a *piedra imán*." His eyes brightened. "Rubén Barela gave Dorio Tavera the idea! How ironic! Rubén Barela actually instigated his own downfall."

"There's something poetic about that, isn't there?" Lenor said.

Michael frowned. "But you said Roy told you yesterday that he had some secret plan. Does that mean he hasn't given the fury stone to his father yet? Could he still have it?"

Lenor nodded, then got a faraway look in her eyes. She didn't want to consider the possibility that Michael's summation pointed to. So many years of friendship had gone before, so many happy sunny days with Roy and Apple by her side. Roy had been almost—no, not almost—he had been like a brother to her for so long. Even after she'd left home, they'd telephoned regularly, visited, shared secrets. Roy Baldwin would not hurt anyone in the Tavera family.

"Leonora's rock is probably on a shelf somewhere, waiting for Roy to wrap it up in colorful paper as a present for his father." Lenor pointed to the open herbal on the table. "Without some kind of guidance in reading this book, it would be an almost impossible leap of logic to figure out the truth about the black rock."

Michael scanned the page she was pointing to. "You're right about that," he said. "I'm *still* wondering how you did it."

"With a little luck and a lot of help from Rosa." Lenor thought a minute. "If Miller is innocent, I intend to help him through this. If he's guilty of any of it, I'm going to see that he hangs from the highest tree around. His days of experimenting will be over forever."

Michael gently squeezed her hand. "Does that mean you'll come home to take his place?"

Please don't start that again! Not now! "You look sleepy," she whispered, changing the subject, pulling her hand away.

Disappointed, Michael didn't resist. "Guess I am, a little."

"Why don't I go make the three of us some coffee? We've got a long vigil ahead of us."

"I'll go," Michael said. "They might need you."

"Estelle is here. I'd rather you stay, in case . . ." She didn't want to put her fear into words, and Michael understood.

"Make it good and strong," he said as Lenor and Watson left the room.

Estelle stood up, stretched, then came over to sit beside Michael. "You're going to miss her when she goes back to New York, aren't you?"

"Yes."

"It's hard to say good-bye, even when you know the separation is only going to be temporary," she said knowingly. "My husband travels." But when he comes home, it's like another honeymoon all over again." She smiled and cocked her head to one side. "You two make a very handsome couple. Have you set a wedding date yet?"

"We haven't talked about marriage," Michael said.

"Is that a fact? I could have sworn . . . I mean, the way you look at her, the way she—" Estelle shrugged. "I guess it's just a matter of time."

"Tell me about your husband," Michael said. "What kind of work does he do?"

Estelle warmed to the subject, and they talked in whispers until Michael thought he heard footsteps outside the door. "That was quick," he said as he crossed to the door.

Estelle watched as he pulled it open. She saw a flash of silver.

Michael crumpled to the floor. Instinctively, Estelle started toward him.

Then everything went black.

Watson sat beside a large tray of woven willow branches that held cups on saucers, sugar bowl, creamer, spoons, napkins, herbal tea in a tea ball, a thermos of hot water, and an electric pot full of fresh, strong coffee. While the coffee had brewed, Lenor had rummaged through the refrigerator and found the perfect snack, a small bowl of nutrient-packed pasta and vegetable salad. Since she'd skipped the beef stew at supper time, she forced herself to eat all of the salad. The food made her feel much better, but when she lifted the heavy tray from the cabinet, she felt suddenly weak.

Deciding against more food, Lenor went to a cabinet at the other end of the kitchen, and pulled out an almost-full jar of honey. From long-enforced habit in the hospital, she examined the label, read it, read it again.

HONEY OF AN APPLE
Pure Natural Apple Blossom Honey
Uncooked Unfiltered

She looked up at the line of identical honey jars that started at the front of the cabinet and neatly stretched all the way to the back. The Tavera family was one of Sheriff Apple Hardy's best customers.

Lenor looked down at the jar in her hand, then up at the first jar in the long line. Something was different about the one she held. What? She read, then reread. The words were exactly the same on both the tan-and-brown labels. She took the other jar down, held it next to the first, and looked again. There was a tiny straight-line nick in the paper at the upper left corner.

Quickly, Lenor examined the other jars. Only the first had the clean, distinctive scratch. She tried to duplicate it with her fingernail. The paper scuffed, then tore. The fine, almost-invisible marking had been made by something like a pin or a needle or a razor blade—and she was sure it had been done deliberately.

Suddenly light-headed, Lenor caught hold of the countertop and steadied herself. The murder weapon, still in her hand, was now covered with her own fingerprints. But she didn't need the police to tell her whose fingerprints were under hers and her grandparents'. They would be Roy Baldwin's.

How could I have been so obtuse? How could I have offhandedly rejected the idea that some foodstuff was the vehicle for the poison? My whole family could have been poisoned! Why couldn't I put the obvious two-and-two together?

Perhaps because of her muddled thinking over the past few days, perhaps because of her feelings about Roy. She had no idea what he would do next. Roy had the intelligence to unravel the secret of the fury stone. Roy had the background in human anatomy to know exactly how to aspirate blood from the heart. With the *piedra imán* in his possession, he might try almost anything.

Though Lenor knew that normally Michael could physically handle Roy, Michael had no weapon, and the fury stone would tip the balance heavily in Roy's favor. Without her help, Michael might not have a chance. After concealing the honey jar on a shelf behind a stack of clean kitchen towels, she hurried to heft the tray again and get back to the library.

For whatever reason they'd done it, Lenor was glad the library door had been opened. The tray she carried was getting heavier by the second. *We're all so tired,* she thought. *We'd probably better start taking turns getting a few winks of sleep.*

She stopped just short of the door. *I really am tired . . . not thinking straight. Neither Estelle nor Michael would have opened that door.* Lenor's body trembled. The cups tinkled softly against their saucers. It took all the control she could muster to keep from dropping the whole thing as she lowered the tray to the tile walkway. She picked up Watson, then stood, holding him. "Stay with me. I'm going to need your help," she whispered. Quietly sidestepping along the wall, she reached the entry and peeked around the doorframe into the room.

For an instant Lenor was frozen with horror. Juanita Chavez was bent over Magdalena's sleeping body. She held a twenty-five-cc glass syringe with a long shiny needle positioned exactly over Magdalena's heart. Michael and Estelle were on the floor, either unconscious or dead. *Juanita Chavez?* Lenor's mind whirled frantically and came up with only one idea. Watson dropped to the floor. Attack!

A silver-topped cane leaned against the foot of Magdalena's bed. *Miller Baldwin's cane?* Lenor ran into the room, grabbed the staff, and swung it at Juanita's head. The woman gave a short grunt of pain as she reeled backward from the glancing blow that had struck her shoulder. For a second she seemed stunned, about to topple over, then shook her head and rallied. Watson jumped at her from the bed, but Juanita fended him off with a quick chop, and he fell to the floor, dazed.

Juanita walked forward; Lenor moved back, glancing intermittently at her mother. Magdalena was asleep and breathing normally; her nightgown was undisturbed, unmarred by any telltale spot of blood. Relieved, Lenor backed to the table and, without looking dug into the black bag of supplies she'd brought from the hospital. Her hand closed over the plastic syringe she'd filled earlier, and she kept it hidden behind her back as she pulled it out.

Juanita was within striking distance. Lenor swung the cane. Juanita ducked out of the way, then lunged. The cane clattered out of reach.

Ordinarily, a woman Juanita's size would have been no match for Lenor. But Lenor was weak and Juanita had the strength of a demon. She pinned Lenor against the table. Lenor's hand, holding the syringe, was trapped. Juanita's eyes burned with hatred. The horrible odor of vomitus almost gagged Lenor as Juanita spoke.

"What good fortune," she whispered. "I would much rather have the power *you* possess than that of a mere *curandera*."

Lenor's mind leaped from one approach to another. Juanita's

appearance had taken her completely by surprise. All she could think was that Michael had brought Juanita to her grandfather's party. It gave her an idea.

"So I was right about you, wasn't I? You're in love with Michael."

Juanita was confused for a second; then her mouth twisted into an evil smile. "And I'll have him, too," she rasped. "You're willing to give up a little of your heart's blood for that good cause, aren't you, Dr. Tavera? All you doctors are willing to sacrifice to forward science." She brought the needle up and pressed the tip to the center of Lenor's chest. "You'll hardly feel a thing. Rosa didn't. Of course, I put her to sleep first." She made a dry cackling sound. "But you'll want to stay awake, won't you? You wouldn't want to miss a learning experience, would you?"

Juanita did this to Rosa? Impossible! Lenor felt the sharp tip of the needle prick her skin. *Watson, come here!*

"It won't hurt very long, Dr. Tavera. I'll just fill the syringe with air first. "Like this." She pulled the plunger back as far as it would go. "Then I'll just give it a little push. Like this."

When she jammed the plunger in, the needle sank deeper. Lenor could feel it stop against the bone of her sternum. She swallowed hard. "I'm disappointed in you, Juanita. You should have studied anatomy first. You're going to break that needle right off if you try to go through my breastbone to get to my heart." Out of the corner of her eye, Lenor saw Watson slink under the bed. *Come here, Watson!*

Juanita sneered. "I was just getting your attention, lady." Her eyes widened. "Oh, but you're not a lady anymore, are you?"

"What do you mean, Juanita?"

"Michael took you to his bed yesterday, didn't he? He made love to you—" Her eyes narrowed with an evil grin. "He raped you. Yes! He had to, because you're a cold, inhibited bitch. You've teased him and tormented him for years." She shook her head slightly. "It doesn't matter. I have Gilberto now. And I've already forgiven Michael."

Juanita shifted her weight a bit. It was just enough relief—

Lenor could get her right hand free. At the same time, Watson jumped up on her shoulder and swiped sharp claws across Juanita's face. In that fraction of a second, Lenor pushed the needle attached to her own syringe into Juanita's side. She rammed the plunger down with all her strength, and the powerful sedative began to take effect almost immediately. Juanita dropped her syringe, slumped heavily forward. Lenor slid out of the way, grabbing Juanita around the waist to ease her fall, as she collapsed, head first, across the table.

It was as if all the lights in the greenhouse had gone out when Juanita had lost consciousness. For a moment Roy hadn't been able to figure out exactly what had happened, but he'd quickly come to his senses. He'd halfway expected Juanita to fail him, and he was prepared.

Things had been working pretty well up to this point. In spite of Lenor's quick thinking when Magdalena had started hemor-rhaging, his plan would continue to work. There was no way Lenor could know about the tiny shreds of castor bean he'd mixed with Magdalena's chamomile tea. Rafael, who so frequently rode out alone, would be an easy target, his death readily blamed on an errant, anonymous rabbit hunter. Grandpa would be happy to join his wife, one way or another.

Roy took a momentary break from his work and went into the back room of the greenhouse. His father was still unconscious, lying on a makeshift pallet of blankets. The combination of Percodan and Valium Roy had injected would keep Miller out of harm's way for a good long time. "Rest well, Father," he said, carefully tucking a light quilt around the sleeping man. "Very soon, you'll be the happiest man alive."

For a moment all Lenor could do was close her eyes and try to catch her breath, but it didn't take long for her mind to get back to the next emergency at hand. She opened her eyes, hurried to examine the three women, who, unbelievably, were still sleeping peacefully. Then she knelt beside Estelle.

Estelle had received a blow to the back of her head and had a slight swelling but no blood. She was unconscious, but her breathing was steady and her pulse was strong. Lenor checked her ears for bleeding, a sign of skull fracture, and was relieved to find none. Pupils normal. Estelle would come around shortly, probably with a bad headache.

Michael's head was bleeding, but there was no sign of blood coming from his ears. His pulse and breathing were even, pupils okay. Juanita had struck him on the right temple, and the well-placed blow had been enough to instantly knock him unconscious. Lenor knelt beside him and dabbed at the stream of blood with a strip of sterile gauze she'd taken out of the black bag. "Michael? Can you hear me, Michael?" She thought she saw his lips move, but his body remained motionless. "Michael, it's over. We can all relax now. Michael?" *Oh, please let him be all right!*

His eyelids fluttered.

"Michael? It's Lenor. Watson and I are right here with you. You're going to be just fine. Listen to me. It's all over. We're safe." Michael moved his head slightly, and Lenor's heart leaped for joy. "You can hear me, can't you, Michael? Mama's safe. Rosa's safe. Paula's safe." Watson began licking Michael's hand. Michael didn't move.

She stared at the blood that still seeped from his wound. *So much blood has already been spilled this day,* she thought. *Good people don't deserve to suffer like this.* His eyelids fluttered again, and Lenor rejoiced.

"That's right, Mr. Martino, good people don't deserve to suffer. You've suffered your share, haven't you, Michael? But you've come through it just fine."

The paintings he'd done of her over the years flashed through Lenor's mind like beacons. What had he said about the last one? ". . . like someone else had been painting it . . . no control over my brushes." How would Nemesia's well-intentioned magic affect his emotional equilibrium? Could he accept that the magic was real and his feelings, delusion? Would he . . . ? *Keep talking!*

"Michael? Talk to me. You've been lying here quite long

enough. It's time to wake up and help me figure something out. You've got to tell me about Juanita. I need to know about Nemesia's—"

As soon as she said the name Nemesia, Michael shook his head. It was a slight movement, but a definite reaction.

Hooray! "Tell me about Juanita," she said.

Michael didn't move.

"Let's talk about Nemesia," she said.

Again, the shake of the head.

Hooray again! Lenor picked up his hand and began rubbing it between both of hers. "Please wake up, Michael. Talk to me!"

Twenty-nine

"I'LL TALK TO YOU," A VOICE SAID FROM THE OPEN doorway.

Lenor's head jerked around toward the sound. A young man stood there, dressed in a dark suit, with a pale purple flower in the buttonhole of his lapel. It took a moment for his identity to register. Junior Garcia! A slide-action shotgun was propped against the doorframe next to him, and a tortuous smile was spreading rapidly across his flushed face.

Watson stepped up onto Michael's chest, putting himself directly between Junior and Lenor.

"I've been wanting to talk to you ever since you got here. I wanted to thank you for the advice about school. Don't look so confused. I said I'd do it, but I didn't. I've lied to you before. This is just the first time you've known about it."

Smart, but rather lazy, quiet, and sleepy, this cocky youth was *not* the Junior Garcia Lenor knew. His eyes were wide, pupils dilated; his nostrils flared, breathing rapid; his left hand twitched, as if he were trying to snap each finger against his thumb. If his speech patterns weren't so complicated, Lenor would have guessed he was sleepwalking. Observing the boy's agitated, possibly drug-induced state, Lenor decided to keep quiet. She'd seen people in the throes of a psychotic reaction turn violent, their hostility and aggression triggered by just one wrong word or phrase. But even irrational, he'd been right about her confusion. First Juanita, now Junior Garcia. Absolutely nothing was making sense. She didn't dare take her eyes off him. He leaned casually against the doorframe and crossed his arms over his chest.

"You'll remember all the other times I lied when I tell you about them," he went on. "Like the time I told you that you should date Randy instead of Sam. I lied. You should have been dating *me*."

Lenor had no idea what he was talking about. When she'd been dating, Junior Garcia had been just a baby.

"Like the time I told you I didn't care whether you decided to let Robby kiss you. I lied." He unfolded his arms and took a step closer. "I *did* care!"

Lenor glanced to her left. The walking stick was out of reach.

In one smooth movement Junior knelt down on the other side of Michael's body and grabbed Lenor's arm.

Using Michael's chest as a launching pad, Watson leaped at Junior's face. As if he were no more than a pesky fly, Junior batted him away, and Watson thumped against the end of a bed.

"I *did* care. Do you hear me?" Junior whispered harshly. "And you're going to pay for all those lies you made me tell. Especially the one I told you on the day you left for college. Remember that one?"

Lenor shook her head.

"I told you that you were smarter than I am." He scowled and gave her arm a painful jerk. "I lied." Then he smiled again. "But you know that now, don't you?"

His grip tightened unmercifully as he stood and pulled her up with him.

"Now step over your lover and come with me, little sister."

Lenor couldn't help herself. "My lover?"

He grabbed her other arm and forced her to take a step over Michael's body. "You don't fool me," he sneered. "I know all about you and the reclusive Mr. Martino. Did you know that you even call out his name in your sleep?" Lenor frowned, afraid to say any more just yet. "Well, you do." He mimicked her voice. 'Michael!' Sound familiar?"

"You were in my room?" she asked, then watched as the boy's expression completely changed.

"Of course," he said, in the same high voice. "Who else would have brought you such a lovely gift all tied up with a pink ribbon?" He frowned. "Maybe you didn't think of it as a gift. You're right. Another lie." He smiled. "Old Woosey wasn't a gift. He came to pay you back for teasing my son."

Again his face and voice changed. Lenor stared at him.

"But after we're married, there won't be any more teasing, will there?" He started to pull her through the doorway, but changed his mind and pressed her back against the doorjamb. "Would you like to powder your nose before the ceremony? You'll want to look your best."

Lenor nodded. Just the chance she'd needed. *Now, Watson!*

"No. You don't need any powder. You never did." A dreamy expression crossed his face. "We're going to make my father so happy. Steven will die. Magdalena and Rafael will die. Everyone will die." He winked at her. "Then you will inherit the ranch. Then I will inherit the ranch."

Which means I will have to die, too! It was time to risk talking to him. "Junior, you're such a sweet young man. You really deserve a wife who would be happy staying at home, taking care of you."

He shoved her outside, spun her around, then jerked the strip of bloody gauze from her hand. In a fraction of a second he had the wet cloth wrapped and tied securely around her wrists. She heard a scrape of wood against tile, heard Watson give a weak screech of pain when the wood thudded against bone. *Watson!* Then she felt the double barrel of the shotgun press into her back.

"I'll decide who I want to marry," he said gruffly, then continued sweetly, "We're taking a short ride. We can't keep the priest waiting. I even have a beautiful wedding dress for you."

Thirty

MICHAEL COULD HEAR VOICES, BUT HE COULDN'T MAKE his muscles behave. No matter how hard he tried, he couldn't open his eyes to see who was talking. The words, a senseless conversation about a wedding, seemed to be drifting through a fog. Didn't they know that the library was too small for that kind of crowd? He'd have to tell them to change their plans—just as soon as he could get his lips to move.

At last he could curl his fingers and actually feel his fingertips touching his palms. He bent one elbow, the other, one knee, the other. His head hurt. Hands across his chest, he lay still for a moment, then opened his eyes and looked cautiously from side to side. Somebody else was on the floor with him. Who?

Reality struck him all at once. Rolling to his side, he got to his feet in one smooth motion that sent shafts of pain stabbing through his temple. He blinked, trying to clear his vision.

"Estelle!" He looked at the beds. The three women seemed to be sleeping. Estelle began to groan, then move. "Lie still!" He knelt beside her. "Don't move until you know nothing's broken."

"What happened?" Estelle whispered.

"I'm not sure. The last thing I remember is opening the door."

"Look!" Estelle pointed. Juanita lay bent over the table.

Michael looked around the rest of the room. Watson was staggering a bit as he came through the door. "Where's Lenor?"

"I haven't seen her."

Michael hurried to the door and looked out. The coffee tray lay on the tile, untouched. "Something's very wrong." He crossed to the phone, dialed Rudolfo, and asked him to bring Nemesia and come over right away. "Bring Rafael and a gun, too." He hung up, called Apple Hardy, then turned to Estelle. "Will you be all right?"

She rubbed the back of her head. "I'll be okay," she said, smiling weakly. "Pretty good headache, though. You're bleeding. Let me—"

"I'll stay till Rudolfo gets here, then I have to find Lenor," Michael interrupted, then went into the bathroom and splashed cold water on his face until he felt a little more alert. He was toweling off when Rudolfo and Nemesia walked in. "Estelle will explain. Neither of us knows much about what just happened, but Lenor is missing."

"I thought I heard a car drive up," Rudolfo said. "Be careful, Michael."

"I will."

Outside, Michael looked around. There were no unfamiliar cars in the carport. The sky was cloudy, and a few drops of rain were beginning to fall. There was a strange smell in the air. Ozone? He hadn't heard any thunder or seen any lightning, but then he hadn't heard or seen much of anything for some space of time. The odor was familiar. *Think!*

Diesel! The car that Rudolfo had heard must have used diesel fuel. Whose car? His head was hurting so badly that he could hardly keep his mind on one thought long enough to make any sense of it. *Damn it, man. You're wasting precious time.* Diesel. The distinctive clacking sound. He'd heard it just recently. Where? As he walked toward the carport, the odor became stronger. Something clicked. A four-wheel-drive. John Garcia! Of course. He'd be the only one who could get through Apple's guards.

Now what? Had Lenor been right about John Garcia? Had the sheriff of Mora County put Old Woosey in her bed? The mist in his brain was beginning to clear. Before Lenor had left to make coffee, they'd been talking about the Tavera Legacy . . . and motive. Motives. Michael walked further up the driveway and the diesel smell disappeared. He backed up. The odor seemed to be coming from his right now, so he moved in that direction. He'd find her by his sense of smell if his brain wouldn't work. Motives. Envy. Jealousy. Revenge. Greed. Greed stuck in his mind. They'd talked about it. "How could the Tavera property fall into the hands of someone who desperately wanted it?" "All the heirs die intestate, and it's auctioned off by the state." "There's another way." "Marriage."

Had he been dreaming about a wedding taking place in the library, or had he actually heard someone say the word? He'd walked all the way across the front of the house and was on the road that curved behind the bunkhouses. The diesel smell was still strong. Michael began to run. The road also led to the chapel.

Thirty-one

LENOR COULDN'T BELIEVE HER EYES. IF IT WEREN'T FOR the shotgun pressing against her body, she would have enjoyed the lovely scene before her. She'd never seen so many candles burning at once. They were everywhere in the little Tavera chapel, on both ends of every pew, along the floor in the center aisle, lining the two shallow steps that led up to the massive wooden altar table. There were more candles on the altar, on either side of a beautiful arrangement of fresh flowers.

Fresh flowers. *Where did I just see these same kinds of flowers? In Roy Baldwin's greenhouse. How did they get here? Did Roy bring them?*

A groan drew her attention to the front pew on the right. Just seeing the back of the head of the man seated there, she knew instantly who he was. Father Rand.

"Pretty clever, huh? I lied to him, too. He thought he was coming to give poor Paula the last rites. He can do that later tonight." Junior gave Lenor a push toward the front of the church. "I really thought Paula would be gone by now. Guess I'll have to rethink my dosages when your turn comes around. Maybe I'll make yours simple, like I did for Jovita. Simple, relatively painless, and no guesswork for me. A little bit of honey makes the medicine go down," he crooned in a high voice.

Junior grabbed Lenor's arm, then pushed her around to face Father Rand. "Meet my bride, Lenor Tavera," he said to the man, who was bound and gagged. "She'll just be a minute getting ready." He lifted the lid of the large box on the pew next to the Father, untied Lenor's wrists, then stepped back, keeping the shotgun leveled at her heart. "Don't take long getting undressed, my dear. I think the good Father is getting uncomfortable."

Lenor didn't move except to look left, then right. No light except candlelight. No movement except the flickering flames and the shadows. Junior's face brightened with a sweet smile.

"No help in sight," he said in the higher voice. "It's just the three of us. Cozy, don't you think?"

Should I be relieved that Roy Baldwin isn't here?

Junior swung the shotgun to his left and pressed the muzzle against Father Rand's temple. "I said, don't take long getting undressed, Lenor," he growled.

Once again, she was almost sure Roy Baldwin was here with her. At least part of the time. But how could Roy be here? And who was the other presence, the feminine one? Vaguely familiar, but—for now, she would have to obey. She took off her boots, her jeans, her shirt, then reached for the fluff of white material in the box.

Junior grabbed her hand. "Didn't you hear me? I said *undressed*. My mother wouldn't have worn anything under it."

Father Rand closed his eyes, and Lenor breathed a prayer of thanks, but Junior had a different idea. He gave a hard little jab with the gun. "Open your eyes, man," he said in his woman's voice. "You're a 'father.' Fathers and mothers are allowed to look at their children naked. And they're allowed to touch them. And they can make their children do anything they want. In about nine months, I'll show Lenor how it's done. Such fun." Junior looked at Lenor and grinned. "See how smart I am?" he said in the deeper voice. "Not everyone can be witty. The priest is a father. Get it? You have to be very clever to make jokes like that one."

And we're both going to have to be very clever to get out of here. Lenor directed the thought straight at the priest with her most determined look—and he blinked. *Good heavens!* Father Rand blinked again. He would help if he could!

Lenor started talking again. "I've always known you were smart, Junior. How could anyone else have been so clever as you've been tonight?"

With luck she might be able to divert Junior's attention long enough to snatch the shotgun away or hit him over the head with some handy object. *Look around.* As if the gyrations were necessary to the task of undressing, she turned to her right, then to her left, as she reached back to unfasten her bra. The only objects heavy enough to accomplish the job she had in mind were the two brass candlesticks on the altar. Heavy, they were. Handy, they weren't. She pulled off her socks, stepped out of her panties, and reached for the dress.

"So, Junior. When did you find the time to go shopping for this beautiful wedding dress?"

"Didn't have to shop. It was my mother's." He grinned. "Hope it fits."

It wouldn't. Mrs. Garcia was a petite five-foot-four, with a figure to match. Even as thin as Lenor had become, she had no hope of fitting into it. She dropped the dress over her head. Surprisingly, she didn't have to force her arms through the long satin sleeves. Though too small, this dress did not belong to Junior Garcia's mother. "I hope I don't tear it," she said. "It's a little snug. Can you help me with this back zipper, Junior, please?"

Junior took a step toward her, then stopped. "Oh, no, you don't. I'm too smart for that trick." He poked Father Rand in the ribs. "You help her. Go on. Stand up. This'll probably be the thrill of your life, priest."

Lenor turned around. The Father's hands were shaking so badly he could barely get hold of the slide. "Maybe if you'd untie his wrists he could do a better job of it," Lenor suggested.

"There you go again, trying to outthink me. Well, you can't do it. Just give the poor man time. The problem's not his tied hands, it's your bare back that has him shaking out of his pants." Junior threw his head back in raucous laughter. "Get it? Shaking him out of his pants? Get it? Probably his first time." Junior gave out a low, guttural growl of anger. "But it won't be the first time for me. Will it, Lenor? Just like my mother. You do that to me every day. Every day. Every day. Every day. Start *zipping!*"

Lenor helped all she could by holding on to the full skirt just beneath the bottom of the zipper. Mercifully, Father Rand finally got the thing started. Lenor exhaled and tried to make herself as small as possible. She could barely breathe. *Think of something, damn it!*

"Now turn around so the groom can see his bride," Junior said. "Isn't she pretty, sir?" He pushed the priest back down on the pew. "Isn't she just about the prettiest thing you ever did see?"

Father Rand nodded warily. Lenor thought she would probably explode out of the dress if she moved even one muscle or dared to breathe more than a tablespoon of air at a time. Her ribs were painfully compressed, her arms were rigidly encircled, her breasts were spilling out of the low-cut satin bodice. She looked at Junior. His eyes were fastened on the rise of her bosom. *Distraction!*

The hair first. She pulled the combs that held the heavy knot and let her hair fall down her back. Leaning forward, she pretended to smooth the full skirt, pressing her breasts closer together, making them round even higher. She put her hands firmly on her waist and pushed down hard against the line of gathers, while she moved her shoulders forward, then back. She could feel her skin straining against the material as the neckline slipped lower and lower. She sent another silent message to Father Rand. *Watch him! Catch him off guard! Watch for the chance to do something!*

Junior's eyes were great round orbs. She let all the air out of her lungs, leaned slightly forward again, and tugged as hard as she dared without ripping the skirt away from the top. Junior was completely entranced, and Lenor pretended not to notice that her nipples were now fully exposed. She swung her hair to one side and began smoothing it with her hands, curling it around one breast, tempting him to step forward by brushing her fingertips across the rising nipples. If he moved toward her even a few inches, the shotgun would no longer be pointing at the Father's head. *Come on! Come on!*

Junior moved, shifting his weight from one foot to the other. He put his hand over his crotch and groaned softly—but he didn't move forward. "Mother, don't do this," he said softly, never taking his eyes off Lenor.

Mother? Lenor moved her shoulders as if she were uncomfortable, then reached back and unzipped the top of the dress as far down as she could. She let out a sigh, as if relieved, and moved so that both her breasts were completely free. "That's better," she breathed, then ran her hands under and around her heavy curves. "How do I look?" she asked in a sultry voice.

That did the trick. Junior took a long step forward and reached out his twitching left hand to touch her. Father Rand lifted his bound legs and kicked forward, catching Junior at the knees. Junior fell to the floor, and one barrel of the shotgun went off, leaving a gaping hole in the end of the opposite pew.

"Bitch!" Junior cried.

Lenor kicked at his head, but barefoot, it had no effect. She ran to the altar, grabbed one of the brass candlesticks, then turned and tried to bring it down in an arc on the top of his skull.

Junior ducked, pumped another shell into the shotgun's chamber.

Lenor's wrist was caught in a steely grip, and the shotgun's cold metal was pressed roughly against the center of her left breast.

"Now we'll see who you can tempt with these, after I blow them all over the good Father's altar."

Lenor stared past Junior. The door at the back of the chapel was opening. It could only be Michael! Watson scurried in and disappeared under the pews.

The chapel looked as if it were full of twinkling stars and ghosts. Michael felt like he was hallucinating. But the sheriff's four-wheel-drive parked outside had been real. Michael looked around for John Garcia. Something moved up near the altar. He stepped inside.

"Don't come in here!" Lenor shouted.

Junior whirled around. "Get out!"

Watson sprang from the shadows and dug his claws into Junior's leg.

"Yeow!"

Michael, an easy target standing in the doorway, gave Lenor enough time to act. She brought the candlestick down on Junior's head. The shotgun went off as Junior slumped to the floor.

Lenor looked up. "My God! Michael!" His shoulder was bleeding, as he ran up the aisle. "You've been hit!"

"Just a nick," he said, then grabbed her and held on as tightly as he could. There was no use trying to speak; it was impossible. A crazy child had tried to kill both of them. Thank God, he'd failed. All Michael could do was offer silent prayers.

"Michael?" She looked up and saw tears in his eyes. "Michael. We have to help Father Rand." His arms loosened a bit. "We have to untie the Father, Michael."

He turned his head, then looked back at her. "Are you all right?"

Lenor quickly adjusted the skimpy dress to cover herself as best she could. "I'm fine. He didn't hurt me. Go."

While Michael untied the cloth gag and the ropes around Father Rand's wrists and ankles, Lenor checked Junior to see if her attack had done real damage. It hadn't, but he'd be unconscious for a while. She started to fuss over Father Rand's abrasions.

"You don't have to worry about me," he said. "I'm not too much the worse for wear." He stood up and shook his head in bewilderment. "I never would have guessed that Junior Garcia would ever do something like this."

"He didn't," Lenor said.

Michael looked at the boy on the floor, then back at Lenor. "Drugs?" he asked.

"No, not exactly."

"He was acting so strangely," Father Rand said. "I don't think he was in his right mind. On the way out here, he told me he was going to give his father the thing he'd wanted most in all his life."

"What was that?" Michael asked.

The Father looked perplexed. "The Tavera Legacy?"

"Tavera Legacy, my butt! I had a hell of a—" Hurrying up the aisle, Apple Hardy stopped short. "Oh, excuse me, Father. Uh . . . I had a heck of a time trying to find you guys. Just lucky Steven was still staying at Angelina's and looking out the window at Jovita's grave. But hey. I'm too late."

Father Rand stepped forward. "We're glad you're here, Sheriff."

"Doesn't look like I'm needed," Apple said. "What the— that's Junior Garcia. What's he doing here?"

"I'll explain later," Lenor said. "Right now you should go pick up Roy Baldwin."

"Roy Baldwin?"

Lenor nodded. "For the murder of Jovita Tavera . . . and other crimes. He'll probably be in his greenhouse behind the general store. If you hurry, he might still be sitting in a wooden chair about halfway down the first aisle of greenery."

"How do you know—? Never mind. Anything else I should know?"

"Just one thing," Lenor said. "He'll have a smooth black rock with him, about the size of my fist. He won't want to give it up, but I'd appreciate it if you'd bring it back to me."

"Evidence?" Apple asked.

"Sort of," Lenor said.

"What about Junior here? Shall I cuff him?" Apple asked, reaching behind her waist.

"No need. He'll be fine as soon as he comes to," Lenor said.

Apple shrugged, then started down the aisle. "Okay. I'll get on the horn to John Garcia. And, Lenor—" she looked back "—a little advice."

"What's that?" Lenor asked.

"Lose the dress."

Thirty-two

LENOR SNUGGED JUNIOR'S SUIT COAT AROUND HIM, checked him more thoroughly, then fussed over Michael's wound. One, maybe two, pieces of buckshot from Sheriff Garcia's Defender had entered his shoulder, in almost exactly the same spot that Thomas had been hit.

"Will you stop?" Michael complained. "It's just a scratch."

"I'll stop if you'll hold still. I want to get a good look at this."

Michael relented, but only until she started talking about surgery. "Oh, no. That little slug can stay right where it is," he said, backing away.

"Well, that's the rub. It might decide not to stay where it is," Lenor said. She put her hands on her hips and smiled. "Besides, what would Thomas say if he could see how you're acting right now?"

Silence. Michael had watched a brave little boy let Lenor tend to the same kind of wound. He could still hear Thomas's words, "If you get hurt, she would fix you right up." "We'll see," Michael said finally, then, "Shall I carry Junior out to the car?"

"I don't want to move him until he starts coming around," Lenor said. "It shouldn't be long now."

While Lenor hovered over Junior, Father Rand and Michael walked down the two outside aisles and blew out the candles on the ends of the pews. When Junior began to move and make little groaning sounds, the two men hurried toward the front of the church. Lenor held his hand. "Junior? Can you hear me?" she asked.

"I'm dizzy," he whispered, then rolled toward her.

"You might be dizzy for a little while longer, Junior. Not long," Lenor assured him. She started gently rubbing his back.

"I'm thirsty."

"When you can stand up, we'll take you down to the house and get you a drink of water," Lenor said.

Junior looked at her, then closed his eyes tightly shut. When he opened them again, he turned his head and glanced around. "Where am I?" he asked, looking at Father Rand, who was standing at Junior's feet.

"You're in the Tavera chapel," Lenor said.

The boy's brown eyes filled with terror. He rolled over and tried to crawl away from her, but Michael blocked his path.

Lenor moved to Junior's side. His left hand was still twitching, and she took it in both of hers, applying gentle pressure to a spot between his thumb and index finger. "You're safe here, Junior," she said, lightly rubbing the back of his hand. "No one's going to hurt you. I promise you that."

The terror slowly disappeared from his eyes as he looked from Lenor to Michael to Father Rand.

"You're going to be just fine." She helped him to move back, to sit propped up against the end of a pew. "Do you understand what I'm saying, Junior?" she asked. She removed the purple flower from his buttonhole and slipped it into the bodice of the wedding dress.

"I understand . . . How did I get here?"

"You drove your father's patrol vehicle," Lenor said. "Remember that?"

Junior shook his head, and a strand of soft brown hair fell across his forehead. "Huh-uh."

Lenor moved her hand in front of his face, catching the wayward strand with her fingertips, pushing it back into place. "Well, maybe your headache is making you forget," she said, continuing to smooth his hair to one side. "It's okay to forget." She smoothed again. "You don't have to remember."

Michael knelt down on the other side of the boy. He'd seen Lenor use a similar technique on Thomas: touching in rhythm, speaking hypnotically, suggesting. Junior's left hand was no longer twitching. Michael gave Lenor a questioning look over the boy's head. Her answer was a slight shrug and an I-don't-know-yet tilt of her head.

"I'm going to ask you a couple of questions. Is that all right with you?" she asked, still holding his left hand.

"Okay."

"Junior, can you tell me where you've been since you ran away?"

"What?" He looked confused. "I didn't run away."

"Your parents have been worried about you," Lenor said.

Junior frowned. "Roy Baldwin gave me a ride into town this morning. We had a Coke together before I went to the library. Why should Mom and Dad be worried? They knew I'd be gone all day." He made an effort to get up, and Michael took his hands and helped him to stand. "Can I go home now, Dr. Tavera? I've got one hell of a headache, and I have to register for summer school tomorrow."

Lenor put her arm around his waist and gave him a little hug. "Just as soon as we get you that drink of water and call your mother. All right?"

"All right."

"Michael is going to take you and Father Rand down to the house now. Can you walk outside to the car?"

Junior nodded, took a tentative step, and swayed. Michael and Father Rand moved to support him on either side.

"You're doing just fine, Junior," Michael said as they moved toward the door.

"The keys are still in the ignition," Lenor said. "After you call

Mrs. Garcia, will you call the Mora Clinic and have them send the ambulance for Juanita? She'll need gastric lavage. Tell Estelle to start a saline IV."

Michael stopped and looked back at her. "Aren't you coming with us?" he asked.

"I'd better get the rest of these candles put out first. I'll be right behind you."

Michael nodded in agreement. "Don't take too long, or I'll come back for you," he said.

"Don't worry about me. Just let everyone know everything's fine. And Michael?"

"Yes."

"Juanita's going to need your help when she wakes up. Comfort her, will you?"

Michael frowned at Lenor, nodded, then started moving toward the door again. He'd do as she asked, but he wasn't going to relax until she was safely home.

With the candle snuffer on the altar, it shouldn't take longer than five minutes to put out the remaining candles, Lenor thought as she took off the dress and reached for her clothes. It felt so good to pull on her sturdy Levi's and blue work shirt. Somehow the familiar attire made her feel safe.

At last the nightmare was over. Apple would pick up Roy, seize the fury stone, and he would go with her under protest. Apple would be safe from harm, since Roy's focus was limited to getting the Tavera land and Apple was well armed.

He would go to jail, be tried and found guilty. He'd probably be sentenced to serve a very long time in a psychiatric hospital. Lenor could only hope that his illness was organic rather than functional. A lesion could be excised, a temporary psychosis cured, a murder forgiven. Roy's brilliant mind now knew the secret of the *piedra imán,* a cancer of a different sort. But Lenor's repossession of the fury stone would remedy that.

Watson sat next to the wedding dress that lay heaped in the

box. He was curious about the small purple flower that sat on top of it.

"*Azuncena de Méjico,*" Lenor explained. "It should have registered when I first saw Junior's lapel flower and his symptoms—dilated pupils, red skin, aggressive behavior. Roy must have administered small doses of the belladonna to keep Junior disoriented until he was ready to use the boy for other purposes."

"Eee?"

"Oh sure. Rub it in. I should have figured out what was wrong with Juanita sooner. I had some of the clues. The strange behavior and symptoms I saw in the woods, when we were looking for Thomas; the iced tea with the thick layer of undissolved sugar in the bottom of the glass, at Grandpa's party; the rapid deep breathing, when I went to Michael's house; the vomiting tonight. Something should have clicked when I saw the *blighia sapida* tree in Roy's greenhouse, but I missed the poison-induced, prediabetic condition altogether—until Junior's flower reminded me of the possibilities. Juanita's being a sleepwalker helped, but it was even easier for Roy to control Juanita in her weakened condition."

Watson seemed satisfied with the explanation as Lenor picked up the dress and gave it a good shake. Holding it against her body at the waist, she brushed her hand down the skirt to get the wrinkles out before folding it. Someone—*not* the petite Mrs. Garcia—had taken very good care to keep the dress in perfect condition. Something Junior had said still puzzled her. "My mother wouldn't have worn anything under it." That didn't sound anything like the Mrs. Garcia Lenor had known these many years.

Involuntarily Lenor shivered. *What else did he say?* Something about parents seeing their children naked, touching them. *Sexual abuse.* Of Junior? Not likely, especially if she gave any weight to the fact that Junior had referred to himself in the third person. "Turn around so the groom can see his bride." Lenor started shaking in earnest as she hurried to fold the dress and put it back in the box. Junior had been speaking for Roy. Gloria Baldwin had been the abuser!

Suddenly everything made terrifying sense. Roy Baldwin had spent his whole life trying to please two parents: his father, the perfectionist; his mother, the molester. With instruction from the *Tavera Herbarium* and the help of the *piedra imán,* Roy was now able to control not only his own quintessence, but the desecrated spirit of his mother.

Lenor had theorized before, but now she knew—the two voices channeling through Junior Garcia had belonged to Roy and the imprisoned spirit of Gloria. Roy was out for revenge and restitution. If he could please his father in the process, so much the better. And until Apple arrived at the greenhouse, Roy was still free.

A distant rumbling made Lenor spin toward the altar. Thunder. Candle flames danced as if stirred by a gentle breeze. It had just started to sprinkle when she and Junior had left the house. The candles would have to wait until she closed the door against what might turn out to be a downpour.

Picking up the dress box and the shotgun, Lenor hurried to the entrance, deposited gun and box on the last pew, then stepped outside. The moon winked at her through a swirl of thunderheads. She pulled the door against a sudden gust of wind. The effort left her breathless, and several of the candles at the back of the chapel guttered and went out before she could get the open half of the double door shut. *Well,* she thought, *at least part of my job of candle-snuffing is done.*

Lenor turned to see a giant hawk glide toward the altar. *How did he get in here without my seeing him?* she wondered. It wasn't uncommon for the occasional wayward bird, attracted by an evening light, to fly into the chapel, but the candlelight didn't seem bright enough to be tempting. She sighed. No matter. Watson would help get him outside again. "Watson?"

The cat balanced atop the back of a pew at the front of the church. Facing the altar, he watched intently as the hawk dipped its head up and down. With a flapping of wings, the bird lifted into the air and swooped down.

"Keh, keh, keh!"

"Watson!" Lenor called out as the cat fell to the floor with a yelp of pain, the victim of a low-flying attack. Thin fingers turned icy, Lenor reached for the shotgun. Pumping another shell into the chamber, she gave a little prayer of thanks that Apple had insisted on teaching her the basics of firearms. She didn't want to shoot the beautiful gray bird, but— A hand clamped down on her shoulder, and Lenor gasped.

"That shotgun won't do you any good. The goshawk is only a temporary vessel," a man's voice said as the gray hawk landed on the altar again.

Lenor tried to turn around, but the hand dug in cruelly. She had recognized the voice. "Roy!"

"You won't be needing this." Roy grinned at her as he jerked the shotgun out of her hand and threw it down. It clattered across the floor and banged into the back wall.

"I'm so happy to see that you waited for us," a woman's voice said sarcastically from the front of the chapel.

Lenor swallowed hard, trying to push her fear away. *You can talk your way out of this,* she told herself. "I've been expecting you, Gloria," she said in a steady voice. "I'm not going to forgive you for what you've done to Roy."

The female voice gave a wicked little giggle. "I'm not here for forgiveness, little sister."

"I know," Lenor said. "You don't have a choice anymore, do you? You're here because your son wants you here." Roy started pushing Lenor up the aisle. "Did Miller find out that you were abusing your son? Is that why you committed suicide?"

"Keh, keh, keh!" Gloria shrieked with laughter. "That old man barely knew we existed, much less what we were doing behind his back. And I *didn't* commit suicide. It was just a freaky little accident. I was having a good old time, pleasing myself—if you know what I mean—when that electric vibrator fell into my bathwater."

Lenor got the picture and cringed at the thought. Death by electronic masturbation. *Poor Roy,* she thought as he forced her step after step. *How could all of us have missed this kind of pain? If he'd confided in any one of us, we could have helped him.* Now he would need years of professional treatment. Lenor both feared and pitied her old friend. She had to try to distract him.

"I guess Roy will suffer forever because of you, Gloria," Lenor said, speaking of her captor as if he weren't in the room. If she could somehow trick him into changing his focus, he might release his hold.

"Not too much longer," Gloria said.

"I don't like this person you've created," Lenor said. "I'm going to change him."

"Too late," Gloria said with a shriek.

Roy's hand lifted, and Lenor jumped forward into a run. Before she had taken two steps, Roy grabbed her at waist level, knocking the air from her lungs. She grabbed for the end of a pew, doubled over, and gasped for breath.

"Very good, little sister," Roy said. "You ran right into my arms. Have you missed me so much since yesterday?"

Lenor could neither speak nor resist as Roy tightened his hold around her waist and continued to force her toward the altar. She saw Watson scurry under one of the pews. He sent a garbled message that Lenor couldn't understand.

Gloria's divine?

"Your own father furnished the malmsey for your wedding, Lenor," Roy said. He pushed Lenor down to sit on the steps leading to the altar, then held her fast with one hand on her shoulder. He reached into a knapsack he had slung over one shoulder and withdrew a small crystal decanter. "A sweet, strong wine, made by Rafael's own hand from Steven's wild plums," he said, sitting beside her and wrapping one arm snugly about her shoulders. "With a little addition of my own, of course. You'll feel much better after a draft of this." He looked up. "Bring me the chalice, Mother."

Behind her, Lenor heard the sound of metal falling on wood;

then the hawk flew past, the stem of the silver communion goblet clutched tightly in its claws. The goshawk made a low pass in front of them and dropped the chalice on the floor.

"Talk to me, Roy," Lenor said, frantic to divert his attention.

"I'd be glad to, little sister, as long as the talk doesn't interfere with our wedding."

Lenor tried to look into his eyes, but he was turned away from her, reaching for the cup. She put her hand lightly on his thigh.

"Don't do that! You can't touch me yet."

She jerked her hand away, shocked by the violence of his reaction. In this state of agitation, talking to him would not be easy. "I know you're troubled, Roy. I want to help you."

"Help me?" He laughed. "I don't need that now. I have all the help I need."

"Do you think the fury stone is the answer to all your problems?" Lenor asked.

"Problems? I don't have any problems." He finally looked at her. "All my problems are being eliminated, one by one, perhaps even as we speak."

Lenor chilled. She'd been right about her whole family being in jeopardy. *Keep digging.* "What problems are being eliminated?" she asked.

Roy's eyes narrowed in a cunning look. "Remember *The Piano Bird*?" he asked.

A tremor of fear shook Lenor's body. It was a book they'd both read as teenagers, in which hot dogs had been skewered with oleander branches. The results had been fatal for the picnickers. "The honey you gave to my grandpa for his birthday?" she asked.

Roy smiled. "Every drop from the Jericho rose."

"You stole Apple's beehive."

"Of course. This project called for a lot of honey."

Lenor wove her fingers together and squeezed as hard as she could. He'd been planning this for at least two years. *Keep your head!* "Who else, Roy?" she asked.

"You mean you don't know? Now that's a first, Miss Know-It-All little sister." He cocked his head to one side. "You know about Jovita. Paula's and Magdalena's exits will take a little longer, now that you've interfered, but are inevitable, nonetheless. The castor bean never fails." His hold around her shoulders tightened. "I have a different plan for Rafael and Steven."

Stay calm! "Why Paula?" Lenor asked.

"She fancies herself an expert in pharmacology," he said in singsong tone. "Got a little too interested in my greenhouse. Asked too many questions."

"Anyone else, Roy?"

"Well . . . there's George, of course."

"George?" Lenor closed her eyes and swallowed hard. *I should have remembered when I found the honey. I should have called George before I left the kitchen. I've got to get out of here!*

Roy was grinning at her. "Missed that one, didn't you? *Now* who's the smartest of them all, *Dr.* Tavera?"

Panic roared through her body. *Think fast!* She had to work on Roy's own fears. Reason was the only chance she had. "Why didn't you tell anyone what your mother was doing to you, Roy?"

"You think my *mother* is the cause of all this? I forgot about all that—long ago."

"I think Gloria's abuse of a young, innocent boy had to be terrifying," Lenor said, nodding her head. "I think you remember everything. And I think you're still terrified."

"Ha! What could you possibly know about terror? The little girl with the perfect parents, perfect grandparents, perfect home." He turned on her angrily. "You've never been backed into a corner, and stripped of your clothes, and . . ."

His eyes misted with painful memory, and again, Lenor felt sorry for him. Automatically her hand reached out to touch him, comfort him.

"Don't touch me!"

"Keh, keh, keh!"

Lenor jumped with surprise at the combination of ear-splitting sounds. The hawk sailed over their heads, turned, then landed on the back of the front pew.

Roy tightened his grasp, digging his fingers into her arm. "No more questions," he said flatly as he pulled the stopper from the decanter of wine. Awkwardly, with one hand, Roy managed to fill the cup. As he brought it to Lenor's lips, he released her shoulder and grabbed her hair.

It didn't give her much of a chance, but Lenor twisted her body away from him. Not fast enough. Roy's right leg dropped across hers. The hawk took to the air again.

"You wouldn't want to miss your wedding, would you, Lenor?" he said sweetly, drawing her back to a sitting position with a painful jerk on her hair. The goshawk landed beside her, neatly folded its long wings, then hopped up on her thigh and dug sharp talons through the denim and into her flesh.

Watson!

The hawk dodged the fist Lenor rounded at it, then jabbed at her hand and arm with its sharp beak. "Keh! Don't try that again," it screeched, in its high, woman's voice.

Watson bounded at the heavy bird from behind and set his teeth into its neck, but didn't get a good hold amid flapping wings and harsh screaming. Talons sunk deeper into Lenor's thigh before the bird took off, and Watson sent the indecipherable message again.

Gloria's divine!

Roy gave a jerk on her hair. "Look, Lenor. I didn't spill a drop of wine," he said. "Let's toast to a short, steamy marriage, shall we?" With that, he tipped her head back slightly, forced her lips and teeth apart with the edge of the cup, and began slowly pouring the wine into her mouth.

Lenor blocked almost all the sweet liquid. Most of it dribbled out the corners of her mouth. Thankfully, only a few drops went down as she pretended to swallow. A few more went down the wrong way. When Roy released her, she was sputtering and coughing and wiping at her mouth with a bloody sleeve.

"Now that should prepare the flesh for the carnal pleasures," Roy said, smiling.

"Why are you doing this, Roy?" Lenor managed when she caught her breath again.

"You mean the great Tavera brain hasn't figured that out yet, either?" he mocked. "I thought you'd have realized, by now, what you owe me."

"What do you think I owe you, Roy?" Lenor asked, hoping to distract him long enough to get some kind of advantage.

"Ah. Let me count," he said expansively. "You owe me an apology for choosing Apple as your best friend instead of me." He snuggled closer to her. "You owe me an explanation of why you never chose me as your boyfriend." Taking a breath, he said, "And that's just for starters."

Lenor gave him a stern look up and down. "This isn't the man I know. Roy Baldwin would never do any of this."

"You're right—for once tonight. Without the fury stone, I wouldn't have the balls to do anything about the debts you owe." He slipped his fingers down the V neckline of her shirt and grinned. "And you owe me another look. Not through Junior's eyes this time. An in-person peek under these masculine clothes you wear." With a swift downward motion, he ripped all the buttons loose.

Lenor grabbed at his hands when he started pulling her sleeves down her arms, but she moved too slowly. *From a few drops of wine?* Either the membranes of her mouth had absorbed enough alcohol to affect her, or Roy had spiked it with a very potent drug—possibly both. She couldn't seem to make her muscles work.

Roy tossed her shirt toward the knapsack. "No need to struggle, my dear. I'll get what you owe me. The Tavera Legacy will be mine soon enough. But first . . ."

His beautiful model's face twisted into a wicked grin as he pushed her onto her back on the shallow steps. Confused, gazing up into his glittering sable eyes, Lenor wondered why she'd never chosen such a handsome man as a beau. She shook her head, trying to clear her foggy thinking, as Roy pulled off her boots and Levi's and tossed them on top of her shirt. *Perhaps I should* reconsider, she thought through a mist of bewilderment while he removed her underwear. We've always been the best of friends. We've shared everything from clothes to ideas to secrets. And he's quite lovely to look at.

Roy was standing over her now, straddling her body. Fine brown hair covered his chest and, from the lush, dark patch at his groin, scrolled down his legs in graceful whorls. Strong and slender and tall, Roy might have been pictured on one of those calendars featuring beautiful male nudes. But Lenor hadn't seen any nude men, pictured or in person, as endowed as Roy was.

At the spring pool, where they'd gone swimming as children, Lenor had seen Roy in bathing trunks, but she'd never seen him completely naked. How did he ever hide all that masculine equipment in a scanty bathing suit? she wondered inanely.

"I knew you'd be impressed," he said, touching himself in a long, downward stroke. He brought his other hand forward, opened it to reveal a smooth black rock, then held it in front of his thigh. "A dynamite combination, these two," he said, smiling as he cradled his testicles in his palm and lifted.

The already-ample flesh in his hand began to change, to enlarge, pulsing with an elemental rhythm. "Amazing, isn't it?" he said, wrapping his fingers around himself. He frowned. "Good enough for any woman—except you. In your opinion, little Roy was never good enough for the brilliant Lenor Tavera." He stroked himself thoughtfully. "George and Michael can't measure up, now can they? Look at me!" he shouted, when Lenor diverted her eyes. "I'm not putting on this show for anyone else."

Half horrified, half fascinated, Lenor watched as he ministered to himself. Seeing a man masturbate was a new experience. Skillful fingers plied the swollen flesh, urging the muscles to rigid attention, coaxing the egg-shaped glands that swung hypnotically between his legs to issue the balm of lubrication. A droplet blossomed on the tip of the glans and glistened in the candlelight.

"Irresistible, isn't it?" he gloated, then moved his feet closer together, until they pressed sharply against Lenor's thighs. "But you haven't seen anything yet. I'm saving the best for last." He gripped himself tightly. "You may touch me now," he said.

When she hesitated, Roy gave a swift kick to her thigh.

"Touch me," he commanded.

Through an almost paralyzing fear, Lenor tentatively reached out and touched him, then relaxed. *What did I expect?* she wondered. *It's only skin and muscle. A naked man is nothing to fear. Just skin and muscle and—*

Roy grasped her hand and held it still. His erection pulsed beneath her fingers as he moved them up the length and guided them over the fluid at the tip. His soft moans filled the chapel as he forced her fingers to glide in little circles, smearing, smoothing, finally stopping over the distended opening.

A deep breath composed him somewhat. "You can consider this little interlude as our marriage ceremony . . . complete with refreshments," he said, smiling down at her. "If you're a good girl, I'll let you taste."

"Keh, keh, keh!"

Roy's smile widened. "Be patient, Mother," he said. "And consider yourself lucky that I'm letting you watch." He giggled. "Too bad you don't have your little vibrator here. You could show me again how a solitary doctor's wife makes it through long lonely nights." He gave a short laugh. "But that device went up in smoke, didn't it, Mother?"

From somewhere behind Lenor, the great bird launched itself into the air, then landed beside her. Its eyes seemed wide with interest as it looked at Roy. "Keh?"

"No, Mother. You can't have me. I'm not a boy anymore. You do what I say now."

The bird hopped closer to him, a bit of saliva dripping from its beak. "Keh, keh!"

"Yes, Mother. I have a ring." Still holding Lenor's fingers in place, Roy reached down into the knapsack beside his right foot and pulled out a small white envelope.

Something registered in Lenor's fuzzied brain. *What?* She closed her eyes and tried to think. Watson was trying to tell her something. *What?* She could hear him purring. *Purring?* He was contented, while she was in bondage.

Freedom! Lenor opened her eyes and looked up. The hand that had clutched the fury stone now held a white envelope. Roy had left the *piedra imán* in the knapsack. Lenor sat up a little straighter, but the effort sent stabs of dizzying pain through her head. She tried, unsuccessfully, to focus on the satchel, then swayed back against the steps.

"Keh, keh, keh!"

"I agree, Mother dear. The bride is getting impatient. We must proceed with the ceremony." He held up a gold ring. "As much as you want to wear my wedding band, there's only one way to get it." He put it over the end of his little finger, then slid his hand down her arm and pulled her up to a sitting position. "Kiss me," he said.

Once more she hesitated to follow his orders, and once more she suffered. The hawk jabbed at her naked side with its sharp beak, again drawing blood. Her jaw tightened to stay a scream. "Let me go, Roy," she said through clenched teeth.

"Before our marriage ceremony is completed? Don't be silly!" He tightened his hold on her arm. "Kiss me."

"Will you let me go if I do?" she asked.

"Of course!"

Hesitantly Lenor leaned forward and lightly touched her lips to his penis, then quickly withdrew.

"Again!" he commanded.

"But you said—"

He kicked at her. "Again!"

Lenor shook with fear as her lips lightly touched him again. She leaned away from him, further this time.

He jerked her forward. "You owe me more than that, Lenor," he said sweetly. "Just pretend I'm George Murphy." He thought a moment. "No! Not George. You should pretend I'm Michael!" With that, he leaned down so his face was just inches from hers.

In a shimmer of light, the fine-boned model's face transformed. Great black eyes stared down at her hungrily. Beneath wide cheekbones, a dark shadow of heavy beard outlined a chiseled jaw. Lenor's heart beat wildly as she remembered dismissing the fury stone's power to transform. She shook her head. "You don't want me this way, Roy." She looked steadily into the black eyes. "You want me to love you for yourself, don't you?"

As quickly as it had appeared, Michael's face vanished. In its place, Ray grinned down at her. "I said, I want *more!*"

In her drugged state, and weak near the point of collapse, Lenor knew she wouldn't be able to do what he wanted. She tried to kick her legs free, but the viselike grip he had on her thighs made it impossible. Struggling to pull her arms loose, she only managed to give him the opportunity to get a better hold and wear her down further. "I won't give you what you want, Roy!" she said through panting breaths. Instead of getting angry, Roy smiled.

"I suspected it might come to this." He looked at the hawk. "She's not hungry like you always were, Mother. Too bad you can't show her how it's done." The bird's eyes widened as Roy moved his hand down Lenor's arm to capture her fingers. "It's not so tough to do," he said, placing her fingers just so, then gingerly pinching his swollen glans. Another droplet formed. "See. Refreshments. Just like I promised." He jerked her forward. "Now open your mouth!"

"No!" Lenor screamed, shaking her head from side to side, struggling to pull back.

Suddenly Roy let out a roaring groan and let her go. Lenor jerked her head back and stared in horror. She didn't know if she was hallucinating or if the shaft of flesh was actually growing to gigantic proportions. Roy released her and clutched at himself with both hands, trying to wrap his fingers around the expanding mass.

"No!" Roy screamed.

Fascinated, the goshawk hopped forward, head cocked to one side. A long string of mucus dripped from its beak. In the blink of an eye, the bird was airborne; it swooped down, pecking at the quivering, serpentlike appendage.

Roy screeched in pain and batted at the bird. The hawk fell to the floor. Roy's erection collapsed, the tip covered with blood.

Lenor heard two sounds almost simultaneously: the clatter of the gold ring hitting the wooden steps near her right knee, and . . . *Gloria's mine!* Watson launched himself into the air and landed squarely on the hawk's back.

Despite his agony, Roy stretched to retrieve the ring, twisting away from Lenor. She rolled to her left, grabbed the knapsack and her clothes, and uncoiled to her feet. She ran down the aisle toward the door, glancing back over her shoulder, gaining speed, her energy increasing with every step. Roy bellowed, chasing her, pain contorting his face with every step. Lenor hit the wooden door on the run—and bounced back. Locked!

The never-used, rusty latch, jammed into place by a strong hand, wouldn't budge. Frantically Lenor pulled at the knob, but the corroded metal refused to slide back. Though the fury stone was rapidly restoring her strength, it wasn't happening fast enough. Her efforts ineffective, she turned to see Roy halfway down the aisle. For a moment his image filled her field of vision, but a glint of candlelight on stainless steel caught her attention. John Garcia's shotgun!

She shouldered the backpack and whirled to her left, grabbing the Defender by the barrel and swinging the stock into position as she turned. She couldn't remember if it was loaded. One pump ejected a live shell, clicked another into its place, and left two in the tubular magazine. Her right index finger closed gently around the trigger—then released it. *I can't!*

Roy staggered and held on to the side of a pew for support. "You're not getting away from me this time, Lenor," he said, catching his breath.

"I don't want to get away from you, Roy. I want to help you."

"Now isn't that sweet?" he mocked.

"You need treatment, Roy. *Please* let me help," Lenor pleaded.

Roy sneered. "Why would I need *your* help? Without you around, I can continue my studies in peace. And I'll finally be able to give my father everything he wants—and deserves."

"Your father just wants you to be well and whole again, Roy. He doesn't want a criminal for a son."

"He wants what you stole from him, from me, from all of us," Roy shouted. "And I want *you!*"

His brief stop and their conversation gave Lenor time to awkwardly shrug into her shirt, shifting her burdens as she did. With that one piece of clothing on, and the fury stone safely beside her, she felt more secure and determined to get out of this alive—at any cost. But as Roy approached, her determination wavered again. He looked like the little boy she'd played with, the handsome teenager she'd cherished as a brother, the friend in whom she'd always confided. The deadly scattergun that could shred her friend into tiny pieces weighed heavily in her hands—and in her heart.

"You don't want to hurt me," he said, as if he'd read her mind. "You've always loved me."

It was true. As a friend, as a little sister, and as a doctor, Lenor could never deliberately hurt him. She bowed her head and nodded. No harm would come to Roy Baldwin by her hand.

"I knew you didn't have the guts to shoot me!" he shouted, lurching toward her.

Lenor spun around to the door and jabbed at the bolt lock with the butt of the shotgun. Once. Twice. A third time. Roy was almost upon her when the rusty bolt finally gave way. Heaving her weight against the door until it burst open against a slanting rain, Lenor ran straight out, keeping to the path by following the white graveyard fence to her right. She was a dozen feet away from the chapel when Roy caught her by the wrist.

"There's nothing you can do, Lenor. I've made up my mind what I want."

The only illumination was from a distant spotlight at Angelina's house. In the wind-whipped darkness, Lenor could barely see Roy's face, but she could feel the intense heat of his shadowed body close to hers. Then he was backing her toward the picket fence that surrounded the graveyard.

"You don't want me, Roy. You want the ranch," she said. The pointed fence stakes jabbed into her back. She gritted her teeth against the pain and gave thanks for the storm. The cold rain was rapidly clearing her drugged mind.

"The Tavera property will be frosting on the cake," he growled.

The shotgun she still held would have to be her final bluff, but first she had to try another. "I'll give you the ranch, Roy. You don't have to do another thing. We'll sign the papers first thing in the morning. Just let me go."

"Just let you go?" He brought his face close to hers. "Over *your* dead body!" A burst of laughter, then, "You're *mine* until you *die,* Lenor!"

Lenor stiffened her body against the assault of his. "I'm not going to die, Roy," she said firmly, gripping the gun more tightly.

"But that's part of my plan," he said calmly, as if there were no other way to resolve the problem.

"You'll just have to change your plan." She stood up straighter. "I refuse to be part of this one."

With a painful twist Roy bent her elbow and brought her arm across her chest. His hand tightened on her wrist, then he pushed hard against her. Lenor steeled herself for another jab against the fence, but suddenly realized he'd been holding her against the rickety gate. The old latch gave way, and Lenor tumbled, falling down, sprawling backward onto the muddy mound that was her grandmother's fresh grave. The shotgun barrel clanked loudly against the new gravestone.

Her sudden fall had surprised them both, but Roy recovered quickly, and stepped between her legs. With one foot on her stomach, he said, "I will not change my plan! You're just going to have to live with it!" His foot pressed cruelly into her abdomen as he leaned forward. "Or *die* with it," he said on a short laugh. He grabbed at the shotgun.

Lenor tried to swing it out of his way, but he moved faster than she did. He caught the end of the barrel and jerked it toward his body. Lenor leaned forward and screamed, *"No!"* as she tried desperately to free her finger from the trigger.

The blast shattered through the slashing rain and echoed like thunder, again and again, through the nearby hills and mountains. Lenor closed her eyes, her mind praying that when she opened them, Roy would still be standing in front of her.

He wasn't.

Hot tears mingled with cold rain. Lenor bowed her head and cried.

Thirty-three

5 A.M. ◆ A Sunday Morning in July, One Week Later

"YOU REALIZE YOU'VE JUST TOLD ME THE MOST BIZarre story I've ever heard, don't you?"

"I know it's hard for you to believe, George," Lenor said.

"I didn't mean to be—"

"You don't have to explain your difficulties with the paranormal, George, and I don't blame you a bit. You're not the first man to run like hell."

"Lenor, I'm sorry . . . I just can't imagine how—"

"We're still friends. That's what counts," Lenor interrupted. "You don't have to understand anything but that."

"Well, I can certainly understand why you couldn't make it

back on time," George said. "This has been a monstrous week for you, hasn't it?"

Michael had led her away from the grisly scene and comforted her. Apple had kept her away from the site. Steven had assured her that if Roy, sane, had ever remembered what he'd done, he would have wanted to die. But his death still lay heavy on her heart. Lenor's eyes filled with tears, and she shifted the phone to her other ear.

"I guess the police questioning was the worst," she said finally. "I couldn't have gotten through it without the help of your lab work. They were skeptical until I got your package and could confirm everything: the castor bean contaminating the tea; the cardiac glycosides, nerioside, and oldendrin in the honey; the corydalis; the baneberry in Lucielle's cookies, all of it. I'm so glad they're through with me now and everything's straightened out. Thank you, George."

"Like you said, we're friends. I really mean that, Lenor."

She knew he really did mean it. For a week, she'd been a pest, calling to check on her patients, asking for information from patient files that took time and energy to find, consulting with him about treatments and medications. George had been tolerant and gracious through it all.

"Your mother and Rosa are okay?" George asked.

"Better than okay. Mama's giving orders again. That means things are mainly back to normal."

"Here, too," George said. "I'm convinced that Sable didn't get into our computers. She doesn't deny or confirm that she could, but she assures me she would never do it. Wouldn't want to get her Dr. T in any kind of trouble, she says. By the way, she sends her thanks for the package."

"I'm glad she got it," Lenor said. This *bulto* of San Miguel was carved particularly with Sable in mind, and this showed in his dress, his posture, and his gentle eyes.

"Don't know if you heard it from someone else yet," George said. "You were right about Mrs. Hess. She saw an otologist, and she does have Ménière's syndrome. The tinnitus probably caused the headaches. It's hard to understand how anyone can endure constant ringing in the ears. And she has the dizziness and partial deafness to go with it. She's going to have surgery."

"Is Alicia back at Foley?" Lenor asked.

"No. But if she ever gets sick again, she will be. Mrs. Hess came in to see you, say thanks, and apologize. I talked to her. She wrote a letter to Carl Bowder and sang your praises pretty high. Bowder's calmed down considerably."

"Glad I could help her," Lenor said. "Rafael sends greetings to you. And Grandpa sends a warning."

"What warning?" George asked.

"Give up chicken-fried steak."

George laughed. "Tell Steven I'll consider that an order, and thank *you* for the warning about Roy's honey." He was silent for a moment. "Ah . . . guess that's about it from here."

"Have you heard anything from Truelex about my grant?"

He'd hoped she wouldn't ask. He hated to give her bad news over the phone, and was sorry she'd asked him to read her mail. "I don't know whether to call this good news or bad news," he began.

"Did you know that the Chinese kanji for 'disaster' is the same as the pictograph for 'opportunity,' George?" Lenor asked.

George couldn't help his grin. He would miss her optimistic complement to his own pessimistic side. "Truelex wants to talk to you about an opportunity," he said. "They have an offer to make."

"What offer?" Lenor asked.

"Can't tell from the letter, but they imply that if you help them out in one area, they'll reconsider the grant money."

"Interesting. I wonder what they want," Lenor said.

"Want me to try to find out?" George asked.

"No. You've done so much already. This can wait till I get back."

"Speaking of doing so much, thanks for having Apple call me. She explained a lot of the things you didn't have time to tell me."

Lenor smiled. The attraction between Apple and George

would work without benefit of a magic spell. "You're welcome, George."

"Well . . . say hi to everyone for me, will you?" George said.

"I will. And thanks again for the help, George. See you in a couple of days."

5:15 A.M.

Under a white chef's apron, Magdalena wore her best black gabardine slacks, a finely tailored, western-style shirt, and her spring-gray boots. She was mixing the dry ingredients for pancakes. Lucielle stood over a sizzling grill that was covered with strips of bacon, cursing the splatters of fiery fat that attacked her. In her favorite red jumpsuit, Nemesia scrubbed at the scarred wood of the bunkhouse dining table with a soapy cloth. Breakfast preparation for the campers was well under way.

Just like the old days, Lenor thought, as she stacked plates and saucers to carry to the table. With two exceptions, of course. For the first time, Watson sat in a window, watching politely, instead of whining for handouts. And, for the first time ever, Michael Martino was in a Tavera bunkhouse.

Last night, when Michael had called to volunteer, Lenor had asked him why, and after a couple of evasions he'd confessed. He wanted to spend some time with her on her last day in New Mexico—and he had a few questions to ask. Lenor hadn't seen him all week, though he'd been helping Steven with repairs to the chapel, and she'd had trouble sleeping just thinking about their meeting today.

Lucielle had put Michael right to work. Magdalena was delighted to have someone else to order around. But Nemesia still looked tense and uncomfortable. Lenor knew that there was no easy way for Nemesia to ease her conscience.

"Now that's teamwork," Michael said, his hands full of silverware. "Have you ever seen a better crew than those three in your life?"

"I'd hire them," Lenor said, smiling as she centered plates between Michael's table settings.

Lucielle slid another platter of bacon onto the warming shelf above the grill, then turned around and leaned over the dividing countertop between the kitchen and dining area. "You're damned right you'd hire us!" she said. "We're the best."

Nemesia stopped wiping the table and looked up at Michael, who was waiting to place the last of his silverware. "Sometimes being the best is the worst, isn't it?" she said softly.

"Nemesia, don't blame yourself. Please," Michael said.

"I *have* to take the blame," Nemesia said. "I should have left Ramon and Celsa alone, and I'm sorry you had to be in the middle."

"I can understand why you did what you did," Michael said, putting down his last three pieces of silver. "My mother tried to destroy your life."

"You're being very kind, Michael. If there's any way I can make it up to you . . ."

"You can answer a question." When Nemesia nodded, he went on. "I've never thought too much about magic. If you don't mind telling me . . . just what brand of witchcraft do you practice, Nemesia?"

Nemesia shrugged. "Little of this, little of that. Mexican, Navajo, Nambe, Apache, Wicca. A combination sometimes. Whatever works."

Lenor smiled at Michael. "So you're not going crazy."

You are making me feel a little crazy right now! In well-worn faded jeans and a man's white dress shirt, with her hair in one long heavy braid down her back, she was, without trying, looking more beautiful than any woman he'd ever seen. Michael cocked his head to one side and looked questioningly at his aunt.

Nemesia held up both hands, smiling and shaking her head. "I'm off the case, now, Michael," she said, answering his unspoken question. "You're on your own from here on out. Magdalena's orders."

Lenor couldn't believe her ears. "Mama? Is that true?"

Magdalena looked from Lenor to Michael, then back to Lenor. For the sake of her daughter's peace of mind, she'd decided to back off. And, happily, there was still a good chance Nemesia's work would have a satisfactory result without further interference. "It's true," she said.

"I've never known you to give up so quickly or so easily before, Mama," Lenor said.

"I just finally realized it wasn't fair to put you on the spot like that. You'll have no more trouble from me."

"Oh, I doubt that!" Lucielle said, setting a tray full of mugs next to the coffeepot on the dividing counter. "She'll think of something."

"I don't know what you mean by that, Lucielle," Magdalena said. But there was a devilish grin on her face as she came to the kitchen side of the counter and sat down on a stool next to Lucielle.

Michael, Lenor, and Nemesia sat down on the other side of the counter. Lucielle poured coffee. "Speaking of trouble, I'm glad to know Watson's black rock is back where it belongs," she said.

"Me, too. I've gained ten pounds in a week," Lenor said.

"So the fury stone really *does* work," Nemesia said thoughtfully.

Magdalena gave Nemesia a warning frown.

"Rock or no rock, old Doc B's a lucky bastard," Lucielle said. "Imagine, trying to learn how to be a *curandero*. He's made some pretty bad mistakes and decisions over the years. Like giving Michael a transfusion with Nemesia's blood, knowing that it would either make Michael furious or scare the willies out of him. And all because Miller was still mad at Celsa for snubbing him. Then he turns around and tells Estelle that Michael has hepatitis. What was that all about?"

"I can answer that," Lenor said. "I talked to Miller this week.

He said he couldn't take the chance. Knowing that Roy had delivered some food to Michael's house, he didn't want to risk the possibility that Michael had something circulating in his blood that could harm Magdalena."

"Makes sense. Probably a good decision. 'Course, the *worst* decision Miller made was not coming forward as soon as he knew what Roy had done," Lucielle said.

"That's almost forgivable, when you think about it," Lenor said. "In his heart, he just wanted to protect his only child."

"As far as I'm concerned, he's an accessory after the fact." Lucielle held up her hand against objections. "I know, I know. He didn't commit any crime. But he'd better straighten out his mixed-up mind and tend to business as usual."

"I'm sure he will, when he gets back." Miller had found a young resident in Albuquerque who was willing to take over the clinic while Miller took a leave of absence.

"A vacation would probably do us all some good," Michael said, looking hopefully at Lenor.

"Not till September for me," Lenor said. *And depending on Truelex, maybe not even then.*

"I don't need a vacation," Magdalena said. "In fact, I can't wait for the fall work to start. Gathering calves, separating bulls, breaking horses. It'll be exciting this year."

"Now that's our old Maggie talking," Lucielle said with a smile. "We're glad to see you back on track, kiddo."

"Speaking of being on track . . . I'm still curious about one thing. How did I know to make a *bulto* of *San Miguel*?" Michael asked. "Was I receiving something else I wasn't aware of?"

Nemesia looked a little embarrassed, but encouraged at the same time. "I'll explain," she said. "Michael, did you ever pick up the telephone and hear someone else's conversation?" she asked.

"Yes. Crossed wires?"

Nemesia smiled. "Whether people believe it or not, there are spirits hovering everywhere around us, all the time, just waiting for us to listen. Most people don't believe, even if they give the concept lip service. Like George Murphy. You met Dr. Murphy at Steven's party," she added.

Michael nodded, glanced at Lenor. "How could I forget," he said.

"Well, he's one of those who'll never truly accept the possibility. But it happens. And you just happened to be 'on the line' when Leonora Tavera was talking to Sable Faraday about giving a message to Lenor."

"If my thinking hadn't been so cluttered with the George Murphy problem, I probably would have figured out what Leonora was trying to tell me," Lenor said ruefully.

"George Murphy problem?" Michael asked.

Nemesia frowned. "He walked in on Lenor when she was in trance, talking to Leonora," she said to Michael, then looked at Lenor. "You should never have given him a key."

"I know that now," Lenor said.

"Anyway, Michael," Nemesia went on, "I guess you could think of your interception of Leonora's message as 'crossed wires.' "

"Is that all there is to it?" Michael asked.

"That's about all there is to it," Nemesia said. "Of course you and I had a direct connection when I was trying to get you and Lenor together for a good long talk."

Now it was Michael's turn to look embarrassed. He glanced at Lenor. "Mission accomplished," he said softly.

"I really didn't mean to cause such a ruckus," Nemesia said, looking at Magdalena.

"Just tell me you had nothing to do with George Murphy's little tirade about Watson's 'rock' on the way back to New York," Lenor said.

"You give me too much credit," Nemesia said with a smile.

Lenor lifted a skeptical eyebrow. "Maybe, but—"

"You can't blame me for everything," Nemesia protested, but she was still smiling.

"Well, sure we can," Lucielle said. "Except for maybe one thing."

All four of them looked at Lucielle.

"Don't look at me like that. I was just trying to help," Lucielle said defensively.

"What did you *do*, Lucielle?" Lenor asked.

"It was just a little something I cooked up," Lucielle said.

"Cooked up?" Lenor asked.

"Well . . . you can't work around this place without learning a few things. Pinch of this, pinch of that, a few rose petals . . ."

"Lucielle! You didn't!" Magdalena said.

"Didn't what?" Michael asked.

Lucielle looked at her watch. "Time to get back to work, folks." She left the counter and hurried to the stove. "Pancake batter's waiting to be mixed together, Maggie. Now what did I do with my spatula?"

Nemesia checked the clock on the wall. "We've got about ten minutes until the hungry horde descends."

"I can't argue with that," Magdalena said, then stood up. "Okay, all you lazy bums. Coffee break's over. Hit the kitchen!"

Lenor smiled at Michael. "Now *that's* the *real* Magdalena," she said.

The Land of Enchantment was at its enchanting best as Michael and Lenor rode toward Michael's house after breakfast. Bright sunlight mirrored their happy mood in a sky of brilliant, cloudless blue. The fragrance of ponderosa pine drifted down from the towering Sangre de Cristo Mountains to the west, where the shiny leaves of the quaking aspen splintered the sun's rays into a million shafts of dancing light. Golden yellow false-dandelion blossoms raised their daisylike heads to the warmth of the morning, and white yarrow clusters nodded as the two riders passed by.

Despite the disasters, we can all count ourselves pretty lucky, Lenor thought as the two horses plodded along at an easy walk. Both in New Mexico and New York, things had worked out for everyone. George had even gotten the newspaper to agree to print a retraction of the exorcism story.

"I think that was about the best breakfast I ever had," Michael said as he reined Penny Wise around a tall pine.

"You'd better not let Rosa hear you say that," Lenor warned.

"It wasn't just the food," Michael said. "It was the company." He took a long breath and let it out. "Who would have ever dreamed any of this?"

"Nemesia?" Lenor asked with a laugh.

"Pretty amazing aunt, isn't she?" He smiled.

"Pretty amazing woman."

Michael shook his head in disbelief. "Imagine, Lucielle brewing up a love potion, spiking my iced tea with it at Steven's party. My own aunt, casting spells. It sounds like fiction, doesn't it?" He sighed. "I'm so glad it's over . . . but I'm *so* glad it happened."

"I think Nemesia and Lucielle may have learned a lesson," Lenor said.

"I hope so. I don't think I could handle another two years like the last. The dreams, the unexplainable anxiety, Eloy's temper, and the thing about Juanita. How could she . . . ?"

"You're just about the most handsome man in the world," Lenor said.

"Just about?" Michael asked, grinning.

"Well, you're *not* the most modest, but, okay, you *are* the most handsome . . . and Watson likes you."

"That cat again? I don't know whether to be flattered or insulted."

"You must be a Sherlock Holmes fan," Lenor said. "Dr. Watson can spot one a mile away."

"Can he spot a Lenor Tavera fan?" Michael asked.

"He's been known to," Lenor said.

"Did Nemesia have anything to do with Watson's talents?" Michael asked.

"I suspect she did. She's the one who suggested Grandpa give him to me. Of course you'd have to believe in magic to put any stock in guardian angels."

"I believe now," Michael said, then reined closer. "Who'd have thought that we would have such similar backgrounds?"

"What do you mean?" Lenor asked.

"What with your great-great-grandfather, Dorio, being an *ambulario,* and my aunt Nemesia spending some time in the same black craft, I guess we both have a drop or two of the Devil's blood," Michael said.

"I guess you could look at it that way." Lenor sighed. "Mama told me about a dream she had. She dreamed that a man would come to her and help her through her troubles."

"But how did she know that *I* was the man in her dream?"

"She didn't, but the dream told her, 'He will come to you when you need him most.' When she opened her eyes for the first time in the Mora clinic, there you were. She figures she won't have to do or say another thing now."

"She thinks that you and I? That I'll—?"

"Persuade me to come home," Lenor said.

"Will I?" Michael asked.

"You'll be the first to know, Michael. Right after my mother and Nemesia."

"All this is still hard for a new convert to understand," he said.

Lenor nodded. "I agree. Nobody knows much about *how* it happens, but the mind can do some powerful things. Nemesia's talents are truly rare. Being proficient at practicing the *curanderismo* on both the mental and spiritual levels is a phenomenon that occurs once in a blue moon."

"And speaking of a blue moon, I guess I should thank my aunt for that last dream I had about you," Michael said, a broad smile on his face.

Lenor couldn't help the blush that brightened her cheeks. "I really couldn't say."

"Well, I'll say this. You were wonderful."

Lenor grinned. "Do you mean that even after I had to dig that buckshot out of your shoulder, you still have a kind word to say about me?"

"It wasn't the digging that bothered me. It was the audience. I had to act a lot braver than I really felt to come up to Watson's standards."

She looked at him with round, innocent eyes. "I couldn't deny his request to be with you, now could I? And he did see to it that Thomas brought you some of Lucielle's cookies and a glass of milk to ease the trauma of being—shall we say—exposed."

"Speaking of exposed, want me to tell you about my dream?"

"I'll show you something you've never dreamed of," Lenor said, changing the subject.

Michael's eyes brightened. "What's that?"

Lenor gave Tossa a light jab with her heels, and Tossa took off. "Winning a race to the spring pool," Lenor yelled back over her shoulder as she and Tossa sped away down the side of the hill.

"Hey! No fair!" Penny Wise got the idea before Michael did, and he had to grab the saddle horn to keep from toppling over when his horse bolted forward. Michael protested loudly, "Foul play!"

Tossa was at her delightful best, flying over the ground with sure steps, dodging through the trees with the agility and grace of a jay looking for nuts in a piñon pine. They beat Michael and Penny Wise to the creek by several yards. Tossa looked around to watch Penny Wise arrive, then threw her head back and snorted as if to say, "Gotcha!"

"See, I told you," Lenor gloated as she got off her horse. "Now admit it, this is something you'd *never* dream about."

Michael climbed out of the saddle as if he'd just been on a two-week roundup. "Must be my injury," he groaned, holding his hand over his right shoulder and grimacing with pain.

"Oh, Michael. I wasn't thinking." Lenor hurried to him. "I'm so sorry." She pulled his hand away from his shoulder. "Let me have a look." Pulling at the top snaps of his shirt, she tugged the material aside and peered beneath it. Nothing seemed amiss. "Are you sure—?" She looked up at him. He was grinning. "Are you sure you haven't regressed to being a bratty boy again?" she said, giving him a good hard clout on the arm.

"Ouch! Now that hurt."

"Which? The right jab or the insult?"

"The jab, of course. Being a bratty boy was wonderful."

"Wonderful? For *you*, maybe. At the birthday parties, you used to torment us unmercifully. Remember the snake you put in the lavatory in Apple's bathroom?"

"I was just trying to make your life a little more exciting," he said innocently. "And get your attention." He took her hand when he saw the sad look in her eyes. "It's pretty hard to think about the past, isn't it? I mean, knowing everything now, knowing how I felt about you."

Sad, yes. But not all that hard to think about, Lenor thought as she breathed in the pine-scented air. The pool brought back so many wonderful memories. Lazy summer days had been enlivened by shaky, barefoot walks through tumbling waters, balancing on a jumble of tottering, slippery cobbles. The hiss and pelt of freezing snow-melt, as it leapt into the pool from above and escaped from a languid whirl back into the dancing creek below, frosted ankles and toes to tingling. Daring flops and cartwheeling dives from the prehistoric, basaltic monolith that helped to dam the wide, irregular circle of shimmering water set hearts beating and backsides stinging. Most of the past was a pleasant memory.

Still holding hands, Michael and Lenor circled the huge boulder that rested half in, half out of the water on the sandy east shore, and leaned back against its gently sloping side. Silently they watched the swirling waters of the spring pool, where they'd both gone swimming on the hottest summer days—but never together. Michael finally broke the peaceful quiet.

"I hope you're not sorry I told you all about me," he said softly.

"I'm not sorry at all," Lenor said. "I asked you to, remember?"

"Mainly I remember how sick I felt when you asked me. I don't think I've ever been so frightened in all my life."

"Frightened of what?"

"Your reaction. I was positive you'd hate me, be ashamed of me."

"True feelings are never hateful, Michael," Lenor said, looking directly into his sad, dark eyes. "Uncomfortable maybe, but never shameful."

"I was plenty uncomfortable once."

"When was that?"

"I think it was my second summer back from college. I guess you were a junior in high school then. I came up here after a hot day's work on the ranch."

"I don't remember seeing you here," Lenor said.

"You didn't. You and Apple were stripped down to your underwear." He tried for a smile, but didn't quite make it. "My God, how beautiful you were. My poor old heart could barely stand the sight of you."

"Why didn't you join us?" Lenor asked.

"And embarrass myself to death? Forget about it."

"Apple and I would have been the embarrassed ones. We would have turned into silly fools. You were so gorgeous to look at . . . all those muscles from baling alfalfa hay and breaking wild horses and wrestling ornery colts that were three times your weight." She sighed as she looked back toward the water, then took his hand in both of hers and studied it. "But you never used any of that strength to hurt anyone. That's what makes you a truly beautiful man." She thought for a moment, smoothing her fingers over the top of his hand. "Maybe that's why I've had trouble with the relationships in my life. Nemesia was right. You were the model."

Michael had to smile. "You realize you're embarrassing the hell out of me, don't you?"

"Michael Martino? Embarrassed?" She threw his hand down. "That'll be the day!"

"Let me tell you about the day you and Apple came into Mora and I ran into you at Maria's. This girl I was with had dabbed some horrid men's cologne all over me, and I reeked to high heaven."

"Was she that beautiful redhead?" Lenor asked, trying not to make it any easier for him.

"She had red hair, yes. But the color of my ears rivaled the color of her hair!"

"You could look so innocent and so guilty, all at the same time," Lenor said, smiling at the memory. "Those tight Levi's hugging that cute bottom of yours, your hair all curly and so unruly."

Michael turned and looked down at her, his hands on his hips. "You're just not going to let up, are you? You're just going to keep on teasing and tormenting and—"

"It's the least I can do," Lenor interrupted as she faced him. "I owe you *that* much . . . and a whole lot more." She gave a push against his chest with her hand, and he took a step back. "I owe you for not writing to me after we met at the fair." She pushed him again. He took another step back. "I owe you for keeping secrets from me." She pushed again. "I owe you for . . ." She gave one last push.

"Yikes!" it was all he had time to say before he fell backward into the crystal-clear water of their spring pool.

Lenor brushed her palms back and forth across each other, then crossed her arms over her chest. "Now we're even." But she didn't have time to gloat for more than a second. He was out of the pool, had one arm around her waist, and was steering her straight to disaster before she could resist.

They both came up sputtering, laughing, splashing a soaking barrage at each other.

"Now who's even?" Splash!

"I am!" Splash!

"No, I am!" Splash!

"Say uncle!"

"Uncle!"

They collapsed together, sitting shoulder-deep on the bottom, smiling, looking at each other. Michael slipped his arm around her waist. "This is the way it should have been," he said wistfully.

"Our mothers would have killed us for ruining our boots," Lenor said.

Michael let her go, pulled off his boots and socks, and tossed them up on the bank. "They'll dry out," he said casually. "Here, let me help you." With that, he reached for hers.

Lenor didn't resist. The water felt so good, the company so comfortable. In a moment her boots were lying next to his, and already drying in the arid summer heat. She wiggled her bare toes in the fine sand, then backed up to lean against the boulder.

"Now no one will ever know we played hooky from work in the spring pool," he said, backing up to sit beside her.

"Did you play hooky here often, Michael?" Lenor asked.

He put his arm around her waist again, and shook his head. "No. But if I could have shared the time with you, I'd have been here every day."

"Then we really would have been in trouble with our parents," Lenor said.

"I wouldn't have minded. Your company would have been worth every extra chore they could have given me."

She looked at him. "You really mean that, don't you?"

"And it didn't take a magic spell," he said, turning toward her. "You can give my aunt whatever credit you want, but she had nothing to do with the way I felt then . . . or the way I feel right now."

Lenor couldn't help the tears that glistened in her eyes. "That's a very nice thing to say, Michael."

"I'm not just saying it. I mean it." A finger intercepted a tear and gently brushed it from her cheek. "You've been part of the magic in my life for a long time."

It had been a while—no, not a while; she'd *never* felt this comfortable or contented with a man before. There were no secrets between them, they shared a place and a time, each understood and accepted the other's unique perspective and individuality. If it weren't for the distance that would soon separate them, she could easily give her heart to him. Perhaps she already had. Now, more than ever, she was torn between leaving and staying.

"Tell me what's bothering you, Lenor," he said, after her long silence. "I'm a good listener."

Lenor settled against him and tilted her head to rest on his shoulder. "You've heard it before. I know what work I have to do, and I want to do it, but . . ."

"But you're still feeling guilty about not coming home," he finished for her.

"And disappointed," she said softly.

Michael wasn't sure he'd heard her correctly. His heart sang at the possibilities. Hope soared. "Disappointed?" he asked.

She tipped her head back and looked up at him. "Yes."

He could barely keep the smile off his face. "Care to tell me why?"

It was difficult to put it into words without giving him the idea that she could change her mind. "I'm going to miss you," she said.

It wasn't even close to a yes decision, but it was a damn good start. The smile wouldn't stay in hiding. Michael beamed down at her. "First Watson likes me. Now you do, too?" he teased. "Makes a man wonder how he can deserve so much good luck all at once!"

From sad to happy in the flash of a smile! Lenor grabbed at his sides and found, to her delight, that he was ticklish. He whirled away from her and backed frantically down the sloping bottom toward the center of the pool. About halfway there, Lenor caught up. He smoothly slid out of her way, and she plunged forward into deep water. Some seconds later, she still hadn't come to the surface. Michael began to expect a submarine attack . . . then he began to worry. He dove in headfirst.

Just on the other side of the deepest water, Lenor stood up grinning.

Michael came up frowning, facing away from her, turning quickly around. He stood, water lapping around his belt, hands on his hips. "So this is what I get for being a good listener," he growled.

"No. It's what you get for teasing me about Watson again," she said across the pool.

Michael launched himself straight for her. In three strokes he was beside her, and she didn't resist when he stood and put his arms around her. "You are very touchy about that cat of yours, Dr. Tavera," he said, looking down at her.

"Take that as a warning, Mr. Martino," she teased sternly.

"Warning? Does that mean I'm in some kind of danger?" he asked.

"Yes."

"What kind?"

Lenor reached up and put her hands on either side of his face. For a moment she gazed into the depths of his dark eyes; then she could no longer ignore the temptation. Without any resistance from him, she drew his head down and touched her mouth to his. The feel of him was just as exciting as she'd expected it to be. She rejoiced in the roughness of his cheeks against her palms, the hard lines of his jaw beneath her fingers, the firm outline of his lips brushing hers.

Though cool water swirled around their legs and hips, Michael felt as if he'd been set on fire. He stood still. Time stood still as Lenor's kiss lingered. Her soft, closed lips moved over his, exploring shape and texture, then moved to his chin, then back along the line of his jaw. When she reached his ear, he thought he'd been electrified.

"I warned you," Lenor whispered against the intricate folds.

You should be the one apprised of the dangers here, Michael thought, but he didn't say it. He couldn't. It was all he could do to breathe as she nibbled at his earlobe.

"You should have taken my warning seriously," Lenor said softly, then leaned back. "You could have been safely at home by now."

"Now who's teasing whom?" he asked.

"I'm not teasing," Lenor said.

Michael's heart danced in his chest. *There is no way this is really happening,* he told himself silently. "Pinch me," he said aloud. "I'm sure I'm dreaming again."

Lenor draped her arms over his shoulders and looked directly into his eyes. "If you're dreaming, I never want to wake up," she said.

They stood silently looking at each other, the whisperings of the forest, the music of the stream the only accompaniment to their voiceless communication. In those few quiet moments, pretense evaporated. Fear vanished. Past disappointments dissolved. Only one question remained.

"Are you sure you want this to happen?" Michael asked.

Lenor nodded. "Are *you* sure?" she asked.

He answered with a kiss. Not a phantom touch like hers had been, this was tender, all-consuming. The wall that had always been between them went tumbling into crystal waters, and in its wake, a shimmering heat melted them together.

For a moment, making love in the spring pool seemed, to Lenor, the height of folly. But this was the perfect day for madness, and this was the perfect place for profound communion. Mists of the past were gone. Inspiration of the clear ether awaited. Influenced by universal perception, Lenor made her decision. She regretted not one moment of it.

The sun had climbed to its summertime zenith. The clear mountain air crackled with the heat of noon. Clothing, laid out to dry, steamed on the river boulder. Mother Earth smiled.

Michael and Lenor cooled themselves in the shallows under the dappled shade of a tall ponderosa. "God, I love this place," Michael said, lazing back against the boulder. "How in the world do you handle New York City?"

"You get used to it. Do you think you could handle New York?" Lenor asked.

The straitjacket of a city? Locked doors? Constant vigilance? In exchange for all this? He looked up at the pine trees that towered all about them. "I can give you a qualified answer. I'm sure I could handle the muggers. I might have trouble with the confinement."

"I'm glad you're being honest," Lenor said.

"Do you think you could handle New Mexico again?" he

asked. "I know about a position that's open right now. The working conditions aren't too good, but the pay is worse."

"I still have a lot of work to do that can only be done in New York. But to answer your question, I'm sure I could handle the working conditions and the pay. But I'm not so sure I could handle the"—Lenor gave him a sideways look and breathed an exaggerated sigh—"the dreams."

"Another honest answer. I was hoping for a different—" He sat up in a great whoosh of water. Rivulets zigzagged in glistening streams through the thick black hair on his chest. "Are you teasing me again?"

He had no idea how delicious he looked. Lenor reached out and rescued one droplet that perched on the end of his nose. "*What* different answer did you expect?" she asked.

"I thought—" He wiped his face with his hand, as if trying to clear his thinking. "I expected you to say—"

"Something like, 'Thanks, see you around'?"

Michael grimaced. "Something like that."

"Well, we've been at square one for about thirty years," Lenor said. "What say we try for square two and see what happens?"

Michael smiled, settled back against the rock, and pulled her sideways into his lap. "If square two takes thirty more years, and you take me through another weekend like you just did, I won't make it."

"Sure you will." Lenor pushed away from him and stood up. Leaning against the boulder, she reached into the pocket of her drying jeans, and brought out two highly polished, small black stones. "Remember the *piedra imán*?" she asked as she settled back into his lap.

"If you come up out of the water like that again, I may forget everything I ever knew, except maybe . . ." Michael pulled her closer and began making doodling circles, with playful fingers, just above the buoyant rise of her breasts. "I remember," he said. "Please go on."

Lenor took in a ragged breath that was supposed to fuel her

speech. It almost didn't. "I went into Mora and had Greensun McDowell cut and polish these two pieces for me."

Michael's hand moved lower, his sketching finger drawing spirals now. "He polished them," he said as his palm grazed first one budding tip, then the other.

She'd have to make the story short. "Then I had Nemesia charge yours with magic to keep you safe."

"Safe?"

"And for any more weekends like the last one, it'll make you strong, give you staying power over the long haul," she finished quickly.

Michael was shaking his head, his caution battling with his new belief. "Do you think I need a magic charm for that?"

Lenor smiled at him, then turned in his lap and leaned back against his chest. "After the 'dream' I just had? No. You don't need any help in *that* department." She snuggled down in his arms, took his hands in hers, and tried to relax.

Michael looked down at her reclining body. Even in his wildest dreams he couldn't have conjured a more seductive image. "Then why do I need the talisman?" he asked in a lazy voice.

"You can bring it with you to New York . . . for luck."

"What makes you think I'll visit New York?" Michael asked.

"Elementary, my dear Mr. Martino. You've already purchased an airline ticket."

"How—? What makes you think that?"

"Why else would you ask Grandpa if the New York taxi drivers live up to their reputations?"

"Why else, indeed, Sherlock," Michael said in a dreamy tone. He slid his hands beneath her breasts, and circled the rosy centers with his thumbs.

"So you *will* be coming to New York," Lenor said softly.

"I wouldn't be a bit surprised."

"Then you'll need this." She took his hand and placed the stone in his palm. "Just think of your little *monito* as—"

"My invitation . . . to 'dream' again?" he asked glibly.

His body betrayed the smoothly asked question. A soft moaning sound encouraged Lenor to nestle herself into a new position on his lap.

"See? The magic works."